THE DARK PATH
by WALTER H. HUNT

Fantastic Books
1380 East 17 Street, Suite 2233
Brooklyn, New York 11230
www.FantasticBooks.biz

ISBN 10: 1-61720-940-6
ISBN 13: 978-1-61720-940-6

First Fantastic Books Edition, 2013

I dedicate this book to four ladies in my life:
my dear wife and Bright Wings, Lisa;
my daughter, Aline;
and my maternal aunts, Gloria and Civita, who have been
great supporters and good friends for many years.
I hope you find Jackie to your liking.

Since the original publication of this book,
the aunts mentioned in the dedication have passed on,
as has my original editor, Brian Thomsen.
With this new edition, I am reminded of the place each had in
my life, and I hold them in fond remembrance.

saShrne'e

PULLING ASIDE THE SHROUD

PART ONE

In the dream he saw a battered landscape marred by battle just beyond the brow of the hill. A pall of gritty smoke drifted through the air near where he crouched. He could hear the cries of the wounded and smell the stench of war: blood and fire and death.

He looked at himself, at the ancient ceremonial sword hanging loosely in a scabbard at his waist. His legs were young and strong, not old and withered; it reinforced the dream-state, making him even more aware of it—but the feeling! He had forgotten what it was like to be young.

The thrill of pleasure from that sensation washed away as, in the dream, he realized where his *hsi* had been taken.

This is the Plain of Despite, he told himself as an explosion shuddered through the berm.

The Plain of Despite: where the hero Qu'u had gone to acquire the *gyaryu* he now wore, to face *anGa'e'ren* and perform the *Lament of the Peak.* His familiarity with the legend and the sure knowledge of the symbolic significance of this mental construct sent a chill down his spine.

He willed himself to scramble along the hillside, keeping his head down. Dream-constructs or not, his legs held him up as he made footholds. Still, the activity was unfamiliar and almost alien to him after being an invalid for so long.

He reached the end of the low ridge and came to a wide-open area with large standing boulders. Beyond, the land seemed to slope down to a wide valley. The whole scene was lit eerily by flashes of lightning: or was it artillery?

Beyond the valley was a huge blue-black façade extending outward as wide and as high as he could see. With an enormous effort of will, he let his eyes travel upward until he was craning his neck. At an impossible distance he could make out a fortress of some sort, a sprawling structure with turrets and outbuildings.

The Icewall: the Fortress of Despite.

At least he could look up. Only heroes could raise their eyes on the Plain of Despite.

Your imagination is going to kill you, old man, he told himself, but it didn't seem to reassure him. This was no dream of his own imagination; even he could not conjure up the Plain of Despite, the Icewall and the Fortress … at least not in such detail.

It was the sword sending his *hsi* this way. *You accepted it,* he told himself. It was a *shNa'es'ri,* even if it seemed inevitable.

Sixty years ago the *gyaryu,* the zor sword of state, had been offered to him by the High Lord. He had taken it just as the Admiral had taken it before him. He knew what that meant. He knew what this meant as well.

He walked carefully between the boulders, the *gyaryu* before him. It felt like a live thing in his hands, snarling at the place it found itself. The valley he entered was shrouded in fog. It was a *L'le,* though it was more spread out, more like a human than a zor settlement. There were People there walking or flying, all but oblivious to his passing. As he came close, their wings often seemed to move slightly, as if forming a half-forgotten pattern of deference or respect. In most cases, however, the wing-positions conveyed nothing but despair.

The closer he came to the center of the *L'le,* the fewer active zor he saw. Instead he saw them frozen in position, like statues or grotesque chess-pieces, pinned in place, lifeless.

The Valley of Lost Souls, he thought.

At the far edge of the valley the settlement ended in the dark, blank face of the Icewall. He could make out the Perilous Stair now, a climbing/flying path that led eventually to the Fortress. A zor stood at the base of the Stair with its face turned away, wings placed in a pattern of respect.

As he approached, the zor turned to face him. He stopped suddenly as he recognized the human head atop the zor body.

"Marc?"

"A long time, Sergei," the Marc Hudson-zor said, the crooked smile sneaking onto his face just as Sergei remembered it. The wings assumed a posture of deference. "You look good."

"So do you, for someone who's been dead as long as you have."

"How long has it been?"

"Thirty years," Sergei said, looking away. "I spoke at your funeral. You outlived most of us—Bert, Uwe, even Alyne."

"Alyne." A ripple of affection found its way into the Hudson-zor's wings. Hearing Marc speak his late wife's name chilled Sergei.

"Why am I here, Marc?"

"*esLi* wills it. Or do you want the real answer?" The Hudson-zor smiled again.

"The real answer."

"The real answer is … what has been foreseen is about to begin. The flight has been chosen and the decision is made."

"Do I have to climb that?" Sergei asked, gesturing toward the Perilous Stair behind the Hudson-zor.

"That is for another to ascend," the Hudson-zor said. "It is a *shNa'es'ri* for that person, not for you."

"What does *esLi* will for me, then?"

"What do you think?"

"I think ... that the burden of the sword is great. I have carried it since the Admiral died. I'm not sure that I can accomplish this *a'Li'e're*, my old friend. I have chosen the flight, but I don't know if my wings can carry me where it leads."

"They carried you *here*," the Hudson-zor said, gesturing.

Sergei looked at where he pointed, and saw his own wings, formed in the Posture of the Enfolding Protection of *esLi*.

"enGa'e'esLi," Sergei said to himself, or perhaps to the Hudson-zor, naming the wing-position.

"esLiHeYar, old friend," the Hudson-zor said, and the iridescent fog of the Valley of Lost Souls drifted between them, obscuring the Icewall and the Perilous Stair and the Hudson-zor last of all.

T HE CAPTAIN of His Imperial Majesty's ship *Cincinnatus* had tactfully and politely withdrawn after exchanging courtesies with his distinguished passengers, leaving Sergei Torrijos, the *Gyaryu'har* of the High Nest and Admiral Horace Tolliver of the Imperial Navy, to take their breakfast alone in the captain's mess.

Sergei carefully removed the peel from an orange while watching Horace Tolliver push food around on his plate.

"Another sleepless night, Horace?" he asked.

Tolliver rubbed his neck with the palm of his hand. "How anyone sleeps aboard these ships, I'll never know. I just can't get used to it." He set the fork on the table with military precision. "How about you? You're a long way from your garden in esYen."

"Slept like the dead," Sergei answered, though the echoes of the Plain of Despite still haunted him. "It's about time you woke up."

"I didn't realize that my sleeping cycles were of any interest to you. Especially since you've done your best to avoid me during the entire trip."

The older man coasted his chair to a side table and turned. His wrinkled face was wry and amused. "Not at all, not at all, Horace. I've been meaning to corner you since I came aboard, but I've been kept busy by my handlers."

"All right, then." Horace Tolliver stood and adjusted his uniform in a mirror. "To what do I owe the honor of a visit by the *Gyaryu'har*?"

"Curiosity. And friendship. Hands across the water and all. Remember, I was an officer in His Majesty's Navy once ... long ago."

"Long ago. It was a different navy eighty-five years ago."

The old man looked up, the pain of remembrance crossing his face. "Has it been that long? Eighty-five years. You weren't even born."

"But you digress." Horace looked annoyed as he turned from the mirror and sat down. "All right. Tell me how I can help you with *your* problem."

"Has it occurred to you that there must be a mighty important reason for His Majesty to send you out personally to inspect a border naval base? Especially when accompanied by an official"—he tapped the sword lying across his lap—"representative of the High Nest?"

"Cicero isn't just a 'border naval base.' It's the biggest and most important border base of the Solar Empire."

"But it's still at the *border*. It's at the boundary of—presumably—uninhabited space."

"'Presumably'"

"You certainly don't have to be coy with me. I've read the reports on the disappearance of the *Negri Sembilan* and the *Gustav Adolf II*."

"Those were at the highest clearance—"

"You seem to forget that your government and mine are *allies.* An official of the High Nest—especially the *Gyaryu'har*—is privy to such documents.

"In all fairness, Horace, we'd concluded that the threat is nothing more serious than pirates, operating outside the Empire somewhere. I'm sure the CO at Cicero—Laperriere, I believe her name is?—is competent enough to conduct a sweep of the area, root out the pirates and knock them out. So why send out the brass to conduct an inspection? Are we there to see if she does it right?"

Horace crossed his arms in front of his chest.

"It's really very simple, Horace. The Admiralty suspects that something is wrong and plucked you from your desk and me from my garden to find out what the hell it is."

"I see. Why haven't I been told about this?"

"You *are* being told, Horace. The fact of this excursion is your briefing, and actions speak louder than words. Especially in this case."

"Twaddle." The admiral felt particularly good about telling someone Sergei's age that what he'd just said was "twaddle." He savored it for a moment before continuing. "The Admiralty is expecting a report on the whereabouts of its two missing ships. They will have it, because I intend to find them."

"You … what?"

"I have no intention of sitting on my ass and waiting for them to turn up by themselves. *That* is why the Admiralty is sending a flag admiral to Cicero."

"You're a staff officer, Horace, not a—"

"I am an admiral in His Majesty's Fleet, you may recall. I have a commission and active-duty experience. If Cicero's CO is competent, then no action will be necessary. If she is queasy about taking charge—"

"That," the old man interrupted, "is about the stupidest thing I have ever heard you say. Or ever heard of you having said, for that matter. Border commanders don't get 'queasy' about taking actions against pirates or anyone else. You know damn well there's more to this."

Sergei pushed his chair into motion, moving it toward the door. "Of course," he said, turning at the door with a wry smile, "at my age, you get to say things like that. See you on deck." He coasted through the door, which slid shut behind him. The admiral sat, somewhat taken aback by the way the conversation had ended, which was nearly as abrupt as the way it had begun.

There goes a strange old man, Tolliver thought to himself. *He doesn't even think like a human anymore.*

But after eighty-five years in alien space, carrying the legacy—and the sword of state—of one of the greatest villains in human history—why should that come as a surprise?

What sort of man could have followed Admiral Marais in his war of destruction? What sort of man had Sergei Torrijos been when he was young? It was hardly more than a speculative, academic question now. Admiral Tolliver stood up, picked up his jacket and walked out of the room.

```
20 September 2396
Open Channels TIN/SRO/ADR/CIC
FROM: RADM CÉSAR HSIEN, ADRIANOPLE, FOR ADMIRALTY HQ TERRA
TO: CDRE JACQUELINE LAPERRIERE IN, CO/CICERO NAVAL BASE
```

By order of His Imperial Highness you will accommodate and welcome Inspector-General Horace Tolliver, R Adm ISN, and his escort, *Gyaryu'har* Sergei Torrijos, representing High Lord Ke'erl HeYen of the High Nest. It is expected that you will make Adm. Tolliver and especially Mr. Torrijos comfortable during their inspection tour. Itinerary and schedule are in the attached vidrecs.
EOT

```
20 September 2396
Open Channels TIN/SRO/ADR/CIC
FROM: RADM HORACE A TOLLIVER, INSPECTOR-GENERAL
TO: CDRE JACQUELINE LAPERRIERE IN, CO / CICERO NAVAL BASE
```

Dear Commodore Laperriere:
I am looking forward to visiting the Cicero facility. As a courtesy to the High Lord, I will

be accompanied by a special envoy, High Nest
representative Sergei Torrijos. Though this
circumstance will make the inspection tour
somewhat unusual in nature, I am sure you will be
able to conduct your command in the normal manner
with the minimum of dislocation. If there is
anything my office can do to help this effort,
feel free to contact me.

Tolliver RAdm ISN

Five Vindicator aircraft gathered speed and gained altitude rapidly, leaving
the Cicero landing-field behind. The rising sun, pale and orange against the
horizon, dappled their wings as they flew free. Their afterburners fired as they
rocketed through the upper atmosphere.

Lieutenant John Maisel, Officer of the Watch, turned away from the
receding craft to look at the reflection of his commanding officer in the glass of
the control-tower viewport. She looked tired and worn; he wondered to himself
why she was up at 0600 to watch a routine CAP flight take off.

"Wing Four away, ma'am," he said, turning to face her.

"Very good, Lieutenant."

"Your orders, ma'am?"

"None. Maintain General Quarters until further notice, Lieutenant."

"Aye-aye, ma'am." He turned once again to watch the points of light vanish
in the distance. When he glanced over his shoulder again, the commodore was
gone.

COMMODORE JACQUELINE Laperriere—"Jackie" to those few friends close
enough to call her by name and not by rank—walked slowly along the
glassed-in walkway that led from the control tower to the Admiralty
building. To someone less tired or less burdened, the view of the great naval
spaceport would have seemed stupendous. It hardly captured her attention as she
stopped to watch the flurry of activity as the next wing of fighters prepared to
take to the air.

She knew every detail of the operation; it never left her—a conditioned
response, like the reflex actions that made a good fighter pilot. She had been a
good pilot years ago, before she had been given a starship to command.
Somehow the thrill of piloting a combat aerospace craft still outweighed the skill
to use the firepower and mobility of a ship-of-the-line; yet both were behind her
now. As a commodore in His Majesty's Fleet her post was behind a desk in a
naval base.

Jackie watched Cicero's K6 sun climb higher in the sky. But she wasn't feeling resentment or even regret this morning: It was outweighed by fatigue resulting from the last thirty-six hours she had spent prowling her base. She had walked kilometers along corridors and across the high-impact tarmac, met with subordinate officers and conducted snap inspections of facilities and equipment—all in preparation for the arrival of the Inspector-General, Rear Admiral Horace Tolliver. To the naval base personnel it wasn't a particularly important visit: It wasn't the first time Cicero had been given over to full-dress inspection, and it wouldn't be the last. She had heard this idea repeated any number of times in the last few days—groundhog, pencil-pushing admirals were nothing to be concerned about.

Some of her senior officers—years older and frozen in their positions by choice or circumstance—had taken her to dinner at the Officers' Club four days ago and had tried their best to convince her not to worry about the admiral's inspection while trying also to drink her under the table. She smiled at this memory, remembering the outcome. One of the first things an officer learns is how to drink in moderation, and she'd held up her end in accordance with the best traditions of the Service.

Still, she knew there was something serious going on—it took more than whimsy to bring an old bird like Tolliver, the epitome of a staff officer, so close to the edge of Imperial space. What it meant was that someone at Admiralty had taken notice of the events of the past few weeks—the disappearance of two Exploration Service vessels.

The end result was that the Admiralty considered it worth their attention, and had dispatched the man for the job. Tolliver was steeped in nepotism, the grandson and great-grandson of Imperial prime ministers. He was probably crafty enough to know if he was being deceived, but little enough of a soldier to avoid independent action. It was the way they bred admirals these days, ever since the zor wars and Admiral Marais.

So Tolliver would come out to Cicero, conduct his inspection and deliver some sort of instructions. Official orders were couched in military legalese; real instructions would be conveyed by a cipher like Tolliver. She wasn't sure of the details, but it seemed likely that the orders would be something like, *Solve this problem, or we'll ship you somewhere quiet ... like Pergamum.* A naval base halfway between the Solar Empire and its loyal ally, the High Nest, Pergamum was about as quiet a posting as you could get. It was also the dead end for a naval career.

All right, Jackie said to herself, *I'll solve the problem. It's probably some more damn pirates, just like it was six years ago.* They'd find the base and storm it, seize their ships and confiscate their stores. The pirates would get a taste of the emperor's justice, and everyone would get a medal.

There was doubt somewhere at the back of her mind. She knew the *Gustav Adolf II* and *Negri Sembilan* were too well armed to be prey for a pirate—they were Exploration Service vessels, but they had Marine complements and well-trained crews. Something big enough and clever enough to take on a survey vessel, though … She strode off purposefully, finding a new source of energy to overcome her fatigue.

C H'K'TE WOKE slowly to the sound of a breeze gently rustling the chimes in his front hallway. As he stretched his legs to unkink them, he spread his wings wide in the posture of *esLi-Na'yar,* Greeting to the Day, and offered up a brief invocation to *esLi.*

He sometimes regretted having been posted to Cicero. Though the honor of serving at the largest naval base did not escape his notice, the gravity of the world was a burden, taking away the opportunity for him to fly except in simulators … and he tried not to think about the cold.

He stepped into the 'fresher and slipped protective lenses into his eyes, correcting the harsh light of Cicero's primary to a more acceptable chromatic level. Then he walked to the front room and found his youngest cousin and *alHyu,* N'kareu, waiting for him.

"Greetings to you, noble Cousin," N'kareu said, inclining his head. "Eight thousand pardons for disturbing your meditation."

"It was time I greeted the morning." Ch'k'te walked to the picture window and drew back the blind, letting bright sunlight stream through. "What can I do for you, *se* Cousin?"

"The commander begs the courtesy of your presence, *se* Ch'k'te."

"At this hour?" Ch'k'te consulted his chronometer and noticed the time: 0630.

"She met me in the corridor near the officers' mess, *se* Cousin, and bid me come and wake you. She asks that you meet her in her ready-room after the morning meal."

Ch'k'te watched while a flight of aircraft took to the air.

"Is she there now?" he asked without turning.

"I … believe so, Cousin."

"Very good. Lay out my uniform, *se* N'kareu, while I think for a moment." The young zor bowed slightly and entered the sleep-chamber.

Ch'k'te laid his extended talons on the windowsill and began to clear his mind. He closed his eyes and concentrated on the Circle of *esLi,* the Inner and Outer Peace. Slowly the flickering of the light on his inner eyelids and the small noises made by his *alHyu* faded away, and his mind reached out.

Over the past few years, he had used this morning exercise to familiarize himself with the patterns of the human minds that surrounded him here at

Cicero. He had particularly familiarized himself with the *hsi* of his superior, Commodore Laperriere, and it was that pattern he looked for first.

He felt her almost at once: a strong and extremely alien personality, her mind moving rapidly to outdistance fatigue. As always, when his mind-touch was clear and direct, he could almost see her look away from the report she was reading and speak his name, half aloud and half in her mind.

"Ch'k'te?"

It was accompanied by a wash of emotion. The mind-touch, natural to Ch'k'te as a Sensitive, was a new experience for the commodore. She had approached the idea with some concern, but had become accustomed to the feeling over time; the possibility that it could be used for emergency communication had motivated the experiment in the first place. Ch'k'te, for his part, welcomed the opportunity to further his understanding of the always-confusing human ally.

The afterechoes of the spoken name suddenly rang hollow, as though from the bottom of a deep well. He felt a pressure nibbling at the edges of his consciousness, as if someone had noticed his mind for the first time and was poking at it to see what it was made of.

Ch'k'te?

Dark forms moved through the void. He felt a terrible sinking feeling in the pit of his stomach. Through it all a tide of rapidly rising fear began to wash over him. It was coming from Jackie.

He tried to say her name and found himself strangely mute, as if the effort were too much.

She wasn't a Sensitive and could not form the illusory thought-shapes and constructs to define and constrain assaults of mental energies. Whatever had suddenly touched their tenuous mind-link was assaulting her with raw energies, and she was redoubling their effect through fear.

Ch'k'te? he heard her say again.

The emotions were growing stronger now, the dark forms drawing nearer. He could almost make them out now: huge behemoths, the worst nightmarish forms that *esGa'u* might send to frighten small nestlings. His conscious mind struggled with the idea that his imagination had produced all of this, and he tried to break the link. He found he could not. He could feel his heartbeat race as he turned to meet the apparitions that slowly closed in.

The nearest of the forms reached out to touch him—

"C H'K'TE?"
         Among the People, the reflexes of the soldier are perhaps the most deeply ingrained; he must depend on them for his very life. At

the first touch, Ch'k'te grasped the tentacle that reached for him and raised his hands, preparing to hurl it away with *en-Ga'e'Li,* the Strength of Madness.

Slowly he opened his eyes to see what he had grasped ... and found himself holding a very frightened N'kareu above his head.

Ch'k'te forced his heartbeat to slow to normal as he lowered his cousin to the floor. He straightened the feathers on his wings and allowed his talons to retract.

"It is most unwise," he said quietly, "to disturb a warrior in his meditations."

"Eight thousand pardons, Cousin," N'kareu said, not looking upward. "But you ... looked to be in danger."

"How so?" asked Ch'k'te.

N'kareu did not answer but instead gestured to the sill, where eight deep holes were scored in the plastic, one for each of Ch'k'te's talons.

SERGEI WATCHED as the globe of Cicero Prime grew in the holo above his sitting-room table. He had no particular inclination to watch the approach from the bridge, where Admiral Tolliver now stood; he was content to remain in his quarters.

The bridge of a starship was an alien place to him now, even though he had spent a good part of his adult life commanding from one.

Circumstances had not really changed him. Even standing by as the Solar Empire disassociated itself from Admiral Marais (a lifetime ago, it seemed) had not really affected him that much. Time had had its effect though: It had made him old, taking away the use of his legs and making his arms weak and his breathing careful and measured. Time had taken away his wife, Alyne, and his closest friend, Marc Hudson, after the three of them had followed Admiral Marais into exile.

And of course it had taken Marais himself. He had written a book a few years after the war, but he had never been vindicated in the eyes of humanity. Marais died a villain to the human race. To them, he was a monster who had unleashed the terrible violence necessary to end the conflict between man and zor forever.

It was a conflict that Sergei had not even understood at first. What was more, the Admiral had never admitted remorse or shame for his acts, though the Solar Empire, in an exercise of twisted wisdom, had been more than willing to accept the fruits of Marais' victory.

Marais had gone into an exile from which he would never return. By human standards, the zor should have hated him for the blood-price they had paid, but instead they accepted the Admiral as the synergy of the avenging Dark Wing and the life-giving Bright Wing and had given him the *gyaryu,* the High Nest's sword of state. The act had made no sense to the humans who had exiled them; even decades later they didn't seem to understand it.

hi'i Sse'e had continued as High Lord after the war—poor, blind Sse'e. Chris Boyd, the current envoy's grandfather, experienced a shared dream with the old High Lord in which the Admiral's mysterious aide, Captain Stone, appeared as a cross between zor and human and told *hi'i* Sse'e that he would dream no more.

It was a true prediction. Less than two years after the end of the war, *hi'i* Sse'e killed himself by stopping his own heart. Sergei might be the last living person of either race to remember firsthand the sight of the old zor's broken body lying in a bloody heap on the floor of the former meditation chamber.

hi'i Sse'e's son, *hi'i* Dra'a, had been "touched by the Eight Winds" as well and had died in his garden a year after that. He had also been unable to call forth the dreams of guidance. None of this made much sense within the Solar Empire: They weren't waiting for the insights of the High Lord's dreams in any case.

After *hi'i* Dra'a, the balance of the High Lordship had seemingly been restored by the return of prescient dreams to the High Lord. It had returned confidence to the new bond of friendship between the People and humanity. It had been peaceful for more than eighty years, as each race learned from the other ...

THE YEARS seemed to weigh on Sergei as he sat quietly in his quarters on the *Cincinnatus,* looking at the holo that showed the habitable planet in the Cicero system. Suddenly a wisp of smoke began to rise from the image of the planet and formed it self into a hand, reaching out toward Sergei. He felt fear course through him like a live thing, as a tide of raw emotion welled up from somewhere beyond him.

He found the *gyaryu* in his hands, snarling. He extended his wings to protect himself—

The intercom sounded. "We'll be making planetfall in less than an hour, sir. It's about 0630 local time at the base. Is there anything you require?"

Sergei lowered his arms slowly. He noted that he had assumed the wing position of *enSha'e'esLi,* the Enfolding Protection of *esLi.* He set the sword carefully across his lap. A shiver went through him and the wings disappeared.

"Mr. Torrijos?" the intercom repeated, a hint of urgency in the speaker's voice.

"Yes, damn it," Sergei managed after another moment. "Can't get any peace and quiet around here. No, I don't need anything special."

He looked at his shoulders for an instant longer, almost seeing the wings there again. *Must've drifted off, you old fool,* he thought to himself. *Between sendings from the Plain of Despite and images of wings growing from your shoulders, you can't tell sleeping from waking now.*

He looked at the holo and saw the sphere of Cicero, larger now, but looking like a normal planet.

This is how it begins, he thought to himself. Who had cried out in fear ... and what had reached out to touch him?

An alarm sounded over the ship's intercom, but Sergei was lost again in thought.

chapter 2

A stiff wind blew across the landing-field, snapping the flags back and forth on their poles and tearing through the dress uniforms of the troops that stood at rigid attention waiting for the shuttle to come to a halt. It was a fine, bright, cold morning, uncomfortable enough to make it more than appropriate for an inspection.

Jackie Laperriere waited with her staff; she felt the cold despite her heavy overcloak. She could have delegated the matter to a subordinate, but it gave her a peculiar pleasure to be out on the tarmac rather than inside the control tower. It also gave her an opportunity to meet the admiral and the other members of the delegation personally—especially the enigmatic *Gyaryu'har*, the famous Sergei Torrijos, the last legacy of the wars with mankind's greatest alien ally. They'd have to stand out here and exchange the salutes on her turf.

Ch'k'te had expressed mixed feelings about the upcoming visit, not least because of the unnerving experience earlier that morning. He was a Sensitive, and he had realized there was more substance than shadow to the event.

W HEN CH'K'TE had arrived at her office, close to 0700, she had been upset. She had taken her seat at the conference table; Ch'k'te had remained standing at attention until she directly ordered him to be at ease. He'd taken up his usual position opposite her desk.

"If you could explain to me what happened, I would be much obliged."

"I am humbly sorry, *se* Commodore, for not—"

"An explanation, Commander Ch'k'te," she had interrupted. "I did not ask for an apology."

Ch'k'te's anger rose for a split second but he brought it under control even before his talons could slip a centimeter from their sheaths. Still, the tensing had been enough for Jackie to notice.

"I'm sorry," she said. "This has been a difficult few days. I felt your mind-touch, but then the images … were very sharp. Forgive my impatience. What happened?"

"Something entered our mind-touch from the outside: some thing inimical and alien."

"Alien? Which race?"

"None I know. It was not human, rashk or otran. It was clearly not one of the People, but it *was* quite powerful, *se* Commodore. Our mind-links are nonverbal things even between trained Sensitives. This mind was something much more powerful. It was in total control of the link."

"Was it … what we saw?"

"A Sensitive will sometimes construct a thought-shape to describe a given kind of emotion. Fear was the emotion in this case. My *hsi* built an image based on my own imagination. So … I would say, *se* Commodore, that the owner of the mind may look nothing like what we experienced."

"What do you plan to do about this contact?"

"'Contact' is perhaps too strong a word to describe it, *se* Commodore. But I will do as you order."

"As I order? What shall I order?"

He had not received an answer for that question.

There were few Sensitives stationed at Cicero. There was little need; the Imperial Grand Survey had charted solar systems thirty to forty parsecs beyond Cicero and had found nothing remotely resembling intelligent life. The region of space near Albireo, by comparison, was a hotbed of Sensitive activity following the first contact with the otran at a system then designated only as 79 Vulpeculae. But there was nothing new out beyond Cicero—human settlements outside the Empire, but no sentient aliens … and certainly nothing like what they'd seen in the link.

Nothing at all.

THE ADMIRAL and his staff had settled into visiting officers' quarters in the main complex. For the zor dignitaries, Jackie had arranged ground-level lodging adjoining the extensive hot house garden in the center of the buildings; the front windows of the suite overlooked a tropical scene, immune to the storms that raged above the permaplast dome that protected it. From what little she'd learned about the *Gyaryu'har*, she thought he'd like it. From what she heard when he'd settled in, she was right.

By the first daywatch after their arrival, they were ready for an inspection tour. There was a lot to see, but it was mostly the same: Cicero Prime had been inhabited for just two decades, and it was only tolerable near the equator (where it was merely *bitterly* cold); at the poles the permanent ice caps and vicious winds made settlement impractical. Low axial tilt meant little variation in seasons and thus little relief from the cold.

To no one's surprise, the party remained almost exclusively indoors, reviewing personnel and facilities. Admiral Tolliver seemed most interested in cleanliness and efficiency and found little about which to comment—or complain. On the other hand, the High Lord's representative was very inquisitive about all sorts of things, from people's moods to the cycles of the weather.

"He's amazing," Jackie said quietly to Ch'k'te as they crossed through a large shuttle hangar.

"He is the *Gyaryu'har*," Ch'k'te answered, as if that explained everything.

"That doesn't explain it."

Ch'k'te's wings moved to another position; it could have been anything from deference to amusement. "The *Gyaryu'har* has great wisdom and power."

"As a Sensitive?"

"Not truly." Ch'k'te's wings moved again. "He holds the *gyaryu* and has the power to wield it against the *esGa'uYal*—the Servants of the Deceiver."

"But not much nowadays, I'd guess."

"Why do you say that?"

"Well, he's confined to a power chair, isn't he?"

"Eight thousand pardons, *se* Jackie, but I do not understand how that is relevant."

"You said that he wields—"

"Yes." Ch'k'te's wings changed position a third time. "He wields the sword against the *esGa'uYal*," he repeated. "Confinement to the chair"—he gestured toward the old man, who was patiently listening to a description of the hangar's weather-seal mechanism—"does not present a barrier to his capabilities. The Servants of the Deceiver are—"

"All around us?"

Ch'k'te could not change his facial expression, but his eyes conveyed surprise.

"It would explain his presence here."

"I thought he was here as part of the admiral's entourage. An observer for the High Nest."

"*se* Jackie, the *Gyaryu'har* is not a part of *any* entourage. If he is here, it is because the *gyaryu* is needed here."

"What you saw ... what *we* saw—"

"I fear so," Ch'k'te said, answering her unasked question.

JACKIE ARRANGED a meal for her visitors in the officers' mess, which was cordial on the surface but filled with tension. For her part, Jackie was nervous about the presence of a zor envoy—particularly given Ch'k'te's belief. The *Gyaryu'har* was here for a reason, one possibly as important as the admiral's.

After the meal, the dignitaries assembled in her ready-room around a large polished wood table. It had been brought out to Cicero by Jackie's predecessor, a nobleman wealthy enough to pay the freight to get it there and leave it behind when he was transferred.

Jackie took her own seat at the head of the table. Admiral Tolliver and his staff took a place at the opposite end; the other members of the group—the *Gyaryu'har* and two adjutants—settled in between. Ch'k'te sat to her right.

"Commodore," Admiral Tolliver began. "We have all traveled a great distance to be here. Perhaps you would do us the courtesy of reviewing your report."

"Aye-aye, Admiral." She had been prepared to give such a presentation, and stood up, leaning her hands on the table and surveying the room.

"The Imperial Exploration Service conducts regular surveys of systems from thirty to forty parsecs outward from naval bases at the edge of the Solar Empire," she began. "These surveys serve a variety of purposes, including the location of suitable worlds for colonization or industrialization. The Service is always on the lookout for first contacts."

Tolliver's expression was impassive, but his eyes sent the message: *We know all of this. Get on with it.*

"The Exploration Service is often instrumental in locating potential hazards to the Empire, particularly the havens of raiders and pirates.

"It is important to emphasize that exploration of this sort entails high risks. Most worlds have only been mapped by unmanned probes. Even with the information these probes provide, there are often astrographic and other hazards that have not been previously recorded. This means that systems that have been covered by the Imperial Grand Survey can still present dangers when a manned vessel goes there. Cicero itself was first surveyed by the Exploration Service; though its climate is somewhat less than temperate …" She smiled slightly. "It is a rare find: Earthlike, with a breathable atmosphere. Even Cicero presented perils—a geophysical team was killed during first landing in 2376 when it accidentally caused an ice avalanche during a mapping expedition on North Continent.

"The disappearance of exploratory vessels is highly significant, but this could have occurred for a variety of reasons. Such vessels are well armed and their crews are extraordinarily well trained. Whatever has happened, it warrants our closest attention."

She looked up from her notes and surveyed the room, meeting Ch'k'te's eyes, then the admiral's, and finally the old, old eyes of the *Gyaryu'har*, sitting patiently waiting for her to continue.

"The *Negri Sembilan*," Jackie continued at last, "is a fifth-generation ship of the Malaysia class." A graphic appeared above the table at a gesture to her comp. "We have four other ships of this class on station here at Cicero. While its battle-readiness is below that of a front-line vessel, it is more than adequate to meet anything less than one. It carries a crew of two hundred and seventy-four, including twenty-three officers. The ship's complement includes a scientific team of twenty-five and a Marine complement of thirty-six, consisting of four squads of nine. The *Negri Sembilan* was commissioned in October 2374 at

Cheltham Starbase, and its present captain has been in command for more than eight Standard years.

"The *Gustav Adolf II* is a fifth-generation vessel of the Emperor Cleon class. It is somewhat more lightly armed than the *Negri Sembilan,* but similar in size and crew complement. It was commissioned at Adrianople Starbase in June 2377. The current commander was appointed three years ago.

"Since being assigned to Cicero for exploratory duties in February 2391, each vessel has conducted more than twenty missions. Each has suffered minor damage once." She looked down at her comp. "The *Negri* during a pirate raid at the zor settlement at ElesHyu eighteen months ago, and the *Gustav* from a meteor shower in 2391 during a routine exploration. A complete report of the repair authorizations and tasks are available for your perusal.

"The commanding officer of the *Negri Sembilan* is Captain Damien Abbas." Torrijos' glance caught Jackie's at that moment, making her feel suddenly uneasy. "The *Gustav Adolf II* is commanded by Captain Maria Dunston. Both have spotless service records with several commendations for bravery as well as excellence in the performance of duties—"

"Excuse me, Commodore," Tolliver interrupted, holding up one hand. "Your exposition is most informative, and you are to be commended for its thoroughness. Your assertions concerning the perils of the Exploration Service are noted. The unblemished records of the two vessels, and their commanding officers, are also noted. But the fact remains that the ships are *gone.* Please enlighten us concerning their disappearance."

"Yes, sir." She toyed absently with a stylus, collected her thoughts and continued. "I reported the disappearance of each vessel in accordance with regulations. It is standard policy for an Exploration vessel on duty to send a tight-beam message to the base here on Cicero no less often than once per Standard week. We last received a report from the *Negri Sembilan* four and a half weeks ago, and from the *Gustav Adolf II* three weeks ago.

"Each ship was operating independently and updating the Grand Survey recorded in 2388. The *Negri* was in Sector 19.6.6—" A 3-D grid appeared above the table, indicating human and zor colonies as well as other explored worlds and showing the route of the *Negri Sembilan.* "Its last known position was at this unnamed K3 star." A small arrow indicated the end of the trail. "Its next destination was an F5 main sequence star, indicated by the survey as having eight planets, one possibly habitable. Since the robot probes are considered to be eighty to ninety percent reliable, it is unlikely the probe would have overlooked a celestial body of sufficient size to cause a misjump.

"After the *Negri* failed to make contact at the scheduled time, I submitted a report to the Admiralty and assigned the *Gustav Adolf II* to investigate."

She looked around the room. "The *Gustav* made two jumps. The first jump was to the last known location of the other ship; the second was to the F5 star. We received a report from that system, indicating no debris or unusual radiation. The *Gustav*'s commander conducted a full survey of the system, and reported nothing unusual except for a peculiar incidence of illness among the six Sensitives aboard. Since two were among the landing party on the habitable world, the captain attributed it to a local virus and conducted quarantining and vaccination procedures in accordance with regulations. The illness cleared up after a short time."

"Where did the *Gustav* go next?" asked Tolliver.

"As my report states, sir, we received no further communications from the *Gustav*. I have no data on where they went next. My last orders from the Admiralty were to stay put, to order no further vessels to the site and to await your arrival."

"Very well." Tolliver sat forward and folded his hands in front of him. "Commodore, let me clarify the Admiralty's position regarding the events you have just described.

"Upon consideration of your reports, I have been ordered to inform you that the First Lord considers your actions in this matter to be above reproach. He asked that—once I was satisfied concerning what was known—I convey to you his commendation for your conduct of the investigation."

Jackie tried to read Tolliver's expression and found that she could not easily do so. She gave up. "Thank you, sir."

"Your reports are most thorough on the particulars of the two vessels. I must ask you, however, to provide me with an informed guess as to what you believe has happened to them."

"A … guess, sir?"

"Off the record, of course."

"Of course." Jackie knew nothing ever said to an admiral was completely off the record, but she would have to answer regardless.

She looked down at her notes and at the last report from the two ships and ran the whole matter back through her mind.

The *Negri* had gone to a system for which there was only survey data. It had been previously explored only by an unmanned probe. If it had been attacked there, the *Gustav* had found no evidence of it when it got there ten days later. The system had no other ships in it, no excessive background radiation, nothing. But the *Gustav* had been lost there, too—it had never reported back. Neither captain would have ignored regulations.

It was hard to believe either would have gone pirate or taken off on some wild expedition. They were both too good.

If they had come under attack, there likely would have been some chance for one of them to send a message squirt.

What was left?

"I have very little evidence, Admiral. What I do have, leads me to a conclusion which is highly speculative, to say the least."

"I am prepared to accept that, Commodore. Go on."

"Sir." She put her hands flat on the table before her and looked at them. "It is distinctly possible that we may have a first contact."

The words "first contact" seemed to echo into the silence for a long time. Mankind had experienced three first contacts: the rashk, the zor and, most recently, the otran. Of the three, only the zor had been especially violent. The rashk—a bucolic, reptilian race native to the worlds orbiting Vega—were indifferent to warfare. The otran, discovered by humans and zor in mid-century, were far more warlike, but they were only beginning to explore space.

There were many legacies from mankind's struggle with the zor. Though nearly a century had passed since its end, many old scars and legacies remained—barren Nests destroyed by Marais' fleet, wastelands on worlds ruined by the zor.

And the most obvious legacy: the old, old man sitting at the conference table here on Cicero, listening in apparent calm to the possibility of first contact.

"We have nothing to suggest that is the case, Commodore," Sergei said quietly.

"I was asked for an assessment, *se Gyaryu'har*, and I have provided it. In point of fact, we have nothing to go on at all."

Sergei smiled. "A moment's indulgence for an old man, Commodore Laperriere, before you assert that conclusion. We do have a shred of evidence that may provide enlightenment."

"Sir?"

"We are told," he continued, "that all of the Sensitives aboard the *Gustav Adolf II* suffered some illness during the survey of the system. In my day—" The phosphor caught a facet of an Imperial naval service ring and twinkled. "In my day it was customary to file a daily personnel report. I would assume that the regular transmissions of Exploration Service vessels include these reports. It might be worth consulting the report of the *Gustav*'s chief surgeon; in view of the experiences of other Sensitives"—his smile had disappeared and was replaced by a worried, almost frightened look—"we might well learn something."

Ch'k'te's talons extended a few centimeters. He forcibly retracted them and exchanged a glance with Jackie.

Tolliver looked at Sergei. "What the hell are you talking about?"

"The High Lord has ... dreamed."

Horace Tolliver snorted angrily, "*se* Sergei, are you telling me that you are here merely because the High Lord had a *dream*?"

"I beg your pardon, *se* Admiral," Ch'k'te said. "The precognitive capabilities of the High Lord are well known—"

"They are hardly something to base a campaign on, Commander," Tolliver interrupted. "I will remind you that this is the Imperial Navy and not a psych session for a bunch of damned Sensitives."

"Horace, of all the—" Sergei began, but Admiral Tolliver raised his hand. "Excuse *me*, *se* Sergei."

The older man fell silent.

Horace Tolliver surveyed the room. "I grant the possibility that something might be gained from close examination of the medical records of the *Gustav*. That inquiry will likely conclude that all regulations were followed and all due precautions were taken.

"But I will *not* let the operation of this base and the conduct of an adequate investigation of the unknown danger before us to be determined by the subconscious imaginings of a Sensitive.

"I am particularly unwilling to do so given the mental state of your High Lord. I don't think we can reasonably put any stock in anything he says, sees or dreams. That's what I believe, and the record can damn well so state."

The room was silent as he finished his comments. He looked from face to face, expecting further objections or opposition; but none was forthcoming. Sergei appeared ready to say something, but kept silent.

"Commodore Laperriere, you will conduct a full investigation of the illness of the Sensitives aboard the *Gustav Adolf II,*" Tolliver resumed. "Furthermore, you will issue a general recall order for all vessels under the authority of Cicero Military District and prepare a status report for me concerning the readiness of those vessels to conduct naval operations."

"Sir." Jackie fixed Admiral Tolliver with a stare. "I … It is my opinion, sir, for the record, that an act of overt belligerence is at this time both unwarranted and unwise. I will not accept responsibility for issuing such an order."

"Meaning?"

"I wish it stated, for the record, sir, that if you choose to undertake military operations at this time, with this little evidence, I will protest it. I will of course fulfill my obligation to follow your orders … to the letter."

After a long pause, Tolliver said, "You have your orders, Commodore"—he stood, and the rest hurriedly stood in turn—"carry them out." Trailed immediately by his aides, the admiral walked from the conference room.

chapter 3

He felt the ships jumping from Cicero and knew their doom was sealed. It would strain the bounds of credibility to expect even another Sensitive to believe he knew this, that he could feel it somehow—but he did know. He had felt the brush of that wing years ago, when E'er, his father, had given him the High Lordship by the ritual of *Te'esLi'ir* on his deathbed. What E'er had only perceived as a dim shadow-thing, occasionally preying at the edges of his dreams, had stood out as a glaring, hideous spotlight to the new High Lord; to him, an *e'chya* cutting a dark swath across his visions …

Behind their wings, the lords and courtiers at High Nest had always wondered whether Ke'erl HeYen's mind was indeed scattered to the Eight Winds. Madness in the High Lordship was not a unique thing, nor was it totally undesirable—since madness sometimes opened new vistas to a dreaming Sensitive. But in a time of relative peace, the most violent factions of the People were angered by a weak and half-mad High Lord, who perched in his Chamber of Meditation and dreamed while the *chya'i* rusted in their scabbards.

They did not truly understand; Ke'erl knew that *esGa'u* the Deceiver had prophesied a reckoning with an enemy greater than mere humanity, and it was finally here. While it crept in at the edges of civilization, the sun continued to shine over the High Nest. Ke'erl knew this fact; the *Gyaryu'har* knew it as well and had seen the entire spread of the wing from the Dark Wing to the present, and would now witness for *esLi* at the edge of known space.

And *esLi* alone would judge the outcome.

THE AIRCAR settled to the tarmac at the emperor's personal landing-field on Molokai. After a few moments the hatch opened and Mya'ar HeChra, *esGyu'u* of the High Nest, emerged and drifted slowly to the ground, his wings extended very slightly as he descended the five meters or so; he hadn't waited for the car's grav to lower him.

Dieter Xavier Willem, Solar Emperor, stood on the field waiting for Mya'ar. It was not customary for the emperor to wait for visitors in person, even at his own private enclave; but his visitor spoke with the authority of the High Nest. At Diamond Head, with the Imperial Court watching, this might have meant something different; but on Molokai there were no courtiers, no politicians. Randall Boyd, from the Envoy's Office, stood just behind him.

"*hi* Emperor," Mya'ar said, inclining his head. It had been decided that the emperor was to receive the same prenomen as the High Lord, but the High Nest had learned that humans were uncomfortable with having their emperor addressed by his given name. They also had some stigma attached to touching the emperor's person, so Mya'ar refrained from grasping the human ruler's forearms in greeting.

"*se* Mya'ar," the emperor replied.

"*se* Randall," Mya'ar said to the envoy. Randall Boyd was Nest-child to the first one of that title; he was familiar with the customs of the People, of course, and exchanged the clasp with Mya'ar.

"I thank you for your courtesy, *hi* Emperor," the *esGyu'u* said, as they began to walk across the tarmac. "I realize that your schedule is busy. If the message were not urgent—"

"Then it would arrive by tight-beam," the emperor interrupted. He held up his hand. "I'm sorry that I have not invited you here to Molokai before, *se* Mya'ar. Your honored predecessor, *si* Le'kar, visited here frequently; he presented me with the *surush* blossoms on the far trellis." He gestured toward an arbor, framed by the balmy sky and the beach beyond.

"I hope it will not be my last visit, *hi* Emperor."

"You can be assured it will not … I understand you bear a message from my good friend *hi* Ke'erl?"

"I do. I believe—" Mya'ar looked at Randall for a moment, then back to the emperor. "I believe you will find it disquieting."

"To my friend and brother hi *Dieter Xavier Willem, Solar Emperor, the High Nest sends greetings."* The voice of the High Lord, Ke'erl HeYen, emerged from the holo of his image in the center of the room. *"I regret to communicate with you on such short notice, but it is a matter of some gravity. It disturbs my inner peace, and I fear it will disturb yours as well.*

*"*hi *Emperor, six vessels of your Imperial Navy have departed Cicero System within the last few suns. They were armed for battle with the* esGa'uYal, *but on the Plain of Despite they will find themselves unarmed.*

"I beg eight thousand pardons of you, my brother and friend, but this is an unwise use of our limited resources. We had already placed the Gyaryu'har *on the dark path, and were waiting for the shroud to be pulled aside; Father Sun has now advanced farther in the sky, but I have not received an indication whether this is for good or ill.*

"Regardless of your intentions, hi *Emperor, the fate of these warriors is already sealed. If they return at all, their guise will be*

altered. The esGa'uYal *have already emerged from the Plain, but the one who will ascend the Stair has not yet passed through the* shNa'es'ri.
"Be well, my brother. esLiHeYar.*"*

The holo winked out. The room lights came up at a gesture from the emperor; for a time there was no sound other than the cries of birds and the soft crash of waves on Molokai's northern shore. Mya'ar waited patiently on his perch; Randall sat upright.

The emperor leaned back in his chair and rubbed his chin.

"That was the whole message."

"Yes, *hi* Emperor."

"I … I confess I'm not sure I understand what the High Lord had to say."

"I'm sure that Imperial Intelligence will—" Randall began.

"No," the emperor said. "No, before I turn it over to Langley I want to understand what the High Lord was trying to say. He chose to communicate directly with me for a reason. Do either of you know why? Do you know *what*?

"And what's more," he said, leaning forward, "I don't have any information that any naval force has been dispatched from Cicero. If I haven't been informed, how can he know?"

Randall looked at Mya'ar. The *esGyu'u* had not changed his wing-position, but his eyes seemed to hold some scarcely concealed emotion.

"The High Lord has dreamed, *hi* Emperor. His conclusions are based on his dreams; thus the High Lord guides the Flight of the People."

"But why did he cloak it in … Why did he phrase it the way he did?"

"I do not understand, *hi* Emperor," Mya'ar answered.

"The references—the mythological terms. Surely he must know that I don't have the context."

"He seeks to give you a *sSurch'a, hi* Emperor."

"A *sSurch'a*?"

"A leap of understanding. It is a means of teaching among the People. The elder places the facts before the junior and waits for him to reach the same conclusion on his own. The junior therefore believes in that conclusion, for he has obtained it through his own reasoning."

"I see." The emperor was holding his voice level, perhaps a bit miffed at being referred to as "the junior." "Does he believe that I would not accept him at his word, if he simply said what he knew?"

"Eight thousand pardons." Mya'ar's wing-position changed now, but neither human understood. "Forgive me, *hi* Emperor, but the High Lord has done exactly that. What he *knows* is indeed what he said."

"He speaks of placing the *Gyaryu'har* on the dark road—"

"Dark *path*, *hi* Emperor."

"Dark path, then. *se* Sergei was sent to Cicero—does that mean he was placed in danger?"

"Yes, *hi* Emperor."

The emperor looked at him sharply. "Why? Why was he placed in danger?"

"He was sent to Cicero in accordance with … the High Lord's dreams."

"What could he do? *se* Sergei's an old man, for God's sake. He can't even walk."

"He is the *Gyaryu'har*."

"That is not an answer, *se* Mya'ar. What would he do if a group of—of *esGa'uYal*—turned up in Cicero System? Stab them with his *gyaryu*? Tell them tales from zor legend?"

Mya'ar did not reply, but his wing-position changed again.

"What will happen to *se* Sergei?"

"What *esLi* wills, *hi* Emperor."

"And that is not an answer, either." The emperor stood up and walked to the French doors, which gave out onto a covered lanai. He looked out toward the ocean without comment.

Mya'ar and Randall waited patiently for the emperor to speak.

"If this was so damned important," he said at last, "tell me, *se* Mya'ar: Why does this message come now? Why didn't *hi* Ke'erl provide this explanation—such as it is—before now?"

"And if he was going to put *se* Sergei in danger, why did he not inform me of the peril at Cicero?"

"Surely, *hi* Emperor, he did—by sending the *Gyaryu'har* there," Mya'ar ventured. "There would be no other purpose in such a mission."

"What you are saying," the emperor said, turning again to face the alien ambassador, "is that sending the *Gyaryu'har* was a signal to us: a signal we didn't understand."

"The High Lord was not aware of this misunderstanding, *hi* Emperor. I ask eight thousand pardons again, but it must be noted that the Imperial Court has rarely listened to *anything* the High Nest has had to say."

"The High Lord is our good friend. Surely he does not believe—"

"*hi* Emperor. Whatever *your* feelings on the matter, it is not the position of the Imperial Government. This … This has been coming for some time."

"What has been coming?"

"The attack of the *esGa'uYal*."

"But I thought the *esGa'uYal* were demons. Didn't your people once believe that *we* were servants of *esGa'u*?"

"We were mistaken."

"I am so very glad to hear that, *se* Mya'ar. I wish to be sure that the High Nest is not mistaken again."

EACH MONTH Jackie made a personal visit to Cicero Op, the space station in orbit around the habitable world. The station was the most important facility in Cicero System—it was the anchorage for the Military District fleet and also provided meteorological information for the Cicero Down base and the other installations on-planet.

The recent arrival of distinguished guests had made staff even more unwilling to interrupt her, so Jackie was surprised to hear her door-chime ring.

"Come," she said, and the door slid aside.

She was surprised when she saw Sergei Torrijos' chair hovering in the hall.

"Mr.—*se Gyaryu'har!* I—"

The old man smiled.

She recovered her composure. "Please do come in."

The chair coasted silently into her quarters. "Thank you," he said. "I would have called ahead, but I chose not to discuss my whereabouts with my staff. Given the … current strains, they probably would have demanded that I take an escort."

She led him into her tiny sitting-room, made to appear larger through the clever placement of mirrors and holos. "Can I pour you something? *g'rey'l*, perhaps?"

Sergei looked up at her, surprised for a moment, and then his face composed. "Yes. Thank you, Commodore."

On an impulse she said, "My friends call me Jackie." She poured the liquid into two delicate long-stemmed glasses and handed one to Sergei.

"Jackie, then. My friends"—he said, smiling slightly—"call me Sergei." He raised his glass.

"*esLiHeYar,*" she said and drank, making his face reflect another moment's surprise: *To the glory of esLi.*

He murmured assent. The drink burned pleasantly down the throat into the stomach. "You seem uncommonly well versed in our culture," he said after a moment.

"Thank you." She pushed a wisp of stray hair from her face. "I have a zor exec. *se* Ch'k'te has taught me a great deal about the People." She looked at her half-empty glass, then reddened for a moment. "I mean to say—"

"The two are different entities," Sergei said, holding up a hand and smiling. "I have lived among the zor for eighty-five years, Jackie, since I left Sol System at the end of the war.

"I am the *Gyaryu'har*, but I am not a zor, as—" He lifted both of his frail arms. "—as my lack of wings will attest. Still, like many who went into exile with the Admiral, we have assimilated the culture of the People. Our descendants have had that all of their lives—we are a small, isolated culture among the People."

"I see."

"I suspect that you don't, but it doesn't trouble me. At least you invited me in for a drink."

She didn't have a response for that, except to say, "I'm honored. Ch'k'te is honored as well … Well, more than that. Awed."

"I get that a lot. At my age it goes right past, I assure you." He sipped on his *g'rey'l.* "I'm practically the only one left," he added.

"Of the exiles?"

"Of those who could not remain," he answered. "Exiles. 'Outcasts' might be a better term—we committed the unpardonable sin of winning the war and then went to live with the enemy."

"The sin was in the way the war was won," Jackie replied, wondering where this was leading and whether she should get into this sort of discussion.

"Is that what they teach aspiring officers these days? It's a terrible generalization. There was no other way. None. Two generations of soldiers and sailors and pilots, two generations of civilians, paid in blood because they wouldn't fight the war the way Admiral Marais fought it."

There was a sudden quiet in the room as Sergei said the name of Admiral Marais. That name had overtones: They taught about the war at the Academy— how not? Marais was a villain, pure and simple; he'd even written a book a few years after the war, justifying the campaign in the way Sergei had just described.

She had no illusions. The zor had been an implacable enemy. Ch'k'te had convinced her of that much: She wouldn't want to be in a fight with him.

"The People have long since accepted this. Why do you think they chose the Admiral to be the *Gyaryu'har*?"

"And now you."

"And now me. I am a human, *se* Jackie, but I am a servant of *esLi* and of the High Lord." Sergei moved his chair across the room, reflections in mirrors tracking him as he passed. He turned to face her again. "I suspect that you do not understand this, either."

"I don't know what the *Gyaryu'har* does, if that's what you mean. I asked Ch'k'te, and he gave me a circular answer—that the *Gyaryu'har* carries the *gyaryu*."

"The *gyaryu*." He reached to his belt, and pulled a finely tooled leather scabbard onto his lap. "The *gyaryu* is a *chya*, a very special one." Sergei moved his fingers slowly along the scabbard that held the blade. "Every adult of the People, both male and female, carries a *chya* from the time of *enHeru*, the rite of passage. In many ways it is the perfect zor weapon: a light, flexible and very dangerous blade. It is a talon. In ancient times, a *chya* was not enabled until it was bloodied in combat.

"When the Dark Wing conquered, all of the *chya* were disabled—dishonored. Though we didn't realize it at the time, a majority of the People were willing to use their *chya* to transcend the Outer Peace, because the People had become *hi'idju*."

"*idju* means 'dishonored,'" she said carefully. "*hi'idju* means—"

"The entire People were dishonored."

"And they would have committed mass suicide?"

"Yes." Sergei looked away. "At the point at which the People surrendered to the Admiral, they considered that as a possibility—even though he told them he'd never ask them to do it. You may find it hard to believe."

"I do. Go on."

"In order to change the flight of the entire People, Admiral Marais was given *this*." He drew the blade and held it before him, point up, his hand tightly gripping the hilt.

The *gyaryu* was made of dark-colored metal, just over a meter long. It gleamed from careful attention. As the moment stretched out, Jackie became aware of a barely audible noise, as if from a quickly vibrating wire. Further, the blade seemed to be drawing on all the light in the room, making it dim and shadowy. She knew this was some sort of illusion, but found it strangely compelling.

The old *Gyaryu'har* seemed to be watching her reaction, the way her junior officers did during staff meetings: alert to any indication of dissatisfaction or anger. No, she decided; it was more than that—it was almost as if he was trying to see if she'd noticed *anything* when he drew the sword.

She certainly had noticed, but wasn't sure what that meant.

"*se* Sergei ..."

"Let me tell you something else, *se* Jackie. The High Lord presented Admiral Marais with the *gyaryu* when he realized the Solar Empire—and humanity—was not the enemy, and that it was likely they *never had been*. The war changed so many lives, but it came about as a result of a flawed vision. My life, my career ..."

"Your career was ruined by the war," Jackie said quietly into the darkness.

"Well," Sergei said, "*one* career was ruined." He sheathed the *gyaryu*, and placed his hands over it, one atop the other. "We all took solace from the irony of the situation—that we had had our service to the emperor severed because we did too good a job.

"It was a common belief in the Empire, you know, that in a few years there would be another war, more violent than all of the previous ones. The zor would be even more angry and vengeful for what Admiral Marais did to them."

"It would stand to reason."

"*Human* reason, *se* Jackie. Not zor reason. It was not possible to undo what had been done, but the Flight of the People had been irrevocably changed. We all changed with it: The Empire, the Nests, everything changed ... except that the true enemy, the one we did not see, remained. It's still out there and High Lord Ke'erl HeYen has felt the dark ships at the edge of our space."

"Dark ships," Jackie repeated.

"Horace Tolliver didn't believe me when I told him that *hi* Ke'erl had dreamed. It's curious—your analysis may be exactly correct: What the *Gustav Adolf II* and the *Negri Sembilan* encountered was the enemy that *hi'i* Sse'e felt so many years ago. All these years ... waiting for us, just as he believed."

"Wait." Jackie leaned back against a side table. "Hold on just a minute, *se* Sergei. 'The *true* enemy?' Are you suggesting that the High Nest has known of an enemy ... for most of a century? Why didn't this intelligence come to the emperor's attention?"

"'That the ear does not hear is not the fault of the voice,'" Sergei quoted. "There have been representatives of the People at the court of the Solar Emperor since the Act of Normalization; there is an envoy who is the voice and the ear of the emperor at the High Nest. Do you think that the matter has never been mentioned?"

"Of course not."

"Indeed not. The High Nest has tried to reach out to humanity, but there has been no effort in return."

If there had been any doubt how much exile had changed the old man in front of her, the last comment confirmed it. When he spoke of "humanity" he wasn't talking about himself; when he spoke of the High Nest, it was something he was part of.

"What does the High Nest believe will happen next?"

Sergei looked away, as if there were a response he had in mind but didn't want to express it.

"Horace Tolliver has taken six ships of the line into the hands of the enemy. There's a good chance we will never see them again."

Sergei spoke of an enemy. To Jackie, the idea of an "enemy" was a simple, logical one: a foe, usually armed, whose objectives were opposite to one's own. The armed forces of the Empire existed to combat enemies ... but she realized that Sergei was not speaking in those terms. To him the enemy was a shadowy, almost mystical thing. Following her own intuition, Jackie's mind snapped back to the horror of her shared vision with Ch'k'te: of the tentacled monsters that had comprised her nightmare.

The enemy. The *true* enemy.

She could not speak. It was as if Sergei held her silent, drawing out the moment. She had thought mankind had come to terms with its fear of the dark, the fear of what might be lurking out there beyond the range of its narrow sight. The zor had personified that darkness, calling it *esGa'u*, the Deceiver. Humans had simply rationalized it away.

It remained there all the same.

THEY RODE the shuttle into orbit in relative silence. It was hard to make small conversation with the *Gyaryu'har*. It was not a question of taciturnity on his part; more that she realized a certain ambiguity to everything she thought to say and wondered how he might interpret it.

It was too much for her. The older man seemed to be trying to get her to jump to some sort of conclusion based on the available data. She had thought she understood the zor, with their strange, precognitive culture and their mystical view of the universe. She had thought she understood the unknown, and the way in which it was to be explored. She had thought she had learned to comprehend the vastness of space, especially the seemingly infinite reaches beyond that which man and zor had explored. In a sudden moment of terrible insight, Jackie realized that she had really understood nothing at all.

She *did* understand Admiral Tolliver's position: It was hard to base any sort of sound military planning on the dreams of a High Lord, especially someone like Ke'erl HeYen. They said that the High Lord was mad; even Ch'k'te had confided to her his fear that the zor were being led by an—what was the word he had used?—*alGa'u'yar*. Decadent and weak; short of the standard expected of a warrior. Certainly not a complimentary view.

Nonetheless Ke'erl HeYen, whatever his faults, real or perceived, was a powerful Sensitive, perhaps the most powerful alive. Before now Jackie had always assigned these facts—along with the rest of the insight she had gained into zor culture—to a compartment of her mind in which illogical and irrational perceptions could exist. As a Regular Navy officer, it was inappropriate for her to base her judgment on such things; the idea of having to take such matters into consideration frightened her more than she wanted to admit. Enemies she should understand; bogeymen she could not, or would not, grasp—only fear.

But the idea that they might exist scared her even more.

ONE VISIT a month to the Operations Center was about all Jackie could usually take. Though it was always a pleasure conduct an inspection of the Center, it was almost as great a pleasure to depart. Its CO, Commander Bryan Noyes, was in many ways the epitome of a staff officer: an intelligent, precise, studious man, demanding and accurate, who probably hadn't touched a weapon in ten years. When she had been posted here, Jackie had been advised on Noyes by the former commander of Cicero, who had chosen to leave Noyes behind when taking a flag post somewhere in the inner sphere. "Noyes," the old commander had said, "is a pain in the ass, but he's the best damn pain in the ass in His Majesty's Fleet." Truer words were never spoken.

As she had ordered several days ago, the Operations Center was at full alert. After a long exchange of recognition signals and passwords, the shuttle was directed to a berth at the station. The orbital station was extremely busy, requiring its own traffic coordination; the shuttle was routed along a lane between two large tugs, one coming in from the outer system and the other departing. They dwarfed the little gig.

Noyes had prepared for their visit with more flourish than usual. He met them on the hangar deck, accompanied by an honor guard that mustered all half-dozen zor on board the station.

Jackie and Sergei descended from the gig to the hangar deck. Noyes stepped forward and offered a crisp salute, then bowed to Sergei.

"Permission to come aboard, Commander," Jackie said. It was a ritual phrase, but tradition required her to ask.

"Granted, of course. Welcome aboard, Commodore," he said to Jackie. "Welcome aboard, sir," he said to Sergei. "Is this your first visit here?"

Sergei was taking in the view with what seemed to be the curiosity of a dirt-sider. He turned his glance slowly to Noyes. "Yes, it is. Quite a facility," he added.

"Biggest of its kind, sir." He began to walk toward the personnel access. "Best-armed and more up-to-date than a lot of the bases in the inner sphere."

"Indeed." Sergei looked all about him and saw naval personnel—human and zor both—moving to and fro, attending to their various duties. It all seemed remarkably efficient and thorough. "I daresay it would be hard to take the station by force."

"Impossible." Noyes looked down at Sergei, his face set in a condescending smile. "Properly supported by mobile vessels, this station cannot be taken. Even," he added, almost as an afterthought, "if you could find an enemy to take it."

Sergei let his chair come to a halt and returned Noyes' glance. "I would not be so sure, Commander. There was a time, before your grandfather was born, that we made a similar statement."

"The situation is quite different now, sir."

"Oh." Sergei looked away, and around him at the hangar deck. "Is it really."

"WHEN WAS this station built, Commander?" Sergei asked as he and the commodore followed Noyes from post to post on the bridge. Noyes turned, seeming somewhat surprised at the question. "2381, sir," he answered. "A few Standard years after Cicero Down base was built."

"You maintain complete records, I would assume."

"Of course." Noyes had stopped beside a computer station. He stood— almost striking a pose, one hand by his side, the other on the chair next to him. He looked from Sergei to Jackie, one eyebrow raised a microscopic amount. "Was there … something specific you were—"

"Curiosity merely," Sergei said, motioning with one hand. "2381, you say … That would be just after the chartering of the Imperial Grand Survey, then. Do you have the data of the original probe reports?"

"Naturally, sir." Still appearing a trifle surprised by the inquiry, he sat down and began to enter information. "There is quite a bit of material—planetary and solar data, gravometric analyses, Muir-limit statistics—"

"I am well informed on the subject of planetary surveys, Commander," Sergei interrupted. "I performed nearly two hundred of them during my tour of duty."

The words "tour of duty" rang hollowly through the bridge, already hushed while the inspection was taking place.

"Indeed. Did you have a particular question?" Noyes asked quietly.

"A conjecture merely." Sergei looked up at Jackie, who had remained completely silent during the entire exchange. "Commander," he continued, "as I am sure you are aware, the ultimate objective of this investigation into the disappearance of the two Exploration Service vessels must be the determination of a cause. I reason there is some difference in data between the time when the robot probes originally surveyed the world we quaintly call 'Sargasso' and the time the two ships visited.

"I suspect that the later survey will show something significant: a large mass or perhaps a hidden base."

"If the … *Gyaryu'har* pleases," Noyes replied, "the squadron detailed to investigate Sargasso will soon make all speculation on the subject a moot point. The admiral's investigation will likely explain the disappearance, will it not?"

Jackie was taken somewhat aback by Noyes' comment, and hardly tried to conceal her anger. *Why, you sanctimonious bastard,* she thought.

"The admiral has his methods, and I have mine," Sergei replied, his expression remaining impassive. "Suffer the whims of an old man."

Noyes waited for a moment almost long enough to be insulting and then looked up at Jackie. She hoped that her stern expression offered sufficient guidance.

"Display IGS data for Sargasso System," he said. A display appeared above the console, showing a 3-D representation of the system that moved in slow motion, showing the rotation of the planets around the primary.

"The original survey of the Sargasso System was conducted in 2372," Noyes said, without looking up. "Eight planets, ranging from 0.4 AU to 29.8 AU. One nominally Terran habitable world at the fourth orbital; three inner planets; three gas giants; one outer world. No asteroid belts, little appreciable debris; Oort 0.7 Standard size, all suggesting a mature system and a highly stable primary. Strong hydrogen lines in the F6 sun. The survey shows gravometric analysis, plasma flow lines and electromagnetic data." He poked a finger at the data that hung in midair beside the system display.

"Display *Gustav Adolf II* survey data for Sargasso," he said, and another 3-D display appeared beside the first one and moved to overlay it as Noyes gestured.

Noyes' brow furrowed. "Pardon me," he said. "I seem to have retrieved the wrong image—"

"No," Sergei said. He indicated the identifying icon in a lower corner, identical with the previous image. "No, Commander, this is the correct one. But, as you will see, the data are quite different."

Noyes looked from the screen to Sergei and then to his own display. "Nine planets, two habitable worlds ... an asteroid belt at 6.5 AU; a larger-than-normal Oort cloud ..." He looked at Jackie. "Commodore, I—"

"Belay it," she snapped. "Commander, conduct a complete review of the integrity of your survey data. On the double."

"Aye-aye," he said, looking somewhat bewildered. He stood and strode quickly away toward the pilot's station.

Jackie looked closely at the two overlaid images: the 2372 survey showing eight worlds and the *Gustav*'s survey showing nine and an asteroid belt.

"You expected this," she said quietly to Sergei.

He smiled wanly. "Let me say ... I am not surprised. Take a look at this." He produced a comp from a pocket and handed it to Jackie. A 3-D view of a solar system appeared above it.

"This data agrees with the *Gustav*'s survey! Where did you get—"

"From Cicero Down's comp," he replied. "It was part of the official record of the Grand Survey."

"What does this mean?"

"Commodore." He lowered his voice almost to a whisper, "Your data at Cicero Down have been altered. It means that somewhere on the premises of this base is a spy ... for the *es-Ga'uYal*."

She looked around the bridge, but Sergei placed a thin, bony hand on her arm. "I would expect that the spy could disguise itself as a normal person. It could even make itself look like me. Or you."

"Surely you don't suspect—"

"I would imagine it was someone less obvious than you, Commodore. Also, I would know." He let go of her arm and teed his hand on the sword at his belt.

"Will it tell you who—"

"Part of my purpose for coming up here, Commodore. But I do not know how long it will take me."

"What do you need?"

"Quiet. I do not think my presence has yet been noticed."

Jackie nodded. "Commander," she said to Noyes, "The *Gyaryu'har* and I will be in our quarters."

A HOLO of the planetary system hung in the air over the *Singapore*'s ready-room conference table, with an ID block next to each world and summary information at the base of the display. Admiral Tolliver sat at the far end of the table, scowling. "I don't know, Admiral."

"That's not the answer I'm looking for, Captain Diaz." He turned to the holo. "This data does not agree with the 2372 Grand Survey. There has to be a reason."

"Sir, I am as disturbed about this as you. Despite the log of the *Gustav Adolf*, I expected to jump into the system listed in our survey database. Finding what we found is like jumping into a system without any probe data at all."

"They used to do it all the time."

"I acknowledge that, Admiral. But operating procedure requires—"

"Yes, yes, I know." Tolliver put his hand up to stop Diaz from continuing. "Nonetheless, we are here—wherever *here* is."

"We are at the coordinates we expected, sir."

"Then the survey data is clearly in error … Have the *Johore* and *Andaman* reported in?"

"They've gone into the inner system, Admiral. The current display"—Diaz pointed at the third and fourth worlds—"reflects the information they have gathered since being dispatched there."

"Captain." Tolliver touched his comp. The system display shrank and another appeared beside it. "This is the data derived from the Imperial Grand Survey; it is what we expected to find when we came out of jump. By comparison, the other data"—he gestured toward the original system display, still incrementally updating—"matches the *Gustav Adolf*'s report; it appears that we are where they were. But why are we not *here*?" He pointed to the alternate system. "That is what we are here to find out."

"Admiral, with all due respect, by confirming the *Gustav*'s finding we have accomplished what we are here to do. I'm not sure—"

"I *am* sure. We will examine the habitable worlds and complete our report. Then we will decide where to go next."

"Admiral, I—"

"Captain Diaz, you may consider those instructions as an order. If you do not wish to carry them out, you will be so good as to send me someone who will."

Diaz offered a stiff salute in response to the rebuke, turned and left the ready-room.

THE *CAMEROON* and the *Wei Hsing* remained near the jump point while the *Singapore*, Tolliver's flagship, and its sister ship *Maldive* descended into the gravity-well to join the two ships already there. They took up orbit around the outer habitable world just as the *Gustav* had done weeks earlier; and as Tolliver watched from the engineering station, Captain Robert Diaz ordered a gig with four Sensitives and a Marine guard to the surface to conduct a survey. There was no direct evidence of sentient life, but the first few orbits had shown energy signatures in a range of low hills near the equator.

It took twenty minutes for the small craft to descend through the atmosphere and land on the surface. As it descended, the bridge of the *Singapore* remained deadly quiet; Tolliver's stiffness and the Captain's taut anger hung in the air.

"*Singapore*, this is Ajami. The survey team is inserted." Lieutenant Ken Ajami's image appeared above the engineering station, in front of Tolliver. Vid from the recording cameras sprang to life on holo monitors on the wall. The Sensitives moved out from the landing site, each with a pair of Marines; the cameras began to track across the countryside and showed local flora, along with indigenous insect and animal life. The view was completely normal on the face of it. The teams had the survey data gathered by a similar group from the *Gustav Adolf II*; all preliminary indications showed the same results the *Gustav* had found. The comm channel was full of chatter from the four survey parties as the data was transmitted to the *Singapore*'s bridge.

Abruptly two of the four camera transmissions cut off. Tolliver reached across to the console and touched the controls, then turned to Diaz. "Captain, reestablish contact with parties Bravo and Charlie."

"Alford, Huerta. This is the *Singapore*. Report." Diaz leaned forward in the pilot's chair, turning to face comm station. "Lieutenant, do we have ID on the two teams' locations?"

The comm officer's hands played across the comm console. "No, Skip," he said after a moment. "We've lost them."

"Ajami, report," Diaz said. "Ken, we've lost two of your IDs. that's going on down there?"

Another vid stopped transmitting. The primary camera, following the progress of the Alpha team—consisting of Ajami and two Marines—continued to track, showing a bucolic meadow scene, interrupted by a few low trees set against a clear sky.

"Ken," Diaz said, "if you can hear me, acknowledge."

The bridge had gone completely silent. There was no comm chatter at all, no response from the remaining team, and the screen continued to show the same peaceful scene.

Diaz turned to face Tolliver.

"Gig is lifting off, Cap'n," said Ensign Louise Kahala, the *Singapore*'s helm officer. "It's accelerating toward orbit."

"Get it on comm, now," Captain Diaz said angrily. "*Singapore* sends. Ajami, what the hell is going on?"

The comm officer shook his head. "Gig is not responding, Skip."

"Admiral?" Diaz said, turning to face him. His voice was angry; every captain feels personally responsible for his own people, and he hadn't favored the survey in the first place.

Tolliver didn't answer. Behind him, the breeze shook the branches of the indigenous trees.

"CAPTAIN, I am holding you personally responsible," Tolliver was saying. "I *will* have a complete report, if I must obtain it for myself firsthand." The lift door slid aside, and Lieutenant Ken Ajami, WS4—the highest Sensitive-only rank in the Imperial Navy—came onto the bridge, followed by his Sensitive colleagues Marie Alford, Terrence Huerta and Ivan Asaro. They appeared to be composed and relaxed, which seemed to infuriate Admiral Tolliver even further.

Ajami offered a salute to Diaz, then walked to the gunnery station without a word. The other three remained near the lift doors. Tolliver crossed the bridge to stand before him.

"What do you think you're doing, Mister?" the admiral snapped. "I don't recall ordering you back to the *Singapore*."

"That hardly matters anymore, Admiral."

"What? I'll have your bars and I'll see you in irons—"

"No," the Sensitive answered. He held up a hand, then gestured past Tolliver to the bridge. "No, I don't think so."

Tolliver turned to look where Ajami had pointed. His gaze went to Diaz, sitting in the pilot's chair, and then at each of the other stations on the bridge and the Marines at attention at their posts.

No one was moving. They had frozen in position, staring straight ahead or down at their consoles; walking from one place to another; a hand extended toward a control.

"What ..."

Then, just as suddenly, motion on the forward screen caught Tolliver's eye. What he saw defied description: The planet they orbited, half in shadow, began to *change shape.*

It was a phenomenon he couldn't understand. It was as if it had extended two large limbs or pseudopods made of land and water and atmosphere; as he watched, it engulfed the *Johore,* a quarter-orbit ahead of the *Singapore.* His heart raced: he couldn't move, as fear rooted him to the spot.

A moment later he realized that it was no illusion. The scene on the screen suddenly changed: They had been flung from orbit. The mass-radar confirmed it; alarms rang out across the bridge and across the ship as the sudden change in orbital components stressed its structural members.

"Diaz!" Tolliver shouted. "What the hell—"

Still no one had moved. Tolliver looked from the captain, who sat perfectly still, staring straight ahead, to the Sensitive, who stood with his hands on a guide rail, a sardonic smile on his face.

"What have you done? What's going on?"

"Watch," the Sensitive said, gesturing toward the pilot's board, where transponder codes were rapidly updating. The *Johore* was nowhere to be seen; the *Singapore* was moving rapidly on its as yet uncorrected course. The *Andaman* and *Maldive,* which had also been in orbit, were now flying almost parallel to each other. The mass-radar was recording a series of energy discharges.

Tolliver went rapidly across the bridge to the comm station, where the officer sat rigidly, staring at nothing. He touched a control.

"*Wei Hsing,*" he said. "*Cameroon.* This is Tolliver. Report."

"There'll be no need for *that,* either," Ajami's voice said, as the comm panel erupted in a shower of energy discharge, throwing the immobile comm officer and the admiral to the deck.

It took a moment for Tolliver to get his feet under him, and as he moved to get up he reached for his sidearm. But before he could draw it, he glanced across at Ajami and saw—

*T*HIS IS *almost too simple,* he heard in his head. He couldn't move or see; it seemed as if time had come to a halt and he was floating, immaterial and invisible.

The meat-creatures are as pliable as we had been told, a second voice acknowledged.

Did you doubt?

Of course I did not.

This task is not finished. Those few with k'th's's *must yet be dealt with.*

A trivial matter. Let them destroy each other.

The first voice seemed to be pondering this last comment. At last it said, *Splendid. See to it.*

THE *ANDAMAN* disappeared from the display and then the *Maldive*. The pilot's board showed expanding clouds of debris for several seconds before their density dropped below the sensitivity level.

The *Johore*, *Cameroon* and *Wei Hsing* were nowhere to be seen. Tolliver looked frantically from the holo to the thing that stood in Ajami's place. It looked like a cloud of rainbow-colored gas with a silver sphere hovering in the middle of it.

"You are powerless," the thing said. A tentacle of energy lashed out and struck him, driving him to his knees. "You will not even be able to speak of this. It would be a trivial matter to destroy you, but you may yet have use."

He heard himself screaming, and didn't remember anything more.

chapter 4

Hours later Jackie was summoned to the station's bridge. Moments after she arrived, Sergei's chair glided through the lift doors. They met at the pilot's board in the center of the bridge. All around, crew were at battle stations.

"Report," she said to Noyes, who turned from examining the pilot's board full of transponder codes. The board was complex, like that aboard a carrier.

"An unknown vessel inside the sixth orbital, ma'am. Just jumped in, traveling at just under one-fifth C. Spatial fluctuation indicates that it did not misjump. This was its destination."

"Dispatch a fighter squadron to intercept. Ready a second," she added, looking sideways at Sergei, "and await orders to launch."

"Aye-aye, ma'am," he replied, and did so. The transponder screen was suddenly full of blips: the "bogey," six intercept fighters, and now four starships closing toward the intruder.

"Visual contact," said a tech somewhere nearby. A fighter pilot's-eye view of the approaching vessels appeared near the pilot's board. "Silhouette confirmed," said the same tech. "Bogey is—wait one—an Imperial vessel, Malaysia class. ID beacon not operative."

Jackie looked suddenly at Sergei, who stared stonily at the transponder screen.

"Vessel has taken heavy damage," said the tech. "Reporting … no defensive fields. Bogey has no pressure on the bridge. Fighter leader reports multiple hits on weapon ports and shuttle bays …"

"Order the ships to heave to," Noyes said, and Jackie nodded.

"The *Pappenheim* has already issued that order, sir," the tech replied. "No response."

"Board it," Noyes ordered, after glancing back at Jackie.

The minutes ticked by and the tension aboard the station increased accordingly. The unknown vessel slowed its hurtling descent into the gravity well, proceeding under fighter escort toward the Navy dry-dock, indicating they had been successfully boarded.

At last the tech reported a hail from one of the vessels.

"Lieutenant Tsang reporting," said a voice, and a view of the bridge of a Malaysia-class starship appeared near a console. Tsang was in a vacc suit. "Come in, Cicero Base."

"This is Laperriere," Jackie said, stepping toward the display. "Report, Lieutenant."

"No life support on the bridge, Commodore. The hull has been breached. There are pressurized compartments aft."

"What ship is it?" she asked, dreading the answer.

"I ... seem to be aboard the IS *Singapore*, ma'am." She gestured behind her.

"You're on the admiral's *flagship*? Are you sure, Lieutenant?"

"... Yes ma'am. The admiral—my team found him in the ship's Engineering Section, trying to ... rip out the controls for the maneuver drive with his bare hands. We took him off in restraints."

The bridge of the station was as silent as a tomb.

"There were twenty or twenty-five other crew and officers aboard, all in about the same shape. I took responsibility to have them removed."

"Ask if there were any Sensitives aboard," Sergei said quietly.

"Were any of the survivors Sensitives?" Jackie asked.

"We found six Sensitives in the sick bay, ma'am. All dead by overdose. It ..." she swallowed "... looked like it was by their own hand. Doc says it was cyanide. What are your orders, ma'am?" The young lieutenant looked to be relieved, finally having the opportunity to follow someone else's orders.

"Where have the survivors been moved?"

"I had them transferred to the sick bay of the *Pappenheim,* ma'am. It's inbound for Cicero Op."

Jackie turned to Noyes. "Countermand the *Pappenheim*'s flight orders. It, and every vessel involved in the scramble, are to keep their distance from dry-dock, and from every other installation in this system. No one is to pass within ten thousand klicks of their present location except on my orders. Do it!"

"Ma'am?" Tsang asked.

"Lieutenant, pass a 'Well done' to the rest of the task force. You are to consider yourselves under quarantine until further notice. No additional personnel are to board the vessel unless absolutely necessary, and no one is to come in contact with the survivors except medical personnel unless I order it."

"Ma'am, the Sensitives—"

"Especially the goddamned Sensitives!" she interrupted. "*No one,* Tsang. Pass the word. And I will have the hide of anyone who countermands those orders hanging from the flagpole of Cicero Down control tower. Do it. Laperriere out." She signaled to break the connection.

She turned at last to Sergei. "I suppose you expected this, too."

"No, actually not," he said wearily. "I did not expect them to return at all. Now at least we have a chance to learn the nature of our enemy, before ..."

"Before what?"

Sergei looked up at Jackie. "Before, Commodore, that enemy destroys us."

A STORM was sweeping across South Continent: fierce by any standards except possibly those of Cicero itself. Naval personnel posted to Cicero soon became accustomed to the climate or else they transferred elsewhere; for those inured to it, this particular bout of weather was no more than a garden-variety storm.

From where she sat, Jackie could see the storm beginning to cover the southern hemisphere of the planet, striking the coasts. She could imagine the biting cold wind sweeping in from across the ocean and the clouds chasing each other across the sky in its wake; she could almost see the freezing rain pouring down on the tarmac. In truth, sitting in light uniform blouse and trousers in a pleasant air-conditioned cabin three hundred and forty kilometers above the surface with the planet spread portrait-fashion against the starry backdrop of the Cygnus Arm, the cold seemed completely incongruous.

She had seen this view many times before. Still, it always amazed her, reminding her of the majesty of nature and the sheer size and grandeur of the universe. It was a humbling experience, yet easily taken for granted in an age in which travel between stars was commonplace, almost mundane.

Was this what the unknown planets had looked like to the crew of the *Gustav Adolf II*, the *Negri Sembilan*? Or to the squadron of six that had followed in their wake, looking for a trace of them? The vid log of the survey team of the *Gustav* had shown an Earthlike world that had looked something like Cicero—except warmer. *Like every other Earthlike planet in the universe,* she thought to herself.

She rubbed her forehead absentmindedly. *Gets the thoughts flowing,* as a former lover used to say. In a happier time, he would rub her forehead for her, after a tense stint at the engineering station or on the bridge. Now she did it for herself.

She turned away from the full-length display panel and opened the medical report again, trying to discern some clue amidst the awful evidence provided by the chief surgeon of the IS *Pappenheim*.

```
All surviving crew of the Singapore are suffering
from what appears to be acute schizophrenia,
coupled with extreme paranoia. These psychoses
are directed at anyone and everything, including
each other or medical personnel. This tendency is
especially acute with regard to Sensitives, who
were mentioned in conversations with various
patients. Though there is no evidence in medical
histories regarding personal phobias toward
Sensitive-trained individuals …
```

Of course not, Jackie thought to herself; *wouldn't let 'em aboard a starship if there were.*

```
... several individuals (cf. att. reports 12, 19,
22, 26, 33, et al.) flew into rages when Sensi-
tive examination was recommended in their hearing.
One orderly (cf. att. report 22) was badly
injured and bitten twice by a young female
crewmember, who nearly succeeded in removing her
restraints in the process of hurling herself at
the individual. On two other occasions the re-
actions most closely resembled petit mal seizures.
    From depositions thus far obtained, Sensitives
on board all three ships were forcibly poisoned
by members of their own crew without evidence of
remorse. In one case this act was carried out by
a brother on his own sister (cf. att. report 52),
and during the interrogation the individual in
question declaimed that the sister had "ceased to
be human" and had "become a monster." Other
interrogations (cf. att. reports 19, 26, 38, et
al.) contain similar utterances ...
```

The chime of the door interrupted her. She looked up to see the figure of Commander Noyes standing outside. She beckoned him to enter.

He was still in duty uniform—she had changed as soon as she reached her quarters and felt slightly uncomfortable receiving him in such casual attire. She shrugged to herself and returned his salute as he offered it, cap tucked under his arm at precisely the correct angle.

"I have completed a thorough check of our survey data, Commodore." He cleared his throat. "There appear to be several inconsistencies between original and recent survey data, especially for systems surveyed within the last six years. Cicero Down is out of contact because of the storm"—he gestured offhandedly to the planet behind her—"but evidence indicates that data was altered entirely at Cicero Down and partially changed up here as well."

"*se* Sergei suspects an enemy agent is present here in Cicero System, Bryan." She folded her hands before her on the table. "I'm not completely convinced of that assertion, but if true, the person may still be on-station. I want security to be tight around here. Is that understood?"

"Aye-aye, ma'am." He looked down at his feet, and then at Jackie once more. "Commodore, I would like to discuss something with you off the record."

"You may speak freely."

Noyes walked forward and took a seat opposite his commanding officer. "As you know, I receive—as a matter of course—all reports submitted to you. Documents marked as confidential I generally relegate to a special file devoted to that purpose, to be examined only as your orders permit.

"I made an exception to that rule today. Without specific order from you, I took it upon myself to read the medical report from Dr. Callison aboard *Pappenheim.* I have been in His Majesty's Navy for eighteen years, Commodore, and there is no precedent for what Dr. Callison reports, not in my experience, and not in official record.

"Though you are under no obligation to tell me what is going on, ma'am, I feel that I can best perform my duties if you do."

She attempted to measure him, then to try and see if there was any hidden meaning in what he had said. But behind the professional decorum of the base commander, all she could sense was fear.

"Bryan, I've got a crisis on my hands. This began with two vanished Exploration Service ships, but it was made clear to me by—events—that something far more serious is going on out there. Admiral Tolliver's actions seem to have resulted in considerable loss of life, and I will shortly be filing a report to the Admiralty with my conclusions."

"Which are ... if I may ask?"

"Jesus Christ." She touched the comp, opening up the medical report. "Six ships of the line jump from here armed to the teeth, each carrying a full complement of Marines. Days later just one ship returns, with eighty-five percent of its crew dead, its sick bay littered with the bodies of dead Sensitives. What few crew are left seem to be stark raving mad, including Admiral Tolliver himself.

"They poisoned their own Sensitives, they've taken welders and dug burrows through their own corridors, trying to get away from 'monsters' ... What the hell am I supposed to conclude, Bryan? What happened to them? What did they *really* see?"

"How does the *Gyaryu'har* feel about this?"

"*se* Sergei." She sighed and rubbed her forehead. "This is all tied up intimately with zor mythology. He believes that there really *are* monsters— inimical aliens at Sargasso and elsewhere, including perhaps on this base. He tried to tell the admiral but Tolliver shrugged it off as nonsense. Until a week ago, I would have done the same. Now I'm not so sure."

"But you support the 'first contact' theory yourself."

"Only because—" She swore under her breath. Was she going to tell him about having seen tentacled monsters? "Only because it seemed to fit the evidence. But what about the rest of it?

"The fact remains that there *are* victims of this event and their stories—however crazy—seem to agree. The accounts are not exactly the sort of dispassionate, clinical observations that make up Admiralty reports, but they will constitute the bulk of *my* report once I have an opportunity to confirm Dr. Callison's account personally."

"You're going out there? In *person*? Surely a holo would be sufficient—"

"No." She placed her hands, palms down, on the desk in front of her. "My career may be riding on the way this is reported to the Admiralty, Bryan. I have no choice other than to investigate it firsthand. That means a *person*, not a holo."

"Commodore," he said, sitting forward. "Your orders established a quarantine for the *Singapore* and its survivors. You're too important to jeopardize yourself in this way. For the record, I would like to offer … to visit in your place."

"I appreciate your offer, Bryan." She smiled at him. "But the answer is no. I wouldn't send a subordinate anywhere I wouldn't go myself. Commander Ch'k'te will be aboard Cicero Op within the next watch, and I only expect to be aboard the *Pappenheim* for a few hours. When I return we'll complete my report to the Admiralty together with *se* Sergei."

"*se* Sergei? Surely, ma'am, this is strictly a Navy matter—"

"This is *no longer* simply a Navy matter. The involvement of the High Nest complicates everything. We've waded into very deep waters, and if we take steps in the wrong direction we'll wind up in way over our heads. I agree that *se* Sergei is an enigma—but he may have a better understanding of this situation than either of us. Remember, he was flying starships before your grandfather was born. Zor robes or no, Bryan, he has military as well as diplomatic experience. We need all the help we can get."

A S HER gig touched down in the landing bay of the IS *Pappenheim* a few hours later, Jackie felt far less sure of herself than she had in her conversation with Bryan Noyes. During the trip out she had reread the medical report, with no more peace of mind than the first time through. There was simply no way to reconcile it to actual procedure.

Still, she was haunted by the concern that somehow she could have been able to prevent it. It didn't stand up to close examination: she had made her objections known for the record and had been obliged to follow the admiral's orders. Despite everything that had gone before, naval regulations allowed the admiral to take such extraordinary actions. His decision to take the squadron outsystem had placed the responsibility for its fate in his hands. If he had chosen to ignore the advice of more experienced subordinates he might suffer the consequences from his own superiors. That wasn't certain: Admirals tended to get away with whatever they wanted, and commodores sometimes took the blame. It might come down to patronage.

But if the Admiralty decided to punish Tolliver, what purpose would it serve? Who would punish someone who had lost his sanity?

Jackie wasn't terribly fond of Tolliver. He had ignored her advice; he'd insulted an important official of the zor High Nest. He had ultimately thrown away six ships and nearly everyone aboard.

It wasn't Tolliver who got her sympathy; it was the hundreds of Navy personnel who had undertaken the expedition with him. She still felt responsible for them. She could hardly help it. To Tolliver they might have been no more than names on a duty roster, but to Jackie they were far more than that—they were her *people*: her staff and her crew, and in many cases her friends.

The ones that survived, she reminded herself, *are the lucky ones, insane or not. There are hundreds of others missing ... presumed dead.*

"WELCOME ABOARD, Commodore," said Captain Georg Maartens as she reached the hangar deck. She exchanged salutes with him and with the *Pappenheim*'s chief surgeon, Dr. Arthur Callison. Callison was newly posted to Cicero and looked like he'd simply put on an officer's uniform like a disguise, as an afterthought. Still, she knew his reputation, which was more than enough to make her glad to have him around.

Especially right now, she reminded herself.

By comparison, Maartens was an old friend. Despite his spit-and-polish image as a perfect Navy officer, he always reminded Jackie of a favorite uncle. Several years older than Jackie, he had not commanded anything bigger than a starship.

"Thank you, Georg. I'm ... sorry to be so abrupt with my visit." Maartens led the way off the hangar deck. "I've come to see the admiral."

Callison hesitated slightly as they walked up to the lift. "I ... Well, as you wish, ma'am," he said, seeming to change thoughts in midsentence. Maartens rolled his eyes at his commander behind the doctor's back; *he'd* assumed the request was an order.

"Do you have some objection, Doctor?" They stepped into the lift, and it began to rise slowly toward the heart of the ship.

"Officially? No, not at all, Commodore." Callison clasped his hands behind his back, in a way that was reminiscent of a professor in a lecture hall. "However, I would not advise it, as he is somewhat volatile at the moment. Furthermore he is heavily sedated, though he should be lucid enough to understand you."

"I see."

They rose several decks while Jackie considered her next question. "In your professional opinion," she said at last, "is Admiral Tolliver capable of giving any sort of report on the Sargasso expedition?"

"An *official* report, you mean." Callison rubbed his chin thoughtfully. "That all depends, Commodore."

"On what?"

"Well." Hands returned to lecture-hall pose. "As you know, Admiral Tolliver was found in a very excited condition, Commodore. He was extremely violent and had to be restrained. While considerable medical effort and several doses of quintivalium have worked to ameliorate that condition, I suspect that if the matter of Sensitives is mentioned, he is likely to become enraged—"

"I understand. Several individuals flew into rages when Sensitive examination was recommended in their hearing. Go on."

"The admiral," Callison continued, "will speak quite rationally about his experiences, and his dialogue is internally self-consistent. Note that I say 'internally.'" The lift stopped rising and began to glide laterally forward. "The sum of his remarks, however, is totally at odds with reality as we know it."

"Please explain."

"Admiral Tolliver is capable of delivering a precise, complete and accurate report of the events as he claims to have perceived them. But in view of the subject matter, I am sure that any summary court would dismiss it for exactly what it seems to be: the ravings of a lunatic."

The lift shuddered to a halt, and Maartens looked up querulously, as if to say, *I'd better get this damn thing fixed.* The three officers stepped out into the hall, exchanging salutes with a pair of midshipmen who were waiting for the lift.

"In fact, Commodore," Callison continued, "for the record, I would strongly advise against further disturbing the admiral. I do not believe that you will learn anything more than what *professional* staff have already obtained." They went through a door that slid open at Callison's gesture and found themselves in the sick bay. Callison led them into an inner office and beckoned them to chairs, while he sat and summoned forth medical records, which appeared in midair above his desk.

"I don't mean to question your report," Jackie said after a moment, trying not to bristle at Callison's last comment. "In fact it was quite thorough. Still, the Admiralty is going to be all over us very soon, and I have to be sure of my position. I trust that I make myself clear."

Callison appeared close to framing a reply, but Maartens cut in. "Loud and clear, ma'am."

Callison grunted, exchanged a long look with his CO, and then turned to face Jackie and handed her a comp, which she slipped into a shirt pocket.

"This will give you any additional information you might need. There's an MP on duty outside Admiral Tolliver's quarters, and he will be present in the room during your interview, in case there is a difficulty."

"Don't you think that would inhibit—"

"Begging the Commodore's pardon, but I will *not* bear responsibility for letting you into the admiral's quarters without escort. The MP has his orders in case *my* patient becomes violent. I have my orders as well." He looked across at Maartens.

"It's for your own protection," Maartens added.

"For my own—" Jackie's face reddened. "Listen here. I'm an officer in His Majesty's Navy, and perfectly capable of taking care of myself—"

"Nonsense," Callison interrupted, which stopped her in mid-sentence, making her even more angry. He tapped the desk with an index finger. "In my professional opinion, the admiral is violently insane. At the moment, he has fifty cc's of quintivalium in his bloodstream, about ten times the normal human dosage.

"Last night, under a dosage of *half* that amount, he pulled down a wall section *with his bare hands* because he believed there was a 'monster' behind it, trying to take over his mind. It took three MPs to control him, despite the fact that the admiral is fifty-three years old and is in subpar physical condition. *Three MPs*, Commodore, and a direct injection of enough qv to put a Cicero tusker into a coma.

"The MP has a tranquilizer rifle. If Tolliver makes anything like a sudden move, he will be pumped full of qv darts. The admiral is *my patient*, Commodore, and as such, I will only allow you to interview him on those terms."

"'Allow—'" Jackie began.

"He's got you, Commodore," Georg said, winking. "He has authority."

"All right. I won't disobey your advice," she said after a moment.

"That's settled, then," Callison replied, as if he'd expected that result all along. "Whenever you're ready, ma'am?"

THE ROOM was dimly lit but looked clean and normal. It was a typical outpatient hospital room, not much different from dirtside: There was a single bed, neatly made, in one corner; a couch and two armchairs, with a side table alongside holding several chips and a tablet; a small autokitchen. The walls were painted in a pale pastel and adorned by abstract paintings.

Tolliver sat on the couch with his hands folded. He appeared to be dozing, but looked up when Jackie and the trooper came into the room. The MP took up a position just inside the door, his rifle held ready but pointed downward.

"Commodore Laperriere," Tolliver said quietly. "How good of you to visit."

"It is my pleasure, sir." She took a seat in one of the armchairs. "If it pleases the admiral ... I need certain matters clarified for my report."

She tensed, waiting for something to happen as he raised his eyes to meet hers. He merely gazed at her languidly. "Certainly, Commodore. How may I be of service?"

Direct approach, she thought to herself, feeling the presence of the MP behind her. "I read your deposition to Dr. Callison, but I would appreciate it if you would tell me personally what happened out there."

At the words "out there," Tolliver's eyes grew clearer for a moment, as if he were straining against the effects of the tranquilizer in his bloodstream, then they became glassy again.

"I've ... been thinking that I'd like to talk to you personally, Commodore, and I'm glad you chose to come out to visit me. I've ... It's hard to try and explain it all in report language, even though I've been doing it all my life ... I'd hoped that I would be able to explain in person to another officer, not to some doctor.

"They've decided I'm nuts, you know. Space-sickness. Jump fever." He looked off into one corner of the room and then threw a quick glance at the MP. "They don't really believe what I told them."

"Forgive me, Admiral," she replied quickly. "I didn't come out here to dispute your story, or to cast aspersions—"

"I appreciate that, Laperriere, I truly do."

"—or to cast aspersions," she repeated through his interruption. "I only came out here to listen."

"Perhaps when this is all over I can return the favor." He leaned forward and put his head in his hands for several moments. Then he looked up at her with a pained expression that roused sympathy in Jackie, making her feel a trifle uncomfortable.

The moment passed and his expression was swallowed by lassitude, and he slumped back on the couch. "Where shall I begin?"

"Tell me about Sargasso."

"Sargasso." He looked into space again. "It was a normal planetary system— nine planets, two habitable, and an asteroid belt. We conducted the usual survey, which, incidentally, did not agree with the original survey."

"But it *did* agree with the data from the *Gustav Adolf.*"

"To the last decimal place. But there it was—in ... incontrovertible, on our forward and deep-radar scans. Nine planets, two habitable."

"Please go on."

"I left two vessels at the edge of the system near our jump point and dropped into the gravity-well. I was … primarily interested in finding any trace of the missing ships.

"We explored the system thoroughly and found nothing. Nothing!" He sat forward again, shrugging off a bit of his former calm. The MP moved behind her; Tolliver's shoulders sagged a bit.

"Nothing," he almost whispered. "No unusual background radiation, no debris, no jump disturbances. Then we did a scan on the t-two habitable worlds.

"I sent a landing party down. Four … special officers"—he seemed to avoid using the term "Sensitives"—"and eight Marines. For twenty minutes they sent up survey data on the planet—its ecosphere, flora and fauna—then we began to lose contact with the survey teams. One after another after another." He began to shake almost uncontrollably. Jackie exchanged glances with the MP, who seemed nervous, listening to the admiral's story. She knew what was next in his report; she waited for him to become calm again. Tolliver had changed: his hauteur had melted away and been replaced by fear.

"Then the WS4s came back up from the surface." WS4 was the highest rank for a Sensitive in the field. "They hadn't been ordered up—they just came on their own."

He looked at her with a look of such anguish and despair that she could hardly hold his glance. "Then the planet began to quaver … the mass sensors went crazy. Our ships were flung from orbit … except one.

"The planet *changed shape* and en-engulfed the *Johore*. I heard them screaming …" He put his head down and clapped his hands over his ears. "Screaming …"

She stood and took a step toward him, but he looked up at her suddenly, his eyes ablaze with anger. "They took the *Johore*. They *took* it, do you understand?" He was almost shouting. "Then the *Maldive* and the *Andaman* opened fire … *on each other.*

"I countermanded the order, but no one was listening." He clenched his fists. On his forehead, several veins stood out in stark relief. "No one was moving on the bridge of the *Singapore*. They were frozen in their seats. Everyone but me."

Some of this detail had not reached the report from Tolliver's briefing session. She realized it as the words poured from his mouth. Callison was no doubt recording this. Still, it seemed impossible for the admiral not to have said it all, since the reader (or listener) would have had to hurdle yet other impossibilities to get here.

"I turned to look at the WS4s," he said. "And I didn't see *humans*, Commodore. I saw …"

A look of horror spread across Tolliver's face.

"What did you see?"

He was looking directly at her, but she suddenly knew he didn't see her anymore. He saw something that horrified him beyond all comprehension.

Without warning he hurled himself at her with his arms outstretched. Jackie stepped quickly from his path and pulled him to the deck, her reflexes acting far quicker than the admiral's drug-weakened ones. The MP's rifle coughed several times.

Tolliver struggled, shouting inarticulately, while the drug slowly took effect, until at last he was immobile. Perhaps fifteen seconds had passed.

"Are you all right, ma'am?" the MP asked as they rolled the now unconscious admiral onto his back.

"Forget about *me*," she replied. "Let's get a Sensitive in here on the double—"

She looked down at Tolliver. His eyes were rolled up in his head, and the chest wasn't rising and falling. She began to apply CPR. "How much did you pump into him, damn it?"

"Not enough to kill him, ma'am," the trooper said. "Besides, it wouldn't act that fast."

The look of inarticulate horror gazed off into space, past Jackie, at some imagined terror she would never know.

chapter 5

The surgery door opened and Dr. Meredith Hsu stepped into the waiting room, wiping her hands on a towel. Arthur Callison followed, sliding the door shut. Maartens looked up with questions in his eyes.

"Well?" Jackie asked. "What happened?"

Dr. Hsu tossed the towel into a receptacle in the corner and sat down on the opposite side of the room from Jackie. She swung the chair around to face her expectant commanding officers.

"You'll be receiving a full report from me in a day or two, but I can give you a preliminary analysis."

"By all means."

She looked from Jackie and Maartens to Callison and then back again. "I found absolutely nothing, Commodore. I conducted every forensic test available to me. In my professional opinion, the Admiral's heart simply stopped. There is no evidence of chemical or biological alteration that might have caused the stoppage."

"What about the tranquilizer?"

"Three hundred fifty cc's of quintivalium will *not* produce that sort of reaction, Commodore," Dr. Hsu responded quietly. "His bloodstream simply could not absorb that much in fifteen to thirty seconds before he was subdued."

"The qv didn't kill him, then. What did?"

"There was no evidence that anything did, Commodore. His heart simply … stopped. So did his brain activity."

"Dr. Callison, will you confirm this?" Jackie asked, turning to the older physician.

"My examination will corroborate Dr. Hsu's statements, Commodore."

"Well, it's not good enough." Jackie's voice rose in anger. "You're stating in effect that Admiral Tolliver simply hurled himself at me, and before he could so much as cry out, he dropped dead. I'm terribly sorry, Meredith, Arthur, I can't accept it. I was in that room, and I saw it happen."

"It all happened rather fast. Perhaps you didn't notice—" Maartens began, but Jackie cut him off.

"After this many years in the Service, Georg, credit me with enough powers of observation to notice when a man is dying. He didn't convulse, he didn't have a seizure, he didn't cough up blood. One moment he was alive, succumbing to qv darts, the next moment he was stone dead. People *don't* die like that, Meredith, and you know it."

"He was more than fifty years old—"

"Someone *killed* him," Jackie said, her expression freezing Meredith Hsu into silence. "Someone killed Horace Tolliver before he could tell me what he saw."

"Who? And more importantly—how?"

"I don't know who. It was like the work of a Sensitive, but I don't know anyone—human or zor—with that much power. But whoever it is, the person is still aboard this ship."

Hsu looked angrily at Jackie. "I didn't realize that you'd received a medical degree ... or become a Sensitive."

"Did you consider this possibility in your report?"

"Of course not. I'm a forensic pathologist, not a zor mystic. What do you want—"

"Answers." Jackie stood up and walked toward the door, where she stopped and turned to look at the three officers. "I've got a frightening situation on my hands and it's getting worse. Even if nothing else happens—which I doubt—the Admiralty will be crawling up our asses, what with the Sargasso disaster and the admiral dead. I want answers, and I will have them, and I will not accept your report until you provide them. Is that clear?"

"Your authority doesn't—" began Dr. Hsu.

"Oh, but it *does*. We are in a state of emergency, *Lieutenant* Hsu. I will remind you that this is the Imperial Navy, and that I command here. The murderer of Admiral Tolliver is still at large and likely aboard this ship. A Sensitive might even be able to locate that person, and a Sensitive's examination might be able to determine the actual cause of Tolliver's death.

"I want answers, Doctor, and I will *have* them. Is that clear?"

"I—" Hsu looked down at the floor. "Aye-aye, ma'am."

"I'll be at Cicero Operations. I'll expect your report within forty-eight hours." Without another word Jackie stalked from the room, the door sliding shut behind her.

S HE WAS exhausted when she returned to Cicero Op. She had quarters two decks below the bridge near the outer rim of the station; she went directly from the shuttle deck to her room. She dropped into an armchair, putting her head back against the wall behind.

After a few minutes of quiet lethargy, she stripped off her sweaty uniform and headed for the shower.

Centuries of human civilization had raised the art of showering from the mundane to the sublime, and the Cicero orbital station was equal to the state of the art. For ten minutes she let the water pour over her and the tension flowed out as well.

Then, suddenly, as she stood in the shower she heard her name spoken clearly and distinctly, ringing like a bell in her ears.

She tensed—undoing half of the purpose of the shower in a single moment—and opened her eyes.

se *Jackie,* the voice said again.

"Who's there?" she said over the sound of rushing water. She turned the water off and reached outside the compartment for a towel. "Who—"

She realized the voice was coming from inside her mind. She felt a familiar touch: It was Ch'k'te. She wrapped the towel around herself absently, letting her mind reach out tentatively for contact as Ch'k'te had taught her.

Where are you? She tried to form the words, not sure if the words would be communicated. She received an impression in return: a metal structure, spinning slowly in orbit. She felt the gentle touch of a zor's wing around her.

Look, the voice said. She closed her eyes—

And opened them again. Before her, she saw a high-ceilinged room, the tower room of a fortress. Above, there were high skylight windows looking out on a terrible storm.

Ch'k'te perched in front of her, looking haggard and weary. She'd never felt a mind-touch that had taken visible form before: This was etched sharply before her in sight and sound.

I speak to you from far inside myself, Ch'k'te said over the storm's noise. *He cannot sense my contact with you.*

He?—

Listen to me, Ch'k'te said urgently. *There is not much time. He is here. He took your guise and lured me here and has trapped me.*

Help me, se Jackie, Ch'k'te said at last, his wings curling into a position she knew held some significance she could not interpret. She realized, in some level of consciousness above the present frame of reference, that this setting had some figurative meaning, though she could not recall it at the moment.

How can I help you?

esGa'u, Ch'k'te said. *esGa'u the Deceiver is not far away. He holds me ... he controls me, se Jackie. He is—*

There was a sound to the right. Jackie turned to look at the heavy oaken door and heard a noise, as if someone were trying to break it down—

She blinked and saw her quarters again, quiet but for the occasional dripping of water in the shower. After a moment she realized she was shaking all over.

She slumped into the armchair, still mostly wet, thinking about the sudden contact and the way in which it was suddenly broken off. *esGa'u* ... Ch'k'te had mentioned the name of the zor religion's dark sorcerer, *esGa'u* the Deceiver. He had said he was being controlled by *esGa'u.*

Controlled.

The contact had been broken suddenly, sharply, like switching off a light. Had the control slipped somehow and then reasserted itself? What could it mean?

The discipline learned during years as an officer took over then, pushing fear off into a corner of her mind as she dressed. Without stopping to consider, she pulled on a gunbelt, went through the ritual of stripping and testing her pistol, and holstered it at her side. Jackie was unsure what would happen next but intended to be prepared for it.

CICERO OPERATIONS consisted of a long, thin spindle passing through a wide disk. At the very top of the spindle, just where it protruded from the disk, was the station's bridge. While the station spun, turning on its axis once an hour, the bridge remained stationary relative to the planetary surface in geosynchronous orbit with Cicero Down, located near the planet's equator.

As always, when Jackie stepped from the lift onto the bridge, she had a slight feeling of vertigo. The screens displayed the grim visage of Cicero, a few hundred kilometers away, hanging luminously *above* them, ready to fall on them at any moment. (Or was it *below,* and they were plummeting toward it?) It was no wonder people felt vertigo.

The bridge was a warren of activity. In addition to constantly monitoring the operations of the station itself, Cicero Op controlled the anchorage of the remaining Cicero Military District fleet. It also collected meteorological data from the planet and astronomical data from Cicero System. The Exploration arm was beached at the moment, but when it was engaged in surveying, its reports also filtered through this station.

Jackie surveyed the scene and picked out Ch'k'te. His back was to her, but she recognized him by the pattern of his wings—the slight brownish tint where they joined his shoulders, and the bluish scar near his left wing-talon from the boiler explosion last winter.

HE HOLDS me ... he controls me, she heard in her mind. Without speaking, she slowly looked across the bridge at the forty or so individuals, human and zor, who worked there. Could one of them be ... *esGa'u*? Could one of them be controlling the mind of her exec?

Commander Noyes looked up from a screen and noticed Jackie standing near the entrance to the lift. He immediately walked toward her. She took a step forward to meet him and suddenly stopped, the hairs on the back of her neck rising in alarm. Years in the military had taught her to trust her instincts. There was something about Noyes—the way he was holding himself, perhaps—something she couldn't identify.

Ch'k'te had still not turned from his station. She wanted to shout his name and attract his attention, but she held back.

"Commodore," Noyes said, saluting her. "Welcome back, ma'am."

"Thank you." She returned the salute. "Where is *se* Sergei? I would have expected him to be here."

"*se* Sergei?" Noyes looked directly at her for a moment. "*se* Sergei was ... not feeling well. He is in his quarters—he asked not to be disturbed."

Her glance happened to look past Noyes to Ch'k'te. His neck muscles were bunched, almost taut ... almost as if he were straining to turn around.

"Perhaps," Noyes went on smoothly, "he is feeling the effects of the trip." Ch'k'te's chair swiveled a few centimeters, and his head turned with obvious effort. "I'm sure"—another few centimeters—"he will be better—" She could almost see Ch'k'te's face now. A shiver ran from the small of her back up to her neck. "—in a few hours."

With what seemed to be a great effort of will, Jackie's exec swung his chair completely around to face her. He raised his eyes slowly to meet hers.

In an instant of eye contact that seemed to stretch out to infinity, she felt Ch'k'te's mind reach out to hers. The contact was hastily batted away by some presence. She felt anger and surprise from that mind, as if it had not expected the event to even occur. As fear crept up in her mind, she felt a rising tide of hatred, directed unilaterally toward whatever sentience was controlling her exec and friend.

"Commodore?" Noyes said.

As the contact failed she returned her glances to Noyes.

But she did not see a man there anymore.

Without even thinking, she dived for the deck. The creature seemed to realize at once that its disguise had failed. Before she even reached the deck, a laser shot rang out a few centimeters above her head, detonating in a console behind her.

Not knowing what her chances were of taking out the creature with a single shot, Jackie looked for a tactical advantage. She aimed for a power receptacle near the pilot's board and fired a narrow beam at it.

All the lights on the bridge went out at once. A pale reddish glow replaced the familiar white. Jackie noticed from her crouching position that pandemonium had broken out on the bridge.

"You cannot escape me," the Noyes-thing said, in a croak that still sounded frighteningly like the officer she knew. "I can find you even in the dark, meat-creature."

She refused the bait and remained in her crouch. A shot struck a railing above her head, fired from somewhere on the other side of the bridge.

"I control them as well, Commodore," the half-alien voice sneered. "Silence!" it shouted into the commotion … and it was quiet.

She could hear the blood pounding in her ears as the bridge went silent. In the dim red emergency light, the creature was silhouetted against the bright half-circle of Cicero, and she could see its true outline for the first time. It looked like a crustacean or perhaps a hard-shelled insect, with four legs and two stubby arms. Its head was dominated by a pair of what looked like sharp mandibles, and constantly wriggling tentacles hung down from either side of its head.

"I can smell you, Commodore," it croaked. "I can smell your fear as you hide from me in the darkness. You were so clever. I did not even sense your contact with that egg-sucking zor. It does not matter, however—I can seize your mind at any time. Or I can kill with a single thought."

Just like what must've happened to the admiral, she added to herself.

She saw the alien turn its head toward her. It seemed to be growing in size … becoming larger and larger and reaching out its tentacles to touch her. It was true this time, not a fever dream or a vision shared with Ch'k'te—not some imagining of a madman.

It was true, and she could not prevent it. Her hatred had given way to fright and then to despair. Only a supreme effort of will kept her crouching, rather than allowing herself to be drawn closer to the alien. She could not stop the shaking, and her pistol wavered in her hands—

But before the tentacles from the now giant alien could reach her, a shriek cut across her consciousness like a bright, sharp blade. From the corner of her eye, she saw a figure spring from the darkness, landing atop the creature.

"Ch'k'te!" she shouted.

The alien screamed, and she knew now it was pain that had brought it about. An unarmed zor, as humanity had learned decades ago, is nothing to trifle with—though more fragile than humans, their sharp claws and wing-talons combined with lightning reflexes and uncanny agility made them dangerous even unarmed.

She felt a claw at her shoulder pulling her away, and she found herself half crawling, half running to the lift, Ch'k'te at her side. Laser fire arced through the air as they dived the final few meters into the compartment and the door slid shut behind them.

She took a few breaths as Ch'k'te ordered the lift to descend to the shuttle deck. While it began to drop, she had her first opportunity to look at him.

His face was marred by a number of cuts and bruises and his uniform was torn in several places. His wings appeared to be undamaged, but his chest was sliced neatly and leaking blood.

"Got to get you to sick bay—" she began.

"No … time," Ch'k'te responded. "*se* Jackie." He grasped her arm firmly with a clawed hand. "He … it … already controls this station. We must get off—" He broke off and began to cough. "We—"

"You're in no condition to—"

"Pain … irrelevant."

"Bullshit!" The lift continued to drop. They were in the spindle now, heading toward Engineering Section. "What about your wounds?"

"No … time," the zor repeated, "*se* Jackie. Need … I need your help, your strength."

"For what?"

"Healing. *esLiDur'ar*, the gift of life. Requires—" He began to cough again and Jackie helped him to a seat in the corner of the lift compartment. "Requires internal strength, *hsi*. It is truly a simple matter …"

"If you live that long."

"Need your help," Ch'k'te repeated. "Please, Jackie." He'd even dropped the prenomen. "T-trust me."

"I trust you." She looked up at the lift indicator, and watched them slip down, deck after deck. "What can I do?"

"Open your mind … I will do the rest."

She tried to calm herself and breathed slowly and carefully, squatting on the deck. It was easier opening her mind to Ch'k'te while he grasped her arm. She felt a wash of calm come over her as the contact formed and firmed.

Then, while she watched, Ch'k'te moved his wings into a particular pattern and slowly drew his other hand across the gash in his chest. Where his talons passed, the opening subsided to a pinkish scar … and as she looked, fascinated, the scar faded gradually and disappeared altogether.

Ch'k'te let go of her arm and slumped back against the wall of the lift, breathing shallowly. She felt drained and almost overcome by lassitude; but from somewhere deep inside she drew on strength to fight it off.

She forced her limbs to work again, fighting the lassitude that the *esLiDur'ar* had left behind. The zor's vision seemed to clear.

"I thank you most humbly," he said at last.

"No time for it." She looked up at the lift indicator and noted they were slowing, approaching the shuttle bay at the aft end of the spindle. "Report. What the hell is going on?"

"A few hours ago I … arrived here on Cicero Operations. I had received an order from you to come here. I was met by Commander Noyes on the shuttle deck—except that it was not Noyes at all. He … It seemed to know at once that I had penetrated its disguise. It dominated my mind and controlled me.

"I do not know much more, *se* Commodore. Its intention is to control this base. With Operations under its control it will be much easier for them to seize control of the system."

"How many of them are there?"

"Three—perhaps four. There are at least two more at Cicero Down."

"Half a dozen of them, and hundreds of us? Surely—"

"You do not understand." He pulled himself to his feet, straightening out what remained of his uniform. "*se* Jackie. They can *dominate minds*. They can disguise themselves as anything, even People. As me. As you. We cannot defeat them … They may have already won."

The statement sunk in for a moment and then was interrupted by a sudden, stomach-wrenching thought.

"*se* Sergei … We have to save—"

"He is a warrior. The *Gyaryu'har* will take care of himself." Ch'k'te took Jackie's arm, more gently this time. "We must get off this station, *se* Jackie. If we attempt to rescue the *Gyaryu'har*, we reduce our chances of escape."

"'Escape'? Where do you plan to go?"

"I … thought that perhaps we could use your gig. We could reach the *Pappenheim* or another of the ships in quarantine and then get outsystem."

Before she could frame a reply the lift shuddered to a stop. Jackie stepped back to one side of the door, her pistol drawn and held ready. Ch'k'te had no pistol but held his blade in his hand.

The door slid aside, giving a vantage across the shuttle deck. They flattened themselves out of sight within the lift compartment and glanced carefully around. Jackie's gig was parked on the deck; there were also several small travel pods, each set in a launching tube. The cutter was guarded by four Marines, laser rifles held ready.

"We're expected," Jackie whispered. She nodded to Ch'k'te, and they crept from the lift entrance to a concealed position behind a fuel pod. The Marines did not appear to notice.

"We probably don't have much time," she said, watching the Marines in front of the small craft. "The—thing—that took Noyes' place won't give us a lot of time to plan. We don't stand a chance to get to the gig; looks like we should try to get to a travel pod."

"If the station opens fire on us," Ch'k'te said, his inner eye lids closing and opening rapidly, "we will be debris."

"Do you have any better ideas? We can't go back up to the bridge."

"Decidedly not." Ch'k'te shuddered slightly at the mention of the possibility. "Very well." He gestured toward the nearest travel pod. "The access hatch on the closest pod is partially obscured from the Marine guards. We should have thirty seconds or so to reach it."

"Are you up to it?"

"I was not aware that I had a choice. Besides," he added, "it will be harder to hit a flying target."

Most of the Earthlike planets scattered across the Solar Empire had gravities between nine-tenths and one-and-a-half Standard gravities. By comparison, Zor'a and most of the zor Core worlds were just over half a g. It was there the zor had first settled, and over these worlds trillions of young zor had learned to fly.

Even for the light and hollow-boned zor, nine-tenths of a gravity precluded the possibility of flight; thus many humans had never seen a zor fly, viewing the articulate wing-structure more as an aesthetic part of native costume than as a means of locomotion.

Jackie had seen zor flight at the Academy, in the low-g flight simulators. While human cadets flapped around with artificial wings strapped to their backs, looking for warm updrafts to buoy their earthbound bodies into the air, zor cadets rejoiced in the freedom Earth had never afforded them, and which the narrow corridors of Moonbase did not allow, showing their true home to be the boundless reaches of the sky. Man had always dreamed of flight; the zor had *lived* it, in the truest sense.

In the three-tenths of a g of the station's spindle, Ch'k'te suddenly took flight, rising in an easy arc and attracting the attention of the Marine guards. Jackie was as transfixed as they were for a moment; then she darted out from cover and zigzagged across the few dozen meters of open space as Ch'k'te glided quickly about, easily dodging the miscalculated shots. He arrived several moments before she did. He already had the hatch door open. They dived for seats in the cockpit and sealed the hatch behind them.

The outside camera pickup showed rifle fire splattering against the hull while she feverishly went through preflight check. Before any of the Marines could reach the launch bay she punched the firing stud, spitting the pod out into space, slamming both of them back into their seats.

The instruments were alive in her hands. She had kicked the thrust up to maximum, using up fuel in the process, but it did put distance between them and the station. All the landmarks in space were set out in stark relief: it was powerfully different than the view obtained from inside a starship or space-station. The planet Cicero seemed bigger somehow, and Cicero Operations was likewise gargantuan, a huge child's toy visibly spinning in space, half-lit by the planet and trimmed in vermilion from Cicero's primary.

She was also well aware of the thinness of the pod's hull and just how close she was to the vacuum of space. It had been a long time since she had flown something this flimsy. The *Pappenheim* was four or five hundred million kilometers away: It would be a long flight.

"Bogeys," Ch'k'te said suddenly from the other seat. "Two—no, three. Fighters launched from the station."

"Do they have our bearing?"

"They seem to."

She reached down with one hand and adjusted the comm to the frequency she expected them to use, based on day and watch. The pilots' chitchat told her more than she wanted to know.

She also knew they did not stand a chance against armed fighters in open space.

"Ch'k'te," she said, without looking away from the displays. "See if you can find us vacc suits."

"Aye-aye," he said, and scrambled into the rear part of the pod.

"Ch'k'te?"

"Yes?" he said, beginning to don a suit.

"We can't avoid those bastards in open space and we can't possibly get to the *Pappenheim*. I may have to land this thing on Cicero itself, just to keep us from being vaporized. What are the chances that a ... that an alien has control of Cicero Down?"

"I—" Ch'k'te grunted, and sealed the suit from the neck down. "I would estimate that they are quite good."

She cursed. "Do you have any alternate suggestions? Once I'm in atmosphere, there's no getting out again."

"Prayer to *esLi*," Ch'k'te replied, coming forward and strapping himself in again. He activated the reserve instruments and she turned control over to him. Before she could unstrap, however, he spun the pod end for end and rolled it sharply to starboard, forcing her back against the seat cushions.

"What the holy hell—" she began, and then saw something streak past the front viewscreen of the little craft, wobbling back and forth as it dropped toward the planet's surface and detonated.

"Prayer to *esLi*," he repeated. "Your suit is beside the medikit."

She crawled into the rear part of the pod and quickly began to don the suit. "My friend, if we ever get out of this alive, I will get you a promotion."

"*se* Commodore—" he began, then swung the pod rapidly again to avoid another incoming missile. "*se* Jackie." He turned for a moment to look at her. "The zor sage spoke truly when he advised his pupil, 'Do not set *S'r'can'u* to protect your garden before he has been planted.'"

"I ..." She sealed the suit around her chest. "I think I know that saying." She clambered forward and took her seat again, just as Ch'k'te performed another maneuver that pushed her back into the cushions.

A quick glance at the telltales indicated that the three fighters were almost in laser fire range.

She took the controls again and let the onboard nav computer plot a landing. As soon as it had produced a course, she let it execute. The little pod, burning most of its remaining fuel, sped away from the fighters and toward the planet's atmosphere.

The last thing she remembered, before the g-force made her black out, was the planet growing to encompass the entire forward screen, blocking out the stars.

chapter 6

The commodore's gig rolled forward on its landing gear into the hangar and out of the storm. A med team was already on hand, along with the *Gyaryu'har*'s staff; as soon as the hatch opened, Jackie and Ch'k'te descended to the deck followed by two crewmembers carrying a stretcher.

Lieutenant Daniel Hamadjiou, Officer of the Watch, was on hand to exchange salutes with his commanding officers. Sergei's staff and the medical team attended to the *Gyaryu'har*, who was lying immobile.

"Commodore," Hamadjiou said. "Cicero Down is on alert, as you ordered."

"Very good," she answered. "Have you received any reports of intruders?"

"No, ma'am. Down Control recorded the launch of aerospace fighters from Op. Is everything all right topside?"

"An escape pod was launched. Commander Noyes ordered the launch of a fighter wing, but it fell into the atmosphere."

"We should be able to locate it once the storm passes, ma'am."

Commodore Laperriere looked at him. "You may consider that an order, Lieutenant."

For a moment, Laperriere seemed larger than life and the overhead phosphors seemed to dim. Dan Hamadjiou was afraid for reasons he couldn't adequately explain. He did the only thing he could: he saluted and said, "Aye-aye, Commodore."

SOUTH CONTINENT was completely covered by a low-lying storm, preventing recon planes from flying over the secluded forest where Jackie had finally landed the pod after she'd regained consciousness in the lower atmosphere. Even when the weather started to clear, there hadn't been any over-flights. It was almost insulting, as if she and Ch'k'te didn't matter; but perhaps the enemy simply thought she had crashed the pod and was out of the way.

The map showed that their encampment was a bit over three hundred kilometers southwest of the Cicero Down naval base. She imagined the aliens there on the base, controlling the personnel there, perhaps even assuming her own shape. During the first few days she hadn't thought about it much: she was far more concerned with keeping them alive. Ch'k'te had suffered several stress fractures—his fragile frame was unaccustomed to the g-force of unassisted reentry—so he stayed inside the pod under sedation. She busied herself with the craft of staying alive, using techniques she hadn't needed since her Academy days.

It took her mind off their predicament, and it was probably the best thing. It had all happened so fast—the return of what remained of the Sargasso expedition, Tolliver's sudden death, then the events on the orbital base. She had not really assimilated it all. In one part of her mind, little had changed: She was still commander of Cicero, and still had a crisis to deal with. In another part—the part that crept out late at night when, exhausted, she climbed onto her couch to get some sleep—she knew that it had all changed and that her existence (or freedom, at least) might well depend on the continued indifference of those who had seized control of her command.

The night after the storm broke, she climbed into the pod, shaking the day's snowfall from the cold-weather suit. She found Ch'k'te not only awake, but working on the evening meal at the pod's autokitchen. She got ready to order him back to bed instead of trying to be up and about so fast, but was so glad of the chance to talk that she set it aside. *Ch'k'te is an adult,* she thought. *He can be the judge of his own fitness.*

Without speaking, he handed her a hot cup of coffee and she accepted it gratefully, stripping off the oversuit and squatting in an empty corner of the pod.

"How are you feeling?" she asked, sipping.

"All things considered," Ch'k'te said, gingerly touching his bandaged midsection, "quite good. While I slept, I continued to practice *esLiDur'ar*. The bones should be knitted; I am hardly prepared to run a marathon, but ..." He took a sip of the coffee, making a slight noise of pain as he did so.

"Glad to hear it. Have you been awake long?"

"I was awoken by the sun." He gestured to the forward screen, set to transparency. It had been overcast all day, slate-gray clouds sifting a fine, powdery snow onto the land below. Now the sun was peeking out in greeting to the departing day, filtering through the tall trees and between the distant peaks of the mountains.

"I've been hiking around," Jackie said, "checking avenues of approach. We're not out in the open, but I certainly could have chosen a better spot."

"What are your orders?"

"I ... don't know. Cicero Op is in enemy hands, and I have to assume that Cicero Down is as well. I haven't tried to signal anyone, since that would only give away our location." She set the cup down beside her. "With the ship's stores and the batteries fully charged, we can easily keep alive here for two or three months. There are certainly natural resources to extend that further ...

"It just doesn't accomplish anything."

"What would you like to accomplish, *se* Jackie?"

"This is my *command*, Ch'k'te. I cannot sit by and do nothing while ... aliens control it."

Ch'k'te tucked his legs under him and let his wings settle like a cloak. "My question remains."

"Don't you understand, damn it? We're at *war*, Ch'k'te! Those—things—have control of Cicero! They killed Tolliver—they replaced Noyes—they may have even killed *se* Sergei …"

"We can do little about that now. There are two of us, and I am not fully healed. We do not have a fleet at our disposal—in fact, we cannot even get into orbit."

"I can't stand by and do nothing."

"Well and good. But what *can* we do?"

"I—I don't know." Her hands were clenched into fists. "But we must do something."

Ch'k'te did not respond.

"And if you don't wish to help me, I'll do it myself." She reached for her cold-weather suit—

Ch'k'te moved almost too fast for her to see, reaching out and grasping her wrist before she could reach the suit. His grip was strong and it angered her that she was unable to break it.

The zor was obviously in pain, but he took hold of her shoulder with his other hand and held her firmly, his face inches from hers.

"No," he said, "you will not. We are an hour from darkness, hundreds of kilometers from civilization, and between snow storms. Were you to undertake any sort of action, you would surely perish."

"Let go of me," she said, straining against his grip.

"Forgive me for disobeying," he responded. "I do so not out of disrespect … but rather from affection. I—You are important to me, *se* Jackie. I do not wish to see you transcend the Outer Peace just yet."

She looked at him then, as if she were seeing him for the first time. She had known Ch'k'te for more than four years and she had always considered him a good officer, someone she could trust. Now, with all of the official relationship stripped away, she seemed to finally accept that he was more than a comrade—that he was a dear friend as well.

She wasn't sure whether she really would have stalked off into the twilight alone, but it probably didn't matter. Tentatively she reached out her free arm and encircled his waist, careful not to touch the bandages. He released her other arm and it followed. She felt his arms, and then his wings, encircle her.

She looked up at his face and noticed tears streaming from his eyes. She hadn't realized that zor wept, but somehow it did not surprise her.

"I don't know what to say," she said after a long time.

Ch'k'te did not reply, but instead began to gently stroke her shoulders with his wings. It was comforting, though not arousing—the pheromones were all wrong. She was sure that it represented a significant lowering of barriers for the zor, who had never expressed emotions to her. The "touch" taboo between humans and zor was prominent, and for Ch'k'te to break it was a powerful indication of his true feelings.

After what seemed a long time he let her go. The light outside was gray, tinged with pale orange. She let go carefully and sat back. "Coffee's cold," she said, picking up her cup and emptying it into the recycle system.

"*se* Jackie," he said, as if trying it out. "Jackie. A name full of inner harmony. I ... am unsure of protocol here. Have I just made a commitment of some kind?"

"No ... no, Ch'k'te. It seems you had made your commitment quite a while ago, I just didn't realize it."

"I ... do not understand. I meant to ask whether some mating custom was violated."

"Mating—" She turned and looked at him, smiling. "Oh ... I see what you're asking. No, not at all. I ... have no mate."

"If I offended you in any way—"

"No!" Her voice betrayed alarm. She took a deep breath and added in a more level voice, "No, by no means. I have no mate by choice."

"I do not mean to pry."

"Oh, for Christ's sake—" She reached out and took one of his taloned hands. "My dear friend Ch'k'te. You are the most self-effacing person, zor or human, I have ever met. We seem to be in each other's debt for our lives. Who can tell if we'll even be alive tomorrow to speak of it?"

She released his hand and moved over to the autokitchen. Trying to keep her hands from visibly trembling, she dialed a fresh cup of coffee. "They have— They used to have a nickname for me at Cicero Down. They used to call me 'the Iron Maiden.'"

Ch'k'te nodded, indicating that he understood the reference. "Not really very complimentary and hardly accurate."

She took a sip of the coffee, winced and put it down on the deck beside her. "I had a lover when I commanded a starship, years ago: Dan McReynolds. He was my chief engineer. It was a relationship of convenience, though it didn't feel like it at the time ... When he had the opportunity for his own command, he chose to go, and I didn't choose to stop him."

She turned away from Ch'k'te and looked out at the slowly darkening sky. "Neither of us was willing to put a relationship ahead of a career. I suppose it's like they used to say—I'm married to the Navy." She ran a finger through her hair. "It's probably too late to do anything about that."

"Why do you not seek another mate? Are you afraid the same thing might happen again?"

She turned on him, reddening. "'Afraid'?" she snapped. "I'm not—" Then she stopped, realizing that it had been meant as an observation rather than a criticism.

Psychoanalysis from an alien, she thought. *Well, at least he's objective.*

"Perhaps I am. But it doesn't really matter now, does it?"

"I do not understand. Why should it no longer matter?"

"We're trapped here. You said so yourself: If we were to try anything, we'd most likely die."

"I beg your pardon, *se* Jackie," Ch'k'te replied. "That is not precisely what I said. I pointed out that were *you* to attempt something alone, in the dark, that *you* would most likely perish. I did not mean to imply that all action would be useless."

"You have something in mind."

Ch'k'te flexed his left hand, allowing the talons to extrude from their sheaths and then retract, as if he were trying *them* out. "We still seek to communicate the nature of this emergency, which requires getting off-planet. We have only one way to do so: at Cicero Down.

"We clearly must go there first. Of course, there are certain inherent problems with this plan, not the least of which is the few hundred kilometers of terrain we must cross in order to reach it."

"In midwinter."

"Acknowledged." Ch'k'te looked at the deck and then back at Jackie. "There is an even more important reason for us to reach Cicero Down."

"Another—"

"The *gyaryu.* It is at the base; I have felt it during my contemplations."

"The *gyaryu*? *se* Sergei's sword? Does that mean that he is there also? Alive?"

"Truly, *se* Jackie, there is no way of knowing. I am inclined to believe that he is alive; I would be surprised if the aliens would simply kill him. But since they are powerful Sensitives ... *worse* than Sensitives ... it is imperative that the blade itself not remain in their possession."

"We should've tried on Cicero Op—"

"Eight thousand pardons, *se* Jackie. It was not a mistake to have escaped the station without him. We left *se* Sergei—"

"We abandoned him! If we'd stayed—"

"Please consider. If we had remained, the ... beings would have captured us as well. I believed at the time that *se* Sergei could have withstood their attacks with the *gyaryu.*"

"And he couldn't."

"Apparently not. But the sword is still on-planet."

"I'm guessing that if they realize its importance, they'll probably be guarding it closely." Thoughts chased themselves through her head ... How would they even find it, much less take it away from aliens capable of mind control?

"I am *certain* they realize its importance." Ch'k'te shuddered, as if a chill wind had blown into the cabin. "It is critical that we regain it. If the *Gyaryu'har* is dead, we must return it to the High Nest."

"Why *is* it so important?"

"That is difficult to explain. It is a ... focus, of sorts, for the Inner Peace. To let it be misused by these beings would be a deadly insult to the People as a whole and to *esLi* as well. It would do great harm." His talons clenched and then flexed. His wing-position changed. "It must not be."

Jackie could read him well enough to see he was resolved to do this, even if she ordered otherwise. For all that Ch'k'te was an Imperial naval officer, he was a warrior of the People first.

It struck her as peculiar that he seemed indifferent to the idea the old man might be dead—but that obtaining the blade was vital. Perhaps it was because they would not be able to undo *se* Sergei's death. Regaining the *gyaryu* was possible though unlikely.

There was more to this than what Ch'k'te had already described, but it didn't seem to be forthcoming.

"When will you be ready to travel?"

"Tomorrow or possibly the day after. My efforts at *esLiDur'ar* have been successful thus far, but they are as yet incomplete." He carefully touched his bandaged midsection. "We cannot wait too long, however, or our chances of penetrating the base will be reduced to zero."

"What do you believe them to be now?"

"Minimal," he replied at once. "But that does not mean we should not try."

THE DAY was painted in brilliant white and deep blue, with boundaries etched in stark relief. The featureless plain was a tableau of stark beauty unmarred by the work of man. It could have been a scene from the distant past.

Jackie was reassured by the presence of Ch'k'te, silently sliding to and fro as they skied across the plain. The brilliant orange sun beat down upon them from a cloudless sky, but it gave little warmth. A steady piercing wind whipped up eddies and whirlpools of snow, and while her cold-weather suit effectively retained body heat, she felt chilled by despair.

It was difficult to accept the notion of being on the outside looking in—her sudden transformation to fugitive status had not set well. Once she accustomed herself to the steady exercise it was easy to let her military training take over, giving her more time to think, since she no longer had to consider the movements of her body. Her mind turned almost of its own accord to thinking about the past.

As she moved along, she had a sudden moment of perception in which she felt the instance of the present as the result of all that had gone before, as if it were the logical outcome of every event that had preceded it. It was unnerving to think this was what her life had led to.

She had never been one for speculation on what might have been. She considered it to be an exercise for complainers, those more willing to bemoan their fate rather than to do something about it. Still, she could not help it now, as she reviewed the recent events almost against her will. She thought again about Dan aboard the *Torrance*, years ago, and what they had shared, and why they both had given it up ... When her officers tried to pry behind the facade of "the Iron Maiden" she always claimed she didn't even remember his name, but Dan would always be hard to forget. There had been a time when he had meant everything to her ... *Well, not exactly*, she reminded herself. *The career came first for me, too.*

Of course he had accepted his own command when it was offered. She had realized that her own career was more important than their relationship as well. She had let him go and hadn't stood in the way or protested.

She cursed aloud, bringing herself back to the present. Ch'k'te broke his stride and let himself slow to a stop and she pulled up alongside.

"Is something wrong?" he asked.

"Just thinking about the past." Her breath formed in an icy cloud in front of her. "How are you feeling?"

"Surviving." Ch'k'te touched his chest. "I find myself cursing my own stupidity from time to time."

"Stupidity?"

"For having accepted a posting on the Plain of Despite." He waved his hand around. "This is hardly my climate of choice. An elder cousin in the High Nest convinced me that it was a posting with great honor; otherwise I am sure I would have chosen another."

"It's not my favorite climate, either. This is much colder than Zor'a, then?"

"Zor'a?" He paused, as if confused for a moment, then nodded. "Ah. I see. Yes, it is much colder than Zor'a. Actually," he continued after a moment, "my thoughts were directed toward S'rchne'e, my homeworld."

"Tell me about it."

"It is truly beautiful." He looked around them, as if performing a sort of mental comparison. "I believe that the word 'paradise' would not be inappropriate. My *ehnAr*—'clan' is the closest word—settled there just seventy Standard years ago, and the Nest is fine and new."

"I thought that all of the Nests were centuries old."

"Not at all." Ch'k'te looked away, out across the plains of ice. "You seem to have forgotten your history, *se* Jackie. *esHu'ur* destroyed S'rchne'e—every settlement, every *L'le*, every one of the People on the world—during the war of *esHu'ur*. *Every* Nest on S'rchne'e is new."

There was a long, uncomfortable silence. "If I touched a sore spot, I apologize," she said at last.

"You did not offend." He looked back at her, his shoulders and wings hunching in some unknown position within his cold-weather suit. "What was done was *esHu'ur*'s right to do as an agent of *esLi*. Just as for the People as a whole, he gave S'rchne'e a new beginning and a new direction."

"By destroying everything and everyone? Male and female, adult and Nestling?"

"I do not understand what you would have me say. The deed is done. Every one of the People who defied *esHu'ur* has long since transcended the Outer Peace."

"You don't bear a grudge?"

Ch'k'te fixed her with a glance. "Should I?"

"If someone vaporized Dieron, I think I'd bear some resentment."

"*se* Jackie, if someone vaporized Dieron eighty-five Standard years ago you would never have been born. As for the deaths of Nestlings and warriors of the People I never met, would my anger or resentment bring them back to life?"

"No, but—"

"No indeed." Ch'k'te's shoulders shrugged inside his suit again. "What is more, it is a matter of historical fact that *esHu'ur* had to do this—at S'rchne'e and a number of other worlds as well—in order to accomplish the task at hand.

"I thought that you, as a warrior, would understand this."

They began to move again.

"I still don't see—"

"That is unfortunate. But like most humans, *se* Jackie, you do not understand it from our point of view, *ha'i* Marais did, and we revere him for it; yet his own race cast him aside and made him a villain. That is extremely mysterious to me."

"Mass murder does not sit well with us."

Ch'k'te pulled up short and turned completely to face her. "Consider this, if you will. Aliens of unknown power and capability, but with clearly hostile intent, control Cicero Operations and Cicero Down. These aliens were responsible for numerous deaths at Sargasso and likely numerous deaths here. If you had it in your power *at this moment* to gather these aliens and those who willingly serve them into one place and destroy them with weaponry, would you not do so?"

"Yes, but that's not the same thing at all."

"Eight thousand pardons, *se* Jackie, but I completely disagree. You are mistaking the magnitude of the deed for the deed itself—as if a great act of violence is intrinsically more unethical than a small one. Or perhaps you would suggest that killing *unknown* aliens is somehow more palatable than killing *known* ones.

"Or, perhaps, you suggest that it might have been proper for *ha'i* Marais to make a distinction between combatants and non-combatants that the People themselves did not make.

"As a whole, humans seem to have an extremely bad understanding of the purpose and practice of war. That may be why you fight so many of them."

"I don't believe this." In her mind she was feeling both anger and amusement. "I'm in the middle of a damned wilderness, arguing philosophy with a zor." She pushed off again and Ch'k'te followed alongside. "I don't think I will ever truly understand you."

"'You'? Do you imply singular or plural, Jackie?"

"Plural. The People. The whole race." She took several more strides before continuing. "The mysticism in your culture—I simply can't comprehend it. Like when you contacted me on the station and appeared to me in that castle—"

"Castle? What do you mean?" He looked at her curiously.

"When—when you contacted me on Cicero Op, I got the image of a castle. You were in a tower room, with ... with high windows, open to a storm. It was a laboratory, or something."

"You saw images?" he asked. "I spoke to you—I heard you reply and communicate with me, with more facility than I could have hoped."

"You were a good teacher."

"You have been a good student. The images you saw were ones *you* created, however."

"I don't know how I could have done that—I don't even know what the hell it was."

"It was the Fortress of Despite," Ch'k'te responded stonily. "The stronghold of *esGa'u* the Deceiver."

"An enemy."

"*The* enemy, *se* Jackie. *esGa'u* is the Deceiver, 'the one who turns away from *esLi*.' What you saw, I believe, was his fastness on the Plain of Despite."

"I created that image?"

"Perhaps *esLi* answered my prayers," Ch'k'te answered. "You may have seen the Fortress."

"But I don't have the context. I haven't read the literature, I haven't seen the vids. How could I create that image?"

"I believe you may have seen the *actual* Fortress. You see, we believe that the Plain of Despite truly has a physical existence."

"You mean that it's actually somewhere? On some *planet*?"

"It might be."

"What about *esGa'u*?"

"Our philosophers reason that both *esGa'u* and *esLi* are a product of what might be termed the 'collective unconscious' of our race. If your mind produced an image of the Fortress of Despite, then it is clear that somewhere in me—at least—is a belief that *esGa'u* Himself has truly intervened in this matter."

"Meaning?"

Ch'k'te didn't respond for a long time. They moved silently across the ice plain, with nothing to interrupt but the wind and the back-and-forth sounds of their skis.

"When *esHu'ur* Marais conquered the People, he also demonstrated himself to be *esTli'ir*, the Bright Wing. His was the power to destroy but also to withhold destruction. *esGa'u*, on the other hand, was cast out with His followers in a titanic struggle far back before we began to record history. He has no such obligation to balance darkness with light.

"He will almost certainly show no mercy toward the faithful, *se* Jackie, or toward their allies."

chapter 7

"Come."

The door slid aside and Ch'k'te entered Commodore Laperriere's office. He offered her a salute as the door closed.

"You have an explanation," Jackie said.

"I wish I did," Ch'k'te answered. He walked across to the window overlooking the landing-field. Snow continued to swirl, less fiercely than when they'd come down from the orbital station, but still steadily. "I hate this form," he added. "And I hate this planet."

"I am not interested in your preferences," Jackie answered. "I am interested in the escape pod and your apparent inability to locate it."

"We'll find it."

Jackie's eyes flashed in anger. "Contractions," she hissed. "The zor do not use contractions in Standard."

"No one will notice."

"*Everyone* will notice! This is not the time to create unwanted suspicion. You will perform your assigned task, *Commander Ch'k'te,* or you will yield to someone who can."

Ch'k'te and Jackie locked glances for several moments. Finally Ch'k'te looked away. "Acknowledged," he said. "We will find it," he added. "The storms on this cursed planet—"

"A poor excuse. It must have landed somewhere on this continent; the trajectory should have located the crash site within a few hundred square kilometers."

"Which have already been searched."

Jackie placed her hands on her desk, palms down—a very Jackie Laperriere-like gesture. "It must be there. You must have overlooked it."

"Perhaps the zor Sensitive could have concealed—"

"Nonsense. The zor Sensitive is not strong enough to effect a concealment of that sort; his human companion has no Sensitive ability at all."

"What about the old man?"

"He is comatose," Jackie answered. "He has not stirred since the sword was taken away, and I suspect all of his power comes from it. He is no threat.

"I warn you, Commander. Find the escape pod. I have received word that this operation is to be completed soon, and I wish no loose ends."

OMETHING WOKE her from troubled sleep. At first she reacted like a soldier, crouching and reaching for her weapon: she wouldn't expect mercy from the things that had been lurking in her dreams. Then she realized she was alone in the small tent. The still-warm impression of Ch'k'te's body in his sleeping-roll indicated that she had not been alone for long.

She sat up slowly and pulled on a gunbelt and holstered her pistol, then pulled on her outside clothing and made her way out of the tent. It was a chill night with a stiff wind blowing from the top of a nearby bluff; the tent itself was in the lee of the wind, but she could see loose, powdery snow swirling, wraithlike, by the light of Cicero's two tiny moons.

She could see Ch'k'te standing with his back to the tent, only partially dressed in his cold-weather suit. His wings shivered in the breeze. He held them stiffly, with his arms held loosely at his sides; his head was inclined downward.

She had not intended to disturb his contemplation, but the crunching of snow attracted his attention and he turned. Again, as had happened so many times in the last few days, Jackie was taken aback by his thin, disheveled appearance, his eyes red-rimmed even through their protective lenses. Zor were clearly not intended for postings of worlds like Cicero.

"An elder cousin in the High Nest convinced me that it was a posting with great honor."

"Is everything—" she began, but stopped, seeing the look in Ch'k'te's eyes.

He looked at her curiously, as if seeing her for the first time.

He held a hand out, shivering in the cold. She took it and he grasped it tightly.

"He is ... *alive, se* Jackie. I heard him cry out."

"Who?"

"The *Gyaryu'har. se* Sergei. I heard him as I dreamed. He is ... The blade and the wielder are linked. They share a deep bond, and when it was taken from him by the ... It pained him. I can scarcely fathom the depth of anguish I felt."

"Is he dying?"

"Nothing so ... easy. They will not let him transcend the Inner Peace, especially with Cicero Down's facilities at their disposal." Ch'k'te turned again to face in the direction of their next day's travel.

The last few days had been difficult at best. A storm had come up suddenly, forcing them to dig a snow-cave along an escarpment to evade the biting wind. As they came closer to Cicero Down, they had also been forced to elude the prying eyes of overflying aircraft.

It had troubled her all along that they had little in the way of a plan. The journey itself had occupied their waking hours; they traveled from sunup to sundown, stopping infrequently, taking a few minutes out at the end of the day to cook a hot meal and collapse for the night to regain their strength. Not surprisingly, survival had made all other concerns take second place. Now here was a new wrinkle: the *Gyaryu'har* was alive and was in the hands—or rather the tentacles—of ... the aliens.

"We left him behind once, Ch'k'te. We won't do it again. You told me that he was a warrior, but we're going to rescue him if we can. The last time it was about survival. This time it's about *duty*."

Then, as she looked at Ch'k'te, something occurred to her. "You heard him cry out, you said."

"That is correct," the zor replied, letting go of her hand.

"Was it the first time you ... felt his mind? Since you were on the station, I mean."

"This is almost the limit of my range—perhaps twenty kilometers," he replied. "I was not even sure that *se* Sergei was alive until this night."

She thought about this for a moment. She still didn't know how to approach the problem: the unknown capabilities of the aliens and their ability to invade minds and to assume different forms clouded her thinking.

"I—" She sighed heavily, wondering how to broach the subject. "Ch'k'te. Do you think you could contact him?"

"Touch his mind? The *Gyaryu'har* I ... may not."

"Why not?"

"It is not permitted, *se* Jackie. Except for the High Lord, no one may touch the mind of the *Gyaryu'har*."

"If he is in danger—"

"It is not *permitted*."

"For God's sake, Ch'k'te, this is an emergency! If we can reach him ... if he can help us get to the *gyaryu* ... Without *se* Sergei's help, we'd be walking in there blind."

"I—I do not know if I could even reach him over this distance. The amount of energy required is great."

There was a long silence, except for the wind.

"Can I help?"

"It would not be easy. They might be monitoring his mind. Even with your strength added to mine, we might not be able to reach him. What is more—"

He fell silent and looked away from her.

"What's wrong?"

"The process of drawing upon another's mind is one of ... forced intimacy. It is more than the mind-touches we have as yet undertaken. It can only be performed in harmony with someone one knows and trusts. It is more than a simple linking of minds: it involves the lowering of all the barriers, making all avenues available."

"I trust you," Jackie replied. "I have nothing to hide from you."

"It was not you with whom I was concerned. It was myself."

Ch'k'te stood in the cold, shivering as the wind gusted above. "Opening one's mind to a mate or even a close member of the same *ehnAr* is one thing. But you are an alien, a *naZora'*. Eight thousand pardons, *se* Jackie, but if our minds proved to be incompatible—"

"We've served together for years, Ch'k'te. How could we be incompatible?"

"Our *minds*, *se* Jackie. You are important to me, as a friend and comrade. I have affection as well as respect for you, but it is a thin veneer of custom and behavior that allows us to enjoy our relationship. There is no hiding when the mind is bare, no duplicity. There may be things lurking within that we would rather not have exposed."

"I'll take the chance, thank you. Without any idea of what's going on at Cicero Down, we don't stand a chance of getting in there."

"I am not sure this is a wise course, *se* Jackie."

"Oh?" She put her hands on her hips. "Well, I'm not sure as we have much choice. I don't like walking into a trap.

"I can order you to do it," she added.

"Indeed you can," he retorted at once. For several seconds they stood facing each other, neither speaking, each waiting for the other to look away.

At last Jackie dropped her hands to her sides. "I can't really get you to do so against your will. Look." She took his arm and began to lead him toward the tent. "We aren't going to get anywhere, except together, as a team."

She stopped, and turned to face him. "I'm afraid of it, too. It's not any easier for me, thinking about letting down my barriers—all of them—to a, a zor. It just may be easier for me to admit to the fear."

B Y RELAXING and breathing slowly as Ch'k'te had taught her, Jackie put herself in a receptive state to prepare for the mind-link. Unlike a simple touching of minds, the link involved a total fusion of consciousness. It was done infrequently, and only in response to a particular need. Reaching *se* Sergei, if it could be done, was just such a need.

As she drifted, hearing the distant howl of the wind outside he tent, she felt the tendrils of Ch'k'te's mind reach for her …

"*se* Jackie."

She awoke with a start, finding herself in the tent. Opposite her sat Ch'k'te, but instead of appearing grim and haggard, he appeared healthy and strong. He was draped in a crimson robe, belted loosely at the waist; his wings were raised slightly. All around him was an almost imperceptible glow.

She looked down at herself and saw that she was wearing a similar garment, though it was cut differently for her human form.

"What—"

"A construct," Ch'k'te replied. His voice seemed fluid, as if it were echoing the strumming of some alien instrument. "An illusion, if you will. It is customary for the one guiding a link to provide a framework within which to form it." He drew back the flap of the tent.

Jackie looked past the open flap, bracing herself slightly for the inrush of cold air ... but outside the tent she saw nothing but a featureless expanse of gray. She could not suppress a shudder.

Ch'k'te let the tent-flap fall from his hand. "I did not intend to frighten, *se* Jackie, merely to illustrate. Beneath the veils of reason and logic, all is illusion. To a Sensitive, much of what he sees in ... reality"—she thought she heard a distant chiming of laughter in his voice—"is illusion as well. It is all of a piece."

Jackie let one hand trail along a bare leg. "And all this?" She fingered a seam of her garment, noticing in passing that it was all she was wearing. "What is the significance of all of this?"

"My ... mate gave me this robe," he said, running a taloned hand along the lower hem. "She fashioned it herself. I tried to provide a comfortable fit."

"A bit short," she replied. "But your knowledge of human customs must have told you something about undergarments."

A wave of embarrassment struck her almost physically and she felt a pang of fear. Ch'k'te reached out for her hand as the image of the tent began to waver.

She took the offered hand and the scene stabilized. "No, no," she said, smiling. "I'm sorry. I'm not offended. I'm actually quite touched."

"If you require something, you can fashion it easily," Ch'k'te replied carefully.

Thinking slowly, Jackie tried to imagine undergarments, and presently found them forming around her. After a moment's adjustment, she looked up at the zor.

"Much better. Now, how do we contact—"

"Patience," Ch'k'te said, cutting her off. "We are only at the surface." He paused, and she tried to reach out to him, but his thoughts were guarded.

"Is something wrong?"

"I thought my ... framework would make this an easier task. Instead I fear that it has made it more arduous."

"I don't understand."

"I did not expect you would." He absently traced a pattern before him with the talon of one hand. A faint glow stayed visible for a moment. "You see, the linking of minds is most often done in conjunction with a ... particular custom in zor society. It is often practiced as a ... in prior to—"

"Mating," Jackie finished for him.

"Yes. Mating." Another wave of embarrassment spread out from Ch'k'te and this time Jackie forced it back herself, consciously trying to make the scene stabilize. It solidified at last, though she noticed from the corner of her eye that a wall of the tent now bore a holographic painting of Sol System and part of her Academy diploma—both of which hung on the wall of her office at Cicero Down. Further, she could feel her day uniform forming in place of the ceremonial robe.

No, damn it! she thought. *This is Ch'k'te's mind-link, you're going to screw it up!*

Ch'k'te looked up at her, his eyes focused and intent. The holo vanished, but the Academy diploma remained, tauntingly, hanging on a corner of the wall. Her suit faded away.

"Mating is a spiritual as well as physical experience," Ch'k'te said. "Especially among Sensitives. Mating partners unite with one another, sharing experience and feeling, until they are truly one."

"Where is your mate now?"

"She has transcended the Outer Peace," Ch'k'te replied, looking away.

"I'm—I'm sorry."

"I appreciate your sympathy," he replied. "But you must understand, *se* Jackie. I feared this link because of that situation. My mate was a strong Sensitive, and ... she was the last person with whom I attempted as deep a mind-link as we now require. I have determined that she left some of her *hsi* behind. I retain an image of her personality in my mind."

"I don't understand," Jackie repeated. "—I seem to be saying that a lot."

He looked away. For a moment, Jackie saw the faintest image of a different zor hanging in the air beside Ch'k'te's head. "Those that transcend the Outer Peace continue to exist only in memories. But a considerable amount of the *hsi* of my mate appears to have remained."

The image of the other zor disappeared suddenly. "I do not think the two of *us*, even combined, can reach the *Gyaryu'har*. But with the *hsi* of my mate ... But to introduce that personality might destroy the link, or do grievous damage to your psyche—if it were forced upon you."

"But with her strength, you might be able to reach *se* Sergei."

"Yes." He looked down at his talons, partially extended from their sheaths.

"What would that entail?"

"Bringing her forth? If it were possible ... *se* Jackie. You are not a Sensitive, and you do not possess certain skills to protect yourself if her *hsi* proved to be strong enough to take over the link. Still, with her strength ..."

"What if I ... let you do it?"

Ch'k'te's head snapped up. "I could not take the chance, even if you would trust me to do so. The temptation—"

"Temptation? To bring her forth and—"

"And leave you trapped."

Jackie smiled, though she could almost see her own uneasiness in the air around her. She ignored it and continued. "You are too noble a being and too good a friend to try and do that."

Ch'k'te did not speak.

"I *trust* you, damn it."

Ch'k'te looked up at her. "*se* Jackie, I—"

"You need my help. I'm putting myself in your hands. Get on with it."

The zor sighed deeply. "Very well." He reached his hands out to either side of him, raising his wings in a position of supplication.

As Jackie sat, trying to compose herself, she felt something on her back begin to move. Her shoulders began to hunch against her will; she reached back with her hand to find that her back had begun to sprout wings! As she brought her hand slowly back into view, she noticed that her fingers were elongating and melding, the fingernails extending into sharp talons, four replacing five.

That was not the only change. As she watched, the room began to become perceptibly brighter, almost unbearably so. She put her transformed hands over her face and realized that her head, too, was changing shape: her mouth was forming into a sharp beak and her ears were elongating and flattening.

Somewhere in the back of her mind she could feel a stirring, as if a long-dormant part of her brain were awakening. A wave of fear swept over her and cascaded as alien perceptions followed, one after the other, fighting for her attention. She felt herself slipping, then being pushed, farther and farther back in consciousness. Shortly she could only barely feel the transformations that were rapidly taking place. There was another personality in her mind: it was first surprised, then hostile and then jealous, binding and gagging her, trapping her within her own mind, controlling her so that she could not even scream.

As the light in the room dimmed in response to Ch'k'te's mental command, she let her hands drop from her face, to look at the handsome form opposite her.

As the aura of emotion washed out from her form, she heard herself say, "In the name of *esLi* I greet you, my mate."

chapter 8

At A'alu Spaceport (named for the High Lord of the Unification) traffic was as heavy as always. On the diplomatic concourse, inaccessible to any but officials of the Solar Empire and High Nest, the bustle and commotion was no more than background noise; workers and lesser officials kept a respectful distance as T'te'e HeYen, High Chamberlain of the High Nest, swept through with his entourage on the way to the berth of his private shuttle.

T'te'e cut an imposing figure most times—he was taller than many of the People, and his wings were often held in a haughty posture as befit his rank—but as he passed through the largely empty concourse this afternoon, he conveyed a taut anger that made him even more to be avoided. This emotion made those on the concourse even more eager to please or avoid him.

When he reached his berth, however, he stopped short and re-formed his wings to the Posture of Polite Approach when he saw who was waiting for him.

"*se* Byar. I am honored," T'te'e said quietly. "I did not expect to see you here."

"I thought it appropriate," Byar said. "If you have a few moments before your voyage …" He gestured offhandedly toward the 3-V reporters, kept at a respectful distance, but still permitted to record and report. The Act of Normalization with the Solar Empire had created this circumstance, which T'te'e still felt to be an affront; but there was nothing to be done for it but to endure.

"Of course."

The two flew up to a quiet alcove a dozen meters above the concourse and turned their backs to the invasive cameras. Their wing-positions would be partially visible, but their speech could at least be concealed—and Byar touched a control on the comp tucked into a sleeve of his robe to mask it even further.

"Is it done, then?" Byar asked.

"It seems so. I will know more when I reach Adrianople. *hi* Ke'erl has felt the *esGa'uYal* at Cicero."

"And the *gyaryu* …"

"Taken. Even *I* felt that. There is no conclusive evidence that *se* Sergei has transcended the Outer Peace, but prolonged separation from the blade can only lead to that."

"It pains me to think of this."

"I know." T'te'e's wings formed the Enfolding Protection of *esLi*. "Nonetheless, *se* Sergei is a warrior; he understood the danger when we first chose this flight. We all did: *si* Th'an'ya, *se* S'reth, the High Lord himself … *esLi* wills this, *se* Byar. Nonetheless, one thing is clear: Qu'u may not emerge as we expected."

"If Qu'u does not emerge—" Byar began, alarmed, but T'te'e's wings changed to a posture of reverence to *esLi*.

"Peace, *se* Byar. I did not say that Qu'u would not come—merely that he will not take the form we had thought, *hi* Ke'erl has dreamed this as well."

Byar thought about this for a moment, then placed his wings in a similar position, indicating assent. "Did the humans respond to *hi* Ke'erl's message?"

"*se* Mya'ar said the emperor understood the gravity of the warning, but did not sense the wing of *esGa'u*. It could hardly be otherwise." T'te'e's wings dropped to a posture of distaste; he glanced over his shoulder, and noted the interest of the 3-V reporter below.

"We cannot defeat the *esGa'uYal* without the humans, *se* T'te'e. I need not remind you of that."

"*esLi* protect us. I pray that we can defeat the *esGa'uYal even with* their help."

A S THE aura of emotion washed out from her form, she heard herself say, "In the name of *esLi* I greet you, my mate."

While the transformation had been taking place, Ch'k'te had remained frozen in position. He was unwilling or unable to move as he watched the image of his dead mate slowly replace that of his commander and friend. Emotion and a terrible longing had welled up in him, making him realize how painful it was to know she had transcended the Outer Peace and that this was just a memory.

"*li* Th'an'ya," he began, and then stopped. Her eyes looked back at him, the eyes of his recollection of their last meeting, just before she departed Zor'a with the exploration team.

Somewhere within the image of his lost mate was Jackie Laperriere, who trusted him … It was such a temptation to give her *hsi* away—

No, he realized. *This must not be.*

"*li* Th'an'ya." He sighed heavily. "I … have summoned you back to aid me with your Sensitive skills."

"Summoned me back? What do you mean?"

"I … You are a memory, my dear soul-mate. I have used the *hsi* of my link-partner and overlaid your personality, though my joy is mixed with pain."

"Link-partner?" She looked at him quizzically. "But am *I* not your link-partner?"

"No," he said slowly. "You are not. There is another in this link, one who yet lives."

"Another? I—" Th'an'ya stopped and looked down as if contemplating. Then her head snapped up in anger. "A *naZora'e* female? What madness is this?"

"*se* Jackie is my friend and my commanding officer. I needed her strength, but I need also your skill. She gave me leave to summon you forth. I have used her *hsi*-form to house you. I cannot betray her trust."

"You would choose a *naZora'e*—over me?"

"She lives, *li* Th'an'ya, and you do not. And she placed herself in my hands. I am *idju* if I trapped her *hsi* in this way."

"You need not make that choice," Th'an'ya replied. "*esGa'u* has toyed with you, but I will rectify matters on my own."

"No, you will not."

Th'an'ya had raised her hands and wings in an invocation. She stopped and looked around her as a voice sounding remarkably like Ch'k'te spoke those words. She looked across at the image of her mate, but he, too, was looking around.

"Though it pains me to have summoned back your memory," the voice continued, "I am in dire need of your skill. Yet I need also the strength of my link-partner. I had not expected you to thrust her aside so suddenly, yet I am sure that you will not and cannot destroy her. You can only destroy yourself."

The tent-image faded away; yet they remained suspended in the void, surrounded by an ethereal image that enfolded them. It was the image of Ch'k'te —a sort of meta-Ch'k'te, less tangible but measurably more powerful.

"It is not a part of the Th'an'ya I remember, to destroy beings out of wanton anger. I need you, my dear one, and in this crisis I have formed a link with a human, untrained and unready, yet brave and trusting. I need her as well."

"Crisis?" Th'an'ya asked quietly.

Neither Ch'k'te nor meta-Ch'k'te replied, but the void slowly formed itself into images, vignettes depicting all that had happened in the past few days: the return of the Sargasso expedition, the transformation of the Noyes-creature, the hurried escape from Cicero Op, their trek across the ice, and finally the searing, bright cry of anguish when the *gyaryu* was torn from the hands of its keeper.

When it had all faded away, another image surfaced and played itself out—a scene on a space-station, parsecs distant and years ago, the last farewell between the two. It was a touching of minds that revealed to Ch'k'te for the first time that Th'an'ya had known then that she was parting from him forever.

"It was my choice. I recall this now, mate of my soul: I gave my *hsi* to you so that I could be here for this *shNa'es'ri*. But with so much of my *hsi* here, then …"

Her wings altered to a position of submission. "I am lost," Th'an'ya whispered. "I have transcended the Outer Peace."

"Part of you still lives," meta-Ch'k'te replied gently. "And you will live on forever, as long as I live."

"What of this *naZora'e*? I hold her *hsi*."

"If her *hsi* is strong, she will summon herself back by Remembering. If she cannot, I may have to dismiss you to return her. But if I do so I will have failed, for I need both of you to accomplish the task."

"Does she have the skill to realize this?"

"I do not know. But we can pray to *esLi* that she does."

IN THE void Jackie could feel her own body, strangely altered by the process it had just undergone. Her hunched shoulders could feel the weight of their articulated wings; her hands were now four-fingered claws with sharp talons; her face ended in a pointed beak … and yet in another sense she had none of these things at all. She was curled up, fetuslike, in a dark nowhere, waiting for something to happen.

She was terribly frightened. The transformation and sudden emergence of Ch'k'te's mate had only accentuated that fear, making it even more apparent that the entire experience was out of her control.

It was beyond her comprehension. The Th'an'ya personality had thrust her aside without even thinking, casting her out of her own body with a thought—

No, she thought to herself, and at once a pale-colored sense of wonder washed over her, realizing that there still was a "self" to think to.

No. She did not cast me from my body. My body is still in the tent, out on the Cicero ice plain. This Th'an'ya is a memory, a construct, just as Ch'k'te said— she no more has a body within Ch'k'te's mind than I do.

He has linked his mind with mine for a purpose; he has summoned her back from his memory for a purpose. The purpose is to contact se *Sergei and to learn what has happened to him.*

She opened her eyes and saw the gray, featureless plain she had seen from within the "tent." She saw her own body floating there, halfway through the transformation from her own figure to that of a female zor.

She touched her taloned hand with her human fingers and flexed her single wing.

I am Th'an'ya ehn E'er'l'u na HeYen, she thought. *I first held the Inner Peace on the twenty-fifth day of the month of the Bright Sun, in L'le E'er'l'u of Sharia 'a.*

I am Jacqueline Laperriere, she thought. *I was born on March 18, 2359, in Stanleytown, North Continent, Dieron.*

I live, thought Jackie/Th'an'ya. *I live.*

I remember.

Remember the fine bright days in the hills of E'er'l, when the sun would play down on the waving grasses, and the wind would blow the clouds tumbling across the sky / and the deep forests of North Continent, with their hidden streams teeming with life / remember running through the brightly decorated halls of the L'le, bare-taloned feet taking purchase in the soft wood floors that would spring back into place when we would pass / and feeling the hot sand of the beach between our toes / and the waves crashing onto the shore / and the thunder in the mountains at night/

Some of those are not my memories, she thought. *They belong to Th'an'ya. Remember your own past, as painful as it might be.*

Remember Jackie Laperriere.

Once again she felt that odd sense of progression, one event leading to another, each bringing her closer to where she was now. The events stood out in stark relief as images etched in the void, taunting her with the choices she had made and the turnings she had made her life take. She was alone now, lacking even the ability to cry out.

Remember, she told herself. *Accept the past that is yours.*

Slowly she felt the talons retreat again into fingers; her shoulders relaxed as the remaining wing shrunk and gradually disappeared. But the memories were bright lights in the darkness, twinkling like stars …

THERE WERE always the stars, to be gazed at and longed for, in reach and yet unreachable. Our ancestors did not have the power to escape the binding confines of the surface; yet we had learned to navigate the depths of space and to try and fathom just how limitless it all was.

The Academy was at Moonbase, man's oldest space facility, built in the twenty-first century: before the War of Accession, before the Empire. There were still parts of the base that had ancient inlaid tile floors bearing the blue-and-white symbol of the international organization that had built it. It had been a traditional challenge for cadets to find every location inside Moonbase that still had a recognizable United Nations emblem.

It was strange after all this time to remember that particular bit of trivia, but it was of a piece with the rest of the Academy experience. Centuries of tradition weighed heavily upon everything they did, from survival training in the vacuum wilderness of Luna, to breaking out sail on a clipper at sea on Terra's Pacific Ocean. Intimidation and humiliation were part of it, too—what the instructors liked to call character-building. But when they stood on the parade ground at Admiralty HQ in Greater St. Louis with the Imperial banner snapping in the wind and gave the salute to their commandant, there was no doubt they were truly the cream of the crop. The last cadet in the class—the so-called anchorman

—was kilometers ahead of non-Academy officers and felt it, too. Many came before them and many would come after, but that slice of time was theirs eternally, like a framed portrait on a wall, as if it were all that had ever been …

Jackie had specialized in navigation. She had served for a while on the carrier *Charlotte Amalie*, piloting aerospace fighters; it hadn't been as exciting —or as dangerous—as it had been decades before, when the Solar Empire was fighting the zor, but it had been a thrill ride all the same. After two years of survey and rescue missions, she had been posted as a junior navigator to *Kennewick*, named after an Imperial estate in central Washington in North America. The chief navigator aboard was a burly man named Bartholomew Fredericks. When she first came aboard, she'd addressed him as "Commander Fredericks," and even (once, in a staff meeting in the Old Man's ready-room) as "Astrogator Fredericks"—his official title, though the term "astrogator" had never really replaced the more archaic "navigator" in the hearts or official dispatches of the Imperial Navy.

But after a few weeks aboard *Ken*, she took to calling him "Big" just like everyone else did. Big Fredericks was a hard-drinking, hard-fighting officer who doubled as the Old Man's chief of security. The Marines assigned to his command seemed to identify with him because they thought he was much like them.

Those who served under Big knew better. He had a fierce loyalty to the Empire and to his comrades; he was a stabilizing influence for young officers on their first deep-space cruise … He had a big heart and turned out to have the same love of folk music as Jackie did. One off-watch when they'd drunk too much, he took her off to the ship's hydroponics section and confessed his love for her, but Big was too much the father and not enough the lover figure. She'd laughed it off—which had hurt him.

Less than a month later, the *Kennewick* took a broadside from a rebel ship during the insurrection at Allara. Big Fredericks, the Old Man and the rest of the bridge crew were blown into the vacuum. Somehow the *Ken* had limped home under Jackie's command, leaving her shattered survivors on the beach for three months: R&R at half-pay, waiting for another opportunity to ship out.

For some of them that chance never came, but the door was always open for an Academy grad. Her next opportunity came with the *Royal Oak II*. After two years, attrition and the Thompson's World rebellion had promoted her to chief navigator, one of the youngest in His Majesty's Fleet. It took two more years for her to obtain her own command, as CO of the newly commissioned starship *Torrance*.

It was during her tour with the *Torrance* that she met Dan McReynolds. They were from different worlds, really—he had been conscripted by the

Mothallah System defense force and had clawed and scratched his way into engineering school. He had originally intended simply to acquire a skill so that when his hitch was up he wouldn't have to return to his poor home-world and go "on the dole," as they called it in Mothallah. But a brave and foolhardy emergency repair conducted during battle convinced someone in the Imperial Navy that his talents were too good to let escape.

The Imperial Navy bought his contract from Mothallah System. The patron who discovered him made sure that he entered Officer Candidate School. By the time he was assigned to the *Torrance* as its chief engineer, he had as good a reputation as any engineer in the fleet. He had a way with machines. It was almost as if he spoke their language; his memory was phenomenal, his diagnostic skill uncanny. He could make anything work … with one notable exception.

He fell in love with Jackie almost from the start. His over-confidence and brashness struck her as rather boorish; she mentally labeled him as an ass, then as immature. Then there'd been the rescue mission at the Tsing research colony, where they'd worked for forty-eight hours saving thousands of people threatened by a biodome collapse. In the end, all of her barriers broke down and she found herself drawn into an affair that was the talk of the Fleet. They seemed so incompatible at first: one partner outspoken, the other reserved; one optimistic, the other gloomy; one an officer the hard way, the other Academy-bred. But it worked somehow; each found in the other the missing element that had made them restless and unfulfilled.

It worked until Dan was offered his own command. He accepted at once; he gave over his formal request for transfer with a stony face, without hesitation. It was probably career suicide to refuse, especially given his background and the stiff competition. She agreed with his logic and signed the transfer, accepting it then as she had a thousand times since.

She hadn't stopped him. He never looked back. Her promotion to commodore had given her the Cicero command, but it had never been the same.

Now at last, back in the present, somewhere in the deep and unstructured void of her mind she put her head in her hands and cried as she had not done in many years, and another part of her cursed herself for feeling self-pity. It wasn't as if feeling remorse or anger or pain could change the past …

Jackie.

Slowly she lifted her head up again, taking her hands away from her eyes, to behold a scene of wondrous beauty. In the void, no longer formless but filled with pastel-colored patterns that slowly changed according to some unknown harmony, were three crystalline figures: herself, Ch'k'te and a zor female she knew to be Th'an'ya—two zor and a human, two living and one but a memory, two Sensitives and one untrained … and over and around them, she perceived the ethereal enfolding wings of another mind, Ch'k'te and yet not Ch'k'te. It was a sort of meta-Ch'k'te, a name she attached to the protective consciousness that held them all and protected them from the gently shifting chaos all around.

What has happened? Jackie asked, looking at her translucent hand and through it at the void around her.

Breakthrough, meta-Ch'k'te said, from all around. *We have brought forth* si *Th'an'ya, whose skills we need, and you have Remembered in sufficiency to restore your persona.*

I am sorry if it was a painful experience, se *Jackie*, Ch'k'te said. *My soulmate,* he added, gesturing toward the crystalline form of Th'an'ya. *My comrade-in-arms*, he said to Th'an'ya, pointing to Jackie.

Your hsi *is strong*, Th'an'ya said to her.

We must reach the Gyaryu'har, meta-Ch'k'te said.

Without indicating assent, Th'an'ya's mind reached out across the void, taking the other entities with it.

It was a profoundly skillful mind. Th'an'ya was more adept than anyone Jackie had ever experienced—certainly more powerful than Ch'k'te, and more than a match for any of the Sensitives that had examined her when she entered the Service. It was more than just power. While the Navy Sensitives had almost made her skin crawl with their disdainful, burrowing minds, Th'an'ya was like a sculptor or even a graceful dancer, weaving a pattern from the chaos even as they seemed to hurtle through it.

As they traveled, the light around them grew brighter, pulsating rhythmically. Slowly shadows and shapes began to form, then whirling, geometric patterns of two and three and more dimensions—and suddenly Jackie recognized what they were: minds, human as well as alien. The human minds seemed to be arranged in patterns that were almost familiar, spinning off stray surface-thoughts like sparks from a pinwheel during an Emperor's Birthday celebration; the zor minds seemed familiar as well, though their patterning was totally different and betrayed far less of their inner composition.

But there were other minds as well, and Jackie felt them as distant, hovering shapes, waving tendrils in the ether, as if they sensed a presence but could not determine its location.

How will we find se *Sergei?* Jackie asked.

By his pattern, Th'an'ya replied. *I can see it.*

Jackie looked ahead of her and noticed that a shape was coming into view: a pattern of eleven glowing points, with the helix of a human mind hovering within.

He dreams, Th'an'ya said, hovering at a respectful distance. *Surely we intrude—*

The need is great, meta-Ch'k'te said. *We must wait for the dream to pass.*

THEY HAD placed a mask upon his face, that he might not see them; they had taken his blade, that he might not fight them. Thus, blind and unarmed, he came at last to the Fortress, high in the crags of the Icewall. The storm raged, though he felt no rain upon his back; the lightnings split the sky, though he felt no fear.

The force of Despite had no power over him as he journeyed, for it no longer inhabited this land. It had come to him during his travels and it had slain him, though his body lived on.

The Fortress jutted from a great promontory, overlooking a flight of steps spanning uncounted kilometers. He had climbed them all, impervious to cold and pain and fatigue, a young man in his dreams; the steps had not been difficult to traverse, for Despite welcomes those who come to it willingly.

As he expected, there was a guardian.

"Admiral," he said, for he was able to see in this land.

"Sergei, why have you come here?"

"I have chosen this flight, Admiral, *hi* Ke'erl dreamed that the *esGa'uYal* would come here."

"As they have." A flash of lightning illuminated Marais' visage, looking stonily down at him. "The Deceiver, who once sought to separate the People from the *naZora'i,* has sent his minions here. Now he brings another race to bear, delivering both *naZora'i* and the People into his hands. Still he knows that we are not weaponless before him."

"I do not understand."

"You could *not* understand. It is beyond *your* comprehension, just as it was beyond *mine. esLi* knows, for He knows *esGa'u.* He has sent me to bring you a message in this hour of dishonor, to plant the seed of *esGa'u*'s destruction."

"What seed shall I plant?"

"*esGa'u* cannot destroy the body, so he shall destroy the soul. In the hour of darkness, He shall provide one to lead you into the talons of Despite and thus destroy yourselves. It will be a matter of *enGa'e'Li*: the Strength of Madness.

"You shall be free and you will destroy; for this you will be judged. *esLi* has seen this. You will plant the seed of the hatred, Sergei. This seed that was formed while I lived and when you were young. The road is long and narrow, but ultimately leads only one way."

"Who will tread this road?"

"The Destroyer," the Admiral answered. The lightning flashed again and he saw the Admiral reach to his face. Sergei realized with a start that the Admiral, too, was wearing a mask: a smiling, sneering caricature of the face he had worn in life. As he pulled it aside, Sergei found himself backing away, while his eyes remained riveted upon the true face of Admiral Ivan Marais: *esHu'ur*, the Dark Wing, bringer of destruction, the awful, grinning visage of death ...

Sergei toppled from the high cliff and fell into infinity, feeling the grasping tendrils of the *esGa'uYal* upon him. He opened his eyes, praying that the mask would not prevent him from seeing these predators before he perished. Instead he felt himself buoyed up and saw instead familiar *hsi*-forms: two zor and a human.

SUDDENLY THE crystalline form of the *Gyaryu'har* materialized before them, as if it had fallen from a great height. It was *se* Sergei and yet not, for his form was enfolded in a zor's wings.

"*se* Sergei," Ch'k'te said. "You were dreaming ... I humbly ask eight thousand pardons for the transgression of touching your mind, but the need is great. My *Ssthe'e*-self will protect us for a short time."

He gestured around them, indicating the ethereal form of meta-Ch'k'te. "We are several hours away," Ch'k'te continued. "We sought to recover the *gyaryu*, and we hope to rescue you as well."

"You are truly ..." Sergei's mind was in clear turmoil for a few moments as he looked from face to face. "The aliens have stolen your form, *se* Commodore, as well as yours, *se* Commander, though I am the only one who could tell the difference. They have restrained me so that I could not see them.

"As for you, *si* Th'an'ya—I see that what you foresaw has come to pass."

"*saShrne'e*," she answered, inclining her head. "The shroud is pulled aside."

Ch'k'te looked at her for a moment, his wings forming in a position of curious inquiry.

"How many aliens are there?" Ch'k'te asked.

"Six at least. I cannot be sure."

"What others have they replaced?" Jackie asked. "Do they have the run of the base?"

"Commander Noyes and my aide have been replaced," Sergei replied. "It appears they have kept to the same routines in order that they might not attract attention. There was a report of trouble at Cicero Op, but that appears to have been passed over. At the moment it is as if they are waiting for something."

"We'll get you out of there."

"The *gyaryu*," Sergei said, reaching a crystalline hand down to touch an empty scabbard. "That is far more important—I am not; at least not without the sword—I am merely an old man. Recover the blade and return it to the High Nest."

"You're damn important—" Jackie began, but she stopped suddenly as the pastels of the void suddenly became dark and milky. Swirling patterns of light formed themselves into tendrils that struck against the form of meta-Ch'k'te.

"Go. Quickly." Sergei raised his wings in an invocation to *esLi* and vanished.

The buffeting grew stronger, and the echoing silence of the void was replaced by a peculiar buzz. meta-Ch'k'te raised his wings in alarm as the tendrils buffeted him, breaking shards away from his form. Th'an'ya extended her wings to cover Jackie, and a rainbow of light sprang from her in all directions—

Somewhere in the distance a dark and quivering form became visible. It was a huge misshapen thing with many tentacles; it seemed to reach across an enormous distance to grasp them. There was little hope in trying to outrun it.

meta-Ch'k'te braced for its touch and a cloud of dread swept through the link, as each awaited the attack of the alien mind. Instead, however, the reaching member struck meta-Ch'k'te like a sledgehammer, shattering him into uncountable fragments and sending the others spinning into the void, unable to control their flight.

Jackie saw the cliffside approaching, its surface sparkling with jagged ice. It was immense, extending for as far as she could see up or down. She knew she would strike it, and that it would shatter her, leaving her easy prey for the monster behind.

It was the Icewall, the boundary of the Plain of Despite, the insuperable barrier that kept the minions of *esGa'u* from escaping onto the plane of normal existence. Its presence meant that *esGa'u* had come at last, bringing the Plain of Despite with him, to rule and conquer ... and there was no escape.

She struck the wall and shattered. Each of her tiny fragments cried out in pain until, at last, darkness overtook them.

"*se* Jackie."

She let her eyes open slowly, fearing what she might see this time.

What she saw was the tent illuminated by the pale reddish rays of a sun low on the horizon. They struck Ch'k'te, cloaking him in crimson.

She looked at herself and took inventory. She was solid *(Good start,* she thought) and in human form, though her shoulders felt like they'd been in a vise for several hours. She was still wearing her cold-weather suit and she was dripping with sweat inside it. Ch'k'te looked exhausted; his wings drooped and his arms hung loosely at his sides.

It suddenly felt strange for just the two of them to be there. Jackie had become accustomed to the feel of Th'an'ya and to the enfolding presence of meta-Ch'k'te, even though it couldn't have been more than a few hours. Similarly, the tent felt close and confining after the limitless reaches of the void through which their minds had traveled.

Then the memory of the Icewall came back to her. It was like a physical blow.

"Christ," she tried to say, and found that her mouth was dry as dust. Ch'k'te held out his canteen to her and she drank slowly, watching the sun set through the transparent flap of the tent.

She looked at her chronometer and confirmed that it was evening. Nearly a full day had passed since Ch'k'te had forged the mental link to reach the *Gyaryu'har.*

She turned to him. Every muscle proclaimed its agony. "Report," she said.

"The link was broken. Something detected us. *se* Sergei separated, and then something forcibly destroyed the link."

"Does this 'something' know now that we're alive and nearby? Did it overhear what *se* Sergei said to us?"

"I do not know. It is possible."

"Shit." She tried to settle herself into a less uncomfortable position. "We're screwed now, Ch'k'te. We're completely screwed. We might as well walk up to the goddamned landing-field gate and wave an Imperial banner. They know we're coming and they'll be waiting for us."

Then, as she sat trying to unkink the muscles in her lower back, her expression changed. "Wait a minute …

"*se* Sergei said there were only a few of these aliens at Cicero Down and that they'd taken the place of key personnel, including the two of us, but that most people on base didn't even know a switch had taken place.

"Suppose we carry it a step further—suppose we make no attempt at disguise but simply go in disguised as *ourselves*. Only a few individuals *can't* be fooled by that, and we're not going to surprise them anyway."

"Surely they will know of our presence sooner or later."

"Yes, I imagine they will." She looked away again, out through the tent-flap. "But hopefully we can reach my office first."

"Your office?"

"Commander's privilege," she said. "I'll explain if we get there."

Ch'k'te remained silent, unwilling to inquire further.

"Six individuals, Ch'k'te. We may only have to worry about six individuals, two of whom will look exactly like us."

"If they indeed know we are coming, there is considerable risk. And even if they do not, what if we meet 'ourselves'?"

By way of answer, Jackie reached for her gunbelt and secured it around her waist.

T HEY CROSSED the snow plain under an almost moonless sky, making them virtually invisible to visual surveillance. There was no sound other than the ceaseless howling of the wind. It was even colder at night, though with the cold-weather suits and facemasks, it hardly penetrated to their bodies. The necessity for keeping warm enforced isolation, preventing conversation while they were moving.

While they were resting from a particularly strenuous uphill climb, Jackie broke the silence.

"I want to know what happened, Ch'k'te, but first I want to clarify something else, *se* Sergei knew *si* Th'an'ya and didn't even seem surprised to see her."

"*li* Th'an'ya was known to the High Nest," Ch'k'te said. He bent to examine the bindings on his skis.

"Nice try."

Ch'k'te straightened and looked at Jackie. "I beg your pardon?"

"He *knew* her, Ch'k'te. Not only that, he was not surprised to see her *even though she's transcended the Outer Peace.* You didn't expect to find her *hsi* in your mind ... but he did."

"I am not certain of that. But if it is true, what does it mean?"

"I don't know. But he told her that what she'd foreseen had come to pass. He told me several days ago, in not so many words, that he had come to Cicero *precisely* because he thought something was going to happen here."

"I am certain that *se* Sergei was here for that reason, *li* Th'an'ya was a powerful precognitive; I am sure that is what he meant."

"There's more to it than that."

"Perhaps so. I cannot say."

Jackie looked away at the dark sky, filled with the diamond points of distant stars.

"Tell me about what happened."

Ch'k'te turned away. "Eight thousand pardons, *se* Jackie—"

"I'm not asking for an apology, just an explanation. I want to understand it."

"It was a dangerous thing to do, especially with an alien mind, but I was ..."

"Desperate."

"An accurate description. I realized that I was not strong enough to reach the *Gyaryu'har*. Then I sensed the presence of my soul-mate's *hsi* ... and with her help I realized that I might be able to succeed. She did not know that she was ..."

"A memory? And you had to convince her?"

He looked at her then, the profile of his face etched in starlit shadow.

"*li* Th'an'ya was assigned to be a part of an exploratory mission, which was lost. We linked and mated the night before she departed; the ship misjumped or crashed. In any event she never returned.

"She left her *hsi*-pattern within my mind. The *hsi* I found during our link was far stronger than I would have expected. When I sensed it, I realized that she had left much of herself behind in me."

"What does it mean for her to have left her *hsi* behind that way?"

"She was a powerful Sensitive, *se* Jackie." Ch'k'te looked down at his hands. "She could not have continued to function thus without so much of her *hsi*. She must have *known* that she would not return.

"Every person's *hsi* is different, never seen before, never to be repeated again. With her pattern so strong, I reasoned that I could make use of that strength. What happened ..."

"You didn't expect her to take over. To take *me* over."

"I expected ... No. I did not expect that. I can only again ask eight thousand pardons and thank *esLi* that your *hsi* was strong enough for you to Remember."

"I remembered, all right, though I don't think I'd ever really forgotten."

"There is a difference between Remembering and remembering." She saw his shoulders flex in a certain way, as if he were trying to position his wings. "Th'an'ya displaced you in such a way that I might have had to break the link if she had permitted me. As it was, you reached a rather primitive point of self-awareness and worked back through your Academy and Service experiences until your emotions returned you to us."

Her mind jumped across several of the images she had experienced the night before: Moonbase, Big Fredericks, the time on the beach, Dan McReynolds ... "Wait a minute. How do you know—"

"I ... we ... observed the process."

Jackie's stomach jumped. "You were *watching*? I spilled my guts out! I was fighting back from whatever damn place your mate put me in, half zor and half human, torn apart from all the crap that I went through over the last fifteen years, and you sat by and *watched!*" Ch'k'te didn't reply.

She grasped him by the shoulders. "You *bastard!* You put me through that and you didn't raise a talon to help?"

"There might have been some therapeutic effects—"

"I don't need therapy, damn it! I didn't need to have it all thrown back at me—"

"—and further, it was not something I could control. I had no choice."

"What the hell do you mean?"

He reached his hands up and grasped her arms, a trifle more tightly than she would have expected of a zor. She felt tension in his grip and saw it in his eyes, as if he were trying to restrain powerful emotions.

For just a moment she felt a pang of irrational fear, wondering what sensitive spot she'd rubbed this time.

"I did not expect to have my soul-mate's *hsi* stamped upon yours. I did not expect you to have to suffer so in order to restore you. If the need had not been so great, I would not have attempted such folly—I would not have even attempted the link. If your power, and the strength of your *hsi,* were not so great, your Remembrance might not have even been possible.

"Once Th'an'ya had emerged it is not even clear that I would have been able to break the link at all, for to do so would have resulted in dismissing Th'an'ya ... *forever.* Even given my soul-mate's scrupulous adherence to the morality of the situation, I am not sure she would have allowed me to do so."

Jackie searched his gaze and replayed his words in her mind. "If I couldn't— If I hadn't been able to break through, where would that have left me?"

Ch'k'te did not answer, but she saw—and somehow felt—a terrible sadness in him.

"Answer me, damn it," she whispered.

"I do not know, Jackie. Perhaps you would have remained thus."

"You risked my—my *hsi* that way?"

"At your request and order. But you could not have known; I do not think that such a warning would have deterred you. I can only offer you my sincerest, my humblest, my most heartfelt apology. If your honor is somehow stained, I am ready to transcend the Outer Peace at your request." He let go of her arms and stepped back a pace, then laid his gloved hand on the hilt of his *chya.*

It took a moment for the words to sink in. When she realized their implications she felt as if a trapdoor had opened under her feet and that she was falling down into a bottomless pit. A moment before, she had been incensed, incredulous that someone she considered to be a friend and comrade had placed her in such danger, with no way of telling if she—if they—could have escaped it. Now, because of that outrage, Ch'k'te had reacted the only way he could: not with righteousness or apology, but with a simple statement of intent.

"If your honor is somehow stained, I am ready to transcend the Outer Peace at your request."

She wanted to take him by the shoulders and shake him for offering such a crazy solution. Her honor, "stained"? It was something like that; what bothered her most was not having any control over the situation, being directed by things she didn't even understand.

On the other hand, she wasn't ready to adjudicate between life and death for her executive officer and friend. There was no doubt he was serious about spilling his life out here in the middle of—

In the middle of the Plain of Despite, a voice in her mind said.

She must have started, for Ch'k'te looked directly at her.

"se Jackie?" he asked.

This is my command, she thought to herself, dismissing her surprise. *Everything that happens is my responsibility.*

"You followed my orders, Ch'k'te," she said quietly. "You were aware that there was some risk, and you warned me in advance—or tried to. I understand you better and maybe myself as well. Your actions and your concerns were correct.

"Your apologies are accepted. I only hope that … I have not dishonored you by suggesting anything to the contrary."

"Not at all," he replied at once. "You understand me so well, I must continually remind myself that you are not *ehnAr'u*, a clan-sister."

They embraced, with the wind blowing snow-devils. Jackie could almost feel the presence of ethereal wings enfolding them.

FOR THE rest of the night they did not break their journey. The strenuous exercise helped work out the muscle soreness resulting from prolonged inactivity; they made good time skiing, as if some burden had been lifted.

Just as false dawn was brightening the sky, they saw a groundcar in the distance, heading across a flat part of the plain in the direction of Cicero Down. They stepped quickly out of their skis and covered them with snow, then headed on foot to intercept the car.

Its bright headlights picked them out and slowed to a stop. The driver's-side hatch opened, and a uniformed figure leaned out.

"Commodore!" he shouted. "Commander. What are you doing out *here*?"

They approached warily on foot. Jackie kept her hand near her pistol; she could sense Ch'k'te's tension as his hand hovered near his *chya.*

"We were on our way back from inspecting Coast Station," she answered. "Our groundcar broke down and we had to go on foot. The weather interfered with our radio. We'd like a lift if you have room."

"Plenty of room." They approached close enough to see features on the driver: it was Lieutenant John Maisel, one of the tower watch officers.

They stepped inside the cab. The car was empty but for Maisel; Jackie took the other front seat, while Ch'k'te climbed in behind the young officer.

"I hadn't realized that you were off-base, Commodore," Maisel said as the car picked up speed, heading toward Cicero Down.

"It was a high-security mission."

"But—following your own directives, ma'am, it should've been on the day roster." He looked her up and down as he drove and his expression became puzzled. "Besides, it's more than four hours to Coast Station by groundcar, and I just reported to you when I came on watch at midnight—"

The road turned sharply and Maisel had to give his attention to driving the car. When he looked back Jackie had her pistol drawn, aimed at his chest.

"What the … ?"

"It would be wise for you to make no sudden moves, Lieutenant," Ch'k'te said from the rear seat. Maisel turned a few centimeters, enough to see the tip of a very sharp talon held near his right carotid artery.

Maisel looked very deliberately from his commanding officer to the zor and back. He didn't move his head more than a millimeter in either direction.

"Lieutenant, I have not been on base for nearly a week. Neither has Commander Ch'k'te. The commodore you have been reporting to is an impostor."

"Huh?" Maisel looked forward, concentrating on piloting the groundcar for a few moments. "An impostor?"

"An alien impostor," Jackie added. "Aliens have seized Cicero Down, taking the place of myself and other key personnel."

"Alien impostors?" He didn't say anything for several moments but his eyes were surprised, scared, confused. "But—"

Ch'k'te's talon moved quickly and drew a spot of blood on his neck. Maisel pulled away and then remembered the zor's warning. He froze.

"I don't believe this is happening," Maisel said, concentrating on the driving once more, trying not to move his head.

"I wish it was not. *We* are who we seem to be, Lieutenant," Jackie said, exchanging a look with her exec. "The aliens who have taken our place have mental powers far surpassing the capabilities of human or zor Sensitives." She shivered momentarily, thinking again of the tentacled monster that had invaded their mind-link and sent her crashing into the Icewall.

"How do I know *you're* not the impostors?"

He felt Ch'k'te tense in the rear seat and tried to remain even more immobile.

"You don't," she said.

"This is ludicrous." He drove silently, aware of the sharp talon at his neck and the gun pointed at his chest. "*Somebody's* the impostor, and someone's not telling the truth—either you or the ... *you* back at Cicero Down. You claim that you and Commander Ch'k'te have been replaced by aliens with Sensitive powers. How come no one else has noticed?"

"I don't know. Ch'k'te and I had to bug out of Cicero Op and never reached the squadron."

"The escape pod," Maisel said. "You—she—said that it had been launched by accident."

Jackie exchanged glances with Ch'k'te. "It's possible the squadron has been taken over, as well. If that's the case, none of this may do any good. Even if we rescue *se* Sergei, we won't be able to get away from Cicero."

Maisel looked at Jackie with a curious expression. "The old man representing the zor High Lord?"

"The *Gyaryu'har*," said Ch'k'te from the back.

"He's dead."

"Dead? When did he die?" *Oh shit,* Jackie thought to herself, wondering if they'd brought it on.

"Almost a week ago, ma'am," Maisel replied. "He arrived at Down under medical supervision and died about eight hours later."

"Did anyone see the body?" Ch'k'te asked, as Jackie relaxed slightly.

"I didn't see it personally. But I have no reason to doubt—"

"*se* Sergei is being held prisoner by the aliens. He is very valuable to them."

"The old man?"

"He's more than he seems, and he had his own reasons for coming here." She could see the lights of the landing-field in the distance; the road led directly to an arched gate. "We intend to rescue him from captivity and find a way offworld if we can. We can use your help, John. *I* can use your help."

"You should be aware, however, that the price of duplicity will be very high," Ch'k'te said to him quietly. With another lightning-swift motion, Ch'k'te drew his talon along Maisel's neck, leaving a thin slit in its wake. Blood formed along it and Maisel winced, though he still did not move.

"Commodore ..." he began, never looking away from the road, perhaps gauging how much time he had before he reached the gate.

Maisel was only in his mid-twenties, with no real combat experience, despite being stationed at the edge of the Empire. Other than the occasional colonial revolt or pirate skirmish, there had been little opportunity for such experience.

The proximity of death had probably never been so great. The likelihood of suffering it at the talons of a violent, totally unpredictable alien, brought forth a fear John Maisel had never felt before. He knew all about being a good officer, operating by the book—but this was something new.

"Choose," Ch'k'te said levelly from the backseat.

Maisel's face reflected the overhead lamps that lit the approach to the gate. He looked from the gate to the somewhat bedraggled figure of his commanding officer. Her pistol remained aimed at him and her eyes were cold and emotionless.

"If you're the commodore," he reasoned, "I do my duty by helping you. If you're an impostor, I'm a traitor." His shoulders sagged. "All right. I can only die once. What are your orders, ma'am?"

Jackie looked at Ch'k'te, who nodded. He withdrew his talon; Maisel sighed with relief.

"I need to reach my office," Jackie said. "We're likely to meet resistance along the way. There may be no avoiding it. I need you to help get us on base, since the … aliens will be expecting the two of us, alone, on foot." She holstered her gun and took a small pressure-bandage Ch'k'te handed her, applying it to Maisel's neck to cover the damage the talon had caused.

Maisel lowered the driver's-side window and reached for his gate-pass. "You're going to trust me. Just like that." It was a statement rather than a question, as if the young officer had lost all energy for further questions.

"We only have one other alternative." She settled back into her seat, her hand remaining close to her holstered weapon. "By the time this is over, there'll be enough blood spilled. There's no need to get any more on our own hands."

THE SKY was still mostly dark when the groundcar pulled up in front of the post headquarters. Maisel had shown his pass and come on base with his two superior officers crouching, hidden, in the rear seat; it was still quiet at midwatch with much of the base asleep.

The three officers entered the building, exchanging cursory salutes with on-duty Marines and going directly to the lift. Even though everything seemed normal, Jackie was on edge, as if every wall had eyes in it.

Or tentacles, she told herself with a shiver.

The lift rose quickly and deposited them on the top floor at one end of a dimly lit hallway. Through the glass panels at the far end of the hall, the horizon was painted with the faintest touches of morning.

Jackie gestured to the door, her pistol in her hand. The door slid aside at once, revealing the familiar office. It was tidy ... and empty. She beckoned to her junior officers, who began to methodically search the office for hidden transmitters or listening devices. She walked to the wall containing a holo of Sol System.

For just a moment, she paused and looked above and to the left where her Academy diploma hung. After all that had happened during the past few days, it (like all of the trappings of this office) seemed to be slightly out of line with her memories, as if they belonged to a previous life ... or to another person. There it was, big as life: Jacqueline Therese Laperriere. There she was.

Or was she?

She reached out to the holo with her right thumb and touched Earth's Moon at approximately the latitude of Moonbase. A voice said, *"Print identification positive."*

"Voiceprint record on," she said. "Commodore Jacqueline Therese Laperriere."

"Voiceprint positive."

Ch'k'te and Maisel had concluded their search and stood watching this process. If Jackie had turned to look, she would have seen surprise and curiosity in her exec's eyes.

"Retinal scan on."

She took a step to her right and stood opposite the holo image of Mars, which hung at approximately eye level for Jackie. A beam of pale greenish light sprung from the orb and struck her right eye for a few seconds, then flickered and disappeared.

"Retinal scan positive. Awaiting your orders, Commodore."

"Transmission, closed channels, Priority Alpha One One Null. To the commanders of all vessels on station in Cicero Military District, from Commodore Laperriere. Relay to Adrianople Naval Base and Admiralty Headquarters, Sol System. Voiceprint confirmation attach.

"Begin message.

"Mayday. Cicero Down is presently under the control of alien beings whose capabilities include, but are not limited to, the ability to assume alternate forms and to control human and zor minds using Sensitive techniques. Aliens have seized Cicero facilities and are responsible for the death of Admiral Horace Tolliver. They are also probable culprits for the disappearance or destruction of several Imperial vessels.

"End message. Read that back."

As she turned from the holo to face her companions, her own voice began to repeat the words. She was sure she'd quavered as she gave the message, but it sounded clear and firm.

Suddenly there was a noise in the hall—the soft *whoosh* of the lift. "Belay readback," she said, and the voice cut off. Maisel flattened against the wall; Ch'k'te took refuge behind a filing cabinet. Jackie crouched beside her desk, pistol in hand.

Footsteps came down the hall toward the office and stopped outside. The door slid slowly open and a hand reached within and touched the phosphor beside the door, clearing away the shadows and illuminating the room.

A sudden rush of nausea came into Jackie's stomach as she crouched behind the desk and saw the figure standing in the doorway. It was the image of Commodore Jacqueline Laperriere.

chapter 10

The image of Cicero's commanding officer looked around the room, replicating Jackie's mannerisms perfectly. She wouldn't have seen a better image of herself if she looked in a mirror.

"I sense you here, Commodore," the alien said in Jackie's voice. "You were a fool to return, and a bigger fool to expect that you could pass unnoticed.

"There is no escape," the voice went on, as the door closed. "They"—a casual wave of the hand—"will believe whatever I make them see. They will see you as alien monsters." A flicker of a smile mixed with a sneer came across "her" face. "They will shoot you like animals."

Jackie stood up from her crouch, pistol in hand. She could hardly contain the fear rising from deep in her chest.

"Ah, Commodore. At last we meet," the other figure replied. "Although I feel that I know you already all too well."

"You've got a lot of guts, making jokes while I've got a gun pointed at you."

"Should I be afraid?"

Anger mixed with fear now: anger at this *thing* taking her form, taking her command. "Maybe I should blow your goddamned head off."

"If you can."

"All I've got to do is squeeze this trigger."

"If you can," the alien replied, in the same maddeningly calm tone of voice.

"For the moment let's assume I can." Jackie wasn't sure she was ready for cold-blooded murder just yet. "Suppose you answer a few questions."

"Nothing I tell you could possibly change matters. Very well."

"Who are you? What are you?"

"I am …" The creature smiled. "R'ta. In your tongue, I would be titled 'drone.' The best approximation of my race's name is *Vuhleissicha'a'*n*o'ulu' *eeei*." At three points within the word, the alien made a sound almost irreproducible by a human throat: a sort of gargling *click* voiced almost in the windpipe.

"'Vuhl.'"

"As you wish."

"What happened to the ships we sent to Sargasso?"

"We destroyed them," R'ta said almost offhandedly. "A few specimens were retained for the … Great Queen's consideration."

Jackie shivered slightly; she didn't like the sound of *that*. She was aware that her gun arm wavered a bit. The alien seemed to notice as well and the smirk became more pronounced. Jackie made a mental note to never smirk again; she didn't like how it made her look.

"What do you control in Cicero System?"

"Cicero Down and Cicero Op," the alien replied. "The squadron is being held in quarantine … at least until our reinforcements arrive."

"And they are not aware that anything is amiss?"

"No." R'ta took a step forward. "Their minds were easily manipulated, just like yours."

"Don't come any closer," Jackie said, trying to hold her pistol steady. "I'll—"

"What will you do?" asked the alien, stepping forward again.

"I—"

"You have already lost."

"I …" Jackie's gun arm began to come down and fear transfixed her. She felt numb, as if she had no control over her own movements.

At the edges of her perception, her sight began to go dim and R'ta became the center of her vision. The alien seemed to grow larger and brighter with each step it took, tendrils of vaporous light extending toward her. With the narrowing of sight she could feel an undercurrent of fear: chilling, unreasoning fear that she couldn't dismiss.

"Hold it right there," Maisel said, standing up, his pistol trained on the alien. "Don't take another—"

The alien diverted its attention for a moment and looked directly at Maisel. "*Die*," it said.

Her body seemed still held in check, but for a single moment Jackie's vision cleared. She watched the alien speak the single word and the tendrils retracted a few centimeters.

She knew that she could not possibly raise her arm to fire the pistol, but she did have another alternative.

"Transmit," she said, as she heard rather than saw Maisel collapse to the floor. The gun he had been holding skittered into the corner near the door.

The alien turned again toward her, its face trapped in a look of surprise as it heard the message being spoken in Jackie's own voice.

"*Mayday,*" the message said. "*Cicero Down is presently under—*"

"You—" it began. The tendrils of light leapt across the intervening distance toward her—

"*—the control of alien beings whose capabilities include, but are not limited to, the ability to assume alternate forms—*"

She felt the tendrils grasp her, hatred flowing through them like electricity. Agony gripped her and she fell to her knees, crying out in pain.

"There might have been a chance for you to live," the creature said. "There was information you might have provided. But you will perish now."

"—and to control human and zor minds using Sensitive techniques—"

The alien came closer and closer as Jackie writhed in pain, every nerve-ending sensitized to the energy the being poured out. Jackie knew that when the alien touched her it would be the end. Images crossed her mind: of Dan McReynolds, of Big Fredericks, of Ch'k'te ... of the Academy, of home in Stanleytown, of the starry backdrop of space—

"—Aliens have seized Cicero facilities and are responsible for the death of Admiral Horace Tolliver—"

Suddenly there was a surge of pain so intense that she could not contain it. It was as if someone had trained a laser pistol at her head and fired it from point-blank range. She could even hear the sound of a blast, and could even smell the awful aroma of cooked flesh ...

"—They are also probable culprits for the disappearance or destruction of several Imperial vessels. End message."

As she began to lose consciousness she perceived a strange image: a silvery globe, hovering in a tank filled with rainbow-colored mist. There was an intelligence in the tank, something aware and malign ... and it seemed to be registering disapproval.

The Jackie-alien's body fell to the floor. Its body was already changing, losing its human appearance and taking on the form of an insectlike alien with a hard carapace and mandibles, with tentacles on either side of its distended jaws. It writhed in pain ...

... And as it writhed, Jackie's vision began to clear. The pain that had moments ago been so direct and forceful was already fading as the creature completed its transformation and stopped moving on the carpet.

Ch'k'te did not let go of the trigger until he had finished playing the laser over the creature's head. Then, he turned to his commanding officer.

"Are you all right?" he asked, as Jackie stood carefully.

"Yes. What about—"

"Dead."

She went to Maisel's side and looked for a pulse. "His heart's stopped, but there's a medical case in the closet. Ch'k'te—"

"Do not bother. The alien shut off his aura."

She looked up at Ch'k'te, who was calmly reloading his pistol with a spare power-pack from the shelf above her desk. "What the hell does that mean?"

"It means," he said, stopping for a moment, "that the lieutenant's brain has been rendered inert. Even if you restarted his heart it would do no good."

Ch'k'te's voice was level, but his hand talons were partially extended; his anger was clearly only barely held in check.

She clenched her fists as a surge of hatred flowed through her. With a thought, the alien creature had willed the young lieutenant to die—and it had happened.

"I will have my revenge, Ch'k'te," she said quietly.

"You shall not stand alone." He switched the pistol from reload to ready. A low-pitched hum filled the air. "Are you—"

"This is the IS *Pappenheim* calling Cicero Down. Acknowledge." The voice of Georg Maartens, the *Pappenheim's* CO, filled the room.

Jackie exchanged a knowing glance with Ch'k'te. "Computer, verify voiceprint," she said into the air.

"Verified as Captain Georg Willem Maartens, Imperial Navy."

"Acknowledge. Open a scramble circuit with this frequency."

"I assume," Ch'k'te said, "that there is some reason that you did not inform me of this communications circuit."

"Regulations. Every base commander has one, usually built into some piece of office equipment. Just in case the regular comm gear is jammed … or in enemy hands. It's a last resort, to be used in direst emergency. I think this qualifies." She shrugged. "Of course, we probably just alerted every alien on base that we're here."

Ch'k'te gestured toward the headless corpse strewn across the office carpet. "They may have already received that warning."

"CICERO DOWN acknowledges, sir," the communications officer said, turning to face the captain. "We have a scramble circuit, audio only."

"This is the *Pappenheim*. Go ahead, Commodore," Maartens said.

"Georg, there's very little time for me to describe what's going on. Regardless of previous orders to the contrary, you and the other ships in the belt are to proceed at once to Cicero planetary orbit."

"Acknowledged," he said. "Do you have further orders, ma'am?"

"I want a landing party of thirty Marines at Cicero Down on the double. They should go through normal landing procedures, but if they meet resistance … have them shoot their way in. Also, I want you to maintain absolute radio silence except when I initiate contact using this frequency."

"Aye-aye, ma'am," he said.

"I'm counting on you, Georg. This is a matter of life and death."

"We'll be there in about four hours."

"Good luck. Laperriere out."

The connection terminated. Maartens rubbed his chin thoughtfully. "Damn strange," he said.

"What do you intend to do, Captain?" his exec asked, coming to stand beside him.

"How long have you been in His Majesty's Navy, Christoph?" Maartens asked, looking up at him.

"I was commissioned four and a half years ago, Captain."

"Then the answer should be obvious. Beat to Quarters, son. Comm, give me a channel to the rest of the squadron. Helmsman, plot a minimum-time course to Cicero orbit."

THEY CREPT carefully down the six flights of stairs, avoiding the lift in case the power was turned off. They reached ground level without meeting another living soul of any race. There were several Marines in the lobby, rifles in hand, receiving orders from their squad commander.

"Ch'k'te?" she whispered.

"What is it?"

"Can you induce fear in another person, if that person isn't a Sensitive?"

"It is most distasteful to do so," he said, concentrating on the scene in the lobby.

"That's not what I asked. Can you *do* it?"

"Yes."

"And would that person be able to tell where that fear was coming from?"

"Not unless he or she was a Sensitive. It would otherwise be no more than a feeling of fear."

"Of you?"

"Of … whatever I chose."

"Of me?"

Ch'k'te looked at her. "You are not considering—"

"We don't live five minutes otherwise. But if I can make them believe I'm … If I can take *its* place, we might be able to walk out of here."

Moments later, she could feel the hairs at the back of her neck stand up as she walked across the lobby toward the main entrance. The squad commander, a Marine sergeant named Ames, intercepted her near the door.

"If you would stop right there, ma'am," Ames said, drawing a pistol from his holster and aiming it directly at Jackie's chest.

"What's the meaning of this?" she answered, glancing briefly at Ch'k'te.

A hint of fear crept into Ames' eyes. "There is—We received a report of an intruder, ma'am. We were told to look for someone … for someone …"

Ames' fear was palpable and visible; Jackie had to keep herself from reaching out and reassuring the young Marine. Her stomach churned at using the tactic.

Ch'k'te turned up the intensity. Jackie prayed that her expression remained grim and hostile.

"You were told to look for someone who looked like me, I suppose?"

"Y-yes, ma'am, I—"

"And who issued this order?"

"Commander N-Noyes, ma'am."

"Commander Noyes—" Anger swept through her at the mention of his name, but she restrained herself. "The commander is ... most efficient. But for the assistance of Commander Ch'k'te, an intruder might well have killed me less than ten minutes ago. You will find its remains on the carpet in my office. Send two of your detail at once to investigate it."

Ames looked her in the eye, obviously frightened but trying to control himself. Suddenly there seemed to be a flash of recognition in his eyes, as if the mask Jackie had assumed had slipped aside and crashed to the floor.

And just as suddenly, with half a dozen laser rifles pointed at her, it was Jackie's turn to feel fear.

"Baker!" said Ames. "Terry! On the double."

Jackie looked at Ch'k'te. His face remained impassive as the two Marines hustled across the floor.

"You heard the commodore," Ames said, looking away from Jackie and lowering his pistol. "Go up and investigate. On the double." The Marine squad leader looked at Jackie once more. "Your orders, ma'am?"

"There might be other intruders on base, Sergeant. I want every entrance and exit to this place covered, airlock-tight. Nobody in or out, except on my orders. Understood?"

"Aye-aye, ma'am," the Marine said, standing aside to let her pass. Slowly, without turning, Jackie and Ch'k'te crossed the few meters to the door. As it slid aside they walked into the bright, cold morning.

T HE HOLO over Georg Maartens' ready-room table showed Cicero Prime as it appeared on the bridge's forward screen. He could see Cicero Op as a tiny pinprick in opposition to the *Pappenheim*'s current position, still more than an hour downrange.

He looked up as the door-chime rang. "Come," he said, looking from the holo display to the door.

Christoph Kim, his exec, came into the room. The bustle and conversation from the bridge drifted in and then vanished as the door closed. "You asked for me, Skip?"

"Yes, Chris. I wanted to go over a few things about our deployment."

"I've filed the tac plan already ... Sir, may I speak freely?"

"Of course."

"Sir, I've been thinking about our orders. Commodore Laperriere has been … Well, Skip, she's been under a lot of stress. Do you think she's …"

The young XO's sentence trailed off. Maartens hadn't interrupted but he placed his hands on the table, palms down, and regarded his second in command.

"Chris, you've been my exec for two years. I've known Jackie Laperriere for more than a dozen. She's stubborn; she's sometimes a little stiff-necked; and Lord, she has a temper sometimes. But one thing she is *not*, is crazy. If she says there are aliens, then there are aliens."

"Aliens that can assume human form."

"If she says so."

"Aliens that can control minds."

"If that's what she says. Are you questioning her orders, Commander?"

"No sir."

"That's good, because—"

"No sir." He looked directly at Georg Maartens, taking a step to the left so that no part of the holo display lay between them. "I'm changing them."

"You're ch—" Maartens looked at his exec, trying to process what he'd said. " … ch—" he began again, and suddenly realized he was unable to reply.

Or move.

Or look away. Christoph Kim was visible as if at the end of a long tunnel. A hard, sardonic smile crossed the young man's face, and something flashed in his eyes: a glint of some intelligence Georg Maartens didn't recognize.

You'll belay the order for the Marine drop, the exec's voice echoed in his mind. *There's no need for it now.*

But my orders … he thought. A profound lassitude prevented him from even completing the sentence. Then he found himself shivering: though he could not look away from Kim's eyes, his peripheral vision told him that the ready-room had disappeared from view—indeed, the entire ship surrounding them was gone. It was as if he were floating in space, with nothing but liquid darkness surrounding him, the sky filled with stars, the vacuum hard and bright and cold—

Fear gnawed at him, a living thing. He'd just taken a breath: when he exhaled he would suffocate in space.

God oh God oh God—

"Excuse me, Skip, but I—" came a voice, and the ready-room materialized around him as abruptly as it had disappeared. He felt the mind that held him in its grip slip just a bit.

He exhaled.

"What the hell—" said the other voice. Maartens felt his hand rest on the scale model of the *Pappenheim* that stood on the ready-room table, a heavy brass thing that weighed five or six kilos. Knowing that he had only one shot, he stood and flung it with all his might at Kim, aiming for the head.

It must have been a piece of blind luck. The model caught the exec full on the side of the face. He toppled over, one hand extended toward Dante Simms, the *Pappenheim's* Major of Marines, who had come into the ready-room. He hadn't rung the door-chime—he never did; he must have caught Kim by surprise.

Simms looked from his captain to the exec, whose features were shifting even as he held an elongated hand to his head. He delivered a sharp kick to the other side of Kim's skull—something short of a killing blow, but enough to give Simms a second or two to draw a pistol.

There was no need. The exec was unconscious, but was absolutely no longer Christoph Kim, the *Pappenheim's* second-in-command. Three or four of the bridge crew were already in the doorway, responding to the noise. At least one other crewmember had drawn a pistol.

"Dante," Maartens said quietly, leaning on the table, "if I ever give you a rough time for coming in here without knocking, you give me one good slap to the side of the head. Do you copy?"

"Aye-aye, sir. Loud and clear, sir."

"Good. Comm, find Dr. Callison and get him here on the double. Dante, if that—thing—moves a centimeter, you kick it again."

chapter 11

It was strange and frightening to walk among naval personnel on base and know that some of them might be enemies. After years here Jackie knew most of them personally; she returned their salutes, hoping that she appeared calm and in control. She couldn't simply be *herself*—whatever she had been to her subordinates had been destroyed. She had to be the being that replaced her: feared as well as respected, familiar yet totally alien.

They must have known, she thought to herself as she and Ch'k'te crossed the parade ground in front of the command center, heading for officers' quarters. *They must have sensed a difference, a change in style or tone, something.*

Nothing could replace her so completely and go undetected.

She watched as a flight of Vindicator interceptors shot into the morning sky, leaving contrails behind them. She had seen it countless times, but now the sight seemed new and unusual.

How could an alien have truly replaced her? Did her people know her so little, that this—R'ta, this *vuhl*—could have taken her place without so much as a second thought on anyone's part?

Poor John Maisel had not known at all until she'd told him. He'd probably not completely believed it until he saw it with his own eyes—just before the alien had killed him with a single casual thought.

There are deeper questions here, she thought to herself, as she put one foot in front of the other, straining against a stiff wind. If R'ta had truly replaced her, what was *she* now—an impostor? A stand-in for a stand-in? If so, what did it mean? What was her real identity now?

She stopped walking, reeling with the consequences of her thoughts. Ch'k'te stopped as well, his hand near the pistol of his belt.

"*se* Jackie?" he asked quietly, tension evident in his voice.

"I …" She looked at him and then away, toward the low buildings. The wind changed direction, making the flags at the edge of the field snap, their pull-ropes ringing hollowly against the metal poles.

Even if an alien had not taken her place, the events of the last few days had made her an intruder now. It was almost as if she saw Cicero Down and everything in it through different eyes, eyes that were open to different impressions.

"*se* Jackie."

It was terribly hard to reconcile it all.

"*se* Jackie. We are being watched."

The flags snapped again in the breeze, making a dull, hollow chime in the morning air. Jackie looked at Ch'k'te again, as if she were seeing him, too, for the first time.

"What … What did you say?"

"We are being watched. I believe we were just probed by a powerful Sensitive. It would be unwise to remain out here waiting to be shot at."

"Yes … yes, you're right, of course." They began once again to cross the field, as Jackie shook her head to clear the thoughts that had been crowding into it.

WHILE FOUR vessels dived into the gravity-well, the remainder of the fleet stayed at a distance near the Orionward jump point that Tolliver had used on his exit from and return to Cicero System.

As the *Pappenheim*'s bridge monitored the deep-radar, which registered mass and jump disturbances, readings would suddenly appear and disappear. Single ships and then groups of several at a time showed up and then vanished.

There was something out there—something that might be waiting for a signal to materialize. It wasn't comforting to Georg Maartens to have an enemy near a jump point with a large part of the defense fleet deep in the gravity-well. From a tactical perspective it was a frightening prospect.

JACKIE AND Ch'k'te crossed to the main building where the *Gyaryu'har*'s assigned quarters had been located. *se* Sergei's rooms adjoined the hothouse garden, which included many plants found in zor gardens—it was one of Ch'k'te's favorite places to meditate, and he had been able to furnish it well during his tour on Cicero.

The building was deserted at this hour of the morning. As they moved through the corridors, the sound of their footsteps seemed to echo unreasonably, like the report of an automatic weapon. No one came out to challenge them.

It was disarmingly simple to make their way to the suite's door in the interior of the building. This was a bit frightening: there were no guards, no defenses, no evidence the enemy was preparing for them.

At a wave of Jackie's hand, the door slid aside to reveal the apartment. Like her office, it was tidy, clean and vacant. On the near wall was a sleeping pallet. A handle had been extruded from the wall, presumably to aid *se* Sergei in getting in and out of bed. A small table in the center of the room held an extremely old and exquisitely crafted 3-D chess set, with pieces shaped in the forms of zor heroes and demons.

On the far side of the room was a transparent floor-to-ceiling wall fronting the atrium. It was half-covered by a drawn curtain, but the glass door stood partially ajar.

Jackie looked at Ch'k'te, then walked slowly forward, pistol in hand. She gestured and he took up a covering position.

She pushed the door open slowly and stepped into the garden, squinting against the bright morning sun that penetrated the bubble skylight that domed it.

She froze, startled. The garden was always a delight: Visitors were assaulted by the sights and smells of growing things, familiar as well as alien. This time there seemed to be nothing at all growing. There was a stench of decay that sent a shiver down her spine.

She could feel Ch'k'te behind her. She cast a quick backward glance; when she turned again to look at the garden, she saw Sergei's powered chair, motionless under a thasi tree facing away from her.

She resisted the temptation to speak his name aloud. Instead she walked forward, the sound of her footsteps echoing on the flagstones of the garden path. She had almost reached him when the chair turned slowly to face her.

The familiar features of the *Gyaryu'har* looked back at her, the frail human form wrapped in a quilted zor robe inlaid with intricate *hRni'i* designs. He had a gray blanket spread across his chest, with his old, knotted hands folded in his lap.

"*se* ... Sergei?" she asked of the person in the chair.

In a flash of insight, she knew he was not. It was the eyes that gave it away: they burned with a fierce and frightening anger. It was a caricature of *se* Sergei, no more; the deep pools of those eyes seemed to grow and enlarge to drown and encompass her.

"I think we have met this one before," Ch'k'te's voice said from behind her. She tore her gaze away for a split second; when she looked again at the figure in the chair, the image was blurring and melting into another human form.

She raised her pistol with a great effort of will and pointed it directly at the image of Bryan Noyes.

"Commodore Laperriere," he said in a painfully familiar voice. "How nice of you to come. You might as well put it away," he said, backing the chair off a meter or so with a flick of one finger. "Perhaps you could break foolish R'ta's Domination. Do not expect the same good fortune with me." He stood and removed the robe, dropping it on the chair, then took a step toward Jackie.

She tensed and tried to squeeze the trigger but found that she could not. The alien had captured Noyes perfectly: his mannerisms, his walk, even the peculiar inflections in his voice.

"I told the Great Queen that R'ta was too young and inexperienced for this role, but she refused to listen to me. You have been more clever than I expected, Commodore, you and your zor catamite here."

Jackie heard—*no, felt*—Ch'k'te's talons come out, but found she could not even turn her head to look at him.

She felt a mild probe and heard Ch'k'te speak her name in her head.

"Oh, there'll be none of that. Sleep," Noyes said, glancing for a heartbeat at Ch'k'te.

Jackie heard her exec collapse to the ground, his left wing brushing against her leg as he fell. A chill of fear rippled through her and it bore Ch'k'te's name.

"Now then," Noyes said. "I believe this game has gone as far as it is going to go."

"Meaning?" she managed to say.

The alien crossed his arms before him. "Just like a meat-creature to miss the obvious. You remind me of R'ta—except"—he smiled, his eyebrows arching— "except, my dear, you do not *disgust* me as she did. A pity you were born human: You would have made a fine drone, perhaps worthy even of me.

"But since you do not realize what is about to happen, I will be happy to explain it to you." He took another step forward. Jackie felt her hand slowly lower without her assistance. "It is imperative that we have the dispositions of your bases and fleet duty stations. If our takeover of Cicero had not been interfered with, we might have been able to do this more painlessly. Regrettably"—he walked forward two more steps, almost in arm's reach—"your interference has made this task far more difficult and, for you at least, far more painful. If R'ta had been more attentive to your surface thoughts, I suspect that she would be alive to see this. Perhaps"—a snaky grin crossed his face— "perhaps she might even have learned something."

He took one more step forward and reached out to touch her head—

And everything exploded.

T HEY CALLED her "the Thane" but not to her face. It was an obvious reference to her Highlands origin, of which she was extremely proud, even though half the personnel in the fleet had never heard of Scotland, having never spent time on Earth. She was best known for her temper, legendary far beyond Cicero. Still, in just a few years, Captain Barbara MacEwan had risen from fighter pilot to carrier commander, winning nearly every award for performance and bravery the Imperial Navy could bestow. She had also won the loyalty of her subordinates wherever she went, and the crew and officers of the fleet carrier IS *Due d'Enghien* were no exception.

Now, as she stood on the bridge watching the patterns of fighters fly across the holo image of Cicero, she thought about the orders she'd received from Maartens. They had been explicit: Gain air superiority over Cicero Down to cover an air drop of Marines to take control of the base. The *Due d'Enghien* had launched two waves of aerospace fighters, with orders to control Cicero Down's airspace.

It was clear from the radio chatter between ground and fighter interceptors and among the fighter pilots themselves that some sort of illusion was being created, disguising the true form of the *Due* and its fighters. It was difficult for Barbara MacEwan to truly believe this was possible—but it was clear that the ground-based defenders weren't recognizing their comrades at all. Thus she had to face the unpleasant task of launching attack waves to shoot down the interceptors that contested the base's airspace.

Don't hesitate, Maartens had said. *Do what you can to avoid casualties, but land those Marines.*

These were from Jackie Laperriere's orders. Maartens had sent them scrambled to her; she had looked them over again just before she came up to the bridge to supervise the operation.

The commodore had always been welcome on her bridge: Barbara had a distaste for groundhogs, regardless of rank, but Jacqueline Laperriere had flown an aerospace fighter and knew what it meant to command. Still, the orders had been bizarre and had suggested the near-impossible—that something or someone was powerful enough to fool instruments of ships-of-the-line. The ghosts hovering at the edge of mass-radar detection and Maartens' report of his exec's attack had been enough to make her believe it. Though it made her uncomfortable to turn the weapons and energies of the *Due d'Enghien* against fellow soldiers, the mission demanded it.

It was like an exercise mission except it was for real. *Aim for the engines,* she thought: *You don't have to flame 'em to shoot 'em down.* Except that when you're fighting for your life at 10,000 meters and Mach 5, you don't have much chance to think about the other guy.

THERE WAS a certain perverse excitement about dropping through the air in a clear ablative capsule at hundreds of meters per second, with flak blooming all around. It was the same thrill felt by paratroopers over the centuries, something lying between climax and abject fear.

Strange, Marine Master Sergeant James Agropoulos thought to himself, as he plummeted through the atmosphere. *All the bizarre things that run through your head when you're counting down, waiting for the parachute. Did I drop off next week's duty roster with the lieutenant? Did I remember to lock my footlocker?*

Will I get hit by a flak fragment and be scattered in microscopic particles across the landscape? And even if I don't, will the parachute open and keep me from becoming pate on impact?

Relax and enjoy the ride, he told himself. That's what Dante Simms always told the recruits, just before they closed the capsule and fired them off on the training drops. Look at it this way, he thought. If the flak hits, or the parachute fails, there isn't anything you can do about it. And if you make it, there's a hell of a lot of other things to worry about once you get down there.

He thought briefly about his long-gone ancestors, who filled the earth and sky with gods and demigods, who offered or capriciously withheld help from the superstitious mortals who worshiped them. If his parachute were to fail, there would be no Zeus to reach out a mighty hand and rescue him, but there would also be no jealous Apollo to cut the cords and put his life at risk. Still, it wasn't comforting to realize that his life lay in the hands of greater powers in any case.

Relax, he repeated to himself, giving a quick glance to his wrist-chrono. *Relax and enjoy the ride.*

S OMETHING HAPPENED.
Ch'k'te woke, his mouth dry, his right shoulder aching and numb. A cold breeze blew across him. He was still in the garden, but Jackie and Noyes had disappeared.

He reached to his belt, and found his pistol gone, but his *chya* was still in its scabbard. He sat up and drew it, feeling the familiar mind-touch of its *guy'u*—

Suddenly a chill, much greater than that of the cold air blowing through the cracked skylight, ran the length of his body. He probed carefully within his mind and felt unfamiliar patterns, heightened and lowered potentials, barely concealed neural configurations. His mind had been probed ... No, that was too gentle a word.

He had been Dominated and then tossed aside.

Anger and fear and shame cascaded through him, fighting with each other, as he realized the consequences of what had happened.

Shame won out. He grasped the *chya* with both hands, feeling it softly hum through his hands as he turned its point toward his chest. He began to speak a litany, invoking the blessing and forgiveness of *esLi.*

He stopped after a moment and dropped the partially charged *chya* on the flagstones. He looked at his talons. The *guy'u* in the blade seemed to snarl in protest, but he ignored it.

You have an obligation, he told himself. *Death can come later, when you are finished.*

Rage rose in him and he forced it back down, grasping the blade in both hands and standing. He clenched it tightly and concentrated, closing his eyes.

When he opened them, he looked upon his *chya* as it reflected the sunlight along its length. Looking up through the broken permoplast above, he saw two fighters streak across the sky, one pursuing the other. He knew that his course was laid out for him.

A s JACKIE lay there deprived of sight, she felt the alien's mind enter hers, neither gentle nor careful. It began to search methodically. She recoiled in horror and fear, but it only made it more painful.

She was blind and confronted with a power so great that she could do nothing to counteract it. The fear was a powerful drug in a way, but like most such drugs, it had a saturation point. After trying to fight or even avoid the vuhl's mental incursions, resulting only in greater pain, she began to realize that there was a limit to her fear, past which she would feel nothing.

Images and memories she had long forgotten drifted past her conscious mind —*the sound of a shuttle landing on a hangar deck, its landing-gear squealing, metal on metal ... the geometric precision of a dozen arms saluting ... the faintly antiseptic smell of fresh linens in the hospital on Shannon's World ...*

She was afraid. Still, the point of paralysis had been reached and passed and left far behind. She had known worse, though her mind was now open to all of the horrors and fears she had kept concealed behind a wall of reason.

She had known death on the battlefield. She had watched a starship disintegrate and explode under concentrated fire.

She had watched John Maisel collapse and die at a single thought.

Hatred fueled anger, an awful growling thing forming first in her chest, making her hands clench and her arms and legs tense. She had never been very emotional—*a good soldier*, they would say: kept her head, never gave in, tried not to get involved. But this was no ordinary enemy, and this was no ordinary hatred. A creature so powerful, so inimical, so ... evil ... deserved death at her hands, at this moment.

A voice inside her head spoke to her then: *This is enGa'e'Li; the Strength of Madness.*

Slowly she realized the mental probing had stopped and that her vision was clearing, though she could scarcely make out the outlines of the room or the irregular shape hovering over her.

I would not have expected Sensitive talent of you, the alien said. *But you will not live long enough to use this secret.* He raised his hands and a wedge of pain was driven into her forehead. She screamed as it drove farther and farther into her skull, growing white-hot. She could see more clearly: the room was filled with vuhls, some half-transformed from human or zor form, some completely metamorphosed. There were familiar faces among them: Marine NCOs whose service records she had seen, officers from the squadron ... even —Ch'k'te—

"Not you, too?" she said weakly, as the ember of pain burrowed into her mind and she watched Noyes fall away, out of her range of vision. Ch'k'te—or whatever it was that looked like Ch'k'te—stepped forward into her range of vision, his tentacled/taloned hands reaching to touch her forehead. She managed a supreme effort of will and pushed him away, getting unsteadily to her feet.

" … JJJaaacccckkiiieee …" the aliens said, swaying around her. She was somewhere in officers' quarters but not in her own rooms. She could feel a buzzing in her head.

"Won't … get me, you b-bastards …" she said. With a last straining, scrambled for the door. She found herself in a long hallway and saw light at the end: an open window. Cold air streamed in toward her. It would be several floors above ground level, but it gave her a chance, some possibility of survival. The vuhls here wouldn't give her that chance. She ran toward the window, grabbing the wall for support.

"Donnnnn'ttt lettt hhher rrrreeeeeaccch ttttheeee wwwwwinddddowwwww …" she heard behind her. The footsteps were an irregular staccato.

She swung one leg through the open window and gazed uneasily down. It was twenty or thirty meters down, and pavement below. She swung the other leg out and braced herself.

Suddenly a tentacle wrapped around each of her arms. She struggled, hearing a babble of voices behind her, but her captors were too strong. With a heave they pulled her back within the corridor. She braced for impact, but instead landed gently in several pairs of waiting arms.

Arms.

She looked at the tentacle wrapped around her right arm. As she blinked and looked at it through blurring eyes, it became a taloned hand, scarred and scratched. She followed the hand to the arm, where it disappeared inside a cold-weather suit. Her gaze traveled up and saw a familiar face.

"Ch'k'te?" she whispered, not sure what to believe. Was it a vuhl, transformed into the image of her friend? Was it Ch'k'te himself? What was real, and what was hallucination?

There had been a voice in her head sometime during the interrogation. She'd heard that voice before, but at the moment couldn't place where or when.

And what had the vuhl—Noyes—said about Sensitive talent? … *I had not expected it of you.*

She *wasn't* a Sensitive! She hated the thought—human Sensitives had always turned her stomach.

"What …"

"We got 'em, Commodore," said a familiar voice. "Six of the creatures survived. After they were knocked out, the interceptors and ground artillery just stopped firing."

She turned to look, and saw that she was being gripped by Dante Simms, the *Pappenheim*'s Major of Marines.

"Glad to have you with us," he said.

chapter 12

One of the Marines—Agropoulos, Jackie remembered his name—offered her a small flask that contained something Marines were not supposed to carry on duty. She took a long sip and then handed it back to the young man.

She looked around her at the Marines and officers in the room. They had half carried her into a vacant suite and helped her into an armchair. Eventually the room had stopped tilting at a crazy angle, though her head continued to buzz uncomfortably.

"Thanks," she finally said, smiling briefly at the Marine.

"Ready for a report?" Captain Georg Maartens asked. He stood next to his Major of Marines in the doorway.

"Go ahead," she said, rubbing her forehead with the fingers of one hand.

"Cicero Down is secure. After the Marines established a command post, they located a source of high-frequency radiation. When they altered its broadcast characteristics, it created some kind of feedback response, which bothered hell out of the aliens. We reached you just before the one that was messing with you lit out. We'll catch him if we can."

"Where are the aliens now?"

"Three of them are in the control tower, under heavy sedation. The others are in other places on the base."

"And ... *se* Sergei?"

"We found him down below. He's in some kind of trance, but seems to be stable. I had him transported to the *Pappenheim* so that Callison could take a look at him."

The news calmed her. "So the base is in our hands again."

"That's right," he said, exchanging glances with a subordinate. "But probably not for long."

"What do you mean?"

"Deep-radar detected several bogeys. They'd jumped from the general direction of Sargasso. They're now less than twenty hours downrange."

"Vuhls," she said, and the name echoed hollowly in the quiet of the room. From the corner of her eye, she noticed Ch'k'te shudder.

"'Vuhls,' ma'am?"

"Our friendly aliens. They're getting their reinforcements, just as R'ta said they would."

"If I may suggest," Maartens said, "we may be able to fight a rear guard and send a mayday to a nearby base—Adrianople, perhaps—"

"We wouldn't stand a chance."

"We really have little choice—"

"Georg," she interrupted, grasping the arms of the chair, "these creatures can control our *minds*. Do you realize what that means? They could turn us against each other, make us see anything they choose. There is only one alternative that will save the greatest number of lives.

"We have to abandon Cicero."

There was a long, heavy silence in the room.

"Commodore," Georg said at last. "Jackie. It's been my sincere pleasure to serve under your command these past few years. In my opinion, you are among the finest officers in the fleet, and I put great faith in your judgment. The past few weeks' events have put you under a lot of strain, the sort that no one back at Admiralty HQ could possibly understand.

"And they *won't*, Jackie. Take it from an old sailor. They'll take you *apart* for abandoning an Imperial naval base without even a fight."

She sat forward on her chair. "I don't give a damn about the opinions of a bunch of fat-ass admirals. They can't—I won't let them—toss me out of the Navy for refusing to commit suicide."

"Politics is politics, J—"

"The politicians are far away right now. They don't even realize the threat the vuhls pose to the Empire. They've never had their minds probed …" she trailed off, leaning back in the chair. "A few of them took over Cicero, Georg. Imagine what two or three *thousand* could do—if we gave them the chance. They probably have the entire disposition of the Imperial Fleet by now, ripped out of my head like seeds from a melon.

"We have a few of the creatures as prisoners; we have a sample of their technology. We have less than eight hours to evacuate this base and destroy every piece of data that might be of use to them." She stood up a little unsteadily, but shook off the arms that reached out to support her. "I know what you're thinking—that it'll cost me my career. To tell the truth, I'd rather have my life than some posthumous medal for bravery under fire."

She looked around her at her personnel. *Hers,* she thought: people who were ready to follow her orders, whether they were wise or foolish ones.

"Well?" she asked, looking around from face to face. "Let's get to it."

E IGHT HOURS. With bogeys closing in on them from the outer system, time seemed to be running fast, slipping away in increments. There was so much to do, more than could possibly be done in such a short time. She decided at once that if anyone was to get away, they *all* were. There were people to transport, records to destroy and things to dispose of one way or another. She had a damned good team around her—experienced Marines, talented pilots and the crews of half a dozen of His Majesty's ships. In the shadow of whatever the future might hold, they prepared to abandon Cicero to aliens with unimaginable mental powers. No one questioned whether their CO had made the right decision: It was a truth they already knew and had already accepted.

On the holo in the control tower, she watched as the ships nearest the Sargasso-side jump point updated information on the position of the enemy. Data on the enemy vessels was being stored as it arrived; they were gradually assembling a composite image of the ships. It had started off by displaying a cone image. As data had been added to the picture, it had slowly transformed into a great irregular cylinder, nearly twice the breadth and length of an Imperial starship, with a number of light and dark patches, like crenellations along each side.

Energy readings, such as there were, further chilled her as she looked at the slowly evolving image: they indicated a total power-to-mass ratio far in excess of any Imperial ship. The only advantage lay in her chosen route out of Cicero System: the jump point for Adrianople was a third of the way around the circumference of the volume, and more than forty degrees of declination separated from the Sargasso one.

The wing of esGa'u *is not bright or dark, but neither and both: it moves with great speed, and encompasses all—*

"What the hell?" she asked herself as unfamiliar words buzzed through her head, like a scrap from some conversation overhead in a crowded room. The tower officer of the watch looked up as she said it and opened his mouth to reply.

"Incoming message," the comm officer said, cutting off the comment of the officer of the watch.

"Laperriere," she said. The display changed to reveal the bridge of the IS *Due d'Enghien.* Barbara MacEwan sat in the pilot's chair.

"Commodore," MacEwan said, "how many more of those damn dirtsiders are you going to send me? The stupid sons of bitches don't have the sense that God gave a horse when it comes to bringing their birds into the hangars. They think they've got two kilometers of runway to deal with—"

"Barbara," Jackie said, "I—"

"We've only got s' much room here, ma'am. I've put six fighters in a landing bay before, but they all knew what the hell they were doing. But your damn Downers come crashing in here—"

"Barbara—"

"—and I'm going to have problems raisin' from the atmosphere if they clip my directional sensors again. Where the hell did you get those—"

"Thane!" Jackie shouted, half angry and half amused. Barbara MacEwan's rolling monologue stopped in midsentence and Jackie could hear some amused chuckling off screen. MacEwan slowly swiveled her chair away from the vid pickup and said something to someone on the bridge in some incomprehensible Terran dialect. Then she looked back at Jackie.

"If ye'd be so kind as to pass on my concerns to the ground-based pilots, ma'am, I'd be much obliged," MacEwan said quietly, her face reddening ever so slightly.

"I'll do that." Jackie tried to compose herself. It was difficult not to appear amused. "Have you had any report from the distant flyby?"

"Aye, Commodore. I've just finished transmitting everything to the *Tilly*, and I'm expecting another report shortly. We got some good shots, but your orders were to keep more than a hundred thousand klicks away so there's nothin' too clear."

"Where are you deployed now?"

"I have a wing on CAP, Commodore, and a wing on flyby. The other two are alternating on close support, one in dock while the other flies. I thought it best not to deploy the oiler, by your leave, ma'am." The oiler was a support craft that let fighters refuel without landing.

"No, that's fine ... but where are the ground wings? Nearly three full flights should be up there by—"

"Beggin' the commodore's pardon, but as I *tried* to tell you, I wouldn't trust the dirtside flyers as far as I could throw Cicero Down. Even if they deployed right comin' out of the chute, I could hardly trust 'em to land."

"You've—you've got three interceptor wings in *hangar*?"

"Damn right," MacEwan replied. "Ma'am," she added.

"Launch them."

"Beggin' the commodore's par—"

"You've already done that, Barbara. Launch the bastards, one carrier wing for one ground wing. Leave it to the wing commanders to work out the details."

"I don't believe it's wise—"

"That's an *order*, Captain," Jackie said, and watched fire leap into MacEwan's eyes. "Look, Barbara. We've got an enemy force bearing on us. I'd rather have every bird up and flying, despite the technical details. Those pilots are the best we've got and that makes 'em damn good. I flew a fighter for a while, so did you—flyers have their own language. Leave it to them to get it straight; just put your best out front, the rest will follow."

MacEwan did not respond for a moment, then nodded. "I'll give the orders."

"Good. I expect you'd try more strenuously to talk me out of it if you *really* thought it was a bad idea. I pay you to think, Barbara, and don't you let me forget it."

"Aye-aye, Commodore." She looked offscreen and rattled in her dialect. "My XO will get right on it."

"Glad to hear it. Anything else?"

"No, not for now, ma'am. But tell them to be *careful*, would you?"

"Aye-aye," Jackie responded. MacEwan nodded, and broke the connection.

S HE PACKED up what little she could take: her entire life collapsed to a few kilos. As an officer, especially one commanding a major Imperial facility, she rated as much as she wanted to carry; but she was unwilling to grant herself luxuries she could not readily extend to her people, who were having this forced on them. It didn't matter that much—she had always traveled fairly light, leaving her life's treasures at the farm near Stanleytown back on Dieron.

She watched her last sunset on Cicero and then boarded her gig, the last ship to leave the base. The single sun seemed alien somehow, as memories of Dieron's double suns flooded through her mind. There was an emotional attachment to Cicero, but nothing more than that. It had never been home, no more than the deck of a starship had been: just another post, another assignment.

Home was Dieron, under Epsilon Indi's double orange suns.

Home will be what the gyaryu *can vouchsafe, when the* hsi *of* esGa'u *blankets the sky.*

She heard the words fly through her mind just before the shuttle's acceleration hit, forcing her into the cushions of her couch; her consciousness raced trying to determine their source, but they had vanished like the fragmentary wisps of a dream, dispersed by the waking mind.

A S THE outer airlock door sighed open she heard the strains of bagpipe music rise and echo through the hangar bay. Below her, a dozen Marines snapped to attention and then presented arms. She and Ch'k'te descended slowly to the deck; she offered a salute to the officer waiting for her there.

They waited, patiently, for the howl of the ancient Earth instrument to make its way through its arduous tune. When the last echoes of the strain had finally died away, Jackie said, "Permission to come aboard, Commander?"

"By all means, ma'am. Welcome aboard, Commodore."

"Thanks, Ray." She shook hands with the young man and proceeded between the ranks of Marines presenting arms. "I wish my—visit—could have been under more pleasant circumstances. I assume the Thane's on the bridge."

"Still complaining about the dirtsiders, ma'am, that's right." Ray Santos, Barbara MacEwan's exec, led Jackie through a sliding door into a lift and activated it. "But I've got to hand it to you, ma'am, you were right—leave it to the flyers to work it out."

She smiled. "They'll curse each other a lot, but they'll get the job done. How are things coming?"

"The bogeys are down to medium range. We've pulled most of our wings in to fly CAP, and only have two on close flyby."

"And the rest of the fleet?"

"Tilly's still in high guard; the rest are scouting ahead, awaiting your orders, Commodore."

The lift door slid open, revealing the bridge of the *Due d'Enghien.* It was a hive of activity, with several officers huddled around the holo display forward of the pilot's board. Barbara MacEwan, wearing what looked to be some plaid garment, noticed her come in. She muttered something to a subordinate and walked over to give her a salute.

"You're out of uniform, Barbara," Jackie said, smiling.

MacEwan took off her cap and bowed slightly. "MacEwan tartan has seen more battles than Imperial blue, ma'am. I thought it appropriate, were we to come to blows with 'em."

Jackie's smile disappeared. "Let's not discuss that possibility. You don't want that to happen."

"Aye-aye," MacEwan replied, a question remaining, unspoken, but scarcely concealed in her voice.

"What's our status?"

"Awaiting your orders, ma'am."

"Fine. Let's get under way."

MacEwan saluted once more and turned away to sit in the pilot's seat. Ray Santos took the helm. She barked orders, thankfully in Standard, and they watched as the scene on the forward viewscreen shifted.

The formation began to move out on a course perpendicular to the plane of the system. It would provide them the earliest opportunity to escape from the gravity well of Cicero System if they couldn't reach the jump point.

As they moved, Jackie kept her eyes on the pilot's board, watching as the wings of aerospace fighters began to circle away from the steadily advancing bogeys, heading back for the safety of the *Due.*

Suddenly the bogeys changed course, altering their direction so quickly and at such high velocity that Santos began to check his instruments to make sure they were reading correctly. He turned, surprised, to face his commander.

"Everything checks out, ma'am," he said. "They're comin' after us."

"Range?" MacEwan asked.

"Two hundred twenty thousand kilometers, Skip."

MacEwan looked over her shoulder at Jackie. "We can stage a delaying action, Commodore, to cover the fleet's escape. I have eight wings ready to—"

"Pull them all back, Barbara."

"The recommended tactic in this case, Comm—"

"There are *no* tactics on the book for this," Jackie interrupted. "Pull every fighter back to close support, and prepare to run like hell. Give me an open channel to the other ships."

"Commodore, I—"

"Do it," Jackie said, crossing her arms. "On the double, Captain!"

MacEwan held her glance and, without looking away, said, "Ray, call them all back." She gripped the sides of her chair and swiveled it to face Jackie. "Commodore, I've been doing this for years, and if they're as strong as we think they are, they'll surely blow our ass out of the sky if we don't delay 'em somehow."

"If they weren't … who they are … I would agree. But they are dangerous even at great distance. They can control *minds*, do you understand? They can take these ships without firing a shot."

"Turnin' tail and runnin' doesn't sit well with me, ma'am," MacEwan retorted levelly.

"I don't give a damn what—" she began, then stopped and leaned on the railing in front of her. "It's the best policy, to save the greatest number of lives. I've lost too many good people already"—*like John Maisel*, she reminded herself—"and I don't want to lose any more."

"We let 'em take Cicero without firin' a shot?"

"Goddamn it, Barbara, this isn't a glory campaign! *Six* of them took Cicero Op and Cicero Down, and no one noticed. As far as I can see, we have two choices: Leave here—or die here. It's on *my* head, not yours."

There was a signal on the pilot's board indicating the other ships had acknowledged and were waiting for her message.

Barbara MacEwan gazed at her, anger in her eyes.

"Attention all hands," Jackie said. "This is Laperriere. Your orders are to proceed with all possible speed to the Adrianople jump point and to jump on your own mark. Contrary to any established procedure or regulation, or any future orders, you are not—I repeat, *not*—to descend into the gravity-well of Cicero to come to the aid of another vessel.

"Let me make myself quite clear. Even if orders are given *in my name*, or with my voice, in contravention to this order, they are to be ignored. We'll see you all at Adrianople. Laperriere out."

"This is madness," MacEwan said quietly.

"This is survival," Jackie said, trying to remain impassive. "If they"—she gestured toward the rapidly advancing aliens in the holo—"if they take control of a ship, even this one, it could be used to lure others into their control."

"You're afraid of them."

"Damn right. We can't fight them, do you understand? We can't resist."

In the quiet of the bridge, Jackie and Barbara held each other's gaze for a moment that seemed to stretch out to infinity.

But you can, a voice inside her said. *You already know the way.*

"Captain?" Ray Santos' voice interrupted their stares. "Captain, I'm not getting any response from the Green wing."

Jackie and Barbara tore their attention away from each other to look at the board. Each of the fighter wings had returned to take up formations close by the *Due d'Enghien*—except for one flight, which seemed to be headed on an intercept course with the aliens' formation.

"What's their range?" MacEwan asked.

"Seventy-three—no, seventy-two thousand kilometers to the bogeys and closing."

"What the hell are they doing? Stupid sons of—They'll be out of range in twenty or thirty thousand klicks. Prepare to come about."

"Belay that order, Commander," Jackie said, looking at Santos.

Santos looked from MacEwan to Jackie and back, not sure what to do.

"We're talking about *lives* here, Commodore. Those fighters can't jump. I don't want to leave 'em behind—Schoenfeld, Garret, Sidra, Leung, Khalid, Cox. They're *my* people out there."

"Not anymore."

They watched the line of fighters advance inexorably toward the enemy formation. Then, abruptly, the fighters began to slowly circle, as if they were going to fight each other.

"God," MacEwan said, watching the circle.

"Energy discharge," Santos said. He named a figure.

Moments later, the sensors of the *Due d'Enghien* showed a bright ball of fire, expanding for a moment and then vanishing.

One of the fighters' transponder codes winked and went out, followed immediately by two more. Two more explosions brightened the starry sky behind them.

"God," MacEwan repeated. The bridge was silent, and the ghastly scene began to play itself out. The aerospace fighters continued to battle each other, destroying themselves one and two at a time.

"Time to jump?" Jackie asked quietly.

"Three minutes and ... twenty seconds, ma'am," Santos said after a moment. MacEwan remained silent, scarcely able to comprehend what was happening to the fighter wing.

One by one, the transponder codes winked out, until there was only one left. It advanced slowly toward the alien formation and then abruptly vanished.

"Garrett," MacEwan said in a whisper.

"Two minutes to jump," Santos said.

Jackie swallowed, feeling an emptiness in the pit of her stomach from what she had just witnessed. A wing of aerospace fighters, expertly trained—among the best in the fleet—had been lured into a trap like flies caught in a spider's web. Then they had been ... taken over ... and made to fight one another, perhaps to provide entertainment for their masters.

And they had destroyed each other, all but Green Five. Lieutenant Owen Garrett, aerospace pilot, had been taken by the aliens.

"One minute."

The alien fleet was turning away now—as if they were finished with their sport and unwilling to exert themselves to follow the escaping humans. Cicero was theirs now, what was left of it. She had done the best she could to hold them off, and it wasn't sufficient—it wasn't even marginally effective.

"Turnin' tail and runnin' doesn't sit well with me," Barbara had said—and they couldn't do it forever.

"Thirty seconds to jump."

Would they run from Adrianople?

Would they run from Dieron?

"Fifteen seconds."

And what would happen when they could run no more? She shuddered to think about it, knowing that there was only one answer.

And the voice in her mind said, *There is another answer, and you already know it.*

"Jump."

And the Imperial Fleet vanished, the pattern of stars swirling into milky gray and then vanishing into the inky night of jumpspace.

seGa'Mrha'u

DESCENT TO THE PLAIN

PART TWO

interlude

That the High Lord dreamed and that his dreams were the prescient gift of *esLi* was not in question among the noble Persons of the great Nests. The gift of foretelling was integral to the *hsi* of the one who led the People; how else would he know the right Path from the Deception?

And yet for all that, there was a certain uneasiness about the prescient gifts of *hi* Ke'erl HeYen, the High Lord of the People, and the way in which he used them. He had given over much of the day-to-day operation of government to his High Chamberlain; he had stopped attending meetings of the Council of Eleven to discuss policy. He spent most of his time dreaming in the Chamber of Solitude, sometimes emerging after half a sun to wander the eyries and halls of the High Nest still wrapped in a stupor. Other times he would bring *alHyu* and warriors running with a shrieking and howling, only to dismiss them all and close himself off from the world to dream once more.

He is mad, they said. *He is unfit to be High Lord*, said others—but never loudly, and never to *hi* Ke'erl. Perhaps he would have agreed.

He felt the madness growing within him as his world withdrew from The World That Is, closing more and more upon the world of dreams. He could not help but receive what *esLi* bestowed upon him: insights into the coming embrace of *esGa'u*. While it repelled and angered him, it made him yet more frightened to know with an awful clarity that only a High Lord could perceive that it was the truth.

He could not communicate this perception to his subjects or his advisors. Each day that the madness gripped him more closely, they granted him progressively less credence. As they spoke to him of fleet deployments and the political posturings of the Imperial Senate, he replied by speaking of the calamity that lurked beyond the edge of the Empire and by telling them of his own coming death and the destruction of the High Nest save that which the *gyaryu* itself could protect.

Calamity, they said. *Can we not fight it?*

They humored him by asking this, only half believing what he told them.

And he replied, *The People are warriors; the* naZora'i *have learned to be warriors, despite their rejection of* esHu'ur. *But there is no weapon we can use against this thing. It works so well against it for ... it can* be *us. It will take our place and make its own.*

And they inclined their wings and said, *We do not understand.*

And he placed his wings in a posture of supplication to esLi and said, *Indeed, neither do I.*

chapter 13

The First Lord had arrived during low watch while Jackie was lost in haunted dreams. Word of his arrival reached her officially by dispatch while a steward brought her breakfast.

She had read the message with some amusement: Rumors traveled faster and with greater accuracy than official channels, at least on a naval facility. The news itself was sobering, recalling the situation even more acutely.

While she ate her breakfast she caught a glance of herself in the cup of dark, swirling liquid that passed for coffee here at Adrianople Starbase. The reflection was dim and muddy but still it showed a haggard and almost gaunt face. So many things had changed in the past few weeks; so many idols had been smashed and so many illusions shattered. Since she had arrived, she had walked through the gently curving halls of Adrianople Starbase like some sort of ghost, a survivor of mankind's first grim encounter with the inimical alien vuhls; most of the regular personnel had kept at a respectful distance. Perhaps they didn't want to overhear something.

It was easier to utter an expletive to no one in particular and go on eating one's breakfast than to think about it. She didn't truly give a damn about the timid staff officers of Adrianople. She also didn't really give a damn about being beached, since it had happened before, years ago. At the moment her posting was to Rear Admiral Hsien's staff, good enough for her (and Ch'k'te) to avoid half-pay while without a regular assignment, and good enough to get fresh baked bread and real orange marmalade.

Not good enough to get real coffee, she thought to herself, idly playing with the cup and watching the brown liquid roll around inside it.

And whenever the surface was placid, the same haggard face gazed back at her, a grim old veteran.

If there had been any doubt before, that face would remind her that it had all really happened. Cicero was no longer hers: it belonged to the vuhls.

She shuddered. Fear began to prey at her—fear of the unknown power of the aliens that confronted humanity. It was too difficult to put down.

Before it had advanced very far, though, the door-chime sounded. She composed herself and said, "Identify."

Her comp projected a holo of the corridor outside her quarters. Before the door stood a familiar figure.

"Come."

The door slid wide and Ch'k'te entered the room, a small package cradled in his arm. He hesitated near the entrance to the alcove where she sat.

"Have you eaten?" she asked, beckoning him to a seat. "There's plenty."

He gestured at the other chair, which molded itself into a perch. He took his position, placing the package on the table beside him.

He picked up a slice of bread. "Rank certainly has its privileges," he said, carefully spreading the marmalade on it. "My accommodations were ... a bit more spartan."

"You should have let me know." She managed a smile, though she hardly felt like smiling. "We won't be on old Hsien's staff forever. We might as well enjoy it."

Ch'k'te did not reply as he ate. Jackie played with her coffee cup, trying to think of something to say.

"I received a message just after I awoke," Ch'k'te said at last, carefully wiping his hands with a napkin. "The High Chamberlain *na* T'te'e HeYen has arrived on-station. He has ... requested my presence."

"Really? What about?"

"There is an ancient tradition, *se* Jackie, that any new discovery—especially in the area of Sensitive phenomena—is to be immediately brought to the attention of the High Lord. In ages past, the High Lord would command the individual to attend him in the High Nest, where a mind-link would take place. As this is impractical in this case, the High Chamberlain has brought the High Nest here to Adrianople.

"The mind-link is called the *Dsen'yen'ch'a*, 'the Ordeal of Experience.' The High Chamberlain will investigate what took place at Cicero."

"And he intends to ..." She let the sentence hang, trying to imagine what the ritual was like and what it meant to Ch'k'te.

"I really have little choice regardless of his intentions, *se* Jackie," Ch'k'te replied. "It is my duty."

Jackie put a hand on his arm. "Are you afraid of this ordeal?"

"Of the ordeal itself? No. Certainly not. *se* T'te'e is a skilled Sensitive. It should be neither painful nor unpleasant. But I cannot and will not conceal what the High Chamberlain will learn.

"I have been dominated by the mind of an alien being—laid open as if I were a helpless *artha*." Ch'k'te's talons intertwined as he laid his hands on the table. They were clenched; Jackie could see the muscles ripple along his arm inside the uniform jacket. "They took it all from me. Everything I know. Everything."

"They were stronger than you are."

"I am an officer in the Imperial Navy."

"They took over your mind, for God's sake!"

"I am also a Sensitive, *se* Jackie." He looked at her, anguish in his eyes. "There is always one option available to a Sensitive."

It hung in the air for what seemed like a long time. Finally, Jackie grasped both of Ch'k'te's forearms. "There is no way I would ever order a person under my command to commit suicide." As he started to protest, she rushed on.

"By extension, I would never expect you to undertake something on your own I would not order you to do. This is a very frightening time, not just for you and me, but for all of the people of both our races. If they don't know it, they will soon.

"You know what they did to you. They did it to me, too, without the benefit of Sensitive skill. How do you think I feel? Your mind-touch is alien, but gentle. Theirs was—" Her hands trembled. "There are no words to describe it. Even if I wanted to remember."

"We are hardly in the same position."

"You're damn right. I outrank you. It falls within my authority to give you orders …

"Now hear this: You will not—I repeat, *not*—feel anything short of the profoundest sense of well-being for the responsible fulfillment of your duty toward His Imperial Highness' Navy and toward me. Is that clear?"

"*se* Jackie, I—"

"I believe that was an order, Commander." She squeezed his arms.

"Yes ma'am." He returned the grasp, retracting his claws into their sheaths.

"That didn't really do a damn bit of good, did it?"

"It does not really solve the problem," he replied. "But it does make me feel better about the favor I am about to ask of you."

"Ask it."

"If there were a clan-brother or clan-sister present I could lawfully call upon them to stand by me during *Dsen'yen'ch'a*. However, there are none here." He reached for the package he had been carrying and handed it to Jackie. "But perhaps in lieu of such a person I could call upon you to accompany me."

Jackie carefully removed the paper concealing the contents of the package and uncovered a folded crimson cloth. As she uncovered it she recognized it at once: the special robe Ch'k'te's mate had made for him.

She sat silently, fingering the garment in her hands. Zor society was so filled with subtleties it was hard to tell what commitment she might be making by agreeing, or what Ch'k'te's reaction might be if she refused.

Was this just a point of honor with him? Would the Chamberlain really wish to accuse him of treason, because a horrible alien gutted his mind against his will?

And what would happen in this ritual, assuming the Chamberlain indeed permitted her to "stand by" Ch'k'te? She wasn't a Sensitive; she certainly didn't fully understand the zor. What did Ch'k'te expect of her? When she was just his commanding officer, or just his friend, their relationship had been simple. What was she to him now? Some sort of replacement for Th'an'ya?

"Ch'k'te, I ... don't know exactly what to say. I'm honored, of course, that you place such faith in me as a friend. But I am not one of the People, and don't know if I can take the role of one."

"You are a friend. That is enough, *se* Jackie. We have shared life and death, and we have opened our minds to each other. What closer trust could I give to someone?"

She had always been told that the zor face was inscrutable and alien, and that it was improper—and occasionally dangerous—to anthropomorphize, to attribute human meaning to something a human might read in it. *"They do not express pain or anger or sorrow the way we do,"* her exoculture professor back at the Academy used to say. *"Theirs is an alien mental state."*

But as she sat there with the ceremonial robe in her lap, the so-familiar face opposite hers seemed to convey nothing but the sincerest affection and respect. Perhaps those authorities who could not recognize familiar features in the zor face simply hadn't looked closely enough.

"All right," she said at last. "Tell me what you want me to do."

JACKIE FELT uncomfortable in the dress uniform, supposedly cut to fit her specifications some hours ago at the base's haberdashery. Her own custom uniforms had been left behind on Cicero; the new one was stiff and didn't seem to fit properly. She waited outside the door for the bailiff to return from reporting her arrival to the board.

When at last the door opened she walked slowly into the room to face three men seated behind a long table. There was a smaller table and straight-backed chair facing it. The bailiff beckoned her there and then returned to the doorway.

She placed her portfolio on the table and saluted. "Commodore Laperriere reporting as ordered, sirs."

She drew off the white dress gloves, placing them on top of the portfolio. She extended her right hand, palm down and then up, and then raised it beside her. It was a tradition descended from the old Earth one; convicts were branded on the right hand so as to distinguish them.

The officer chairing the board was advanced in years; his clean-shaven face was cavernous and pock-marked like the chipping façade of an old building. It was a familiar face, from dozens of official circular dispatches: the First Lord of the Admiralty, His Grace William Clane Alvarez, Duke of Burlington. She had never seen him in person; he had never chosen to visit Cicero, and even Adrianople was a long way to come since the outcome could simply be transmitted to him by some subordinate to peruse at his leisure. It was an indication of the importance of the inquiry to the Admiralty.

"This board of inquiry," he began, "is convened to investigate recent events that have transpired at Cicero. You are called before this board to explain your actions. Do you understand the reasons and scope of this inquiry?"

"Yes, Your Grace," she replied. "And I recognize its authority."

"Very well. Bailiff, you will administer the oath to Commodore Laperriere."

"Do you promise to tell the truth, the whole truth and nothing but the truth, so help you God?" the bailiff intoned.

"I do."

"Please be seated," said Alvarez. He beckoned her to the chair, in which she sat carefully. "Commodore," he began, "I will commence these proceedings by reviewing this matter. For the record, the board acknowledges its appreciation of your promptness in attending our summons.

"It is our understanding that by your orders, the personnel and vessels under your command were evacuated from Cicero Military District. According to your report ..." Alvarez peered at a comp in front of him, then back at Jackie. "You indicated that your reasons for doing this was the alleged presence of hitherto unknown hostile aliens." In clipped, succinct and efficient sentences, he set out the reasons for the inquiry: the departure of the Cicero squadron from its assigned base, the evacuation of personnel and equipment, and the rest. Though it was exactly what she'd expected to happen, hearing it described by the highest ranking naval official in His Imperial Majesty's Government gave it a chilling aspect, as it was devoid of emotion.

She listened patiently but uneasily. Her report was brought forward and presented, then entered by reference into the record.

The First Lord concluded softly, "This board is empanelled to examine the circumstances surrounding the loss of His Majesty's fleet base at Cicero. In and of itself, it is not empowered to conduct a court-martial of the officers involved, but—" He raised his right index finger and tapped it against the table several times. "But it can, and may, make specific recommendations to the Judge-Advocate General regarding disciplinary measures for those culpable."

Neither of the other two line officers spoke. They seemed to be deliberately avoiding Jackie's eyes. She did not like the tone of the inquiry thus far, but she did not reply, simply returning the First Lord's glance measure for measure.

"This board has considered your official report, Commodore. We found it very informative and complete."

"Thank you, Your Grace," she said.

"I must point out to you, however, that there are many questions still remaining unanswered. It is my intent to see that they are answered in a fashion that will satisfy His Highness the emperor. Do you understand?"

"Completely, sir."

"The abandonment of a naval facility is an extremely precipitous decision, Commodore." He gazed at her with a hawklike stare—passive yet clearly hostile. "The emperor does not willingly surrender sovereign territory of the Solar Empire. Are you aware of that?"

"The decision was not made precipitously, Your Grace. Nor was it made without due consideration of the consequences of such an act."

"And what did you perceive those consequences to be?"

"At the very least a board of inquiry, sir. At the worst, I would imagine, court-martial and possibly even ... criminal prosecution. But any of that—all of it, I daresay—would be preferable to remaining behind."

"And why would that be?"

"I did not wish to ... subject myself to Domination once more."

Alvarez folded his hands on the table in front of him. "Commodore, your report was liberally sprinkled with this term. As I understand it, you claim to have been, er, mentally contacted by these alien creatures. Yet a thorough review of your personal record—" He touched his comp. Her Service record appeared in the air above the table; he peered at it over the top of his nose. "—indicates that you have no previous record of Sensitive talent. Your E3G test in May 2384 indicates that you might have some Sensitive abilities, but you are completely untrained in this capacity."

He looked up at her, his gaze narrowing, his brow deeply furrowed. "Let me clarify my position, Commodore. You are not a Sensitive; yet various portions of your official report make extensive use of Sensitive terms such as 'Domination' and 'Resistance.' Since you are not professionally qualified to use such terms, especially before a board of inquiry, I recommend that you refrain from doing so either in verbal or written form. Do I make myself clear, Commodore?"

"You—you place me in a most uncomfortable position, sir. I—"

"You may interpret my recommendation as an order, Commodore."

She took a deep breath. "I understand your need for clarity at this proceeding, Your Grace." She felt her hands clenching and her voice rising in intensity. She restrained both. "However, if you choose to restrict my form of response to this board's inquiries, you not only compromise my ability to adequately defend my actions but also jeopardize the ability of the board to reach the truth. If it please Your Grace."

"Are you telling me—"

"*Asking* you, Your Grace. Asking merely that you not order such a constraint to my choice of terms. For the good of the Empire, if nothing else."

"A trifle melodramatic, don't you think, Commodore?"

"Sir?"

"'The good of the Empire' is hardly something you can comprehend, Laperriere, especially after your actions at Cicero. I daresay it is your *own* well-being you should be more concerned with."

"If Your Grace would be good enough to expl—"

"We are speaking of criminal negligence here, Laperriere!" the First Lord exploded. "We are discussing *treason*. I consider myself a consummately fair man; I could already have you in irons for abandoning your post."

"I did not abandon my post, sir," she replied icily.

"You *abandoned* your post, Commodore!" The First Lord frowned at Jackie. "Without orders to do so, you evacuated a perimeter naval base of the Solar Empire. This is a court-martial offense. If the evidence to support your actions is not overwhelming—and at present I do not think it is—there is an extremely high likelihood that the board will recommend that you, as well as several of your most senior subordinates, be summoned before a full court-martial to answer these charges in detail.

"Is that *clear*, Commodore?"

"If it please Your Grace—"

"A question was asked, Commodore. Is it clear to you what the logical consequences of these actions will be?"

Alvarez was moving the inquiry exactly the way he wanted it; Jackie could feel anger begin to rise as she took a moment to reply.

"I understand what the consequences of improperly evacuating Cicero would be, Your Grace. If the board holds that my actions were indeed improper, I am sure that the full penalty of military law will be assessed. I knew that when I gave the orders, and I know it now. If the matter were a simple one, none of us would be here."

"Your point is granted," Alvarez replied. He seemed somewhat annoyed; it was clear he had not received the meek response he wanted. "To return to the original point, Commodore, you should be more concerned with the defense of your position than with the fate of the Empire as a whole. However … in the interests of fairness, the board is willing to hear a justification why it should listen to inexpert testimony on the subject of, er, Domination."

"Thank you, sir," Jackie answered, not letting go his gaze. "If the board is willing to hear expert testimony, it is available from my executive officer, Commander Ch'k'te HeYen. While the presentation of witnesses is irregular at a board of inquiry, it is not without precedent.

"I would also call to the board's attention that the surname *HeYen* indicates Commander Ch'k'te's clan-relationship to the High Nest. He has ample Sensitive credentials. I am confident he will offer satisfactory evidence in support of my official report."

Alvarez did not seem to like this comment either and turned aside to discuss the matter with his two fellow officers. Jackie knew he had every right to turn down this request, but that to do so would show beyond any doubt that he was determined to hang her from the yardarm.

He could've done that without a board of inquiry, she thought.

After a moment Alvarez said, "There will be a short recess to discuss this matter." As they all rose he nodded at Jackie, who seated herself once more.

Alvarez waited for the other two panel members and the bailiff to depart the room as well. Then, when the door had closed and they were alone in the room, the First Lord stood and walked to the drink dispenser in the corner of the room. "Black coffee," he said at it. It hummed for a moment and produced a plastiform cup.

"Would you like something to drink, Commodore?" he said, without turning to face her.

"No thank you, sir."

He took his coffee to the table and sat behind it once more. "Official record disable," he said to the comp in front of him. "Commodore, I assume you are aware that the zor High Chamberlain arrived on base late yesterday, only a few hours ahead of me. His presence here, along with the condition of the—of Mr. Torrijos—complicates matters immensely.

"I received extremely precise orders from His Imperial Highness before departing Sol System: *Find out what happened at Cicero and who was responsible.* His Imperial Highness learned, through the offices of the zor High Nest of all places, that an expedition was launched from Cicero; from your report, I understand that this was on the orders of Admiral Tolliver. But it was on your orders the base was evacuated.

"The emperor's orders are my charter, Laperriere. I am not interested in academic discussions or protracted legal battles; I am not even interested in summoning a court-martial. This report of yours"—he pointed to the comp on the table—"while precise, authoritative and complete, simply will not satisfy His Highness. I have you by the ... by the epaulets, Laperriere, and I need a reason to hear you out and give you a chance to defend this ridiculous series of actions."

"I can only give you one reason, Your Grace. It happened just as I have described. The medical reports, along with Admiral Tolliver's testimony—"

"I can't possibly admit that as reliable evidence. Horace Tolliver was a friend of mine, a good friend. I can't have his career end with something like this."

"He attacked me, sir—"

"Prove it. And while you're proving that, prove you didn't have your MP shoot him with something that would have killed him."

"You're accusing me of *murder!*" Suddenly her unease became anger. "Your Grace, less than two weeks' jump from this base there are aliens with incredible Sensitive talent that are bent on destroying the Solar Empire. *They* killed Admiral Tolliver, *they* captured Cicero Op and Cicero Down, they very nearly killed *me*. They are real, the danger is real, and the report I gave you is firmly grounded in reality.

"I realize that you have the power to bury this matter, and me along with it. You'll forgive me for fighting back, since I'm not enthralled by the prospect of making big boulders into smaller ones for the rest of my natural life.

"But before you ignore my report and sweep it and me aside into the recycler, let me remind Your Grace of one important consideration. If I'm not telling the truth—if I acted improperly—if there really aren't any aliens at Cicero or Sargasso or anywhere else, I wind up in the same place I would have been. But if I'm right, and you ignore me …"

She didn't even have a good idea of where to end the sentence and so just let it hang in midair. She looked away from the First Lord and noticed that she was gripping the desk so hard that her knuckles were white. She was angry now, though she knew it would do her no good to let it loose.

"I'm not going to bury you, Commodore," Alvarez said at last, so softly she hardly heard him. "I don't know what I'm going to do with you, but just burying you was never an option. You'll get your hearing, although the board of inquiry will sit in closed session. But now hear this, Laperriere: I will *not* be played for a fool. There may still be leg-irons waiting for you if I see no alternative. I just had to be sure of what—of whom—I was dealing with.

"When the rest of the board returns, we will consider the matter of allowing your exec's testimony. In the meantime, Laperriere, I want to know, off the record, just what the hell happened out there."

THE SHOWER washed away most of the frustration and anger, leaving her more or less refreshed. Her stomach was still churning in anticipation of the evening's events. Ch'k'te had left a message for her giving directions to the Chamberlain's quarters and the time of the ceremony; by the time she came out of the shower, she had only an hour and a half to prepare herself for it.

Tentatively, remembering the mental link, she took the crimson robe and pulled it on, securing it at her waist with a sash. It had a peculiar odor, a faint zor-smell along with something else she couldn't identify. Still, it felt soft against her bare skin. Unlike the garment Ch'k'te's mind had fashioned for her, it reached nearly to her knees; it had been designed for a tall zor, with enough gather to allow wings to protrude from the back.

She walked barefoot to stand before the mirror in the sleeping-chamber. She looked at herself wearing only the robe.

And a zor looked back at her.

She stepped back in alarm out of the range of the mirror, feeling vertigo for a moment. She dropped onto the edge of the bed and looked down at herself, only to see a perfectly normal human body.

She took several careful breaths and then stood and walked once more to the mirror and, after hesitating for a moment, looked again at herself.

To her relief this time she saw herself, clad in the ceremonial garment. She reached up and absently pushed a strand of hair from her face.

I'm not a zor, she thought. *What the hell am I doing?*

"If I did not know him as well as I do," a voice said, "I would ask the same question."

She whirled to look at the room, her eyes darting from place to place, to seek the source of the voice.

"But I believed in him and trusted him when I lived, and he places faith in you. I can only do the same."

Jackie's stomach jumped. *What's happening to me?* she thought. "Th'an'ya?"

"Yes," said a voice from behind her. Slowly she looked over her shoulder at the mirror, and in the reflection of her sleeping-room she saw a figure standing behind her own reflection.

When she turned back, the room was empty.

"I did not mean to frighten," the zor said quietly. In the mirror, it walked forward and stood by the reflection of the bed. "In fact, I had hoped to do just the opposite."

Jackie walked to the bed and sat down, watching as her image took up a position beside Th'an'ya in the mirror.

"Where are you? What the hell is going on?"

"I am inside your mind."

"My mind? How can you—" She put her head in her hands. "This is crazy. First I look in the mirror and see a zor instead of myself, and then I'm—I'm talking to a ghost."

"I am not a 'ghost,'" Th'an'ya replied.

"I know goddamned well what you are!" Jackie answered. "You're some kind of imprint inside my mind. You're a *hsi*-image. Why don't you get out? I don't want you there, especially after what happened at Cicero Down."

She felt the faintest touch within her mind and the memory of the Noyes-thing's mental probe began to surface. It was as if a door were slowly being opened, revealing an awful brightness beyond.

"Stop it!" She stood and ran to the mirror, pounding on it with her fists. "Stop it! Get out of my mind, you—"

The probing stopped. "I am sorry," Th'an'ya's voice said.

Jackie leaned her head on the surface of the mirror. "I must be going crazy."

"Most assuredly not."

"How the hell do you know?" Jackie stared into the mirror at the zor sitting on the bed. "What do you know about madness, especially in humans?"

"I know a great deal about madness, *se* Jackie. And I understand what the onset of Sensitive talents is like."

"Sensitive ..."

"When I was twelve turns old, my Sensitive talents began to emerge. Normally this happens closer to adolescence. Few of my Nest knew how to handle someone too immature to produce shields or to restrain the outpouring of surface thoughts. What was more, I was a powerful Sensitive even at that age.

"It was worse than the normal agonies of puberty. It was madness, friend of my mate."

Jackie stood up straighter. "What ... did you do?"

"Suffered, mostly. When I was a few years short of adulthood, I went to Sanctuary, a sort of ... asylum? No, that word has the wrong connotations. It is a retreat and place of contemplation."

"A monastery?"

There was a slight, gentle probe within her mind. "Yes, that would be a good description. The ... keepers sent me on a journey through my own mind and taught me control from within."

"A journey through your own mind? I don't understand."

"They shut off all of my sensory input, and introduced a specific kind of hallucinogen into my bloodstream." She snorted, in a tone that always meant amusement when Ch'k'te did it. "Later I learned that it had a forty-forty chance of killing me."

"How did you survive?" It seemed a strange question to ask of an apparition.

"I pierced the Icewall."

Jackie understood that term with more certainty and clarity than she would have liked to admit. She stood and walked to the mirror. She stood before it and reached her hand out; it blurred slightly. A zor four-taloned hand reached out to meet it. She put a hand to her face and felt what she thought was human skin, but the image-hand met the rough, leathery visage of a zor.

I know what I am, she thought. *I am a human Imperial naval officer, not a zor. This is like a Sensitive's fever-dream.*

"But you *are* a Sensitive," the mirror-image of Th'an'ya said. "You are a Sensitive more than you know. And though you are not one of the People, the honor my mate has bestowed upon you is one that any of the People would envy."

"I'm not sure I can go through with this," Jackie replied, fingering the hem of the crimson robe. "Whatever I am to Ch'k'te, I cannot be a zor to him."

"That is not what he expects. I am also sure that he did not expect you to demonstrate such innate ability. It is for this reason that my *hsi* has come to you. I foresaw my own death in a prescient dream years before it occurred; I gave most of my *hsi* to *le* Ch'k'te so that he might have it in time of need. When he linked to you it summoned me forth. Though I did not know it then, I know it now: my *hsi* was meant to assist you. It is why I am here."

"Why me?"

Th'an'ya did not answer that question. "*se* Jackie, I live no more except through you. Though it will pain *le* Ch'k'te to know that I am now gone from him, he will understand that it best serves *esLi* that I become your teacher and guide—and also, I hope, your friend."

"By forcing your way to the surface? By spouting zor poetry in my mind all the time?"

"I … do not understand." Th'an'ya's image stood and walked toward the mirror, while Jackie's reflection blurred again and returned to normal. "This is the first time I have attempted to speak to you since our link was broken on Cicero."

"You've been talking to me for days! You've been—There was the line about the wing of *esGa'u*, telling me I knew how to resist the vuhls."

"I have not, *se* Jackie. I have done nothing of the sort."

Jackie frowned and looked at Th'an'ya's image. "In any case, what right do you have to—to set up housekeeping in my mind? Don't I have enough damn problems?"

"It is the will of *esLi!*"

"You'll have to do better than that."

"Ch'k'te is a talented Sensitive with a strong will, but he will never be as powerful as you will become. Ch'k'te cannot do what you *must* do, and for this you will need my help. It is the will of *esLi*."

"A more powerful …"

Suddenly Jackie felt cut adrift, more than she had ever been in her career or indeed in her life. From the corner of her eye, she glanced at her own reflection.

She looked very frightened, and felt it. With a great effort, she sought to calm herself by taking a deep breath and standing up straight as if she were on the bridge of a starship.

"The Imperial Navy," she said after a moment, "employs about four hundred human Sensitives. As far as I'm concerned, they're a fairly disgusting lot who have no regard for discipline or responsibility. They can hardly respond to their own physical needs and they seem to exhibit little in the way of personal hygiene. When I graduated from the Academy, and again when I held my first commission, I was given routine tests for Sensitive talents.

"I failed my E3G tests both times. They drugged me and I lost forty-eight hours of my life while these—*civilians*—crawled around inside my head like vermin, searching for some elusive talent I didn't even believe mankind truly possesses. At the end they said that I *might* have some abilities, but based on what I'd seen I didn't want to become one of them. I *won't, si* Th'an'ya, even under your tutelage, even at your urging, even if it is the goddamn will of *esLi*. It doesn't matter what you are or who you are. Sensitives are everything I am *not*: they exhibit every characteristic I abhor. If you think I'm going to change into—to submit to such—sloth, you should reconsider and go find some other host body."

Jackie looked at herself in the mirror, and suddenly the robe seemed foolish, like a costume for a masquerade.

"I understand your concerns. But it seems to me that you are frightened of your own talent."

"You're right!" She turned away from the mirror and undid the sash on the robe and began to remove it. "You're damned right. I can't do this—I can't go through with it. I know what my limits are."

"You have no idea," Th'an'ya's voice said quietly. "You can not comprehend."

Jackie stopped, half undressed, and turned back to the mirror. "That's right," she said at Th'an'ya, pointing at the zor in the mirror. "I have no idea. I've had no idea since this entire thing started. Always—" She let her hands fall to her sides and looked at the floor. "Always it came to something I *do not understand,* something I *cannot comprehend.* I am a naval officer, a veteran of many years in His Majesty's service, and I am told that I cannot understand the full impact of my actions.

"Now you tell me I'm a Sensitive, and this is also beyond my understanding.

"I won't stand for it, Th'an'ya. I won't stand for it. If I am to continue as an officer, if I am to be a … Sensitive, it must be my choice and I must have control of my own actions, my own body. *Mine*, do you understand?" She pointed a thumb at her chest. "No wings, no talons, my own features, my own mind, with me in control. If you are in my mind to be my teacher and … my friend, you must do so on *my* terms, with no tricks of any kind. If you're not prepared to do that, you'd best be prepared to get the hell out right now."

"I … will do nothing without your consent, *se* Jackie."

"Even during this … Ordeal?"

"Even during the *Dsen'yen'ch'a, se* Jackie. It is your body and your life. I am, I pray, the agent of *esLi* in this matter: I shall not interfere, but I will always be ready to help."

Jackie looked down at herself and then at the zor-image. She secured the robe around her and walked forward to stand at the mirror, watching as the image of Th'an'ya did the same, until it overlapped her own reflection. Slowly, as if with great trepidation, she reached up to touch the mirror, watching the zor before her do the same. For a moment it almost seemed as if their hands touched.

chapter 14

He was walking on an elevated platform, a hundred meters above ground level. The noise struck him first: voices, traffic, machinery, the sounds of thousands of people around him.

The last thing he remembered before that was that he was hurtling through space in his fighter, with an impossibly huge alien craft looming in front of him.

Owen Garrett turned aside and grabbed the railing as if he were holding on to the whole world. For the life of him, he couldn't connect the two events: the last place he remembered and the place he was right now. In eight years as an officer and a gentleman he'd misplaced a few hours, but never … never—

What am I doing here? he asked himself. *How did I get here?*

The answer came back in his mind: *You are on your way to work.*

All right, he thought. *Get a grip.* He'd been a fighter pilot for four years; he was trained not to panic.

He let go of the railing and began to walk toward work: a power plant here in the biggest city on Center. He looked up at a nearby skyscraper which displayed a chrono; he had thirty minutes before he was due to start his shift. There was time for a cup of coffee.

A few hundred meters farther on, he stepped into a crowded shop. He reached into a pocket of his overalls and drew out a comp, which he waved at a sensor on the counter. "Small coffee," he said.

A panel slid aside and a cup of molded plastic appeared. The familiar smell of badly brewed coffee wafted toward him. He drew out the cup and took a sip; it tasted pretty much like he'd expected.

He drew his comp out again. *Maybe there's a clue here,* he thought. He checked the time and date; it was twelve days since the battle—

Battle.

Oh God, he thought, a terrible feeling in the pit of his stomach. He remembered now: the other pilots in Green Squadron circling and firing on each other, fire blooming in the darkness and reflecting against the rocky alien angles of the huge ship. *They killed each other.* Aaron Schoenfeld, Devra Sidra, Steve Leung, Anne Khalid, Gary Cox.

All of them but him. His fighter wasn't pulled into the combat; it was pulled into … into—

"Are you okay, pal?"

Into the ship. He was pulled into the ship by—

He felt a hand at his elbow. He jerked it away, but looked up to see another man in similar overalls.

"I'm fine. Just—just a little tired," he answered. "I didn't sleep too well."

"Right." The other man was bigger; he was also familiar somehow, though Owen couldn't place him. "Don't worry, we've all had mornings like these."

"Look," Owen said. "I don't think I belong here—"

"Sure." The man's face betrayed a moment of alarm, then the look vanished. "Sure, pal. What you need is a breath of air." He took Owen by the elbow and steered him quickly out of the tiny coffee shop and onto the elevated walkway.

"What's the idea—"

"Keep walking," the other said. "And keep your trap shut for a minute." He took Owen across a bridge, noisy with traffic from the level below. There he stopped and let go of him. "We can talk here, but only for a few minutes. You almost blew it back there, pal."

"I don't know what you're talking about."

"Eyes and ears." The big man looked around: up in the air, left and right. "There's always someone watching and listening. You know that."

"No, I don't."

The other didn't reply for a moment, sizing him up. "You don't, huh? Did you just get here?"

"I don't know. I ... don't remember. Five minutes ago I walked into that coffee shop and it was like waking up from a dream."

"You an Imperial citizen? Imperial Navy?"

"Yes."

"What ship?"

"None of your damn business."

"Look, pal. You play straight with me, I'll play straight with you. We're all here for some reason, and if we wind up enemies ... it'll be just what *they* want."

"'They'?"

"The Overlords. The rulers of this world. The enemy, you scan? The people who captured us."

"All right," Owen said after a moment. "I'm ... Owen Garrett. *Due d'Enghien.*"

"The carrier?"

"Yeah."

"Rafe Rodriguez. Engineer's mate. From the *Negri Sembilan.*"

"The *Negri*? The ship that went missing from Cicero?"

"Right. I'm guessing something similar happened to the *Due* and that's how you got here."

"Not really. The *Due* was evacuating Cicero and my fighter wing got pulled in by …" Owen pressed his hands to his forehead. "I don't know," he said. "I don't remember."

"There's some reason for you to be here, pal. The Overlords don't leave loose ends. Look, we can't talk here. After your shift"—he gestured toward Owen's work uniform—"come to the Shield. It's a bar where we hang." He named an address. "Looks like you've got a new piece of the story to add."

THE WORK shift went by slowly. He'd apparently been here a week or so, working as a machine operator; there were people who knew him and he did his best to seem the same as he must have appeared for the last few days. Of Rafe Rodriguez he saw nothing; all during the shift he had the feeling he was being closely watched, but couldn't place by whom.

At last he made his way to the place Rafe had mentioned. He located it by querying his comp. Just after he'd looked it up he realized that someone or something could have noted that inquiry—but there really wasn't anything he could do about it. He wasn't sure what he'd find there: A nest of conspirators? Some sort of underground resistance cell? Was he being sent there—as he had been sent *here*—to root them out?

He really had no idea, just as he had no idea whether he was spinning this out in his mind because he had no other way of occupying it at the moment. Whatever the case, he tried to compose himself the best he could and made his way across the city, a few kilometers in distance and several levels down.

The Shield was really a miserable little place, wedged between a hospital dispensary and some sort of dance club, thirty meters below the surface of the city. As he went in, two men and a woman forced their way past him into the crowded street, bouncing along on their way to other distractions.

Rafe was at the long metal bar, which looked as if it had been fashioned from the hull of a spaceship. There was noise, light, conversation and half a hundred vaguely familiar faces, all of which overwhelmed him. As he wavered in the doorway, Rafe forced his way through the crowd to him, seized him by the elbow as he had done that morning and guided him back by way of the bar—grabbing his drink as he passed—and through a doorway into a private room where several men and women stood, talking and drinking.

"Skip," Rafe said at the door, and one of the group turned around to face them.

"Lieutenant," he said to Owen, "I believe you know Captain Damien Abbas, late of the *Negri Sembilan*."

A FTER THE end of the wars with the zor, humans had spread out in every direction, exploring and settling well beyond the edges of the Solar Empire. The official position of the Imperial Government was that civilization extended no farther than the worlds where the sword-and-sun banner flew; everything beyond that was pirates and stragglers.

The truth was quite a bit different. The century of peace had created all kinds of opportunities. The Imperial Navy decommissioned ships and sold them to enterprising merchants and exploratory societies; corporations invested in expeditions to worlds outside the Empire, seeking new opportunities. Many of these journeys ended in disaster; but some resulted in prosperity and success.

Sixty years ago, a religious group dedicated to the veneration of technology had set out from Denneva, a heavily populated world in the Imperial Core. They were well funded and equipped with industrial nanofactory equipment, and were searching for a world rich in heavy metals; fifty parsecs beyond the edge of the Empire they found Center, which was more than adequate for their needs. The Imperial Grand Survey had not reached Center in the 2330s; it would be more than forty years before the Imperial Navy built a base at Cicero to organize further exploration efforts in the area.

Being outside the Empire gave the settlers of Center wide freedom in developing their society just as they wanted it. It also made them vulnerable. There were no naval vessels to protect against attacks by pirates ... or, as it turned out, by conquerors.

T HERE WERE officers and crew from the *Negri Sembilan* and also from some of the ships that hadn't made it back from Sargasso. The Imperials had gradually made contact with each other, adopting the Shield as their meeting place; neither the technophiles of Center nor the Overlords who had taken control of the world seemed to take much notice of them.

"We didn't know what we were dealing with at the time. We'd heard there was a free port in our survey area—a place the free traders called Crossover. We planned to visit there, show the flag and get a look in case there was something happening that might pose a threat to the Empire."

"And you didn't find a free port."

"No," Abbas replied. "We didn't even find the solar system we expected. It didn't match the survey data at all."

"Sounds familiar." Owen described the discrepancy that had been found at Cicero Op.

"The Sensitives on board had already changed sides—or had been replaced by Overlords."

"Aliens."

"That's right," Abbas said. "Nobody knows what they *really* look like—except they can take human form … or at least look like they've taken human form. We tried to fight but … they could make us do whatever they wanted.

"They made us take out the *Gustav*. They jumped here and left us behind, at least some of us—I don't know why. Every day I see someone else from the *Negri*: same story. As for the other ships—we know something else happened at Sargasso, some admiral who came out with the Cicero squadron."

"I didn't see the report, but the commodore did. She managed to take the Down base back from the aliens."

"How'd she beat them?"

"No idea. The *Due* was out flying high guard and was only ordered to Cicero Prime orbit to retake the base. We were barely in the air when the Down CAP patrols turned aside and gave us control of the airspace. It happened so fast—less than a Standard day—then we were ordered to evacuate."

"You *evacuated* Cicero? Jackie Laperriere *evacuated* Cicero?"

"It was that or …"

The huge alien ship crossed Owen's mind again. They'd taken him inside it and—nothing. He didn't know.

"And you got left behind somehow."

"Not quite." He explained what had happened to Green Squadron and to his own fighter, as far as he remembered: the sudden quiet on the comm, the other Green fighters turning and fighting each other, and his controls going dead as the other alien ship grew larger and larger in his forward screen.

"You were *inside*?"

"I must've been. I don't remember."

Damien Abbas' face grew very serious. He took a moment and cracked a few of his knuckles, then leaned forward and said, "Now hear this, Lieutenant. You've *got* to remember. It's the most important thing in the whole damn world: You've been to a place that no human has ever seen. If we can get that intelligence back to the Empire, maybe we'll learn something to help us beat these bastards. Do you read me?"

"Aye-aye, Captain," Owen replied.

"*h*A T'TE'E, the commodore has arrived."

The High Chamberlain opened his eyes slowly and let his gaze travel from object to object in the chamber, finally resting on the young *alHyu* standing near the door.

"Very good, little brother. Show her in." T'te'e HeYen recited a few verses in his head to calm himself, surprised that his meditations had been unable to dispel the tension about what was to come.

It was not a comfortable position to be in. He had left Zor'a and the High Nest after a lengthy and distressing interview with his cousin the High Lord, whose prescient madness was deepening with each passing day. He had arrived at Adrianople to find the *Gyaryu'har* without his blade, trapped in a coma-like trance that seemed impervious to his ministrations. He had expected it of course, but the reality of the situation was still disturbing.

T'te'e was not afraid of decision or of action: His life had depended on these things more than once, before he had pledged his *chya* and his *hsi* to the dignity of the High Nest. But with little assistance or advice, either from the High Lord or the ranking human in the High Nest, it made it a difficult route to fly.

The *alHyu* showed the human into the chamber and the door slid softly shut, leaving them alone.

"*se* T'te'e," she said, inclining her head slightly. She had no wings to assume any posture of deference; it made her even more difficult to read. He knew that she was a warrior of the race of *esHu'ur*—therefore he could accept that she had honor—but without being a part of the Flight of the People, he could not understand where her duty lay. *This is what we have come to*, he thought. *Did* se S'reth *and* si Th'an'ya *foresee this?*

"*se* Commodore. Be welcome to the High Nest," he replied ritually. Wherever he traveled, the High Nest traveled with him.

"Thank you, sir. It is an honor to make your acquaintance and to be allowed to participate in the Ordeal."

"It is my brother *se* Ch'k'te's decision, *se* Commodore, not mine."

"Sir?"

"It is rare that any *naZora'e* participates in this sort of event, Commodore. I advised my brother *se* Ch'k'te strongly against it. If it were my choice, I would have forbidden it."

He could feel a powerful, unformed anger radiating from her.

"Are you telling me that I should get the hell out?"

"I cannot tell you such a thing without becoming *idju*."

"I'm afraid I don't completely understand."

"*se* Ch'k'te ... said he would transcend the Outer Peace if I forbade your participation. To forsake his rights, especially on those terms, would have dishonored me. Therefore ... I have permitted it."

The anger subsided somewhat. "He said that?" she asked.

T'te'e inclined his head and postured his wings to convey the Oath of Truth Before *esLi*, but she did not seem to notice.

"So I'm to remain, though you don't like it."

"My feelings in this matter have been rendered irrelevant."

"I hardly think so, since you chose to bring them up," she retorted. "You're telling me I don't belong here, and that you'd be more than happy if I volunteered to withdraw, since Ch'k'te won't back down. I don't think your feelings are irrelevant at all, *se* T'te'e.

"I'm to trust my ... *hsi* ... to you. After what I went through at Cicero, I'm not happy about doing so in the face of such hostility."

This was hardly the mode of speech a warrior of the People would use toward an official of the High Nest, and he was not exactly sure what to make of it.

"'Hostility' is not the proper word," the zor replied. He closed his eyes and perched there for several moments, while Jackie stood at parade rest, forcing her anger down. She could read something from him ... Was it disgust? No—it seemed a lot more like confusion.

"What is the proper word, then, sir?"

T'te'e's eyes opened and looked at her once more, his proud head seeming to droop. "'Trepidation' is a closer description of what I feel. Perhaps 'fear' might be appropriate, though my training lets me put most of that aside.

"I have seen what the High Lord has seen, *se* Commodore Laperriere. I understand why he is slowly losing his sanity, as his clan-father *hi'i* Sse'e did: He knows with terrible certainty that the legions of *esGa'u* have the power to destroy all that the People and our human friends have built, in a way that would make the conquests of *esHu'ur* seem as nothing."

"But didn't Marais—*esHu'ur*—nearly exterminate you?"

"There are worse fates than death, *se* Commodore."

"I am aware of that, *se* Chamberlain." She watched him settle his wings in another pattern, but she did not understand its significance.

"But you do not truly understand it as one of the People."

"I—" She fought down anger again. "I understand it more thoroughly than you can imagine, *se* T'te'e. My mind was invaded by them, just as Ch'k'te's was—and I have linked my *hsi* to Ch'k'te. I have been shattered against the Icewall. Do not tell me I do not understand."

At the mention of the Icewall, T'te'e shivered slightly, as if he felt a cold breeze waft through the room.

Perhaps, he thought, *I have underestimated her.* se *Ch'k'te is one of the People; he knows well what is to come. For him to be willing to transcend the Outer Peace for a* naZora'e ...

And there was something else about her that he simply could not read.

"*se* Commodore," he said at last, "I recognize your worthiness to participate in the Ordeal and ask eight thousand pardons if I have offended you in some way. No offense was meant, nor dishonor intended. As with any one of the People, I give you an assurance upon my honor that I will extend the wing of the High Nest over you during the *D'sen'yen'ch'a*."

"No offense was taken, sir."

"Will you agree to abide by the honor and custom of the People during the Ordeal?"

"Upon my oath as an officer, to the best of my ability, sir."

"Very well," he replied. "Let us proceed."

THE SERVANT who had admitted Jackie to the Chamberlain's presence touched her softly on her left arm and beckoned to her. She followed into a side-chamber, lit for humans rather than zor. The small room held a low table and two chairs. One of the chairs contained a human. He rose as she approached; the young zor withdrew.

"Commodore? I'm Martin Boyd, from the Envoy's Office." He extended his hand and she took it. They sat at the table. "It was felt that I should make you aware of certain matters prior to the start of the Ritual."

"A briefing."

"Quite so." She took a moment to look him over. Martin Boyd was a middle-aged man of small proportions. Her first impression was that Boyd was officious like a bureaucrat. Still, he seemed to be at ease with formality, like a well-trained ambassador.

"Will you be participating in the Ritual?" She realized offhandedly that she had capitalized the word, almost as if she understood its meaning.

"Participate? No, of course not. It's unusual—in fact, it's quite remarkable —for a human to be allowed at all."

"*se* T'te'e made that issue quite clear."

"The High Chamberlain is … conservative. Nonetheless, the arrangement has been agreed upon, and I am here—"

"To assure that I don't make an ass of myself."

"—I am here," Boyd continued, patiently, "to assist you in any way I can and to apprise you of events from a different perspective."

"What do you mean?"

"The Admiralty, especially His Grace the First Lord, is rather skeptical of your account. Isn't that correct?"

"Yes, sir. Their Lordships seem to be having a difficult time with it."

"Yet you are certain that the things you describe *did* happen."

"More certain than of anything I have ever known. What's your point?"

"My *point*, Commodore, is that the High Nest knows and has known for some time that there are hostile aliens beyond the boundaries of the Solar

Empire. The source of this knowledge is the prescient dreaming of a High Lord whose sanity comes more and more into doubt. The ever-rational humans—and even a number of the People—have discounted *hi* Ke'erl's visions, in some cases dismissing them entirely.

"The People have learned skepticism from humans about the rule and guide that has directed them for millennia. The gift of *esLi*, the gift of prophecy—of prescience—is a bright and terrible burden that has been the sorrow and the joy of the High Lord since the Zor'a was united thousands of years ago. Sometimes, including *this* time, the awful knowledge of what is to happen brings about madness. But this makes the truth no less true.

"Almost a year ago, the Council of Eleven presented their fears and concerns to the Solar Emperor and asked that the Imperial Navy be put on war alert. The naval forces of the People have been partially mobilized for the whole time, even though the majority of worlds under the authority of the High Nest are on the opposite side of the Empire from its present threat. Needless to say, the emperor declined. He was gracious and polite; he offered to take the matter under advisement, but he declined nonetheless."

He paused to let it sink in, or perhaps just to gauge her reaction. She kept her face impassive, betraying nothing, not even fear. Inside, though, her mind was racing.

The High Nest knew about the vuhls, at least a year ago—and no one acted, she thought.

"Do not judge your admirals too harshly, Commodore. Consider what you would have done with the news: not *now*, but before your recent experience. You may be ready to believe now. Would you have believed then?"

She looked away at her hands folded in her lap, pale against the crimson of the ceremonial robe.

Am I that different? she asked herself. *Have I changed that much?*

The mighty river flows from a hidden source, the voice in her mind said to her.

She must have looked alarmed. Boyd reached out and touched her arm. She jerked away at the touch, turning to look at the far wall. It was adorned with a multihued tapestry depicting some scene from zor legend: a warrior, glowing *chya* in hand, climbing a steep road toward a distant tower crowned with lightnings.

"Commodore?"

"I'm sorry; you startled me. Please go on."

"Without cooperation from the Admiralty," Boyd continued, "the High Lord sent the *Gyaryu'har* to Cicero. His reasons were twofold: first, as *se* Torrijos is a former military officer, his assessment of the situation would be valuable to the Council of Eleven; second, because he was presumed to be safe as long as the *gyaryu* was on his person protecting him. It had been dreamed that the talon of state would be able to guard against the *esGa'uYal.*

"Just before the *Gyaryu'har* began his journey, the Admiralty relented and prepared an inspection tour for Admiral Tolliver to coincide with *se* Torrijos' itinerary. Less than a month before they arrived at Cicero, the first of the two exploratory vessels disappeared.

"Several weeks ago, the High Lord sent a message to the emperor informing him that the *esGa'uYal* were beginning to stir. He sent this message just after Admiral Tolliver jumped from Cicero.

"The rest I believe you know."

She took a few deep breaths. "The … *Gyaryu'har* alluded to his mission. What I didn't realize was that the inspection tour was his, and not really Admiral Tolliver's at all."

"As I am sure the Admiralty wanted."

"I have a question for you, sir. Why are you telling me all of this now—just before the—just before whatever it is happens?"

"It may help to clarify matters for you somewhat. To the People, you see, every person and every thing has a role, a place that *esLi* has arranged. The mystical nature that the 'rational' human perceives as chaotic is actually based on the trust in that harmonic arrangement, and the security that one's role will somehow be made clear. It is the reason for the code of honor—for the dreaming of the High Lord—and for the *Dsen'yen'ch'a.*"

"My role is as an Imperial naval officer, Mr. Boyd. Nothing less will suit, or satisfy."

"Your point is taken, Commodore. But you underestimate yourself."

"What do you mean?"

A gong sounded in the outer chamber and Boyd stood. "We must go. The High Chamberlain is ready to begin."

"What do you *mean*, dammit?" She grabbed his arm and nearly pulled him back into his seat.

"I—I may have spoken out of place. Please, Commodore, we must attend the High Chamberlain." He loosened his arm from her grasp and walked away. Not knowing what else to do, she rose and followed.

C H'K'TE STOOD perched in a torus that hung near the rear wall of the chamber. His eyes were shut, but they opened as Jackie and the Chamberlain approached; he stepped from the torus and fluttered gently to the floor. He reached out and gently grasped Jackie's forearms.

"Thank you for coming," he said, as the Chamberlain stood at a respectful distance.

"I keep my promises. I'll do my best."

"More than enough," he replied, giving her a gentle squeeze on one forearm and then letting go. "Did the Chamberlain say something to trouble you?"

"He tried to suggest that I should not be here."

Ch'k'te turned to look at the Chamberlain, and Jackie felt the tension increase. "I set him straight," she added hastily, half expecting to see claws unsheathed.

"Did he—touch your honor?"

"No. And he apologized afterward. He's consented to my participation, and I'm as ready as I'll ever be."

Ch'k'te held the High Chamberlain's gaze for another moment and then looked back at Jackie. "*esLiHeYar*," he said at last. *To the everlasting glory of esLi.*

"I do not know what form this Ordeal will take," he said quietly to Jackie, looking down at the deck. "The Chamberlain is obliged to satisfy himself and therefore the High Nest that I have not transgressed and made myself *idju*—No, please let me finish," he said, as she tried to protest. "You have been willing to give up anything, even control of your own *hsi*, on my behalf. I believe you to be a truly exemplary human because of it.

"But you still are not cognizant of our culture, and I assure you that I may have transgressed in a way you can not understand. If the Chamberlain finds me to be wanting, I must submit to his, and *esLi*'s, judgment." He looked over his shoulder at the torus. "Regardless of your feelings on the matter, you must surrender to their wisdom if this is the case."

"I ... understand."

"*Do* you? They will not condemn me to life if I am *idju*, *se* Jackie. I will transcend the Outer Peace, and you must let me."

"How could they find you at fault?"

His eyes were full of emotion as he looked up at her once more. "I ... do not know."

I T WAS still difficult to lower her barriers and to expose her *hsi* to another: The first tendrils of the High Chamberlain's mind felt alien and hostile, despite being gentle. *A matter of trust,* she told herself: *he's as afraid as you are.*

So she forced herself to let him enter her consciousness, and slowly she felt herself beginning to drift, as if she were rocking gently in a wide ocean, the waves moving her slowly up and down, up and down ...

She felt Ch'k'te's familiar presence nearby, along with the strong pattern of the High Chamberlain; and there was one other, somewhere beyond or above, only barely showing his/her/its presence: a powerful, all-encompassing one, somewhere beyond the torus that hung several meters away ...

esLi? she asked quietly.

esLi, the Chamberlain said. esLi *commands that the journey begin.* esLi *commands that the ordeal commence.*

esLiHeYar, said Ch'k'te.

I am the glaive of the High Nest.

The gong sounded again, somewhere very far away now, echoing through Jackie's consciousness as her eyes swam.

I am the gyu'u *of the Lord* esLi.

Gong.

I raise my head toward the orb of the Sun and survey the land of my clan-fathers. I scan the horizon and watch for the legions of esGa'u. *Though the searing heat burn away my skin—* Gong.

Though it singe my wings until, blackened, they drop away—

Gong.

Though the madness-of-daylight comes upon me, I shall not swerve from my duty.

Gong.

I am the glaive.

Gong.

I am the talon.

Gong.

I am

Gong.

I

Gongggggggggggggg ...

SOMETHING MADE her open her eyes. Even in the instant before she did, she knew she wouldn't be in the High Chamberlain's rooms aboard Adrianople Starbase; Ch'k'te had prepared her well for the constructs a Sensitive created to house the inner conflicts and meetings of minds.

What she saw, however, was so vivid and breathtaking that she closed her eyes and opened them again to make sure she really saw it. It was even more beautiful than the structure Th'an'ya had imposed upon their link back on Cicero.

She stood at the edge of a great tiled circle set in the stone of a clifftop lookout. It offered a stunning view of rocky country, etched in incredibly realistic detail and bathed in the glow of an orange-red sun. When she compared it to the pastel and crystalline images of her mental link with Ch'k'te and Th'an'ya, it was like comparing the work of a master artist with the drawing of a talented but unskilled child.

She assumed it was drawn from memory; even so, the incredible detail of the scene—from the articulated stonework of the parapets to the carefully defined angles of the distant peaks to the patterns on each individual tile in the pavement beneath her boots—showed a craftsmanship that was almost too skillful to imagine.

It was then she realized that she was alone.

A chill of fear crept through her; she instinctively reached for a weapon at her belt—and felt her hand close around a sword-hilt.

"What the hell?" she said, and her voice echoed oddly in the alien place. She looked at the sash of her robe and saw her hand holding the hilt of an ornately carved sword. She looked at the blade tucked into the sash without a scabbard and *felt* it also, pulsing almost as if it were alive.

A *chya*—at her belt?

She walked to the parapet on one side of the lookout and looked over the side. She saw a dizzying drop onto what looked like sharp rock fangs hundreds of meters below.

"I guess I'm stuck here for the duration," she said.

"Such a pity to be without wings," a zor voice said behind her. She whirled, her hand reaching for the *chya.*

A zor stood in the center of the tiled circle, carefully arranging his wings. From his point of balance, it seemed to Jackie that he had just landed.

"They leave you here while they perform the Ritual of Guard. It *would* be hard for a *naZora'e* to participate, chained to the ground, wingless." The zor examined his talons, an almost human gesture. "Such a pity," he repeated.

She didn't reply. *Where the hell is the High Chamberlain?* she thought to herself. *What am I doing here?*

"So like a human," the zor said, not looking at her. "A military sort, I would guess: honor-bound, dashing into things without the least consideration of the consequences. Is this your first visit to Sanctuary, hm? Perhaps even your first mind-link, little *naZora'e?*"

"Who wants to know?"

"Attack and riposte. Excellent. I cannot read a hint of fear, either; really, quite extraordinary."

"You can read emotions, can you? Well, read *this.*" Impulsively she shot out a whip of anger and resentment: she was tired of being misled and confused, tired of mystery and half-truth—

The mysterious zor stepped back as if struck, fire in his eyes. Continuing to follow her instincts she drew her *chya* and held it out in front of her—

Almost too fast for her to see, the other had a blade in his hand extended toward her. Her *chya* snarled and her stomach lurched: There was something terribly wrong about the zor and his blade. It was glowing unpleasantly.

This was no ordinary opponent; whatever the significance of her gesture had been, it was clear that she was locked in now, like a fencer after the *"en garde"* is given.

"Qu'u," the zor said, holding his blade in sixte. "So, my fine friend. You choose the guise of a *naZora'e* and the battleground of Sanctuary to bring forth the ancient challenge." Lightning-swift, he attacked past her guard but she dodged out of the way, unwilling to let her blade touch his. She crouched, stepping onto the mosaic.

"You are clever, but like the *h'r'kka,* you sometimes choose a guise which hampers you." Again the zor attacked, and again she dodged out of the way, bringing her blade close to her body by tucking her elbow. She edged into the center of the pattern—Suddenly she found herself surrounded by misty, half-ethereal images of herself, mimicking her movement. There were perhaps a dozen of them on all sides, following her steps and her sword-motions, like a gracefully choreographed dance.

"Extraordinary," the zor said softly, surprise in his voice. "Your skill, and your boldness, grows. *A-ei!"* He whirled and sliced through one of the illusions: It burst into silent flame and disappeared. Jackie felt a searing pain in her chest for a moment, and then it passed.

"But you exert yourself. When I am done with the other ten *hsi*-images, you will be weaker still."

She was at the center of ten misty images of herself, a half-dozen meters from the zor. The illusions were somehow linked to her; she certainly felt their pain. One stood directly in front of her enemy—

Again he attacked. She attempted to maneuver the illusion out of the way, holding her sword (and thus its sword) up to protect it, but it only partially blocked his swing. Again the illusion burst and vanished, sending a sharp stab into her shoulder where he struck. A spark of greenish light chased down the length of her crystal-blade and guttered there, giving off a foul smell.

Before he moved again she performed a rapid balestra, thanking God she'd worked so hard at her fencing when she was a cadet, and drove a nearby illusion's blade at the enemy. He whirled out of the way, caught partially off-guard; but the illusory weapon sliced a ragged gash across his front and severed the dark green sash he wore across his chest. The sash dropped to the stone and writhed, then crumbled into dust and swirled away.

The zor recovered quickly enough to slice through his assailant. "Eight *hsi*-images remain, mighty warrior Qu'u. No help in sight for you, is there?"

Jackie stepped back, dodging another of her images around the zor. Suddenly she picked out two specks against the horizon, but she didn't take more than momentary notice; if she paused in her combat, there was a good chance her opponent would know that she'd seen something.

"When fighting a superior opponent," her fencing-master had always said, *"try to use the element of surprise."*

What the hell, she thought to herself. *Here goes.*

Though it frightened her to do so, she whirled and turned her back to her opponent, sweeping her growling *chya* in a wide arc. Partway through the movement her blade met resistance; as she completed her swing, she saw the zor stagger, holding his weapon-side shoulder, and retreat toward the cliff-edge. His own *chya*—or whatever the hell it was—was still held out before him. As he retreated, he slashed at the nearest illusion, striking it roughly amidships. She felt suddenly short of breath; she, too, retreated a few steps, her illusions with her.

"You have now," the zor said, between breaths, "seven images left, *ge* Qu'u. Your skill is even greater than my Master expected." She didn't know what the prenomen meant, but it had been delivered in a sneering voice that made it clear it was insulting, at least.

The distant specks had become the size of fists, and she could make out wings on the figures. She hoped that it was the Chamberlain and Ch'k'te. There was no way to be sure.

Before he could react, Jackie hurled herself forward, an image charging full-bore toward the crouching zor. In a single fluid movement, he executed a perfect stop-thrust and the illusion burst.

"How very arrogant," the zor gasped, "for you to believe that you are so different than I. Tossing away wing-men like that, Qu'u, for no apparent purpose. There are only six of your paltry illusions left." Though somewhat hindered by his injured shoulder, the zor was still skilled and quick, and she was almost unable to react as he feinted toward one of her images and then slashed viciously at another; like the others, it burst and vanished.

A burning pain struck her breasts. She looked down reflexively—

Another illusion was struck and destroyed. The pain lancing through her right leg was so sharp and sudden that she staggered. Without any movement on her part, the four remaining images stepped closer.

The two zor that were approaching—she could almost see Ch'k'te's wing-markings now—had apparently seen the fight. They held their *chya'i* in hand and were beginning to dive toward the parapets.

"I will rend your wings and shred your feathers," the enemy said, his voice a snarling whisper. "I will peck out your eyes and divide your heart with my *e'chya*. You will be carrion for my Nest, a sumptuous meal for my Master." The light in his eyes had changed now and was even more frightening than it had been before.

Jackie was breathing hard, trying to keep her feet. It seemed that her images now moved of their own accord. The other's movements had become exaggerated; he swung wildly, locking blades with one of her remaining illusions. However, as she slowly moved to block his next movements, one of the other images moved forward and swung for the zor's head. As two images engaged the enemy, the other two assumed positions to her left and right.

"You—have—presumed too much, mighty Qu'u," the zor gasped out, retreating toward the cliff. "You have chosen again to fight the Crawler's battles." T'te'e and Ch'k'te had almost reached the cliffside now; she could see the warrior's-gleam in their eyes as they prepared to do battle. Before they could hover for a single blow, the enemy zor leapt to the top of the parapet, still fending off blows. He raised his wings in a posture she did not recognize, but knew—somehow—it was offensive or obscene.

"*esGa'u'Canya'e'e!*" he shouted; then he hurled himself backward and fell screaming, wings outstretched, over the side. Several seconds later there was a terrible crunching sound of bones breaking against rock.

The remaining four images turned toward her and bowed and then vanished.

chapter 15

Two days after his first meeting with Damien Abbas at the Shield, Owen Garrett began to have dreams.

He was unprepared for them at first, but he'd been at something of a loss since that first morning when he'd met Rafe Rodriguez. The dreams had an awful familiarity during the time he was asleep but seemed completely alien when they were over and he was lying awake, shivering at the memory.

He was in his fighter. He could see the impossibly huge bulk of the alien ship blotting out much of the starry backdrop. His attitude control, his comm, and of course his weapons were disabled as his craft was being pulled toward an opening that hadn't been there a minute ago. Unable to control anything on his ship, he laid his hand on the grip of the pistol holstered to the left of his instrument panel. A terrible lassitude gripped him, making him want to do nothing but sleep.

He grit his teeth, forcing his hand to hold the gun. *These are the things that killed my friends*, he told himself.

The fighter was pulled to a halt inside a small compartment, perhaps a meter higher than the plane itself. His interior cameras showed the entrance sealing itself behind, leaving no evidence that he'd entered that way.

He pulled a helmet over his vacc suit and secured it with a touch, then gestured the canopy open. It hissed as the pressure equalized; he clambered out of the cockpit, his pistol in his hand.

There was no welcoming committee. There were also no doors, just a glowing opalescent patch on the wall, a meter wide and a meter off the floor.

As he stood there, he felt the same pressure in his mind, probing, looking for a weak spot. *Lower your weapon,* it said. *You need a nice rest.*

He felt anger rising in him again as he fought the impulse to lie down on the soft, slightly spongy deck. He shot the glowing patch on the wall.

THE FIRST time he had the dream, that action had awoken him with a splitting headache, pain like he'd never felt in his life. He'd staggered to the 'fresher and run his head under the shower until it finally subsided.

The dream had had the ring of truth. He *had* been pulled inside the alien ship. All of his fellow pilots were dead, controlled by some alien intelligence that made them fire on each other. But he'd … he'd—

The next night the same dream came again. It was like an episode of a 3-V action hero, one he'd seen a hundred times before; he was drawn toward the ship, forced into the landing chamber. He climbed out of Green Five, this time giving it a friendly pat right on the sword and sun and saying, "Thanks, old girl. Hope we see each other again."

There was the same mind probe—the same searing pain in his head as he shot the patch on the wall. This time he forced himself to wait until the pain subsided, holding on to the dream with all his might.

This time the wall collapsed and melted, revealing another chamber beyond. He lurched toward it, pistol in hand, and stepped through the opening. Two aliens were standing there; they had black, four-legged insectoid bodies. Past their midsection, the aliens stood upright, with two more limbs that seemed to serve as arms. Their heads were rounded cones with eyestalks; their faces had fanged mouths with sharp mandibles, surrounded by wiggling tentacles that waved like streamers. They were clearly afraid of him; violent confrontation didn't seem to be what they bargained for. He trained his weapon on them, but before he could open fire they scuttled backward through a seam in the wall which closed behind them.

Now it was quiet. Not exactly quiet, actually—he could hear background music, whirling and clicking, faint squeaks and a sound like a pump filling and discharging. The walls themselves, as well as the floor and ceiling, were in constant motion, gradually undulating along their length.

Owen Garrett, he heard in his mind. *Lower your weapon. We mean you no harm.*

"Nothing doing. I'll shoot every wall and every bug in this place until I run out of juice." His anger was a palpable thing now. "I want some answers."

There was no response. He looked around the room for a target; evidently that got their attention. *What are your questions?*

"What do you want from me? Why am I aboard?"

We wish to learn about your fleet dispositions.

That was direct. He'd expected some dissembling, but there it was. "I can't tell you that."

Of course you will, came the reply.

"Of course I *won't*. I'm not about to—"

Of course you will.

The pressure in his mind increased from annoyance level to intrusive to excruciating. He fired his pistol in some direction, but before he could take another step the dream evaporated, leaving him awake and shivering, not knowing what happened next.

T HE REMAINING four images turned toward her and bowed, then vanished. Jackie fell to her hands and knees, gulping in air.

Both the High Chamberlain and Ch'k'te landed beside her and helped her to her feet. She grasped Ch'k'te's arm and stood straight, shrugging off the elder zor.

"May I be of assistance?" the Chamberlain asked, and she shot a glance at him so powerful that he stepped backward with seeming alarm.

"Yes, you can." She tucked the *chya* back in the sash of her robe and wiped her sweaty palms on the crimson cloth. "You certainly can. I'm tired of surprises, *se* T'te'e. I agreed to 'stand by' my colleague and friend during this Ordeal, not stand out in the middle of—on top of—and get into a fight with—"

"A servant of *esGa'u*," the Chamberlain offered. "Shrnu'u HeGa'u. He of the Dancing Blade."

Ch'k'te looked up in alarm. "You knew she would be attacked?" He turned to Jackie. "*se* Jackie, I—"

"Belay it, Commander," she said. "I want some answers, *se* T'te'e. This is the *Dsen'yen'ch'a*, correct?"

"Yes, *se* Commodore, it is."

"But it wasn't meant for Ch'k'te, was it? It was intended for me all along. Am I correct?"

"That is … essentially correct, *se* Commodore."

"Who is Qu'u?"

The Chamberlain did not reply.

"He was a great hero of legend," Ch'k'te offered, looking from Jackie to the Chamberlain back to Jackie. "How do you know that name?"

"This Shrnu'u called me Qu'u. Several times during the battle he addressed me as 'mighty Qu'u' and he referred to my"—she pointed to herself—"appearance as a 'guise.' He seemed convinced that I was Qu'u. Why did he believe this, *se* T'te'e?"

"It is your *hsi*, *se* Commodore Laperriere. You have certain qualities that distinguish you. It is these qualities that make you sufficiently important to warrant such a test."

"Qualities like—"

"Qu'u was a hero of the Unification," Ch'k'te said. "He was—"

"*se* Ch'k'te, my brother—"

"She must know, *ha* T'te'e. With all respect, Honored One, and with eight thousand pardons, I am bound by oath of brotherhood to explain to *se* Jackie what I believe you intend."

"You are risking the High Nest, little brother. I warn you that if she—"

Jackie held up her hand. "Stop talking about me as if I weren't here. Ch'k'te, proceed." She glared at T'te'e.

The Chamberlain's mouth opened, shut, opened again as he considered another reply, and shut again.

"Qu'u," Ch'k'te said, "was the great Champion of the very first High Lord, A'alu HeYen, the unifier of our people. He is said to have descended onto the

Plain of Despite and taken the sword that was reforged into the *gyaryu*. In the Lordship of A'alu, Qu'u was the *Gyaryu'har*."

"What does that mean to me?"

"It is very simple," the Chamberlain said. "The High Lord has need of the *Gyaryu'har*, but he lies in a coma without his guardian blade. I have examined him carefully and have come to the conclusion that without the *gyaryu*, he will never recover ... yet we do not possess it. Even if we did, there are few who can even hold it, much less protect it from the *esGa'uYal*. It *must* be recovered."

"Why don't *you* recover it?"

"I cannot, *se* Jackie."

"You're telling me that you can't—and I can?"

"That is correct."

"What about—What about Ch'k'te?"

"Though the High Chamberlain has not found me *idju*, *se* Jackie, he knows —as I know—that I am not worthy of the Talon of State. While he ... while you were being tested, he performed the Ritual of Guard and was satisfied." His wings altered their configuration slightly. "It is you who are capable of doing this deed, and I would be honored to serve you, mighty Qu'u."

"Don't you start, too! I'm not—I'm not this Qu'u, I'm just an Imperial officer."

Your point is taken, the voice in her mind said. *But you underestimate yourself.*

"No, *se* Commodore Laperriere," said the High Chamberlain. "You are something more. In a very real sense, you *are* Qu'u, and you will journey onto the Plain of Despite to recover the stolen *gyaryu*. With your intimate knowledge of the *es-Ga'uYal* and the power of your aura, you represent our best hope for its recovery."

"What if I choose not to do this?"

The High Chamberlain placed his wings in a position of deference to *esLi*. From far in the distance a gong sounded: once, twice, three, four times.

"THEN, I regret to say, *se* Commodore," the High Chamberlain said from somewhere far away, "both the People and the *na-Zora'i* are doomed to fall to the *esGa'uYal*. *With* it we may yet fail if *esLi*'s face is turned from us, but without it, that matter is a certainty."

Her eyes were still closed. Nearby she sensed the presence of *esLi,* and felt, rather than heard, the gentle fluttering of zor wings.

"The High Nest could command the obedience of one of the People, *se* Commodore. In truth, one of our race with a destiny such as yours would eagerly take up the sacred burden of recovering the *gyaryu*. That you are not one of the People is undeniable. It is a source of great consternation to me. I was prepared to forbid the testing, as you know; that you chose to persevere despite my objections is a testimony to your integrity and honor. I have no means to command you; I must rely solely on entreaty.

"I ... sense that my words will do little to change your attitude," the High Chamberlain continued after a moment. "The testing of the *Dsen'yen'ch'a* is logical and quite proper for one of the People. Yet to you, without preparation or total understanding, it might seem arbitrary and unfair. I ask eight thousand pardons if that will assuage you at all."

Jackie considered her responses. She opened her eyes slightly to see the meditation chamber bathed in dim vermilion light. She was reclining on a sofa of some kind, with Ch'k'te and the Chamberlain standing nearby on slightly elevated perches. The torus of *esLi* hung behind them, silhouetted against the far wall of the chamber.

Her muscles were tense and sore, as if she had truly been engaged in vigorous exercise.

Like fighting for my life, she told herself.

"I'll—I'll have to think about it," she said at last, her voice coming out in a whisper.

The Chamberlain seemed to have expected that response. He fluttered down from his perch. "If you will excuse me, the Ordeal has left me greatly fatigued. *se* Ch'k'te, would you escort the Commodore back to her billet?"

"Honored One," Ch'k'te responded formally and bowed. He settled down on the deck beside Jackie and helped her to her feet; without a word he accompanied her out of the Chamberlain's rooms.

BY THE time they reached Jackie's quarters she was almost too tired to walk. Wearily, she keyed open the door, walked into the front room and kicked off her boots, then went into the sleeping chamber and dropped onto the bed. Ch'k'te trailed behind and hesitated at the entrance to the room.

"C'mon in."

Ch'k'te waited a moment and scanned the room, then walked to the bed and took up a position near it.

Jackie leaned up on one elbow. "What's wrong?"

"I am disquieted, *se* Jackie. I feel as if I have betrayed you."

"Did you know I would be tested in this way?"

"No."

"I didn't think so. This was the High Chamberlain's doing. These are very high stakes he's playing for; he's made you even more of a pawn than he's made me. Don't worry, Ch'k'te old friend, I—" She reached over to grasp his forearm but he shied away. She withdrew her hand and sat up. "What is it?"

"I—Nothing. Nothing at all."

"Spit it out. What are you keeping from me?"

"The High Chamberlain ... asked me many questions touching on my honor and my ... propriety. He asked me if I was your lover."

"Who the hell does he think—"

Ch'k'te held his hand up. "I told him that I was not. As for why it is his concern, which I believe would be your next question, I should think that you already know the answer: I am a sept-brother of the High Nest. If you were one of the People—or I a human—the question would have a different meaning."

"He's still a bastard for playing head-games with you, my friend. Of course, compared with what he's trying to do with me ..."

"He is trying to save the People, and humanity as well, from the *esGa'uYal*."

"'Better living through mythology.'"

"I—Your pardon, *se* Jackie, but I do not—"

"Never mind. It just seems that it'd make more sense if he were to choose a champion who actually *believed* in all of this—in Qu'u, in *esLi* and in *esGa'u*—"

"You do not ... believe in these things?"

"Not as a zor does. Not really, no."

"*se* Jackie, I ..." Ch'k'te stood up and turned to her, his wings elevated. "After all that has happened, how can you not believe? Did you not feel *esLi* in the Chamber of Meditation? Did you not do combat against the minion of *esGa'u* at Sanctuary during the *Dsen'yen'ch'a*?"

"It was an image from *se* T'te'e's mind, Ch'k'te. It wasn't *real*—it was ... imagination."

"I beg your pardon, *se* Commodore, but it was very much real. Though we never physically left the Chamberlain's rooms, what we experienced was *very* real. *esLi exists*, as does *esGa'u*, as do his servants. The High Chamberlain did not ... create the image of Shrnu'u but rather invited him into the mental link. He took a great risk by doing so, especially since you were not aware of the danger that Shrnu'u represented. You could have transcended the Outer Peace, as could all of us."

"That was *mortal combat*." It was more of a statement than a question.

"Yes. If you choose to take up the burden of Qu'u, *se* Jackie, there will be other such combats, some in the physical world and others—elsewhere. They are all *real*. I entreat you to believe me and to grasp this notion. You need a teacher and I hope that I am able to help you."

"You'll do fine," she answered quietly.

Ch'k'te's talons clenched. "I have sought to summon back my mate *li* Th'an'ya, but I have been unsuccessful. Her *hsi* is lost to me, wasted. I fear that she may be lost forever."

"Don't be so sure of that," Jackie replied.

Tentatively she thought: *Th'an'ya?*

I am here, se Jackie. What do you wish of me?

Please show yourself to Ch'k'te. I think he needs to know that you 're here. "*le* Ch'k'te."

He turned away from Jackie to the sound of the voice. In the mirror stood Th'an'ya, dressed in a peach-colored robe with a tan sash, her right hand holding a polished staff.

They spoke rapidly in the Highspeech. It was apparent from the tone of voice that Ch'k'te was deeply moved. Four times he took a step toward the mirror; each time he stepped back, as if he realized that Th'an'ya was only a projection.

I am going now, Th'an'ya said at last. *I thank you*, se *Jackie.*

"She dwells with you now," Ch'k'te said.

"It was her choice. She wants to teach me."

"She will do well at it," Ch'k'te answered, his voice sounding resigned, almost wooden. "She taught me."

Jackie stood and walked over to Ch'k'te, and reached for his forearms again. "I'm sorry—" she began to say. But he backed away from her, his head lowered.

"I must go," he said, retreating. "Excuse me." He turned and walked out through the sitting room to the door.

"Ch'k'te!"

He turned and looked at her for a moment and then departed through the door. It slid shut behind him, leaving her alone.

AT 0700 the board of inquiry was waiting for her, still looking stern and forbidding. There were a few other officers in attendance this morning, however, including Admiral Hsien and—in the very back row of seats—Ch'k'te. He looked as though he hadn't slept; she certainly hadn't gotten much rest either, tossing the *Dsen'yen'ch'a*—and other matters—back and forth in her mind.

"Reporting as ordered, sirs," she said, and took her seat.

"Commodore Laperriere," First Lord Alvarez began, his hawklike features narrowing as he frowned at her over folded hands, "please inform this board what you were doing between approximately 1930 and 2300 hours last night."

"I was attending the—a zor ceremony, Your Grace."

"What sort of ceremony?"

"A Sensitive ceremony called 'the Ordeal of Experience,' Your Grace. It was at the specific invitation of the High Chamberlain T'te'e HeYen." *Not quite true*, she thought, but the High Chamberlain would back up her story—if he expected her cooperation.

"Did you inform your commanding officer of your attendance at this ceremony?"

"I left a message with the admiral's adjutant, sir, at about 1830."

"Which he did not receive until this morning."

"Your Grace, the board did not dismiss me until 1700. Without orders to the contrary, I felt that standing orders regarding relations with the zor, especially distinguished persons of the High Nest, would indicate that the admiral would wish me to attend. I hope that I have not offended the High Nest in any way."

"The High Nest," the First Lord replied, "is by no means offended. In fact, it has given you high praise. It has used a … er, variety of *complimentary* adjectives to describe you. None of which, I might add, adequately describe this board's present opinion of you."

"Sir."

"I assume," Alvarez continued, "that it would be difficult to describe this 'Ordeal' in terms a—layman—might understand. Since it has no place in this proceeding, I will simply note for the record that, whatever happened, you acquitted yourself in proper form as an officer in His Majesty's Fleet. In any case, it has impressed the High Chamberlain enough for him to invoke the Interservice Cross-Training Agreement.

"The High Chamberlain has requested that you be added to his personal staff."

"Your Grace?"

"His *staff*, Laperriere. Effective from this date, 1200 hours, you and your executive officer Ch'k'te HeYen are attached to the staff of the Zor High Chamberlain, T'te'e HeYen. The board of inquiry into your actions at Cicero is suspended until further notice."

"Your Grace, I—I'm not sure I understand."

"Understand *this*, Commodore. The High Chamberlain has asked for you, for whatever purpose, for whatever reason. I can't say I know what this is about, but I can say this: When your tour of duty is done, you will still be answerable to this board. You will still be bound by its decision." Alvarez stood, and the other officers rose with him. Jackie got to her feet hastily. "Until that time, I declare this board in recess."

chapter 16

THE LEGEND OF QU'U

IN THE TIME OF THE WARRING STATES, BEFORE THE
HIERATE OF THE HIGH NEST, THERE LIVED A WARRIOR

[Honor to the High Nest]

IN THE SERVICE OF NEST-LORD A'ALU, WHOSE NAME
WAS QU'U. IN THE HIGH SPEECH QU'U IS A NAME OF
GREAT POWER; BUT THE HIGH SPEECH HAD NOT YET
EVOLVED IN THAT FARGONE DAY. QU'U WAS OF GOOD
REPORT AND WELL-TRAINED, THOUGH NOT OF NOBLE
BLOOD; THE PRINCIPIATE WHICH HE SERVED, THAT OF
N'YEN, WAS CONSTANTLY AT WAR WITH ITS NEARBY
RIVAL,

[Cloak of Defense]

THE MOUNTAINOUS REGION OF U'HERA.

EACH OF THE TWO CONTENDING PROVINCES HAD
SPENT CONSIDERABLE RESOURCES IN TRYING TO SUB-
DUE THE OTHER, TO LITTLE AVAIL. E'YEN, A RICH AND
BOUNTIFUL LAND, WAS DOTTED WITH MANY FORTIFIED
CASTLES, WROUGHT IN STRONG STONE AND WOUND
ABOUT WITH MANY CHARMS AND SPELLS, WHILE
U'HERA, A POORER AND MEANER LAND, WAS GIFTED
WITH MANY NATURAL BARRIERS AND OBSTACLES, MAK-
ING IT DIFFICULT TO OVERCOME. DURING QU'U'S
PREPARATION AND TRAINING AS A WARRIOR, THE TWO

[Wings Contend]

LANDS FOUGHT MANY BITTER BATTLES, SOME BETWEEN
ENEMY ARMIES, AND OTHERS BY MORE SUBTLE AND
LESS HONORABLE MEANS—FOR THE PEOPLE OF THAT
TIME WERE WITHOUT THE INNER AND OUTER PEACE
AND KNEW NO BOUNDS IN HATE OR WAR. BUT
THOUGH THOSE ANCESTORS DID NOT KNOW HONOR,
THEY DID KNOW DESPITE, AND FELT THE HEAVY HAND
OF *ESGA'U* MEDDLING IN

[Barrier Before Despite]

THEIR DISPUTES.

* * *

THE ARMIES OF U'HERA HAD BEEN DRIVEN OFF IN AN
INVASION LATE IN THE SEASON ONE YEAR, AND THE
WARRIORS OF E'YEN HAD TAKEN UP WINTER QUAR-
TERS IN SEVERAL FORTRESSES ALONG THE BORDER
BETWEEN THE TWO LANDS. QU'U, WHO HAD ACQUIT-
TED HIMSELF WELL IN THE PRECEDING MONTHS, HAD
BEEN ASSIGNED WITH HIS CONTINGENT TO THE CAS-
TLE *NE'ESLL'E,* WHICH MEANS "GUARDIAN OF THE
NEST OF *ESLI"*   [Guardian of the Nest]
THOUGH WINTERS WERE HARSH IN THAT PART OF THE
LANDS, THE E'YEN'L WARRIORS WERE MINDFUL OF THE
POTENTIAL FOR TREACHERY, AND MADE SURE TO
GUARD THEIR CHARGES BY DAY AND NIGHT.

ON A PARTICULAR NIGHT, WHEN FIRST MOON WAS
HIGH IN THE SKY, QU'U WAS WALKING ALONG THE
WATCHTOWER SCANNING THE SKIES FOR THE WINGS OF
INVADERS, KEEN OF EYE AND   [Posture of Approach]
BRAVE OF HEART, HE WAS ATTENTIVE TO HIS DUTY
AND WOULD NOT HAVE EXPECTED THAT HIS DILIGENCE
COULD BE EVADED. NONETHELESS, AS HE REACHED
THE END OF HIS POST, HE HEARD THE NOISE OF WINGS
FLUTTERING BEHIND HIM. HE TURNED QUICKLY TO
FACE A DISTINGUISHED ELDERLY PERSON, SETTLING
INTO A PERCHED POSITION ON THE WALL OF THE
CASTLE.

"FRIEND OR FOE?" QU'U ASKED, HOLDING HIS BLADE
OUT BEFORE HIM.   [The Drawn *chya*]
THE STRANGER, UNPERTURBED BY THE OBVIOUS
THREAT QU'U POSED, MERELY SETTLED HIS WINGS IN A
POSTURE OF DEFERENCE TO *ESLI.*   [Deference to *esLi*]
"YOU ARE IN A WAR ZONE, DISTINGUISHED ELDER,"
QU'U SAID. UNSURE, HE LOOKED AROUND. TO HIS SUR-
PRISE, NO ONE ELSE ON GUARD SEEMED TO BE TAKING
NOTICE OF HIS ENCOUNTER, "I MUST ASK YOU TO—"

"YOU ARE QU'U, SON OF CHE'E," THE STRANGER
INTERRUPTED. "WARRIOR OF THE E'YEN?"

                                                            [Stance of Qu'u]

*   *   *

"I AM QU'U," QU'U REPLIED. "AND YOU—"

"MY NAME IS UNIMPORTANT. I AM A MESSENGER AND I HAVE A MESSAGE FOR QU'U."

"WHAT IS YOUR MESSAGE?"

"I BEAR THE GREETINGS OF THE LORD *ESLI,*" THE OLDER ONE INTONED, AND THE HOLY NAME ECHOED THROUGH THE AIR LIKE THE PEALING OF A GREAT BELL. "THE LORD WISHES TO CONVEY HIS RESPECTS AND GRATITUDE TO YOU, MIGHTY WARRIOR QU'U, FOR YOUR DILIGENCE AND BRAVERY AS AN HONORABLE WARRIOR.

[Honor to *esLi*]

"IT IS NO IDLE THING THAT THE LORD CHOOSES TO SPEAK TO YOU, WARRIOR QU'U, FOR HE PROPOSES TO LAY UPON YOU A JOYOUS AND TERRIBLE BURDEN. THE SERVANTS OF THE DECEIVER ARE ABROAD IN THE LANDS, AND SEEK TO DESTROY ALL OF THE NESTS THROUGH A WEAPON OF HORRIBLE POWER; WITHOUT YOUR HELP, THEY MIGHT WELL SUCCEED."

[Descent to the Plain]

"WITHOUT *ME*?" QU'U ASKED. "I AM A WARRIOR, AS YOU SAY. I HAVE FOUGHT IN COMBAT FOR MY NEST, BUT I AM YOUNG AND HAVE NOT AS YET ACHIEVED FULL MASTERY. YOU MUST NOT WANT TO CHARGE ME WITH ANY BURDEN."

"ON THE CONTRARY, MIGHTY WARRIOR," THE MESSEN-GER REPLIED. "THE LORD *ESLI* ASKS FOR *YOUR* SERVICE AND YOURS ALONE. YOU MUST UNDERTAKE A JOURNEY FOR HIM AND UNDERTAKE A MOST IMPORTANT TASK. "YOU MUST TRAVEL TO THE PLAIN OF DESPITE AND FIND THE SWORD THAT WILL BECOME THE *GYARYU,* THE TALON OF *ESLI*."

[Honor to the Warrior]

[Talon of State]

*   *   *

"AND HOW COULD I FIND SUCH A WEAPON OR
EVEN TRAVEL TO SUCH A PLACE?" QU'U MENACED THE MES-
SENGER AGAIN, WONDERING WHETHER HE WAS BEING
DECEIVED. "I AM NOT A SENSITIVE, AND CANNOT
SENSE THE POWER."

"AGAIN YOU DENY ME, MIGHTY WARRIOR QU'U. BUT
ESLI HAS SEEN YOUR FUTURE, AND KNOWS YOUR
WORTH."   [Parting the Shroud]

"WHAT OF MY RESPONSIBILITIES HERE? I MUST MAIN-
TAIN MY POST HERE ON THE WALLS OF NE'ESLL'E,
TO WATCH FOR THE   [Honor of the Warrior]
TREACHEROUS U'HERA. AS YOU HAVE SAID, I AM A
WARRIOR AND MUST PLACE MY DUTY TO NEST AND
LORD ABOVE ANY PERSONAL GLORY."

"I COULD SAY TO YOU THAT YOUR DUTY TO THE LORD
ESLI OVERWEIGHS ANY OTHER DUTY; I COULD POINT
OUT TO YOU AGAIN THE SIGNIFICANCE OF YOUR OWN
ROLE IN THE UPCOMING   [The Dark Wing]
STRUGGLE BETWEEN THE LIGHT AND DARK WING—
BUT YOUR WARRIOR'S DUTY WOULD STILL REMAIN. I
HAIL YOU, HONORABLE QU'U AND ASSURE YOU THAT
YOU WILL BE RELIEVED OF THAT BURDEN ERE YOU
DEPART FOR THE PLAIN OF DESPITE."

QU'U LOOKED AWAY FROM THE STRANGER, THE MOON-
LIGHT CATCHING HIS PROFILE. "THERE IS ONE OTHER
THING THAT YOU MUST   [Confronting *anGa'e'ren*]
KNOW BEFORE YOU PLACE YOUR HOPE AND EXPECTA-
TION WITH ME. THOUGH I AM A BLOODED WARRIOR
AND HAVE BEEN TRUSTED WITH THE DUTY YOU SEE ME
HERE CARRYING OUT, I AM UNWORTHY OF YOUR BUR-
DEN BECAUSE I HAVE TASTED GREAT FEAR. I AM COW-
ARDLY, DISTINGUISHED ELDER, THOUGH IT PAINS ME
TO EXPRESS IT AND IT STAINS MY FAMILY HONOR TO
LET IT BE KNOWN."

"MIGHTY QU'U," THE MESSENGER REPLIED, "IT IS NOT

[Honor of the Warrior]

DISHONORABLE TO KNOW FEAR. IT IS A FOOLHARDY
WARRIOR WHOSE ACTIONS ARE NOT TEMPERED BY
THOUGHTS OF HIS OWN MORTALITY, FOR SURELY
THERE IS NO GREATER WASTE THAN A WARRIOR WHO
GIVES UP HIS LIFE WHILE ACHIEVING NOTHING. TO DIE
IN BATTLE IS GLORIOUS ONLY IF SOME GREAT
PURPOSE IS ACHIEVED, WHAT IS MORE,   [Glory of Outer Peace]
YOU ARE NO COWARD, FOR IT REQUIRED GREAT
COURAGE FOR YOU TO SPEAK YOUR FEARS ALOUD
TO ME.

"I ACCEPT YOU, MIGHTY QU'U. YOU ARE BRAVE, HON-
ORABLE, RESPONSIBLE AND MODEST; YOU HAVE DENIED
ME FOUR TIMES AND I HAVE ANSWERED YOU. WHEN
YOUR WATCH ENDS, GO AND   [Honor to *esLi*]
PREPARE WITH YOUR FRIEND AND COMPANION HYOS
FOR YOUR JOURNEY TO THE PLAIN OF DESPITE." THE
STRANGER CLAPPED HIS TALONS TOGETHER—

AS QU'U WATCHED IN WONDERMENT, A BRIGHT FLASH
OF LIGHT OBSCURED HIS VISION. WHEN HE COULD SEE
ONCE MORE, THE STRANGER WAS GONE.

For a few days, Owen's sleep was filled with images from the same scene, with minor variations. Sometimes there'd be a bit more dialogue; sometimes he'd shoot one of the aliens before it escaped. But it basically ended the same way; they were invading his mind and it felt like they were ripping it apart.

The story didn't seem to trouble Captain Abbas or any of the others who gathered at the Shield. They took it as a good sign that he was remembering anything, but they shrugged it off as a feature of the war with this new enemy. For the regulars at the Shield, it was difficult to deal with aliens they couldn't see—or worse yet, that they couldn't tell apart from a friend.

"This is all the part of those damn Sensitives," Abbas said one night, nine or ten days after the dreams started.

"How do you figure that?"

Abbas looked at Owen. "You don't know? It's the Sensitives—especially the zor—that brought this down on us. From what I hear, they couldn't leave well enough alone. They were casting their minds around the universe and drew the attention of the aliens. That's how they found us."

"I find that hard to believe," Owen answered.

"Well." Abbas squinted at Owen in the harsh light. "I don't really give a damn what you believe. From what I understand, the zor found these aliens eleven years ago and didn't say anything to anyone. Next thing you know they're everywhere: taking over ships, invading the Empire."

"And the Sensitives—"

"Well, they've been *subverted*, haven't they? Ask anyone in this bar what they think of the Sensitives on their ships. They went over to the enemy, as quick as you please. Now maybe—*maybe*—it was against their will, but in the end it comes of meddling in things we don't understand. They stood by on the *Negri* as we … attacked the *Gustav Adolf II*. Now they're all working for the new boss." He took a drink and looked away, as if he couldn't continue.

"Have all of the Sensitives sold out?"

"All the ones on the *Negri* did." Abbas held his drink tightly in his hand. "They didn't have any trouble with it. From what I hear they didn't have much trouble at Cicero either."

"Not true. They got more than they bargained for at Cicero." Owen looked away, thinking about Leung, Khalid, Cox and the rest. "And it still wasn't enough."

"I don't know how it will be. If we can't tell who's human and who's a … who's one of the aliens … Hell, you could be one."

"I'm not." Then Owen found himself continuing: "And neither are you."

Abbas looked up. "Are you sure?" He put his hands on his head and wiggled his fingers. "Booga-booga."

Owen began to laugh, and then suddenly the strangest feeling came over him. It was as if the room had suddenly come into sharp focus. He looked closely at Damien Abbas and knew with absolute certainty that he wasn't an alien. He was sure, though he had no idea why.

Abbas said something, but whatever it was made no sense. All of a sudden nothing made any sense. He looked away from Abbas, letting his gaze travel from person to person; each one looked perfectly normal—

There. There was one man in coveralls sitting all alone near a vidscreen, a drink sitting untouched in front of him, watching his conversation with Abbas.

In the middle of the din of incomprehensible noise he heard the man speak clearly to him.

"You don't see me," he said.

Owen shook his head and looked down at the table—

"Garrett," Abbas was saying, "What the hell—" He'd lowered his hands from his head and was looking concerned.

"You're no alien," Owen said. "But I know someone who is." As Abbas began to protest, he added, "Look over to your right. There's an alien in this room, over near that screen."

"How do you know?"

"I can't say. But I'm sure. And I've got some questions for him." He felt his anger rising again, and it must've alarmed Abbas.

"Are you sure you're all right?"

"I'm more all right than I've been since I got dropped on this rock. Now I'm going to have a talk with this chump. You can help me or not, as you like." He pushed back from the table and nodded to Abbas, not looking at the figure he absolutely knew was an alien.

"I'm in," the *Negri*'s captain said. He took a quick glance where Owen had indicated, then stood up and began to walk in a circle, heading toward the table. Owen took the other direction; from across the room they caught each other's eyes as they closed on their target from two directions.

"Go have a seat," he heard. "Have another drink." The voice was superior and arrogant; the alien was watching him as he moved through the crowd.

He shrugged it off. Again he felt a moment of complete clarity and everything in the room became nothing more than background. The vidscreen above the alien's seat came to life, showing some sort of abstract rainbow pattern; red, orange, yellow, green, blue, violet light cascaded across the alien's face as it turned ever so slowly to face Owen. It reminded him of something, but he couldn't place it.

"I am not here," the alien said, and the edges of Owen's vision seemed to cloud. *I am not here,* he heard in his mind. The man began to smile as Owen stopped, unsure.

Suddenly the room snapped into focus. Damien Abbas' hands had clapped onto the alien's shoulders, turning him away from Owen.

"Is this the one, Lieutenant?" Abbas said loudly, looking away from the man's eyes. "This the one who insulted you?"

Before Owen could reply, the alien looked from him to Abbas and back, real fear in his eyes. "There's some mistake," he heard, and in his mind—*There's some mistake*—but the voice didn't sound quite so arch and superior now.

"No," Owen said. "No mistake." He grabbed one of the man's arms and Abbas grabbed the other. They half lifted, half marched the man out of the bar and onto the busy street.

"You've got two choices," Owen hissed as they pulled him into the alley between the Shield and the dispensary. "You can answer a few questions and then slide off into wherever you belong, or you can die right here and right now." He leaned close. "Time to choose."

"I will answer," the other said. "But I do not understand why—"

Owen shrugged and looked away, then turned and punched the alien hard in the stomach. He doubled over in pain; Abbas was amused and held the alien's neck down with his hand.

"*I'll* ask. *You* answer. What are you doing watching us?"

"Surveillance," the man managed to say. "Directions from ... from—"

"From?"

"Ór," the alien said.

"Or what?" Abbas answered.

"The Ór," the alien said, trying and failing to come free of Abbas' hand.

Owen grabbed the front of the alien's coverall and slammed him against the wall. "What the hell is an Ór?"

"Advisor," the alien managed. "Serves ... Great Queen. You are ... you are—"

"I'm what?"

"Dangerous. Ór ... ordered you to be ... watched. You were immune to the *k'th's's*."

"The—"

"*K'th's's*. You would not understand."

"Try me."

The alien looked at him with a sneer, which made Owen even more angry. But before he could wipe the expression off the other's face, the alien's expression changed, becoming wide-eyed and even more frightened.

"Eh," it said. "Uh."

Then it slumped to the ground and began to change shape.

"We told him we would kill him if he didn't answer," Abbas said, shrugging. "Looks like someone did it for us."

As they watched, the coveralls began to tear apart where limbs and body parts that were far from human began to protrude. When the transformation was complete, Owen could see that it was an alien like the ones from his dream.

"So," Abbas said. "You've been holding out on us, Garrett. How'd you know he was ... what? Whatever *that* is? And what's an Ór? And why are *you* 'dangerous'?"

"Same answer. I don't know how, I don't know what and I don't know why. All I know is that a whole bunch of people saw us frog-march some clown out of the Shield and he's ... well, pretty much dead now." He prodded the thing with the toe of one boot. "And if we wait around here, we're going to be pretty much dead as well."

"Don't be so sure." Abbas jerked his thumb at the hideous alien corpse sprawled behind him. "I don't see that guy anywhere. Do you? Now, come on—you're going to buy me a drink, and we're going to decide what this all means."

JACKIE'S LAST look at Adrianople Starbase was from the bridge of the *Councillor Rrith* as it jumped for Cle'eru, a zor colony twenty-three parsecs distant.

Most of her own task force was left behind: the *Due d'Enghien*, *Pappenheim* and *Tilly* were assigned to Admiral Hsien's direct command along with the *Cincinnatus*, the ship that had brought Admiral Tolliver and Sergei Torrijos to Cicero a lifetime ago. Hsien's orders did not involve offensive action at the outset; it would take him some time to gather his forces in any case.

The departure from Adrianople was far more quiet than the arrival. Within the Solar Empire, events proceeded much as they had been for the past several months.

As for the Duke of Burlington, it did not sit well with him to leave Adrianople without actual resolution of the board of inquiry, much less a clear understanding of what had transpired during the Sensitive ceremony in which the intransigent commodore had participated. But the exigencies of politics, especially those involving relations between the High Nest and the Imperial Household, overruled his desire for justice swift and sure—or indeed a tidy end of things.

William Clane Alvarez was an administrator first, a politician second and a Navy man third and only by association; he left the strategic planning to his fleet admirals at Pergamum, Boren, Denneva, Adrianople, Zhangdu and Eblaar. Still, the testimony of Commodore Laperriere troubled him enough to issue an order to all facilities and ships on-station to maintain General Quarters until further notice. Thus satisfied with his own predilection for caution, he concluded his business at Adrianople Base and, with all the pomp and ceremony proper for a First Lord and a peer of the realm, departed for Sol System to bring the unwelcome news to the emperor.

Jackie found the *Councillor Rrith* to be as uncomfortable as Adrianople Starbase, but for different reasons. She was among only a handful of humans on board; she was lodged in a guest suite normally reserved for distinguished persons of the High Nest. Fitted with special contact lenses, she was able to see normally in the reddish lighting favored by the zor. There was only a short stay aboard the *Rrith*—just under four Standard days, including the normal-space journeys to and from the jump points. The deference shown her by the crew of the ship seemed to border almost on awe; she and Ch'k'te dined at Captain R'le'e's table, and the captain's *alHyu* attended to their every comfort. The rest of the crew kept their distance.

Jackie's isolation aboard the *Rrith* was further emphasized by the new distance she felt between herself and Ch'k'te. He seemed regretful—even apologetic—that he had not recognized her earlier as the avatar of the great zor hero.

She hadn't had enough time to assimilate it herself. She had no duties aboard the *Rrith*; she devoted the trip to exercise and study. She fenced alone against simulated opponents. She reviewed her personal log entries, looking for something elusive that might have given her advance notice of what had happened at Cicero. She spent several hours in the gym. She read, concentrating on zor culture. Working herself to exhaustion and then reading herself to sleep seemed to help keep her mind occupied.

The night before they were to emerge from jump, Jackie had steeled herself to read the beginning of the Qu'u Legend. She had avoided doing so especially when tired, for fear that it might carry over into dreams—with unforeseen consequences. That fear finally made her realize that she would have to face it sooner or later; it was best to be well informed.

Instead of remaining in her cabin she had gone up on the ship's observation deck, mostly deserted during jump since there was nothing to see outside. It was there Ch'k'te found her, reading and making notes on her comp.

He stopped near the entrance to the spacious room, as if he were fearful of disturbing her. She turned away from her studies and indicated a spot opposite. He hesitated then bowed slightly and flew across to settle on the perch she had indicated.

"What can I do for you?" she asked, folding her hands on the table.

"I was interested in your well-being. How are you?" His wings assumed a different posture as he asked the question.

"I'm holding up." Jackie tapped the stylus against a low table a few times, testing it. "Under the circumstances, I'd guess I'm doing fine, dropped into an alien culture and left alone to flounder."

"You are not alone—"

"Damn right I'm *alone*," she interrupted, tossing the stylus on the table. "The High Chamberlain isn't even aboard. He wouldn't answer any questions; you've been keeping your distance—"

"There is still *si* Th'an'ya." Ch'k'te's wings moved again; she thought she'd seen that movement before when he spoke of his mate. He had chosen to use the prenomen for a deceased person, rather than the more familiar *li*, indicating that she had been his mate.

Jackie took a deep breath, realizing how difficult this must be for Ch'k'te even to discuss it. "I haven't talked to her since the night of the *Dsen'yen'ch'a.* I've been a bit scared to call her forth."

"She is—She is there to teach you. She would not hurt you."

"I don't really know that. I've scarcely met her; she keeps her own secrets."

"As do you."

"As do *you*. What the hell did she say to you? What's happened, Ch'k'te? You and I have been through a lot together, but now you're treating me like some sort of idol. I realize ... I know things have changed, that I have changed, in ways I don't understand yet. I can't do it alone."

"You will ultimately have to walk this path alone," he answered, looking down.

"You haven't answered my question."

"I am sorry—"

"I don't want you to be sorry!" She stood and walked away from her seat, facing away from him. "There is nothing to be sorry about."

She stopped, trying to hold her anger in. She turned around again to face Ch'k'te. She spread her hands wide. "We're all alone now. Here, in jump, away from everything and everyone. It's time to come clean.

"I want you to tell me what Th'an'ya said to you."

Ch'k'te did not say anything for a long time, then fluttered down from his perch and walked slowly to the desk where Jackie had been working. He leaned over the table where Jackie's notes were placed and spread his taloned hands wide.

"*se* Jackie, we have been comrades, both as commander and officer and as fellow warriors. Lately we have become close friends, sharing a closeness that People generally share only with their mates. I care for you and respect you; I would even venture to say that I ... love you, as a brother might love a sister.

"I realize also that the aspect of this entire affair that you most despise is that you feel yourself to be a mere pawn in whatever game is being played. You feel helpless, as if the Eight Winds are blowing this way and that, and you along with them. Yet at the very least, you are ... you have the potential to be ... Qu'u, the greatest warrior the People have ever known."

She appeared ready to interrupt; he held both hands up, as if he were trying to ward off her words with them. "Eight thousand pardons, *se* Jackie. Please let me finish.

"You ask me to—as you say—'come clean.' I will be painfully honest with you: you are *very much* a pawn in this most important of games. So am I. What is worse, my participation—and, to a lesser extent, yours—in this affair was preordained and long ago foreseen." He lowered his hands and folded them on the table.

"'Long ago'? The envoy's representative told me that a year ago—"

"Longer ago than a Standard year, *se* Jackie. Long before that."

"Who foresaw it? The High Lord?"

"I could not fathom whether the High Lord foresaw this, *se* Jackie. The precognition to which I refer belonged to my mate, *si—li*—Th'an'ya." He lowered his head; his voice softened to a whisper. "I know ... I feel ... that she loved me. But her joining with me, perhaps even her reason for ultimately *choosing* me, derived from the need for her *hsi* to be present to aid the new Qu'u ... to be here now, within you.

"She used *me* as a way to be present now, when the recovery of the *gyaryu* made her presence valuable and necessary." Once again his wings moved to convey some emotion to accompany his remarks.

"Surely you don't believe—"

"I have thought much about this in the few days since the Ordeal. My mate chose me knowing that I would be available, to play Hyos to your Qu'u." She could hardly hear him as he spoke the final few words. "She named me Hyos when we spoke in your quarters. That ... That is *why* she mated with me. It is why I was condemned to life after becoming *idju* at the hands of the Noyes-alien on Cicero. It is why I am here now.

"I am honored."

"And terribly hurt." Jackie sat opposite him and placed her hands on his forearms. He looked up at her, pain evident in his eyes.

"If this is all true," Jackie said, "and I haven't sorted it all out yet—then you must be feeling ..." She let the sentence trail off. "I don't really know what you must feel right now, though based on what you've said I can make a pretty good guess.

"I'm very sorry, Ch'k'te. I had no idea. I couldn't know, of course, but I should've been more sympathetic."

The sorrow in his eyes seemed to dissipate somewhat. "You have admonished me not to apologize for things beyond my control. You have the advantage of rank to enforce such a request, but I might suggest the same for you."

"Still, it's worse than having her just be gone, to know that she is—that her *hsi* is still present, but—"

"Such false pride is not seemly, either for a warrior of the High Nest or an officer in His Majesty's Navy. I ap—"

She shook her head, as if rejecting his apology before he could let loose the words.

"I will try to put it aside," he said instead.

"I know you will."

He stood, removing his hands from beneath hers. "By your leave, I should like to retire and contemplate."

"Perhaps we can talk later. I still have lots to learn." She gestured to the terminal and her notes. "I've only begun to study Qu'u, and I haven't made a lot of sense of it so far."

"After dinner," he offered. She nodded, smiling, though she still felt tentative. He bowed slightly, allowing his wings to spread out as he did so, and turned away to walk toward the door.

"Ch'k'te."

He turned to face her.

"Don't be a stranger."

He seemed to be laboring with the colloquialism; then understanding appeared in his eyes. He bowed again and departed the room, leaving Jackie alone.

W HEN HE left Jackie and returned to his quarters, Ch'k'te tried to compose himself for sleep but found his Inner Peace severely disturbed. It all seemed unpleasantly clear now: how he'd been brought together with *li* Th'an'ya, been posted to Cicero and finally had become Hyos to *se* Jackie's Qu'u.

The High Nest had arranged this—all of this—based on *hi* Ke'erl's dreams many turns ago: he had seen this—or *li* Th'an'ya had foreseen it.

Had they known he would become *idju* as well—yet condemned to life so that he might serve in this role? Now among the People again, Ch'k'te found it difficult to raise his head and look his fellow warriors in the eye: he felt himself diminished, a *Hssa* in *Ur'ta leHssa*, the Valley of Lost Souls, unable to raise his glance to look upon the Fortress of Despite. *ha* T'te'e had assured him that he was not, but from the time he had been Dominated by the *esGa'uYe* at Cicero Down he had known that he must find the proper time and place to transcend the Outer Peace.

The Qu'u legend was something he knew well—all warriors did. From the moment Qu'u had crossed his first *shNa'es'ri* he was committed to the path that led to the Fortress of Despite; if *se* Jackie were one of the People, she would know this, and would know the Fortress of Despite would mean that she, too, would transcend the Outer Peace. As one overcome by an *esGa'uYe* at the very beginning of the tale, it was an end that Ch'k'te himself would have gladly embraced. Instead *se* Jackie would be Qu'u—a fitting choice, he knew—but one that took the simple end away from him. *enGa'e'Li* was not a choice and would never be again, for he must be Hyos.

Still, it seemed to him there was something about this flight that diverged from the straight path. The High Chamberlain and the High Lord sought the will of *esLi* by applying the Law of Similar Conjunction, in which a flight with the same pattern as one chosen in the path might yield the same results. It all depended on Jackie following the flight to the end … yet, he knew, she might not do that. The Law of Similar Conjunction was like a complex machine, depending on known principles and physical laws. If the participants did not follow these principles and laws, the outcome would be unknown, perhaps even hidden by the wing of *esGa'u.*

He thought about this and offered prayer to esLi, until he was finally able to retire. But his sleep was filled with haunted dreams.

chapter 17

THE LEGEND OF QU'U (continued)

… THEY FLEW THROUGH A NARROW MOUNTAIN PASS
IN THE RANGE THAT IS CALLED THE SPINE OF THE
WORLD, SEARCHING FOR   [Spine of the World]
THE HERMITAGE OF S'TAREU. IT WAS FURTHER THAN
QU'U HAD EVER TRAVELED FROM E'YEN; EVERY
SHADOW SEEMED TO CONTAIN A WING OF *ESGA'U*.

IN TIME THE PATTERN OF THE FOREST BELOW FORMED
THE GLYPH *LI'HS'E'E*,   [The Concealed Truth]
WHICH MEANS "THE CONCEALED TRUTH"; QU'U AND
HYOS DESCENDED THROUGH THE TREES AND FOUND
THE HERMITAGE, JUST AS THE SERVANT OF *ESLI* HAD
SAID. THE HERMITAGE WAS A STRUCTURE OF TWINED
WOOD, A SERIES OF TREES THAT HAD BEEN CAUSED TO
GROW TOGETHER; AS THEY APPROACHED, THEY SAW
S'TAREU WAITING FOR THEM ON AN UPPER LEVEL. HE
DESCENDED TO THE FOREST FLOOR AND OFFERED THE
STANCE OF POLITE APPROACH.

"*SE* QU'U," S'TAREU SAID, "BE WELCOME TO MY
HOME."

"I WAS DIRECTED TO THIS PLACE BY—" QU'U BEGAN,
BUT THE HERMIT RAISED HIS HANDS.

"I KNOW WHY YOU ARE HERE, HONORED WARRIOR.

          [Honor to *esLi*]

AND YOU AND YOUR COMPANION HAVE BEEN SENT
HERE IN THE SERVICE OF THE LORD OF THE GOLDEN
CIRCLE. I AM HONORED TO SERVE THAT LORD AS WELL;
AND HE HAS ENTRUSTED ME WITH THE *HSI* OF ONE
WHO WILL ACCOMPANY YOU ON YOUR ARDUOUS
JOURNEY."

       *   *   *

"THE *HSI* ..." QU'U ARRANGED HIS WINGS IN A

[Duty of the Warrior]

RESPECTFUL PATTERN, "I FEAR RISKING THE *HSI OF*
ANOTHER AT THE FORTRESS OF DESPITE."

"THIS IS A NOBLE STATEMENT, *SE* QU'U," S'TAREU
ANSWERED. "BUT YOU WILL CLIMB THE PERILOUS STAIR
WITHOUT COMPANIONS. WHEN YOU ENTER THE
FORTRESS OF DESPITE, YOU WILL BE ALONE."

During the wars between man and zor, almost any world with an atmosphere and climate suitable for warm-blooded oxygen-breathers was a target for colonization by either side. For their part, the zor preferred planets with lighter gravities and redder suns; humans were more inclined toward brighter primaries. After the Treaty of E'rene'e, worlds were chosen for colonization based on ecology rather than distance from Sol System or the zor Core Stars; after nearly three full generations, the worlds under the authority of the High Nest were spread out across the Solar Empire from the Core to the space near Adrianople Starbase.

Cle'eru had been bypassed by the military; it lay some distance from trade routes and its system was hazardous to navigate. Sometime in the recent past— by cosmic standards—there had been a collision between the moon of the habitable planet and some extrasolar object, perhaps a comet or large meteorite. The impact had resulted in numerous crater impacts on the surface of the main habitable world, and—most unusual for an inner planet—a Saturnlike ring of rock and dust. There was also a wide belt of debris and rock in the inner system. While all of these features made Cle'eru enough of an astronomical oddity to attract scientific scholars from across the Empire, it also made the system a navigational hazard of the first order.

The zor had settled Cle'eru less than ten years after the Hierate treaty. The world had a gravity of six-tenths of a Standard gravity and an orange-red primary that was daily occluded by the ring. Both the local gravity and the sun's color were ideal for the zor.

From low orbit, Jackie and Ch'k'te shuttled to the surface. Stepping onto a world—even though it was no more than the black tarmac of a starport landing-field—was somehow reassuring.

As she stood on the field looking up at the sky, she could pick out tiny shapes flying outside the airspace of the port—zor flying under their own power. The breeze blowing across the field ruffled Ch'k'te's wings as he stood next to her. To Jackie, it looked as if he were ready to take flight himself.

All the fuss about Qu'u had prepared her for a reception when she reached solid ground; instead they were left out in the open, waiting for cargo and their gear to be unloaded. After several minutes Ch'k'te picked out an aircar approaching from the direction of the terminal. It presently pulled up alongside.

A uniformed zor leaned out of the driver's side and said, "*se* Commodore Laperriere?"

Not "mighty Qu'u?" she thought. Then she added, to herself: *Word must not have reached the frontier yet.*

"I'm Laperriere," she said, glancing sideways at Ch'k'te. "Are you our transport?"

"Yes, *se* Commodore," the zor replied. He inserted a talon into a receptacle on his dashboard and the rear hatch, and two back doors slid open. "I am to take you to your lodging, though my orders are to take you to another destination first."

"Another destination? Where else?"

"A ... courtesy visit," the zor answered, "according to my orders, *se* Commodore." They stowed their bags and climbed into the backseat. The zor pilot engaged the car and took it up in the air; shortly they were flying along over a major city.

It was Jackie's first extended visit to a zor world. The scenery was alien below; the car traveled at about two hundred klicks, at an altitude that provided a good view of the buildings. She could see zor flying below the car at slower speeds, descending to land on platforms that extended everywhere from the thin, angular buildings. Unlike human architecture, which had gradually progressed to a point of geometric abstractness, zor structures were intricate and extensively decorated. They bore huge spidery patterns on their sides which Jackie knew to be *hRni'i,* visual and tactile markings that indicated not only the purpose of the building but also its ownership, history and (for all she knew) present market value and number of available rooms. If she were a zor, she could have flown along the walls of the building and read the *hRni'i* with her hands as well as with her eyes.

Such a pity to be without wings. She remembered the voice of Shrnu'u and she had a floating memory of him, his wings held in a mocking position.

"Bastard," she said, burying a fist in her open hand and wondering to herself whether she meant Shrnu'u or the High Chamberlain.

"Pardon?" Ch'k'te asked, solicitous.

"Nothing. I was just ... Nothing."

THE CAR touched down on a wide landing-bay, six or seven levels— perhaps thirty meters—above ground level. There was no railing around the platform. *Of course not,* she thought to herself as she disembarked, a meter away from a sheer drop. *If you step off the edge, you just have to spread your wings.*

"I am to wait for you here," their driver said, and gestured toward a young zor approaching the car. The driver picked up a comp from the seat and activated it, perhaps settling in for a long wait.

They exchanged bows and pleasantries with the zor, who was an *alHyu* for the person they were to meet. He led them into the building, along a railingless balcony that overlooked a sheer drop to the lobby, which was fitted out as a garden. They passed under an archway and came into a sitting-room; there a single zor was perched, as if expecting their arrival. The *alHyu* bowed and left them alone with their host.

The zor was old. She'd never really seen an old zor before; the wrinkled face and drooping wings, the whitened proboscis and balding head, were a bit shocking. The elder one fluttered to the part of the room where they sat; he went to an ornate flagon from a side table and slowly, almost painfully, poured some clear liquid into three exquisite cups, one for each of them. He took one cup at a time from the table and offered it to each guest; then, taking the last one, he slowly made his way back to his own perch. Jackie watched the entire process—she could not look away: it was a compelling scene from the moment she'd first seen him until the time he settled back onto the perch, the disk of *esLi* silhouetting him from behind.

"So," he said, wrapping his taloned hands around the cup and rocking back and forth slightly. He reached one talon into the liquid and drew a small circle in the air.

"So," Jackie repeated.

"So, you are probably wondering what you are doing here."

"The question had crossed my mind, Honored One—"

"Fah," the old zor said, raising his cup. "*esLiHeYar.*" He tossed the contents down his throat. "Aaah," he added after a moment.

Jackie sipped at her cup, which she supposed contained some kind of tea. A fiery liquid several orders of magnitude stronger coursed down her throat, numbing her lips as it passed. "*esLi HeYar,*" she managed to whisper. "What the hell—"

"It is called *egeneh.* Best served warm. Can I pour you some more?"

"Perhaps in my next life, Honored One," she replied.

"Enough of *that,*" he said. "Or else I will feel obliged to lapse into 'mighty Qu'u' every second sentence. *esLi* knows you have probably heard that enough in the last few days.

"I saw you observing me a short time ago, *se* Commodore. *An old one,* you thought. *How unusual.* No, do not apologize," he continued, pouring himself another cupful of *egeneh.* "Even those of my own race are taken aback by my extreme longevity. I remember—Ah, well. Let us not get me started. When I was young, there were no old ones for a simple reason: Your race was busy killing members of my race before we could grow old." His wings altered to a different position; Jackie supposed it conveyed sorrow, but she couldn't be sure.

"Exactly how old are you?—if one may ask such a question."

"Before I answer, let me put your mind at ease. You may ask any question you wish within these walls. However, let me warn you that if I am able, I *will* answer. Choose carefully the questions you ask; and be sure that you wish for me to answer them.

"As to your question, I am one hundred and twenty-four Standard years old, *se* Commodore."

"Jackie."

"Jackie." He thought about the name for a moment, as if he were tasting it. "*se* Jackie. I am S'reth."

"A pleasure." Jackie set the *egeneh*-cup on the arm of her chair and sat forward, her hands folded. "You will really answer all of my questions? No mysticism, no bullshit?"

Ch'k'te shifted uneasily on his perch and looked across at Jackie.

S'reth's wing-position changed. "After a lifetime of studying humanity, I believe I can discern what you mean. Yes, I will answer you directly without any, as you say, 'bullshit.'" The obscenity sounded very strange, being expelled from the mouth of a zor. "Where shall I begin?"

"At the beginning."

"As you wish. Let me see." S'reth settled on his perch. "It is … the wish of the High Lord that you undertake a difficult, perhaps even desperate, mission for the High Nest. Naturally, the High Nest cannot demand this service of you; you are not one of the People. Even the rather clumsy artifice of transferring you to our naval service will not change that biological fact.

"The mission is the recovery of the *gyaryu*, the Talon of State for the High Nest. It was taken somehow during the attack on Cicero by the *esGa'uYal*. It is likely still intact, because our—enemies—would certainly recognize its intrinsic power. If the *esGa'uYal* were to learn to employ the *gyaryu*, its use against us would likely be devastating; therefore, the need to recover it is great.

"The High Lord dreamed that the sword would be lost and then recovered by the greatest warrior of legend: the first *Gyaryu'har*, Qu'u."

"The High Lord knew for sure that the sword would be lost?"

"It was part of the dream, yes."

"He sent the old man to Cicero, and he knew—"

"It was part of the *dream*, *se* Jackie," S'reth replied, as if that explained everything. "The High Lord *knew* that it would be taken, and that Qu'u would appear to recover it. One was necessary in order for the other to occur. In this terrible hour, with the peril of the *esGa'uYal* at talon's length, the High Lord believed that we needed the strength of Qu'u to guard us."

"And they got *me* instead."

"The High Lord is mad, *se* Jackie." Ch'k'te's wings altered position into an unfamiliar pattern and he shifted on his perch at this statement. "But I assure you that your role as Qu'u is neither a disappointment nor a surprise to him. Your presence here is *not* an accident.

"You see, in the High Lord's dream, Qu'u had a human face."

For a moment the image touched off something familiar in Jackie's mind, but she couldn't put her finger on it.

Ch'k'te's wings changed position again and his talons extended a few centimeters in surprise. This revelation was news to him.

"Go on," she said, trying hard to restrain her anger. She knew that S'reth was only a messenger, not the cause of the present situation.

"I sense you are upset, *se* Jackie. I must remind you that the High Lord's distress was greater, for he knew what was to happen. He and *se* Sergei have been friends and brothers for his entire life.

"It pained him to send the *Gyaryu'har* to almost certain death. It frightened him to place the *gyaryu* in the hands of the enemy. But … it was part of the *dream*."

"Did *se* Sergei know?"

"He was a warrior—"

"*I'm* a warrior, *se* S'reth. Are you saying that *se* Sergei would have willingly walked into the hands of the—the *esGa'uYal*—and handed over the sword that has been a part of his body and soul for half his life—as a pawn of some damn game of the High Lord's?"

"*se* Jackie—" Ch'k'te touched her arm, coming out of a stony silence almost for the first time.

"*se* Jackie," S'reth interrupted, "I would hardly classify the fulfillment of the High Lord's prescient dream as a 'game.'"

"What *would* you call it?"

S'reth set his cup on the side table and resettled his wings. They were so thin as to be almost translucent, catching the glow of the indirect lighting behind the disk of *esLi* on the far wall. "I would call it the seeds of madness."

"Well, goddamn it, *I'm* not that mad."

"But the High Lord still *is*, *se* Jackie. And he still dreams … and I regret to say that what he dreams is still a prescient vision of the future."

"What did he dream about Qu'u?"

"He dreamed that Qu'u would return with the *gyaryu*, and with it he will hold the *esGa'uYal* away from the Flight of the People."

"As it happened in the legend."

S'reth did not acknowledge her remark, though his wings rose slightly at her comment. "We believe that in order to save the People, and humanity as well, we must follow the legend as closely as possible. The High Chamberlain has determined that you are to be Qu'u. Therefore we must proceed on that basis. Your companion *se* Ch'k'te must assume the role of Hyos; thus also I will serve in the role of M'hara, who taught Qu'u of the Plain of Despite. There is another role, but no one has filled it as yet: that of E're'a, the spirit-guide. Perhaps someone will come forward."

Jackie exchanged glances with Ch'k'te.

"*se* S'reth, let's assume I'm willing to accept all you've told me so far." She ran a finger along the delicate traceries on her *egeneh*-cup. "Fine. I'm Qu'u, Ch'k'te is my companion, you're my teacher and I'm supposed to fetch back the *gyaryu* from the enemy—the vuhls, the *esGa'uYal*, whatever you choose to call them.

"Isn't there a practical aspect missing here? The Plain of Despite—I'm willing to accept that it actually exists even though it seems to me that it's part of the dream world, the spirit world. *esGa'u* exists, but he's part of the same world. In *this* world, 'the World That Is,' the *real* enemy has the real *gyaryu* somewhere on some planet, probably under heavy guard. When Ch'k'te and I mind-linked with *se* Sergei back on Cicero, we traveled through the spirit world, while our bodies remained behind. No amount of dreaming will actually retrieve the *gyaryu,* even if somehow we can use that method to locate it.

"Aren't we going to have to jump somewhere, sneak our way in, steal back the sword and sneak our way out again?"

"Of course."

"And isn't this going to be damn near impossible against aliens who can Dominate minds and who already reamed us both inside and out before we pulled out of Cicero?"

"Those facts do present an obstacle, yes."

"An obstacle? An *obstacle*? Those facts make this operation an impossibility. We can't do it. *I*—can't do it."

S'reth didn't answer. Instead he lowered himself carefully to the floor and went to the flagon and refilled his cup. He flew slowly back to his perch, made the same gesture with his talon after dipping it in the cup, and took the cup in a shaking hand and sipped slowly from it.

"*esLiHeYar*," he whispered to no one in particular, then continued. "When Qu'u and his companion Hyos left *Ne'es Li'e* after being released from their duties in guarding the fortress, they traveled many days in the wilderness until they reached a hermitage. They had been told that there they would receive instructions on how to carry out their mission. When they arrived, a message was waiting: Servants of the Deceiver were already abroad, looking for them in particular. Qu'u knew he had been chosen for this special duty but could not see how he could accomplish his mission when he was facing the Lord of Despite, who surely could find him wherever he went.

"The hermit replied as follows: *'Despite has more enemies than it can count; the true warrior knows but one.'*

"*esGa'u* did not know who the Lord *esLi* would choose to perform this task, but that a true warrior would recognize *esGa'u* or his servants readily enough. It is possible that the *esGa'uYal* have your scent, *se* Jackie, but I do not believe it is certain. Just as Qu'u could venture unrecognized onto the Plain of Despite, there is some reason to believe that you might be able to pass behind the shadows and enter alien space without being detected as the avatar of Qu'u. It is how you deal with the situation afterward that should be your concern."

"*se* S'reth speaks truly, *se* Jackie," Ch'k'te said, leaning forward and then settling his wings. "It is possible that the *esGa'uYal* that infiltrated Cicero might have been able to provide those on the edge of the system with descriptions of all of the base personnel, but how would they distinguish you and me from the hundreds of others?"

"We'll be pretty obvious. Really, a human and a zor surrounded by aliens—"

"If they take prisoners, they will be both *naZora'i* and People, *se* Jackie. They captured several starships and at least one fighter craft."

"We believe the *esGa'uYal* have retained the prisoners they captured," S'reth said. "You and *se* Ch'k'te would simply be two more prisoners."

"Who could have provided them with everything they needed to know." Jackie looked from S'reth to Ch'k'te. "They read *minds,* remember?"

"I most certainly do remember." She saw Ch'k'te's talons clench and reached out a hand to touch his arm. Then she froze, noticing that S'reth was paying close attention to the exchange.

She withdrew her hand and steepled her fingers in her lap. "I suppose that means we go to Sargasso, then."

"It does seem the logical place to begin," S'reth replied, slowly rocking back and forth on his perch. "It is the entrance to the Plain of Despite."

THEY WERE quartered across the city from S'reth's home in a high-rise hotel that catered both to zor and humans. Jackie's arrival had been anticipated; she was given a suite that provided human amenities—comfortable couches and chairs, a bed and 'fresher that accommodated her. It also had a shrine to *esLi* in an alcove with a torus for contemplation and facilities for receiving zor guests. Lighting and the autokitchen accommodated both races.

Jackie and Ch'k'te returned from their meeting with S'reth weary and not very talkative. Ch'k'te tried to excuse himself to go to his own rooms, but Jackie ordered him directly into her sitting-room, voice-locking the door to the suite behind her.

The lighting was set for zor eyes; she left her contact lenses in. She settled into an armchair. Ch'k'te ran a talon over one of the *hRni'i* on the wall and settled onto an extruded perch.

"All right," she said. "Now we know what's supposed to happen. We're supposed to follow the legend of Qu'u, with me in the starring role. You represent Hyos, who is Qu'u's faithful companion. Is that right, Ch'k'te?"

"That appears to be the case."

"And there's even something for old S'reth to do—he's the representation of M'hara the Sage."

"It does seem to fit the legend."

"But according to S'reth, we also need E're'a the Spirit Guide. Does anyone come to mind who might represent her?"

"You are begging the question, Jackie. I am sure *se* S'reth would reach that conclusion if you had told him that you carry Th'an'ya's *hsi*. I am also sure that you are not attempting to bring me to a *sSurch'a*. Where does this line of reasoning lead?"

"At the Academy, they always taught us that flying solo will get you killed sooner or later. Since I dearly hope to survive this little adventure, I intend to coordinate this little team of ours. That means discussing the plan with all of the team members."

" ... All?"

"All that are going ashore. That means you, me and Th'an'ya. It's time all three of us discussed this."

Ch'k'te shifted uncomfortably from claw to claw. "As you wish."

Th'an'ya? Jackie thought, trying to relax her mind into a receptive state.

I am here.

We need to talk—all three of us. How can I help you appear? Do you need a mirror, or—

No such devices are necessary, se *Jackie. Let me concentrate through you for a moment.*

Jackie closed her eyes, and then opened them again when she heard Ch'k'te's sharp intake of breath. Th'an'ya, in the same peach-colored robe, holding the same wood staff, appeared before them. She inclined her head to Ch'k'te and bowed slightly to Jackie.

"*se* S'reth has suggested we begin our journey by going to the system where the two vessels disappeared and where Admiral Tolliver apparently went mad.

There, it seems, we'll try to assimilate ourselves among other humans and zor, outwit our mind-Dominating, amoral, alien captors, find our way to where they're keeping the *gyaryu,* steal it out from under their noses and get away without shedding a drop of blood.

"Do you like the plan so far?"

"There are some elements that need clearing up," Th'an'ya said at last, her voice sounding thin and melodic pronouncing words in the human tongue. "I can sense ... a sort of amusement, *se* Jackie, even though it is clear that you take this affair seriously. Am I missing some vital aspect of your exposition?"

"It is called 'sarcasm,'" Ch'k'te replied, as Jackie covered a smile and then a laugh with her hand. "She is joking about—That is to say, she is laughing in the face of ..."

He finally gave up, settling his wings in some position that was significant to the two zor but that escaped her. By this time she had totally collapsed into laughter, the tension and resentment of the past several days rushing out of her in fits and starts, until she at last regained some semblance of composure. All the time, Ch'k'te and Th'an'ya's image waited patiently, looking from Jackie to each other.

"As a mere tool of *esLi's* will," Th'an'ya said at last, "it is beyond me to fully understand how He could have condemned us to life after allowing a race such as humanity to conquer us. *le* Ch'k'te, you show great adeptness and depth in understanding to be able to cooperate with *se* Jackie."

"I'm sorry," Jackie said after a moment. "It just ... The whole plan seemed so absurd that I couldn't help it." She looked from Ch'k'te to Th'an'ya, who were waiting patiently for her to continue.

"We apparently have a role for you in this little comic-opera, Th'an'ya, though I suppose you knew it already. You're supposed to be the spirit-guide for Qu'u and his companions. Is that what you envisioned?"

"I expect to be such, yes. With my skills and your own inner strength, you should be able to resist casual invasion of your mind by the *esGa'uYal,* just as E're'a was the protector of mighty Qu'u. But you still do not seem convinced that this is the proper course."

"No, I don't. I still feel as if I'm walking into this blind and unprepared, waiting for things to happen to me rather than taking charge of the situation."

"It does not fit with your Academy training, *se* Jackie?"

"What the hell do you mean by that?"

For a moment the image of Th'an'ya wavered and Jackie cursed under her breath, realizing that her anger was interfering. She willed herself to be calm.

"The People have a different view on the matter of 'destiny' than humans. We believe that things will be as *esLi* wills them to be, and that the Eight Winds will blow where they will, regardless of our desires. Still, the wise person tastes the direction of the wind, and turns his wings to the best advantage.

"If we are to sense what direction to take, it is important for us to understand what *esLi* intends for us to do. This analysis will be most familiar to you, *se* Jackie—for correctly discerning the right course may make the difference between life and death."

"And all we have to go on is the legend of Qu'u."

"It is the basis for this endeavor."

"From what I've read, he sort of stumbles his way along until he reaches the underground passage to the Plain of Despite, and only then realizes that he's on the enemy's playing field and that any mistake will be his last."

"And then," said Th'an'ya, "he must prove to himself just what kind of warrior he truly is."

AFTER THE incident at the bar there was a different dream. Owen was aboard the alien ship again, but this time he was lying in a chamber, on the same spongy, slightly concave floor. He couldn't move, and his head was pounding. He knew why: the aliens had been probing his mind, gathering information.

What light there was came from no apparent source; it was bluish and dim. Still, it hurt his eyes to look around so he kept them hooded, squinting at the curved walls and ceiling. On one wall he saw a luminous oval pattern that shifted frequently, like a malfunctioning 3-V. He guessed he was being watched.

If he had given them everything they wanted, he reasoned, they'd have fed him to the lions by now. So that hadn't happened, at least. But if they were having trouble extracting information, what did that mean? He wasn't a Sensitive; he was no more resistant to mind control than ... than—

Than Devra Sidra or Aaron Schoenfeld, Gary Cox, Steve Leung or Anne Khalid. They'd had no chance; the aliens had made them attack each other. They'd all died in Cicero System; all except him.

"he will do," a voice said from somewhere. Across from him, a red band of light appeared on the wall, shimmering and wavering.

"the other will learn from him," another voice said. This time it was a violet band of color. As Owen watched, four other colored bands appeared between them: orange, yellow, green, blue.

"HE WILL PROVIDE INSTRUCTION." Yellow this time.

"THE OTHER WILL MAKE GOOD USE OF HIS SKILLS." Orange.

"THE DESIRED RESULT WILL BE OBTAINED." Blue.

"THE EXPECTED OUTCOME WILL NOT BE AVOIDED." Green. "THEIR PATHS WILL CROSS."

"THEY WILL NOT AVOID MEETING." Blue again. "THE AGENT WILL DIRECT THIS."

"What are you talking about?" Owen said, feeling for his pistol, which was missing, of course. "What paths? What—"

"CONVEY HIM," said Red.

"CONVEY HIM," the others repeated.

There was a flash of light, and suddenly there was a path across the floor of the room consisting of six colored stripes—each extending from one of the bands on the wall Owen reached out and touched the floor under him; he found it smooth, as if whatever composed the surface had been sanded flat. The nearest wall felt the same way.

"THIS PATH WILL LEAD YOU FROM THIS VESSEL," Blue's voice said from everywhere at once, "WALK UPON IT. DO NOT STEP OFF."

"Not till I get some answers," Owen said. He didn't really expect to get any, but thought it was worth a shot. "The aliens wouldn't tell me anything, but maybe you will. Who are you?"

"BLUE," the voice said. The blue band undulated, "AND THE ANSWER TO THE NEXT QUESTION IS 'NO.'"

"Are you working for or against the aliens?" He asked it anyway, and tried to piece together what the answer meant.

"YOU HAVE VERY LITTLE TIME," Red said, "LEAVE THIS PLACE. DO NOT STEP OFF THE PATH."

"And if I don't?"

"YOU WILL DIE HERE." Green, "WE WILL FIND ANOTHER."

"To do what?" He didn't want to stay; he stood up and reached a foot out toward the rainbow path. He could see it leading beyond the confines of the chamber into darkness beyond.

"YOU WILL TEACH," the six colors said all at once.

"TEACH," they repeated as he took a few steps and watched the alien ship recede behind him.

"TEACH," they said again as the darkness of jump surrounded him.

"'TEACH.'" DAMIEN Abbas looked Owen Garrett in the eye.

"This is a pretty big stretch, Garrett. You're telling me that you *walked* off the alien ship on a rainbow bridge—walked all the way here? And that you're supposed to see something to—Some 'other'? Teach what?"

"Well ..." Owen pointed to his eyes with his thumb and index finger. "I can see them, can't I? We had one drop dead on us, and I've marked two or three others since then. Maybe I'm supposed to teach *that*."

"Well, teach it to *me*, then. If the aliens decide to come and take you away, there'll be no one to do what you can do."

"I wish I could. But I don't know how. I don't even know how this works—but now I know why. And I know one other thing."

"What's that?"

"There's something out there that isn't on the same side as the bugs—in fact, it's more powerful than they are. I don't think it's any friend of ours, either, but it *did* get me off that ship and to this planet for a reason. If I were to guess, it would be because the rest of you are here.

"I think I was brought here to help you. We need to get off this world, and I've been given some talent that will help us do it and some powerful allies to help make it possible."

"What do you have in mind?"

"I think we should steal the *Negri Sembilan*."

"Are you *crazy*? Something that big would be impossible to take. Besides, the Overlords can *read minds*."

"Only if they get close enough." Owen pointed to his eyes again. "They're not going to get close—and they can't control all of us at once. I think they're counting on blending in, Captain. That's just not going to happen."

chapter 18

THE LEGEND OF QU'U (continued)

... QU'U AND HIS COMPANION TRAVELED MANY DAYS AND NIGHTS
FROM THE FOREST OF THE HERMIT. THEY
FOLLOWED HIS
DIRECTIONS AS   [Burden of Day]
BEST THEY COULD. BY DAY, FATHER SUN'S HEAT BEAT
DOWN UPON THEM AS THEY FLEW OVER EVER-ROCKIER
LANDS. BY NIGHT THE MOONS SILVERED THEIR
WINGS AS THEY FLEW EVER NORTHWARD.

QU'U FELT THE HOT BREATH OF PURSUIT, AND COULD
                                              [Approaching Danger]
SCARCELY BRING HIMSELF TO STOP HIS PROGRESS UNTIL
HIS FATIGUE OVERWHELMED HIM.

QU'U WAS YET YOUNG: HE WAS BOTH UNCHANGED BY
THE EVENTS THAT WERE TO COME AND UNTROUBLED
                                              [Cloak of Defense]
BY THE RESPONSIBILITIES THAT WOULD COME LATER.
STILL, HE HAD NEVER FELT AS DRIVEN. HE KNEW THAT
THE SERVANTS OF *ESGA'U* WERE ABROAD AND HE
BELIEVED THAT THEY HAD TO KNOW HIS DESTINATION.
NO MATTER HOW MUCH HE FEARED IT, HOWEVER, THIS
COULD NOT DETER HIM—AND HE DID FEAR IT,
THOUGH HE COULD NOT   [Duty of the Warrior]
COMMUNICATE THIS TO HIS COMPANION, HYOS,
WHO FOLLOWED HIM DEVOTEDLY. ALL THE WHILE, THE
PRESENCE OF E'RE'A REASSURED HIM THAT HE AND
HYOS DID NOT TRAVEL ALONE ...

                                              [Protection of *esLi*]
BUT ALSO THAT HIS LIFE HAD BEEN IRREVOCABLY
CHANGED BY THE NEW MISSION THAT THE LORD *ESLI*
HAD LAID OUT FOR HIM.

AS QU'U AND HYOS CONTINUED NORTHWARD, THEY

COULD SEE MOUNTAINS CLIMBING HIGHER OVER THE HORIZON
UNTIL THEY   [Confronting the Icewall]
CROUCHED, MALIGNANTLY, ACROSS THEIR ENTIRE
FIELD OF VIEW. AS THEY TRAVELED, THE WEATHER
GREW EVER COLDER. WHILE IN FLIGHT, THERE WAS NO
DEFENSE AGAINST THE BITING WINDS AND CRUEL
RAINS, BUT WHEN THEY WERE AFOOT THEY COULD
WRAP THEMSELVES IN CLOAKS AND MOVE LIKE *ARTHA,*
GHOSTLIKE AND SHROUDED.

AT LAST, ON A COLD AND STORMY DAY, THEY CAME IN
SIGHT OF THE LONG CANYON THAT HAD BEEN
DESCRIBED TO THEM. THEY PERCHED FOR SEVERAL
MOMENTS, LISTENING TO THE   [Winds of Despite]
SCREAMING GALES THAT WHIRLED AROUND THE PLACE
AND WATCHING AS THE CLOUDS SCUDDED ACROSS THE
SKY, QUICKLY FORMING AND UNFORMING HORRIFIC
PATTERNS, QU'U GATHERED   [The Drawn *Chya*]
HIS COURAGE AT LAST AND FLEW DOWNWARD TOWARD
THE FAR END OF THE CANYON, WHERE HIS FATE
AWAITED.

For three days Jackie waited for S'reth to summon her back to his presence. His first instructional session after their initial meeting had been—in a word—uninformative. S'reth was even more obtuse and full of anecdotes than the average zor—not that she had any real basis for comparison. She felt the overwhelming need to be patient and careful; it made her even more frustrated with the situation, and particularly with herself and her own lack of control over it.

With no choice but to let the situation control her, she relaxed as best she could and allowed it to happen. *Let the Eight Winds blow you where they will,* as Th'an'ya would say. Still, regardless of her unique position and the burden of the mission, she was still an outsider.

She had begun to occasionally register impressions from the zor in whose society she moved. She tried her best to work with Ch'k'te and especially Th'an'ya to order her mind to deal with these impressions, but it was difficult at best. Still, she received mostly insulting comments such as, "Here comes the *artha*"; it conjured up the image of a four-legged furry creature moving furtively through the mist. It was more of an expression of pity than of contempt, but it beckoned back to a more frightening memory, a sensation from the *Dsen'yen'ch'a.*

... chained to the ground, wingless ...
Such a pity.

She was something of a celebrity on Cle'eru, or more properly a cause célèbre: the human population, several hundred diplomats and merchants, were a society apart. They were ground-bound and uninvolved ... uninformed. Few among them spoke more than a few words of the Highspeech. This was by choice rather than by design, or so it seemed. The humans on this mostly-zor world had a desire to be somewhere else, where the sun wasn't as red, the commerce of human society so distant or the majority of the population so removed, high above them in their own eyries. They didn't seem to hide their contempt very well.

Jackie's arrival on Cle'eru was an occasion; her continued association with the zor was something of a marvel, to be gossiped about in astonishment and with a rather vague horror. Even with allowances being made for her status as an officer in His Majesty's Navy, it was remarkable that she had somehow crossed the line.

Every day when she returned from exercising or touring or some other diversion, her hotel-room comp would be clogged with messages. They were mostly invitations, but sometimes they were obsequious requests for favors or assistance. Disdaining the former was almost as easy as ignoring the latter; but she did desire human companionship. She finally accepted an opportunity to dine at the house of an influential merchant factor on the same night the Imperial consul would be present.

Though not an official occasion, she discarded the idea of evening dress in favor of her own commodore's uniform. She wasn't sure whether she should be wearing it as a member of the zor naval service, but it was clear to her there wasn't a soul on Cle'eru who would gainsay her the right. Thus attired, and armored with the confidence that every flag officer possesses in full dress, she set off alone around the dinner hour to the factor's residence in the human-occupied section of the capital city or, as the zor called it colloquially (and insultingly), *Hu'uren*—"Lowtown."

"COMMODORE, SO *good* to have you with us." As Sir Johannes Xavier Sharpe extended his hand to shake hers, a servant hovered nearby to take her cap and gloves. Jackie took the offered hand: it was ice-cold, in keeping with the chill temperature of the house. She could hear the soft whir of an overworked air circulator, setting her teeth even more on edge. "Thank you, Mr. Sharpe. It's a pl—"

"Hansie, *please.* Call me Hansie; everyone does. May I call you Jacqueline? Such a *beautiful* name," he hurried on, before she could tell him what she thought of the idea. Sharpe was a short, mousy-looking man with darting eyes; she realized she'd taken an instant dislike to him.

"French, isn't it? We've worked so hard at homogeneity these past few centuries it's hard to recall our ancestors' cultural identities. My many-times-great-grandfather"—he waved airily toward a strikingly ugly portrait—"Sir Francis Xavier Sharpe, was English, while I am named for my great-uncle Johann, who was, as you might imagine, a German. One was France's friend in past centuries, the other her deadly enemy. What does that make us, do you suppose?" He smiled, baring his teeth like some pathetic carnivore.

Total strangers, she was inspired to say. "England and Germany were both friend and enemy to France in times past," she replied, as she let him lead her toward the drawing-room, from which random bits of conversation swirled. "I'm actually from Dieron, Mr. Sh—Hansie. So I think we could start from square one."

"Splendid! Well put." He clapped his hands and smiled again. "Well put indeed, madam. Your reputation scarcely does you justice. Allow me to introduce you to the consul. Excuse me," he added before she could follow up his last remark. With a swish of protosilk and a gesture to a tall fair-haired woman in a gown with an unobtrusive emblem over the left breast, he disappeared into the crowd.

As Jackie stood for a moment stranded in the middle of the room, the consul filled up the awkward gap by walking up to her. "Commodore? I'm Ann Sorenson. I represent the Emperor here on Cle'eru." The two women shook hands. "Our host has a fairly limited attention span, I'm afraid."

"I've noticed."

"I'm actually a bit surprised to see you *here.* I've been trying to reach you since you arrived on Cle'eru, but they seem to keep you isolated up there."

"My schedule has been very busy."

"I can imagine. You're really quite a celebrity down here, you know." They walked further into the drawing-room, dimly lit with flickering light. To one side a table was laid with a sumptuous array of delicacies, many of which Jackie couldn't even identify.

"I didn't know. Please tell me about it."

Sorenson glanced at her. "Don't you find it difficult working with *them*?"

"The zor, I assume you mean."

"Yes, that's right." Her nose wrinkled as if she smelled something bad.

"It's a challenge, no question, but they are as dependable and as competent as humans. I don't dwell on it much."

"So I've been told."

"By whom?"

"In this line of work, one hears from all sources … besides, there are officers in His Majesty's Navy who won't willingly work with a zor—and you seem to have one as an exec."

"Your attitude is a bit curious for a consul to a zor world, if I may say so," Jackie remarked.

"Commodore." Ann Sorenson smiled knowingly. "Look around this room: there are no zor here. This is sovereign territory of the Solar Empire. There is no need to deal in platitudes. If you're to be posted here for any length of time, you'll realize that our society is fairly insular; we don't bother much with what goes on up there. Humans are humans and zor are zor; we only need enough contact to get our business transacted."

"I'm afraid I don't share your opinions, Madam Consul. I don't know what purpose your bias serves, but I have worked with zor and will continue to do so."

"I'm not surprised. Excuse me," the consul said with a half-sincere smile, and turned away to walk across the room.

Jackie watched her go, then shrugged her shoulders and turned back to the delicacies. As she stood, alone, for several seconds, a 'bot-tender floated over behind the table and said in a low, throaty voice, "How can I serve you?"

"*egeneh*," she said, looking for something to wash an unpleasant taste from her mouth.

"Hansie doesn't serve it."

The 'bot was still thinking about it; she turned to face the human voice that had answered. It was a tall, rather fashionably dressed man with a half-full plate in one hand and an empty Corcyran crystal goblet in the other. A waiter's tray hovered nearby; in a smooth and no doubt long-practiced motion he set the goblet onto the tray and then extended his hand to clasp hers. "My dear commodore. Such a pleasure to finally make your acquaintance."

"You have the advantage of me, sir," she replied, taking his hand.

"I beg your pardon. Commodore, my name is Ian Kwan. Ian Thomas Kwan. I have the rather dubious honor of being posted to the trade mission here as a representative of the Confederated Press."

"A reporter. You're a reporter."

"That's what my résumè says. And if I do say so myself, I *do* have something of a nose for news." He reached up without looking and snagged a full glass from another tray as it passed. "And I smell a story."

"If your sense of smell is so accurate, why are you posted here?"

"I'm interested in asking you the same question."

She turned her attention back to the buffet table. "None of your damn business." She added several items to her plate almost at random, fairly sure she wasn't really interested in eating them. "What do you want?"

"What do you think I want? A *scoop,* Commodore. I've heard so much about you—"

"Oh?" She looked at him sharply. "What have you heard?"

"It's all flattering." Kwan did his best impression of a sincere smile. "I didn't mean to offend. Let me buy you a drink and we can relax and talk. You're among humans now."

She thought about protesting but decided it would do no good. "Very well, *g'rey'l* and orange juice, if you have it," she said to the 'bot.

Turning on her heel, she took her plate and made her way to a small table near the edge of the room and sat down. Kwan followed shortly, a tray with the drinks just behind him. While she waited, Jackie was able to locate the source of the flickering light: a fireplace with a real fire burning merrily. Several guests were hovering near it, soaking up warmth in the artificially chilly room. Outside, it was almost thirty degrees—a stifling night, even by Cle'eru standards—while it felt like autumn in the Livingston Mountains in Sir Johannes Sharpe's drawing-room.

Her expression must have been evident to Kwan as he sat down. "Beautiful, isn't it?" he asked, jerking his thumb toward the fire. "Hansie must've spent half a million getting it here. And the wood—a couple hundred for every log, at least. Like burning money."

"Pointless extravagance."

"Conspicuous consumption, rather. Appearances *must* be maintained. It's the envy of every human on the planet. Almost," he added quickly. "Guess it doesn't do much for you."

"What do the zor think?"

"Who gives a damn what the zor think?"

"It's their world."

"It's *our* world. We just let them occupy it, 'cause it's too damn hot. But Cle'eru, every square meter of it, is part of the Solar Empire. Has been since the war. You of all people should know that."

"The High Nest might disagree with you."

"*Humans*, Commodore. You're among humans. The niceties need not be observed. Look around the room. Go ahead." He gestured with his glass, handing hers to her as it emerged from the hovering 'bot. "Do you see a single zor here? Even *one!*" He waited for her to take a look. "No. Of course not. That's because Hansie"—he lowered his voice conspiratorially—"Hansie *hates* the sons of bitches. And he's not the only one: most of the people in this room feel the same way. The zor were the enemy eighty-five years ago; now they're clients. But never *equals*, Commodore. *Never.* To the emperor," he concluded, clicking his glass to hers and downing half of it in a series of gulps. "Aaah. Hansie only serves the best."

She held herself back from throwing the contents of her glass in his face. Instead she sipped the drink, trying to look impassive. *At least he's right about one thing*, she thought, appreciating the quality.

For several more minutes, Kwan sought to extract information from her. It was challenging, but her reticence at last bested his inquisitive nature. Good reporters allow themselves avenues of retreat, of course, in hopes of advancing along them in future. At last he withdrew, leaving her alone.

The encounters left her annoyed. It must have showed; no one else approached her as she sat and sipped her drink, occasionally sampling something from her plate. She had learned something, however: there was a huge distance between humans and zor here on Cle'eru, something she could grasp, but simply could not understand. She had learned, also, that Kwan—and the consul—and probably every third person in this room—had a good source of information on her, a fact that made her very uneasy. Who could have given them so much to go on?

She had her answer suddenly, just by looking across the room to the fireplace. A familiar gesture, a face tilted at the right angle to catch the dancing firelight. It was too uncanny to be a mistaken resemblance; she had stopped believing in coincidence some time ago. Besides, it answered too many questions.

With a firm determination she stood, set her glass half-unfinished on the table and walked purposefully across the room. She hardly saw the faces of the other guests who parted in her path. The chatter in the room seemed to quiet suddenly as her objective turned to face her.

"Hello, Dan," she said, the words coming more easily than she would have expected.

"You're looking fine, Jay." The familiar nickname, unused for so many years, struck a note within her as if a weight had been suddenly placed on her chest. She shrugged it off.

"You've been telling tales out of school, Dan."

"I don't know what you mean."

"Did you put that slime Ian Kwan on me? He seems to be remarkably well informed. Even with contacts within the fleet—which I doubt he has—he had to have been briefed on me somehow."

"Jay, don't make a scene."

"Don't patronize me, Dan McReynolds." She grabbed his elbow and steered him away from the fireplace and into an alcove away from the crowd. "It's been years. You went your way and I went mine. I got over you a long time ago, and the universe is a very big place. Now my world's been totally screwed with and you crawl out from under some rock somewhere and I cross your path. You want something. What is it?"

"Why do I have to want something? Maybe I'm here to do *you* a favor."

"I don't need any favors from you."

"Jay … Jacqueline. You don't need to ask; someone *else* asked for you. I came here from Adrianople, just like you did. I understand"—another conspiratorial sotto voce tone—"you want to cross the line."

"'Cross the line'?"

"Go outside the Empire. To a place the Navy calls Sargasso."

"What do you know about Sargasso?"

"I've been there. Lots of us … gray-market merchants"—he smiled; an old, familiar smile—"trade there regularly. I have—how shall I put it?—a landing permit."

Jackie didn't speak, but in her mind, she shouted: *Th'an'ya!*

I am here, se Jackie.

Is this a servant of esGa'u? Can you tell?

I believe that he is not, se Jackie. He is what and who he seems to be.

"Jay, are you all right?" It echoed as if from the bottom of a deep well. Dan's voice echoed concern with some hint of affection. He reached out toward her and she reflexively stepped back, not wanting him to touch her.

"I'm … I'm fine. I may have drunk a bit too much," she lied. "Maybe we should get out of here. Take a walk in the fresh air."

"I'm not interested in some sort of romantic—"

"Neither am I. This is business, and this is hardly the place to discuss business. Don't you agree?"

"I'VE BEEN out of the Service for four years. I left the *Torrance* to command the *Horace*, but after a few years I started getting ready for life on the beach. There's more to the Empire than dress uniforms and spot inspections: Did you ever think about that, Jay? I made enough contacts to be pretty well set up when my hitch was done."

Dan McReynolds leaned on the railing of a little bridge that crossed a stream. It was part of a man-made garden that formed part of Hansie Sharpe's little principality. Above, silhouetted in the moonlight, the fairy towers of zor architecture stood guard.

"In the Navy everything is on the straight and narrow. Look at you, for instance: it's twenty-eight degrees out here and you're wearing a long-sleeved blouse, a uniform jacket and your dress gloves. Appearances are critical because you're a commodore. When I was a captain I had to do the same, and not just with uniforms: my wardroom table had to compare with others in the fleet, I had to participate in the right forums, make the right appointments. For a country boy from Mothallah, it was a different world … a different life. I hated it, and I was glad it was over."

"Even the part you spent with me."

"Of *course* not the part I spent with you. That's old territory, Jay, and we left it behind years ago. But we always were different. You never saw the real world, what's out there beyond the borders, across the line. You probably never will."

"You might be surprised." She had all she could do not to tell him: *I've already seen what's out there. It took my form. It killed my people.*

saShrne'e. *The shroud has been pulled aside*, the voice inside her head said.

"I doubt it," he replied, not seeming to notice the anger in her eyes. "There's lots of action out there, lots of money to be made. Lots of risks to be taken. Jumping to a system that's been charted by the Grand Survey but hasn't been visited by humans is damn dangerous, but finding a source of valuable raw materials, or something to exploit, pays off handsomely.

"I qualified for a decommissioned two-man explorer ship when I mustered out. Now, a few years later, I have twenty times the tonnage and I'm a very rich man. Most of my business is across the line, Jay. I know where Crossover—what you call Sargasso—is; I've been there. I've even seen the *Negri Sembilan* there, the one the Navy has listed as gone missing."

"You've seen the *Negri*?"

"Sure have. It was taking on cargo and was outbound. It crossed the line, Jay, and word has it that it took out the ship that came looking for it. It's a big player out there, supposedly in the pay of one of the big bosses."

"I don't believe you. I've known Damien Abbas for most of his career; he'd never turn pirate."

"Believe what you like. If he wouldn't take the *Negri Sembilan* across, maybe some junior officer would. Maybe there was a mutiny."

She had been about to reply, *Not on an Imperial ship*, but thought better of it. There had certainly been mutinies before: The Solar Empire had been founded on the mutiny of Admiral Willem MacDowell, the first Solar Emperor. And then, of course, there was Admiral Marais.

"Is that the only Imperial ship you've seen there?"

"The only one I know of. The Navy doesn't seem to have followed up. There would've been some pretty serious shooting if any decent-sized force ever came across a pirate haven the size of Crossover."

"A decent-sized force *did* get there ... or so we thought."

"Never happened."

"They got *somewhere*. Every Sensitive on board those ships committed suicide or was killed by his mates; most of the crews went insane. They witnessed something, or met something, so horrible that ..."

She found herself running out of words, though the images continued to flash through her mind: the Noyes-creature ... the destruction of one of Barbara

MacEwan's fighter wings … the octopuslike thing during her mind-link with Ch'k'te. Maisel's death, like a switch being turned off.

Shrnu'u HeGa'u, He of the Dancing Blade.

saShrne'e, the voice inside her head said, the echo of it seeming to thrum in her ears. *You are pulling aside the shroud to reveal the awful face of the Deceiver, who never speaks except in lies and whose truth is falsehood. To defeat him, you must descend to the Plain of Despite. To return, you must pierce the Icewall.*

The Icewall seemed to rush up to meet her, and she put her hands up to shield herself—

—and found her gloved hands grasping pavement, as she looked up from her knees to see Dan McReynolds stooping to help her. Summoning all her will, she shook her head and pulled herself of her own accord to her feet. "You really *did* drink too much."

"No," she said, placing her hands on her now aching temples. "No, I think it's a lot more complicated than that."

"REPORTING AS ordered," Ch'k'te said when she opened the door to her hotel suite. She had called for him as soon as she returned from the party. She and Dan had hardly exchanged a word after their conversation in the garden, agreeing to meet the next day to discuss the plan to cross the line.

She gestured to a perch and with a voice-command lowered the lights to accommodate him. "Ch'k'te, what does the word *saShrne'e* mean to you?"

"It is a metaphorical expression, *se* Jackie." He moved his wings into a different posture. "It refers to an act of honesty, of discarding pretense and dissembling in favor of naked truth."

"'Pulling aside the shroud'?"

"An acceptable translation. In *The Legend of Qu'u,* it refers to the hero's realization that *esGa'u* is abroad in the world and that the servants of the Deceiver walk freely in 'The World That Is.'"

"The voice"—she tapped her left temple with an index finger—"told me that I was pulling aside the shroud to reveal the Deceiver, 'who never speaks except in lies, and whose truth—'"

"'—is falsehood,'" Ch'k'te finished the quote. "From *The Lament of the Peak.* Your voice is well versed in the epics."

"It's the first time the voice has ever spoken to me like that, as if directing me what to do. If I weren't so frightened, I would be angry."

"Have you asked *li* Th'an'ya about this?" His voice seemed almost level.

"She claims to know nothing about the voice," Jackie answered. "Besides, it usually speaks more cryptically. It told me that in order to defeat … *esGa'u* I must descend to the Plain of Despite, and to return I must pierce the Icewall. But it didn't tell me how I'm supposed to do it."

"*seGa'Mrha'u*," Ch'k'te said. "Descent to the Plain. More literally, 'flight through the Wind of Despite.' A chilling metaphor."

To a zor, of course, "chilling" implied "extremely frightening."

"It told me I must do this."

"We already knew that, *se* Jackie. In imitation of the descent of Qu'u to the Plain of Despite, we must travel in search of the lost *gyaryu*."

"Dan McReynolds was at that party."

"Your former mate?"

"Yes," she said after a moment. "While I was with him, the voice spoke to me."

She recounted the details of what she'd learned from him: about "crossing the line," as he put it; about the traders' haven at Sargasso; and about the *Negri Sembilan* now supposedly plying the spaceways out there as a pirate. Her intense mind-link with Ch'k'te weeks ago on Cicero, when Th'an'ya's *hsi* was awakened, had already explained Dan to Ch'k'te. The brevity and precision of her exposition surprised even Jackie—she had expected to be more emotional about Dan, especially meeting him like this after all this time.

"Did he indicate how he came to be here? What part he intended to play?"

"He said he came here from Adrianople and that he was here to do me a favor. He *knew* I was here. He may know about the rest of it—about everything else. I know—I have it on good authority—that he is not a servant of *esGa'u*."

"Then it will all become clear in due time. If you were one of the People, *se* Jackie, I would counsel you to meditate and commune with *esLi*." He gestured toward the shrine. "As it is …" He fluttered his wings and lowered himself to the floor. "I can give you no advice on your own consolation." Politely Ch'k'te excused himself and left Jackie to her thoughts.

The Lord esLi *asks for your service, and yours alone*, she heard in her head as she sat alone. *Ultimately it is your path to tread.*

Before she could react, the voice was gone again, dimly echoing in her mind.

S HE AWOKE to the sound of piano music softly filling the room. Recorded from an actual manual instrument centuries ago, a gift from Big Fredericks, it traveled with her in her personal effects and was currently installed in her hotel-room comp. With a word she softened its gentle tones and rolled out of bed.

"Schedule," she said to the comp, and it appeared in the air above a corner table. A message signal blinked, indicating calls that had come overnight.

She expected to see more of the usual traffic from the human community on Cle'eru, and wasn't disappointed. Her appearance at Hansie Sharpe's house the previous night had excited even more interest than when she had accepted the invitation; it was as if every human on the planet had issued her an invitation. Breakfast arrived while she was still wading through it all, and she worked away at both dutifully.

Two-thirds of the way down the list of messages, she saw a zor glyph that belonged to S'reth. She pointed to it and requested a display.

"*Greetings, Mighty One*," the ancient zor's voice sounded through the air. There was no visual. "*I have contemplated the matter which mutually concerns us. We should now discuss matters further. If your busy schedule allows, I should like to meet with you and your companion just before Father Sun crosses the meridian—or, as you might say, in the late morning. Military procedures notwithstanding, there is no need to confirm this appointment, as you will be welcome when you come. esLiHeYar.*"

After three days of waiting, it might have been a command from the Admiralty. Her immediate thought was to push aside breakfast, throw on clothes and rush over to S'reth's residence. But ingrained habits and discipline kicked in. A soldier rarely passes up a meal when it's already placed on the table, and S'reth had told her to come around noon local time. An order was an order.

After breakfast, she worked it off for two hours in the hotel's gym, which, while equipped primarily for winged visitors, was adequate enough for her needs. After a shower and a change into fresh clothing, she considered herself refreshed and ready for whatever S'reth might have for her.

She was wrong, of course.

A S BEFORE, they were escorted along the balcony into S'reth's sitting-room, but the sage zor was not alone this time. Instead he was settled on his perch, his balding head bent down so that he could converse with his human guest. The man was settled in an armchair nearby with a tiny *egeneh*-cup held in one hand. Cle'eru's vermilion sunlight filtered in through a high window.

It took several seconds for her to react, as she stood in the doorway where the *alHyu* had left her this time. S'reth's guest looked up from his conversation and stood up immediately, walking across the room to meet her.

"Jay, I—"

"Dan, what the hell are you doing here?" she asked, trying not to raise her voice above a whisper. "Are you involved in this … this—"

"I'm here at S'reth's request," he answered evenly. "I'm being paid a tidy sum in cash to do him—and you—a favor."

"A favor."

"You want to go across the line." He turned his back and walked back into the room, not noticing Ch'k'te's claws a few centimeters out of their sheaths.

Jackie noticed, though, and wasn't sure whether to feel alarmed or honored by Ch'k'te's concern.

"What I *want* has ceased to have any meaning, *se* S'reth, I want an explanation." She stalked into the room after Dan and walked up to the old zor's perch. She must have seemed physically imposing to him, for he arranged his wings in the Posture of Approaching Danger and uncrossed his arms, making them ready for action.

"Calm yourself, Mighty One," he said to her.

"I'll be as angry as I please. Dredging up an old hurt is a low trick, and I *don't* like being manipulated that way. I have a court-martial waiting for me back in the Empire and I may be the only person who can run this Qu'u errand for you"—S'reth seemed to wince as she said "errand"—"but I'm ready to call the whole thing off."

"Jay—" McReynolds began, but Jackie turned on him.

"You keep the hell out of this." She returned her attention to S'reth. "Why didn't you tell me, *se* S'reth? You could've dropped it on me three days ago when I reached Cle'eru. I didn't need this deceit."

"Qu'u did not know who would help or hinder him," S'reth replied softly. He changed his wings to the Posture of Honor to *esLi*. "I considered discussing this matter with you, but concluded that meeting him without my presence might trigger—"

"Trigger *what*? Some affection? Not after all these years. Not now."

"Why don't you drop the 'Iron Maiden' act, Jay? I'm not asking you to sleep with me. Besides, looks like you're already taken—Oof!" He couldn't complete his comment because Jackie made fist contact with his jaw. Falling to the floor, he upended a delicate three-legged table, spilling a number of potted plants to either side.

With surprising speed for someone so frail in appearance, S'reth was between them, his arms extended and his wings arranged in the Cloak of Circling Defense. "Stop!" he shouted, muttering something in the Highspeech. Ch'k'te grasped Jackie's shoulder, but she shrugged it off.

"Don't worry, Honored One," she said, rubbing her clenched fist with her upper hand. "I won't hit him again. At least if he doesn't make any more stupid comments."

"Looks like I'm a little out of practice," Dan McReynolds commented, rubbing his chin as he picked himself up off the floor. "Guess I should've stayed in the Navy."

"Guess I didn't hit you hard enough to shut you up."

"Guess not." He brushed soil off of his clothing. "Feelin' better now?"

"Not even a little bit."

"I think," S'reth said, turning to Jackie and leading her gently by the elbow to a comfortable chair, "that I have made a slight misjudgment in my perceptions of human nature." He gestured to an adjacent perch for Ch'k'te. He refused, taking up a guard position behind Jackie. Dan McReynolds found his way to another chair, still rubbing the spot where Jackie's fist had struck, the ghost of a wry smile still playing on his lips.

When everyone was seated and S'reth had reassumed his perch, he took a cup of *egeneh* in his hand and looked at his guests over it. "In the Qu'u legend," he began, "a talented—but inexperienced—warrior is given the responsibility of carrying out a perilous and important quest. He is brought to understanding by a series of trials and revelations, through which he is able to do what is necessary to complete this quest.

"*esLi* in His wisdom could well have apprised Qu'u of what lay ahead of him, but chose to present needed information gradually and slowly at a pace Qu'u was capable of accepting.

"The best reason for the Lord *esLi* choosing to do this is simple. He perceived that if Qu'u knew what lay in front of him—the descent to the Plain of Despite, the confrontation with the *esGa'uYal* and the piercing of the Icewall —then he would be unwilling or perhaps incapable of carrying out the quest with which he was burdened."

S'reth took a long sip from his *egeneh* and glanced quickly over his shoulder toward the *esLi* disk hanging on the wall behind him.

"My human friend, the doctrine of *Dsen'sSur'ch'a*—the Ordeal of Gradual Revelation—is not a matter of deceit. Omens and portents, intuition and insight, are the way in which the People approach the world. This is especially true for a hero, particularly in classical legend. If you were one of us"—he held up his hand and arranged his wings in the Stature of Formal Apology—"this discussion would not be needed.

"One of the People, placed in the position of being the avatar of the mighty Qu'u, would understand that the *Dsen'sSur'ch'a* is necessary for no other reason than to provide triggers for Qu'u to come through." He folded his arms and brought his wings low so that they brushed the perch, in the Configuration of Honored Abasement.

She felt Ch'k'te rustling nervously behind her. "Really, *se* S'reth, that isn't necessary."

"What do you mean?" S'reth answered, remaining in that position.

"I didn't mean to touch your honor: I certainly wouldn't expect you to offer …" Then she realized the import of his question. "I—You, well, I—"

On the Plain of Despite, warriors travel with their gaze directed toward the ground, she heard the voice say. *Only heroes can cast their eyes upward, and thus see the signs and portents of their quest.*

I can read his wings, she said to herself. *What the hell is happening to me?*

"*ha* Qu'u." S'reth's voice seemed to be coming from a long distance away, the voice in her head carrying afterechoes, like eddies in a muddy pool.

"I'm … not ready to answer to that name, *se* S'reth."

He shifted his position at last to an intermediate posture; but in his eyes there was a different light.

"Very well, *se* Jackie, the nature of your journey is just beginning to be revealed. Though you may dislike me for having done so, I have introduced an old acquaintance into this affair"—Jackie suppressed her smile, realizing that S'reth had not recognized the double entendre—"knowing that it might bring about a *sSur'ch'a*. It might produce a further revelation of the path the Lord *esLi* might wish for you to fly.

"But Captain McReynolds' purpose is more pragmatic: he is, indeed, a ship-captain who has been to Crossover, or Sargasso as it is also called. His ship will take you there as the first step on your journey to recover the *gyaryu*."

"I see."

"His services are *needed*, *se* Jackie. It would be difficult for you to reach Crossover without someone reliable—"

"I would hardly classify Dan as *reliable*."

"Now hold it one goddamn minute," Dan said, breaking out of a long silence. "You've got a grudge against me, Jay, but you've got no right to call me unreliable, *se* S'reth and I made a deal to deliver you to—"

"Stop talking about me like I was a rack of *artha*—"

"Why? For the last ten minutes you've been talking to *se* S'reth like I wasn't even *here*. You just told me—and showed me"—he rubbed his chin almost as an affectation, though there was a nasty reddish mark where she'd hit him—"that there isn't anything between us. I'm supposed to get you to Crossover, and I'll get you there."

"Why should I trust you?"

"Why *shouldn't* you trust me?"

"I trusted you before. Last time I did, you let me down in a big way. It's hard for me to forget that."

"You might as well. It was a long time ago and it was business. It wasn't like we were bonded, or ever would be; you were married to the Service then. Looks like you still are."

"Don't be so sure."

"I don't have to be. It doesn't matter to me anymore." He stood up and bowed to S'reth, then walked across the room, staying near its edge. "You'll forgive me if I stay out of range of your fist.

"I'll be in port for three or four more days, *se* S'reth; you'll let me know if I'm to be of service."

He left the words hanging in the air as the sound of his departing footsteps echoed in the hallway.

Jackie looked down at her hands folded in her lap. Ch'k'te's presence just behind her chair was comforting, but she could sense his palpable uneasiness; he knew what Dan had meant to her, and how it had ended. Still, she was unwilling to make some sort of decision on the spot, even though it might be dramatic or even inspiring to do so.

Instead she stood up and walked slowly past S'reth's perch to stand in front of the stone disk of *esLi*, hanging in an antigrav field. Sunlight from outside cut a bright orange swath across it, dividing it into light and dark regions, and etching the *hRni'i* that covered it in dim fire.

If I were one of the People, it would be an excellent time for me to have some blinding symbolic revelation, she thought. *Come on, mysterious voice. Tell me where to go; place my feet on the right path. The shroud has been pulled aside, and I'm ready to cross onto the Plain of Despite.*

Do your worst, she added. *My mind is open and ready.*

The room was strangely silent, as if S'reth or Ch'k'te, in violation of all Sensitive etiquette, were listening to her invitation. Several moments passed, while recent events whirled in her head.

… And nothing happened. Even the sentient weight of the disk of *esLi* seemed distant and unreachable, as if it had withdrawn from her questions and her anger. At last, calling on her own military discipline, she pulled herself to attention. She gave the disk and S'reth each a curt nod, then headed for the exit, Ch'k'te following.

When she was at the door, she heard S'reth speak softly: "What are you going to do?"

She stopped in her tracks. "Ultimately, I don't know." She didn't turn around, or even look aside to see Ch'k'te's expression. "For now, I suppose I'd better pack. My ride won't wait forever."

"*esLiHeYar, se* Jackie."

She felt like turning on him and delivering a retort of some sort, but none rose to mind. Without knowing how to respond, she simply placed her wings in the Posture of Brave Resignation and walked out of the room.

chapter 19

THE LEGEND OF QU'U (continued)

HU'ASCHY'E, THE FEAR OF BEING TRAPPED UNDER-
GROUND, WAS ACUTE AS THEY TRAVELED THROUGH THE
LONG TUNNEL. [Approaching Danger]
THE CEILING WAS TOO LOW AND THE
WIDTH OF THE CORRIDOR TOO NARROW TO ALLOW
FLIGHT: THEY WERE CONFINED TO THE TUNNEL
FLOOR, TRUDGING ALONG IN SILENCE.

AT FIRST THERE WAS NO SOUND BUT THAT MADE BY
THEIR PASSAGE. NEITHER QU'U NOR HYOS FOUND
ENERGY FOR SPEECH; THE [The Drawn *chya*]
GLOOM THAT HAD SEEMED TO DESCEND ON THEM
MADE IT DIFFICULT EVEN FOR EITHER OF THEM TO
RAISE HIS HEAD TO SPEAK TO THE OTHER. SOON, HOW-
EVER, SOUNDS BEGAN TO SEEP INTO THE HEAVY DARK
QUIET; AT FIRST THEY WERE ALMOST INDISCERNIBLE,
BUT GRADUALLY THEY [Warrior Against Despite]
BECAME MORE
AND MORE APPARENT. THERE WERE CRIES AND SHOUTS,
LOW THRUMMING SOUNDS AND IRREGULAR CRASHES
AND THUMPS. WHEN THE TWO COMPANIONS STOPPED
FOR A REST AFTER WHAT SEEMED LIKE A SUN'S WORTH
OF WALKING, THE ECHOES RESOLVED THEMSELVES INTO
A PATTERN THAT QU'U RECOGNIZED.

"THEY ARE FIGHTING A WAR," HE TOLD HYOS QUIETLY,
AND THE WORD "WAR" ECHOED ABOUT THE CAVERN.

AS THEY DESCENDED EVER FURTHER, THE TUNNEL
NARROWED AND CONSTRICTED, HEIGHTENING
HU'ASCHY'E. [Cloak of Defense]
AT LAST THEY COULD NO LONGER TRAVEL SIDE BY SIDE
BUT WERE FORCED TO GO SINGLE FILE; QU'U, HIS
BLADE OUT BEFORE HIM, LED THE WAY. THE WALLS OF

THE CAVERN LOST THEIR ROUGHNESS AND BECAME
SMOOTH AND THEN SHINY, DISTORTEDLY REFLECTING
THE TWO INTO CARNIVAL-CREATURES, THE IMAGES
FURTHER WARPED WHERE THE WALL HAD BEEN BENT
OR DENTED. TO THEIR HEIGHTENED SENSES, IT SEEMED
ALMOST AS IF GROSSLY ALTERED FORMS HULKED
ALONG ON ALL SIDES OF THEM, SHADOWING THEIR
EVERY MOVE.   [Winds of Despite]

THE WAR, FAR OFF AND MUFFLED, GREW LOUDER TO
THEIR EARS WITH EVERY STEP.   [The Drawn *chya*]

Anonymous and unheralded, the avatar of Qu'u and her companion rode up to the Cle'eru orbital station in a civilian shuttle. Jackie had had a fitful night's sleep. S'reth had arranged shuttle passage for them and had provided Jackie with the location of the *Fair Damsel*'s berth. As she thought about Dan McReynolds and his ship, she conceived of a confrontation on the station deck, but she concluded that she didn't give a damn, really, how it came out …

In the deepest part of the night, when she'd felt the most despairing, she dreamed of the vuhls and of the alien image of herself dissolving in the heat of pistol fire after poor John Maisel had been … turned off. It hadn't been that long ago: a matter of weeks, weeks full of lessons too significant ever to be unlearned.

Now she was traveling incognito. She was neither the center of attention nor the object of deference, a curiosity merely be cause she was in the company of, and not merely among, zor.

She was Jacqueline Kearny now, a navigator's mate from Dieron and late of the Imperial Navy. Ch'k'te was Ch'k'te HeU'ur, an engineer's mate. Documents and working papers proved it. The *Fair Damsel* was apparently short at least one crew member in each department, making their introduction into the ship's complement a reasonable cover for their trip across the line.

During the hour the shuttle traveled from surface to orbit she tried to nap, or at least feign sleep, like a cat on patrol. Ch'k'te meditated quietly, perhaps conjuring an *esLi* disk in his mind within which he could perch. Whatever he was doing, he seemed to be a hell of a lot more relaxed. Just as the shuttle was making its final approach to the station, Ch'k'te emerged from his deep and immobile communion by opening his eyes, flexing his hitherto unmoved muscles, and carefully arranging his wings in the Posture of Approaching Danger.

She hadn't yet gotten used to the idea of being able to read wings. She was seated opposite him in a remote nook of the shuttle's viewing lounge. Through the viewport, they could see the hulking station half in shadow, with the blue-green planet huge behind it.

He rose in a single smooth motion. "We seem to be expected," he said without preamble.

"I'd hope so."

"A Sensitive is expecting us, *se* Jackie," he said, his wing-posture communicating a wariness. She resisted the impulse to ask further. Instead she followed Ch'k'te out of the lounge and into the corridor, where passengers were already queuing for disembarkation.

ONCE OUT of the shuttle and out on the station deck, they were assailed by bright, harsh lights that seemed to shine from everywhere. She was wearing a cap; she pulled its brim down to help shield her eyes. Ch'k'te rummaged in his duffel bag while they walked and finally produced a pair of sunglasses and donned them. Even though they were built for a zor, the appearance was comical enough to make her smile, but she was able to hold back her laughter —for the sake of his dignity and perhaps their friendship. In any case, the huge torus of the station was bigger than any ship's deck—even a carrier's launch bay —and she felt small and insignificant. Cargo coasters rushed by, vaguely following lanes painted on the deck. For their own safety, they found their way to the outside wall, where there was a marked, slightly elevated pedestrian walkway.

As they moved along and passed the berths of various commercial vehicles, Jackie watched their reflections in the curved, shiny outside wall. They were elongated like reflections in a trick mirror, distorted where the wall-section had been bent or dented. It was almost as if two grossly altered forms hulked along beside them, shadowing their every move. Ch'k'te seemed not to look at all; since Th'an'ya's emergence, he had been avoiding mirrors entirely.

At last they approached the *Fair Damsel*'s berth. It was less than a quarter of the way around the station from where they docked; they only had to pass through three main bulkheads which separated sixteenth-sections of the torus from each other and were designed to prevent a sudden depressurization in case of collision.

The *Damsel*'s airlock was open, giving direct entry into its rapidly filling cargo hold. Hands were driving canisters up to the entrance, where they were checked against a manifest by a burly, hostile-looking man. He had evidently seen Jackie and Ch'k'te coming from quite a distance; he stood with his hands on his hips and a scowl on his face, waiting for them to come within earshot to deliver his first volley. Jackie almost smiled, knowing just the sort of attack that was coming; Ch'k'te's wings were in a defensive posture that the *Fair Damsel*'s cargo master could not possibly read.

The man actually waited until they were practically at the 'lock before he spoke. "You two the new mates?"

"Kearny and HeU'ur," Jackie said, pointing first to herself and then to Ch'k'te. "Permission to come aboard, Chief." She hoped that was the correct title. Evidently it was; he looked at his comp, scowled a bit and then gave them a curt nod.

"Permission granted. I'm Chief Sabah. Most of the hands call me 'the Sultan' though not on-duty. See Chief Steward Casian for'ard"—he gestured toward the far end of the cargo hold, toward the front of the vessel—"for your bunks and where to stow your gear; then the Old Man wants to see you."

"Aye-aye," she said. "Do we have duty stations assigned yet?"

"Up to the old man. I imagine he's got it all figured out." He looked her up and down, as if he were measuring her for a uniform—or a coffin. Then, abruptly, he turned to Ch'k'te. "That a *chya*?" he asked, pointing to the blade at Ch'k'te's belt, peace-bonded when they came on-station.

"It is."

"I've never actually seen one, but I'm pretty good with a rapier. Maybe I could get a look when you're off-duty."

"I will be pleased to show it to you, sir." Ch'k'te placed his wings in the Posture of Resigned Deference, an ironic supplement to his comment that was not lost on Jackie, but which Chief Sabah would not understand. Sabah appeared to be pleased with the possibility of examining the *chya* and concluded the conversation with a nod, gesturing again toward the rear of the hold.

A FTER STOWING their gear, they asked their way to officers' country; after taking a few wrong turns, they found their way at last to the captain's ready-room. The hatch door was secured open; Dan McReynolds and another officer were going over a manifest, projected in midair over the desk. Both looked up when Jackie and Ch'k'te appeared in the doorway.

"Check on the heavy freight, will you, Pyotr?" McReynolds said.

"It's all aboard, Skip, I—"

"Check on it," McReynolds repeated. The other man looked at him, perhaps trying to read some hidden signal Jackie couldn't understand; then he shrugged and made his way out of the ready-room. As he stepped out he gave Jackie and Ch'k'te each a good long look. There was an annoyance verging on hostility that seemed to follow him out.

"Close the door," McReynolds said after the other had left. Ch'k'te waved at the sensor and then came to stand behind Jackie like a bodyguard.

"I understand you wanted to see us."

"I thought it'd be important to get a few things straight." McReynolds slid a cabinet open and pulled out a plastic squeeze-bottle. He flipped the top off and took a long pull from it and set it casually on the table. "Now that you're on my deck and part of my crew, you're under my command. You'll take my orders or you'll get off at the next stop. Understood?"

"It goes without saying."

"You're sure about this, Jay? It'll take some doing after your previous station. No white-glove dress uniforms here."

"Did you call me here to tell me about life in the commercial service? I know what to expect."

"Do you." He took another pull on the bottle and wiped his mouth with the back of his hand. "Do you really.

"In order to find you and your caddy a spot on the roster, I had to give two good crew members their walking papers. Now, to be fair, I found them berths on other ships with S'reth's help, but it's a hell of a thing to do. They got big enough bonuses that they'll keep their mouths shut, but they had a lot of friends aboard this tub.

"See, in the civilian world, you don't just get an officer exam or a weekly inspection. You get tested *every* day, *every* shift. You screw up once—just *once* —and people will be on your ass, and hard. I can't shield you if that happens, no matter how important this quest is."

"Are you trying to scare me?"

"You're determined to tough this out, aren't you? Machismo was always a strength with you." He tensed and Jackie almost laughed out loud; he looked as if he were expecting her to deck him again. She pushed her annoyance back, knowing he was trying to test her temper.

"Are you trying to scare me?" she repeated.

"No, I'm not. I'm trying to warn you. Watch yourself. You're going to be under everyone's eyes—mine, the department chiefs', your bunkmates', the people you eat with, everyone. I get paid whether you get to Crossover or not, but, as an old friend of yours and of S'reth's, I'd rather you *got* there."

"I guess I should say 'thank you.'"

"Don't strain yourself." He looked to be on the verge of an angry comment, but this time he seemed to hold himself back. "Look. I guess I'm expecting to have to go out of my way for you—for both of you. If I don't, it's just as well. Much as it'd feed my ego to have to help you through this entire trip, it will be better for both of you if we don't even cross paths before you get off.

"I guess that's it. Get settled in and get to work. Dismissed." He tossed them a salute that in the Imperial Navy would've been sloppy; here, it seemed like the height of formality. Without looking at them again, he turned back to examination of the manifest.

*   *   *

THERE ARE a thousand details to be attended to before a merchant vessel can depart from a port. Money matters—port fees, contract settlements and acceptance and transfer of goods—are the responsibility of the cargo crew. On a small merchantman, the cargo crew is nearly everyone.

Most travelers never get to see what goes on dockside. It was an eye-opening experience for Jackie; instead of supervising from the bridge or the station, she was sweating out a deadline working directly under the Sultan, trying to get everything loaded and stowed as quickly as possible. Dock access fees are charged by the hour on-station; for ships like the *Fair Damsel*, a few hours can mean the difference between profit and loss. By the time the *Damsel* cast off, Jackie and Ch'k'te were exhausted and ravenous like everyone else. They went off-duty and found their way to the galley amidships; they found themselves a quiet corner of the commissary to eat their first meal aboard the merchantman.

Their isolation didn't last long. Two crewmembers, one male and one female, dressed in worn uniform jumpers, sat down next to them so suddenly that Jackie saw—and sensed—Ch'k'te's claws extend fractionally out of their sheaths.

"You're Kearny, aren't you?" the man asked Jackie. He'd sat down beside her while the woman had taken a seat directly opposite, next to Ch'k'te. She was studiously spreading butter on a roll, watching her companion from the corner of her eye.

"Jackie Kearny."

"Where do you hail from, Jackie Kearny?" he asked, half turning toward her, letting his arm dangle over the back of his seat. Jackie tried not to look back at it. She set her tableware down in front of her carefully, intentionally trying to avoid the precision of an Academy cadet.

"Dieron."

"Long way from home. But don't you worry; we're one big family here, all good friends."

"Glad to hear it."

"I'm Raymond Li. We'll be working together, looks like, doing route planning across the line."

"You're in Navigation Section."

"I *am* Navigation Section." He laid his hands out on the table, letting his draped arm brush her arm for a moment as it went by. "I'm the chief navigator of this tub and part owner. The Old Man and I go way back."

Not as far back as I go, she thought. She didn't say it, though, instead looking at their other table companion. "You in navigation, too?"

"Engineering," she replied. "Sonja Torrijos."

Her stomach jumped; it must have shown in her face.

"You know the name?"

"I've heard it before—"

"Great-granduncle Sergei, I suppose. Jesus Christ, Ray, it's like I told you: I can't go anyplace without someone making the connection. Well, believe me, Kearny, there's no love lost between me and Uncle Sergei. He's not even human anymore, far as I can tell; he's all but turned into a zor, 'cept for growing wings."

"This is a bad thing," Ch'k'te said softly, without looking up.

"Humans are humans, zor are zor. I don't see any sense in mixing the two."

"Clearly," Ch'k'te said quietly, as if tasting every word before he let it pass, "our captain has chosen a somewhat different course."

"Didn't *mean* it that way," Sonja answered, turning on him. Raymond Li smiled and rolled his eyes as if he'd heard this before. "You do your job, you can be a human, a zor, a rashk or a blue-horned, seven-tailed Arcturian ape for all I care. I got nothing against zor personally."

"Just as a race."

"I got nothing against them as a race, either! Just like your kind to twist my words. I swear, every time I try to talk to one of you I get into this kind of argument. I don't want to talk about it, you read?"

"I understand completely," Ch'k'te said, arranging his wings as best he could in the Posture of Postponed Anger. Jackie tried her best not to notice.

"Don't mind her, friend zor," Raymond interjected. "She's got a chip on her shoulder the size of Adrianople Starbase. Nothing like famous kin to give you an attitude problem."

"Among my people," Ch'k'te replied, "the Nest, sept and clan form such a large extended family that everyone has a famous blood relative."

"What are you, the High Lord's cousin?"

Ch'k'te's wings assumed the Cloak of Affirmation. "I am from a younger and less distinguished clan," he answered. "I do not have that honor." His posture said, *Of course! I am indeed a HeYen.* Jackie quickly looked around the commissary to see if anyone noticed and then gave Ch'k'te a sharp glance. He returned a liquid gaze to her, his annoyance and anger thinly veiled.

"You okay, Kearny?"

We got this far, Jackie thought furiously. *Don't let your damn zor pride get in our way now!*

It does not matter, she heard back from within her head: a cool presence— Th'an'ya. *You are being watched. No one has noticed* le *Ch'k'te's indiscretion.*

"Kearny." She felt a hand, tentative, tugging on her coveralls blouse. "Kearny, you feeling all right?"

She snapped back to the here-and-now. "I'm ... fine. A little tired, I'm a little out of shape, I guess, and the Sultan wears me out."

"He does that to everyone." The conversation topic changed, as the excuse and the brief pause seemed to satisfy her new crewmates.

L ATER, LYING on her bunk, she spoke again to Th'an'ya. *Tell me again what you told me before,* she thought, her eyes shut. *About how we're being watched.*

You have a dangerous enemy on board. He knows what you are, but it will be difficult for him to confront you. Who is he? What does he look like? Who— *So many questions.* Th'an'ya's "voice" betrayed something like amusement; it reminded Jackie of a tinkling, chiming bell. *I have no ability to perceive him as you do. I see him in a different way; this makes me unable to respond to these questions.*

How do you see him, then?

An image began to form in her mind, as if it were being replayed inside her eyelids. A zor, handsome with a noble bearing, a … not a *chya*, but something terribly unlike it. He stood before her in her mind's eye, not looking at her, but examining his talons in an almost human gesture.

Shrnu'u HeGa'u. He of the Dancing Blade.

She sat bolt upright in her bunk, her eyes open; she felt wings pull close around her; her hand reached for a *chya* that wasn't there. Her head collided with the formed plastic of the bunk above and the pain drove her flat again. She must have said something, because she felt, rather than saw, someone beside her.

"You all right?"

For just an instant she felt the impulse to attack the figure crouched beside her bunk, and then she made out a vaguely familiar face in the dim light.

"Sorry," she said to her bunkmate, Karla Bazadeh, a middle-aged cargo hand she'd barely greeted before they cleared port. "Nightmare," she managed to add.

"Need something from the dispensary?"

"No." She rubbed the top of her head, which was already developing a bump. "No, thanks. I'll be okay."

Grumbling, Karla climbed back into the bed above. Jackie rubbed her head and worked on breathing and getting her heart-rate back to normal. After several minutes, she heard regular breathing above her and closed her eyes again to speak with Th'an'ya.

That was a dirty trick.

I fail to understand your meaning, se Jackie.

I had to fight that—I had to fight him. In the Dsen'yen'ch'a, *my* Dsen'yen'ch'a. *He scared the shit out of me. He almost killed me, when I had no way of even understanding the stakes. How am I going to fight him now? I don't even have a* chya.

He does not have his e'chya. You are on equal terms.

He has more weapons than I do.

Are you sure?

You know damn well I'm not sure of anything. What you're telling me is that the Deceiver has placed one of his best agents, who threw himself—or an image of himself—off a cliff—or an image of a cliff—the last time we met. Now he's on board this ship, but doesn't look like a zor, and is looking to kill Qu'u.

Who does not look like Qu'u.

But you say that he knows what I look like.

There is no guarantee of that. His perception of you may well have been different than how you actually seem. He seeks your hsi, se *Jackie, and will only recognize you by it.*

Hard to disguise that.

Impossible, se *Jackie.*

Sometime later she drifted into sleep. Little of her dreams remained with her afterward, except for an impression of a steep set of stairs carved into a mountainside; she was climbing then endlessly, away from some unknown horror below and toward some hidden confrontation at the top.

I̲N ORDER to make a faster-than-light jump, a vessel must navigate out of the gravity-well of a solar system. Some planetary systems are inherently hazardous; for mercantile vessels that lack the sophisticated equipment of military ones, a local pilot comes on board to handle the transit to the jump point.

Cle'eru was such a system. There were two belts of asteroids roughly in the plane of the system's ecliptic, along with a high percentage of comets and meteoric debris. For merchant vessels this made local pilots necessary, and the *Fair Damsel* engaged one before clearing dock.

Jackie was on the bridge when the pilot came on-duty. He was a zor who walked with a slight limp and whose wings didn't settle perfectly over his shoulders. He gave his name as K'ke'en—"Twisted"—a use-name, a joke that was lost on everyone else; as a human navigator's mate, it would have been out of place for her to notice.

It wasn't hard, though, to read the contempt of the bridge crew. As Pyotr Ngo, the *Fair Damsel*'s first pilot, vacated the command chair to make room for K'ke'en, Jackie could see the eyes of everyone on the bridge on the zor. Their resentment, or disgust, or basic racial hatred was clear. Whatever it was, they made no secret of it. She wondered to herself how Ch'k'te was making out.

For K'ke'en's part, he handled it professionally, as he must have been accustomed both to the attitudes of humans (especially on Cle'eru!) and of his fellow zor, who might have looked down on his deformity. It was, after all, more than a physical handicap: it was a speech impediment. The crew might well have disliked taking orders from a zor, particularly a crippled one; but they responded promptly as he gave them. He took advantage of the ship's handling characteristics more and more as he acquired the "feel" of the *Damsel*.

Jackie plotted each step of K'ke'en's course on the helm board. He kept the *Damsel* in the plane of the solar system; but this required numerous course corrections to avoid obstacles, the motion of which she could only guess at. Still, it seemed that K'ke'en's path was unusually complex …

Suddenly, the path as plotted seemed to jump out at her, a familiar shape— or rather a symbol: a zor ideogram. From somewhere in her mind—from Th'an'ya, no doubt—she was able to identify the symbol: *Sha'GaHe'en,* the Danger of Hidden Evil.

As she stood over the board, realization flooding over her, she felt rooted to the spot. She had the feeling of being watched but had to exert all of her will to avoid meeting the zor pilot's gaze. Her first reaction was to think, *C'mon, tell me something I don't already know.*

K'ke'en had gone to astonishing lengths to convey this message, but it occurred to her that he must have had his reasons: hostiles were clearly paying attention, and might notice any more overt means; also, it was possible that K'ke'en wasn't sure to whom he was sending the message and was hoping the intended recipient was listening. Even if he knew, he might fear that he would give away her identity to anyone else.

But who was K'ke'en, to send this message to her?

And who was she, really, to be receiving it?

She never got the answer to those questions. The *Fair Damsel* rendezvoused with the jump-point station near the edge of Cle'eru System; K'ke'en took his credit chip and disembarked, with no further messages.

THE *DAMSEL* jumped. From the outside, if there had been any one to watch, it would have looked as if the ship were under water, her appearance rippling as if a pebble had been dropped in that water sending out echoes of its passage. The water was space-time, making its complaint as the pebble— the surge of energy produced by matter and antimatter annihilating each other in the crystalline trap of the ship's FTL drive—dropped through it. The water shifted, and from the outside, it would seem that the image of the ship shifted with it … and was gone, leaving a soundless echo in its wake.

Transit time to Crossover was about six days. This wasn't a movable feast; in fact, since the very nature of the FTL space in which the ship traveled did not admit the passage of light, it was just as well that the dynamics of jump kept the *Damsel* traveling at a constant speed relative to the real universe even though it didn't pass through it. Distance traveled was a function of direction and time … a novel variation on the three components. It would be six days, two hours, twelve minutes and nineteen seconds in the darkness.

N AVIGATION SECTION doesn't have much to do in jump, but aboard a merchantman there are always things to keep crew busy. Just as on dockside, Jackie found herself assigned to the Sultan, working on cargo inventory. She, Ray Li and Karla Bazadeh, her bunkmate, were a three-person team. It was boring work, and more than once as she unpacked and repacked a cargo canister, she felt her mind casting back to Cicero, or Dieron, or anywhere but aboard the *Fair Damsel* halfway between Cle'eru and Crossover.

The cargo bay had been full of echoes and suddenly she realized that it was silent. She had been engrossed in some irrelevant task, but the quiet made her listen. Even the sounds of Ray and Karla doing the same tasks had somehow faded to soundlessness.

"Ray?" She stood up, feeling strained muscles complain. She set her comp and stylus down on a canister. "Karla?"

Qu'u.

The word boomed around the empty walls. "Ray?" she said again, stepping a few meters out from the loose pile of crates and canisters. She felt her body crouch slightly, assuming a fighting stance.

Mighty Qu'u. I can sense your hsi, *Mighty One.* The cargo bay continued to be silent, but for her heartbeat and the voice that seemed to be all around her.

"Who's there?"

She looked around the bay. It was a huge place, at least in comparison to the rest of the ship: twenty meters floor-to-ceiling, suitable for carrying bulky cargoes. It was forty meters across, plenty of room to hide in. There was no sign of Ray or Karla.

We have met before, Qu'u. Many times, and in many guises. We have both slept for a long time and each of our meetings brings us closer to wakefulness.

She was sure now that the voice was in her head. She scanned the room, looking for a defensible place; she looked in each direction in turn, trying to see if there was anyone else there. A movement caught the corner of her eye and she looked up in time to see someone in the control room, fifteen meters above her head. The lights were cycled into the bright blue-white; she was unable to make out the figure's identity.

What do you want? She said in her mind.

She began to make her way toward the hatchway.

Do you recall, Mighty One, when we first met? You were doing the service of the Crawler even then; my Master had seen you coming across His lands from afar, traveling the dark path. My Master commanded that I confront you with anGa'e'ren, *the Creeping Darkness. Do you remember?*

She did: it was a passage in the legend. It was intended to show up the frailty and inexperience of the great hero. He had almost lost heart and fled the Plain of Despite because of it.

I can see that you do, the voice continued after a moment. *As the shroud is pulled aside, my Master grows ever more powerful, as do his tools—and his servants. We shall see, Mighty One, if you are equal to* anGa'e'ren *now.*

What the hell is that supposed to mean? she asked.

There was no answer. Instead the ominous silence was interrupted by a sound even more frightening. The hydraulics strained aloud. As she turned suddenly to see it, the great clamshell doors of the cargo hatch began to pull open.

She stared dumbfounded for several seconds. If the *Fair Damsel* had been in normal space, Jackie would have been dead almost instantly. She would have been flung out of the ship like the cork from a bottle, decompressed and flash-frozen before she had time to be horrified. It was a revelation to her that all of this was true and that she was aware of it. Explosive decompression wasn't happening as the clamshell doors opened wider and wider.

Beyond them was darkness. Not the stormy dark of Cicero night nor the mere absence of light in a shipboard cabin. It was somehow the *negation* of light, its antithesis, a doom into which light could enter but from which it could never return. The filtering and polarizing screens aboard jump ships dampened this utter dark, made it palatable and encompassable: here, face-to-face with it, the sharp barrier between the cargo-deck illumination and the glassy, obsidian surface of this dark nothing seemed to have vanished. It slopped over onto the deck, as if it could not be restrained.

Within it she could see figures—or were her eyes playing tricks? There were tentacles and pseudopods, dark and greedy staring eyes, faces twisted in fear … articulated wings with a phosphor glow, elongated arms reaching for her … reaching …

Behind her, she heard noises, the scrabbling of claws on the deck, the thumping of many feet. Drawing her *chya* into her hand—it had almost leapt there of its own accord—and settling her wings into a posture of defiance, she turned her back on the creeping darkness to face her assailants.

"T̲HAT'S M̲ARCEL, all right." Rafe leaned past the pillar and then back. They were standing at one end of an elevated walk way; their attention was on a street vendor at the other end, several hundred meters away. "Dr. Marcel Liang and two other sick-bay crew. The *Negri*'s in port, just like Sean said."

"And that's the first you've seen of crew from the *Negri*," Owen answered, taking a look.

"Since the middle of last month. Before you showed up." Rafe looked again. "Are any of that lot aliens?"

"I'm not sure."

Owen put his hand on the pillar and concentrated. It was coming easier now: he needed only to think about the deaths of his comrades in Green Squadron and the emotion would well up within him. The hubbub of the street began to sound distant and remote; he cast his glance across the scene, looking for something out of place.

"That one," he said, indicating the left one of a pair of Marines hanging close to Dr. Marcel and the two others. "He's a bug. He's the only one."

"Do you think they know?" Rafe asked.

"Oh, you can bet on it. Look at the way they act around him," Owen answered. Rafe looked where Owen pointed: Each of the others seemed to defer to the disguised alien who was—very subtly—leading them along the street. Even the other Marine seemed to be a bit scared.

Rafe turned and gave a short chopping gesture to Sean Williams and Desi Rashid, two muscular *Negri* crew also stranded on Center. They began to walk forward along the street, seemingly paying no attention to Rafe or Owen or to the crew at the end of the walkway as they enjoyed the off-duty time. Rafe and Owen took off slowly in the same direction.

"I'll handle the other Marine. You get the bug," Rafe said quietly. "The doc and his boys will go along; they know who I am."

Owen didn't answer. He was walking forward toward the alien who was disguised as an Imperial Marine. Without even summoning the feeling, his anger came forward as a palpable thing, bringing the scene into sharp focus.

At a hundred meters, the false Marine's back was turned to him but his hands were clenched, as if he felt some of Owen's anger flowing toward him.

At fifty meters, the false Marine had turned partway around, taking his attention from Dr. Marcel and the med crew, who had seen Rafe and were looking away from the scene. Williams and Rashid were closing in from the other side.

At twenty-five meters Owen was face-to-face with the object of his anger.

"Take a hike," the alien said, and Owen heard in his mind: *Take a hike.* It wanted him to walk away, to turn aside, to be anywhere but where he was going.

"Why don't you call for help?" Owen asked in a normal voice from fifteen meters away. He knew that the alien could hear him somehow—that there was no one on the crowded street but the two of them. "Come on, get your pals together and let's have a nice rumble right here."

He was ten meters away when Williams and Rashid came on either side of the false Marine. Owen, Rafe and the other two were unarmed; the alien had a regulation pistol holstered at its waist but had apparently never thought to draw it.

"We're taking a walk," Owen said. He heard confusion in his mind: *How could you—How did you—*But he ignored it. They stepped off the walkway into a maze of lifts and stepped accessways; it was a part of the city being redesigned and rebuilt. "Under the stairs," he said.

He shoved the alien in that direction with the help of the others. A translucent block in a nearby building caught the sunlight and broke it up into rainbow fragments spread across the scene.

"I don't know what you want," the alien said. "But you're out of your league."

"Didn't have any trouble with you, did I?" Owen answered. "Tell me again."

He took the Marine by the lapels of the jacket. "I know what you are," he whispered. He could feel the anger flowing through him; even Rafe took a step back. "I know what your kind has already done. It's enough. It's *over*. We're going to get you, every one of you, and—"

"And what, meat-creature?" the alien answered, looking right into Owen's eyes. *You will release me,* it said in his mind. *Or I will end your life this instant.*

Owen felt a pressure in his head like a vise squeezing it. *Release me now, meat-creature,* it repeated.

The pain began to peak; his anger was out of control. The two things collided without a sound. Owen felt as if his head was going to explode; he grabbed the false Marine and dragged him to the edge of the railing.

"No," he managed to say, and pushed the alien over the edge. The two other *Negri* crew looked over and saw the creature fall twenty, fifty, a hundred meters to a platform far below where it lay sprawled, transforming into its native shape, twisted and dead.

Owen had dropped to his knees and was holding his head.

"You all right, pal?" Rafe asked him. "We better make our selves scarce."

"No," Owen answered, slowly getting to his feet. "No. Things are happening so fast, I—Wait. It didn't call for help." He grabbed Rafe's arm. "It tried to kill me itself, with its mind. It couldn't, for some reason, so I was able to kill it."

"Well, yeah."

"They can be *killed*. Don't you see? *There's a way*. Where's the doc? He must've come down from the ship in a gig. That's our ride to the *Negri*."

"They'll be waiting for us."

"No they *won't*. They don't know—it didn't try to call out. They won't know until it's too late."

"If you're wrong, we're dead."

"Look," Owen said. He let go of Rafe's arm and rubbed his temple; the pain was starting to recede. "We've got one chance to do this. We have two pistols, and we've got me. We're going to do it now."

He could feel the eerie calm, the rightness of the thing, the whole world coming into focus.

"I'll get some people together," Rafe said. "I wonder how many people we can get aboard a gig?"

chapter 20

THE LEGEND OF QU'U (continued)

SOMEWHERE FAR OFF, QU'U HEARD THE TOLLING OF
A BELL CALLING THE CUSTODIANS OF THE SHRINES OF
ESLI TO PRAYER, BUT HE KNEW THAT THEY WERE NOT
LISTENING.   [Honor to *esLi*]

IT WAS NOT REBELLION OR BLASPHEMY THAT CAUSED
THEM TO BEHAVE THUS, BUT RATHER INDIFFERENCE
BORN OF DESPAIR. THE BEAUTIFUL AND SACRED
SHRINES TO THE LORD OF   [Despair of the *Hssa*]
THE GOLDEN CIRCLE BECAME UNKEMPT AND FELL
INTO DISREPAIR, UNTIL THEY CRUMBLED AT LAST INTO
RUBBLE. FROM UNDER THE EARTH THERE WAS LAUGH-
TER THAT CASCADED UPWARD THROUGH THE AIR.

"*SE* QU'U."

HE WINCED AT THE SPEAKING OF HIS OWN NAME,
FEELING THAT IT SOMEHOW OFFENDED THE LORD *ESLI*
TO HEAR IT. THE TOLLING BELL AND LAUGHTER CON-
TINUED UNABATED.   [Condemnation to Life]

"*SE* QU'U. YOU MUST AWAKEN: WE MUST SEEK SHELTER
FROM THE BATTLE."

"IT DOES NOT MATTER," HE SAID AT LAST, DEEP WITHIN
THE SPIRALS OF HIS DREAM.   [Cloak of Defense]

"*SE* QU'U, WE MUST SEEK SHELTER. THE SERVANTS OF
THE DECEIVER WILL FIND US."

IT WAS HYOS' VOICE: HE RECOGNIZED IT. THE TOLLING
OF THE BELL BECAME RESOLVED TO BECOME THE
SOUND OF SHELLS EXPLODING, AND THE LAUGHTER
THE INSISTENT HUM AND RUMBLE OF WEAPONS

ENGAGING EACH OTHER. HE OPENED HIS OUTER EYE-
LIDS AND THEN THE INNER ONES   [The Drawn *Chya*]
AND SAW HYOS STANDING OVER HIM, *CHYA* HELD
READY.

TO QU'U'S SURPRISE, THE SIGHT OF A DRAWN *CHYA*
DID NOT STRIKE FEAR INTO HIM, AND ITS GLOW AND
CRY SEEMED A STATEMENT OF DEFIANCE AGAINST THE
WAR THAT RAGED ALL AROUND THEM. THE WAR WAS
OF A VIOLENCE AND INTENSITY THEY HAD NEVER
SEEN, THOUGH CONFLICT BETWEEN THE CLANS HAD
RAGED FOR DECADES.   [Posture of Defiance]
ARTILLERY SHELLS EXPLODED OVERHEAD, VICTIMS
WAILED IN PAIN IN THE DISTANCE; THE SKY—A NIGHT-
TIME SKY, BUT WITH NO VISIBLE STARS—GLOWED
WEIRDLY FROM LIGHT REFLECTING ON THE UNDER-
SIDES OF LOW-HANGING CLOUDS.

                                                               [Crossing the Plain]

"THE QUEST, *SE* QU'U."

"THE SERVANT OF THE DECEIVER HAS THWARTED OUR
QUEST, MY COMPANION. I TURNED AWAY—I FLED—"
                                                               [Stance of Comradeship]

"IT DOES NOT MATTER," HYOS REPLIED. "THERE IS
NOTHING TO BE DONE ABOUT THE DISHONOR. THE
E'CHAYA-BEARER TURNED YOU AWAY AND NOW SEEKS TO
USE THAT TURNING TO DESTROY YOU. YET THE LORD
ESLI HAS NOT ABANDONED YOU. LOOK." HE GESTURED
BEYOND THE ROCKY OUTCROPPING THAT SHELTERED
THEM, TOWARD THE DISTANT, FROZEN MOUNTAINS.

SLOWLY QU'U RAISED HIS HEAD AND LOOKED WHERE
HIS FRIEND HAD POINTED. HE COULD SEE A CASTLE
                                                               [The Perilous Stair]
THERE, SEEMINGLY GROWING FROM THE SHEER ROCK
WALL, ACCESSIBLE ONLY BY A CURVING, TREACHEROUS
STAIR. LIGHTNINGS CASCADED AROUND AND DOWN
UPON THE CASTLE, ILLUMINATING IT WEIRDLY.

* * *

BEYOND IT HE COULD SEE THE GHASTLY WHITE-BLUE
OF THE ICEWALL.

"ON THE PLAIN OF DESPITE, WARRIORS TRAVEL WITH
THEIR GAZE DIRECTED TOWARD THE GROUND," HYOS
SAID, "ONLY HEROES CAN   [Stance of the Warrior]
CAST THEIR EYES UPWARD, AND THUS SEE THE SIGNS
AND PORTENTS OF THEIR QUEST."

QU'U REACHED FOR THE COMFORTING PRESENCE OF
HIS OWN *CHYA* AND FOUND IT   [The Drawn *Chya*]
STILL THERE AND READY FOR USE. *ANGA'E'REN* HAD
TAKEN HIS COURAGE AND PERHAPS HIS HONOR:
BUT AS HIS SENSIBLE FRIEND HAD SUGGESTED, IT HAD NOT
DEPRIVED HIM OF THE BURDEN OF HIS QUEST.

SOMEWHERE IN THE FORTRESS OF DESPITE WAS THE
OBJECT OF THAT QUEST.   [Posture of Resolution]
SOMEHOW, HE AND HYOS WOULD HAVE TO OBTAIN IT.

With a voice that seemed hardly her own, she croaked, "Hyos."

"Ch'k'te," a familiar voice answered through the darkness. "Ch'k'te, I am."
She felt a taloned hand on her own.

She fought her eyes open. Instead of seeing the horrible battle on the Plain
of Despite, she saw a dimly lit sick bay. Thermal blankets were wrapped around
her but she still felt chilled. Liquid dripped from an IV through the blanket
membrane into her right arm. "*anGa'e'ren*," she said. "I—He—"

"You are weakened," Ch'k'te said. "There was ... much concern."

"I'm cold." She pulled the blankets tighter but to no avail. "The darkness ..."
She thought about it for a moment and found her mind still somewhat muddled.
She realized she had no way to end the sentence.

"Jay."

She looked for the voice that spoke her name and located someone near the
door. It was Dan McReynolds; the expression on his face seemed to mix fear and
concern in about equal proportions.

"The cargo doors. Someone opened the cargo doors."

"We got 'em closed," he said. "If I get my hands on whoever opened them,
I'll flush the bastard out into jump. Did you get a look at him?"

"No. Had the lights turned way up. He—spoke to me."

"Did you recognize the voice?"

"It was Shrnu'u HeGa'u." The lights in the sick bay dimmed suddenly; Dan looked around, as if expecting to see someone mischievously playing with the controls. Ch'k'te's sword-hand went to his *chya.* Jackie shivered again and dug herself deeper under the covers.

Dan gestured to Ch'k'te, drawing him away from the bed. Quietly he asked: "Who the hell is—"

"The one mentioned is a—a demon," Ch'k'te answered. "He is a legendary servant of *esGa'u* the Deceiver, an enemy of *esLi* and therefore of Qu'u. He ..." Ch'k'te let the sentence trail off.

"A *demon*?" Dan turned away from the zor and ran a hand through his hair. "Someone tried to vent one of my crew, and you're telling me it was an imaginary being?"

"'He of the Dancing Blade' is not imaginary, *se* Captain. *se* Jackie has already met him once, during the Ordeal of Experience."

"She's met a demon?"

"In mental combat."

"A dream."

"You may use whatever terminology you wish, *se* Captain. The fact is that a servant of *esGa'u* attempted to kill her. That means—"

"The fact *is*," Dan interrupted, "some real live flesh-and-bones being aboard this ship tried to kill her. We're in jump, so there's no one but crew aboard; so one of my own crew tried to get rid of her. Pyotr Ngo thinks that the hull breach might've even destroyed the ship."

"The Deceiver would have willingly sacrificed one of his servants to destroy Qu'u."

"But she's *not* Qu'u!" He gestured toward Jackie, huddled in the hospital bed. "This is a conflict between Jay and—"

"And who?"

"How the hell should I know? I'm just doing S'reth a favor. I didn't agree to risk my ship for her. Now someone opens the cargo doors in jump, for Christ's sake, and I find her on the cargo deck, gone so far over the horizon so I have to sedate her. Small wonder, with the doors opened out on—"

"On *anGa'e'ren*," Jackie said.

"On jumpspace," Dan continued, annoyed. He walked back toward the bed. "This has gone far enough for me, Jay. I want you to tell me what the hell is going on, free of all this mystical shit. I want to know now, who's really after you, who opened the doors."

"The darkness," Jackie said, turning away from him, her eyes grown wide with horror. He reached for her shoulder, intending to turn her back to face him—

—And found himself being thrown back and away from the bed, toward the far wall. He regained his balance and lunged forward—

But Ch'k'te had interposed himself between him and the bed. The zor held his *chya* before him, which glowed with a radiance that did not come from the sick-bay lights.

"I can vent you into the vacuum for touching me," McReynolds said quietly. "Get out of my way."

"I recognize your rights, *se* Captain," Ch'k'te said quietly, unmoving. "I respectfully decline to allow you to proceed with your interrogation. You will not pursue this course any further."

"Why, you—" McReynolds took a step forward, but heard a snarl … not from Ch'k'te, but rather from the *chya*. Startled, he froze and looked from Ch'k'te to the blade and back.

"I will not allow you closer, *se* Captain. If I must remain in this position until the ship leaves jump, I will do so, following which I will escort *se* Jackie from your vessel. If you choose violence, however, I will use my *chya* and you will die."

The finality with which he spoke those words, his voice level, sent a chill through Dan McReynolds.

"I could have you removed by my security."

"Perhaps. No doubt several of these persons would die as well, and you might still not obtain cooperation from *se* Jackie. You are welcome to try, *se* Captain; I am ready."

Neither man nor zor spoke for several moments.

"Ch'k'te, put your *chya* away." It was Jackie's command voice. Dan looked past Ch'k'te to see her sitting up in bed. She had the bedclothes wrapped around her, but her gaze, though still haunted, was clear and steady. "Dan, back off. Nothing is accomplished by this scene."

Ch'k'te stepped back carefully to stand beside the bed, returning his *chya* to its scabbard. It made a final complaint as it was put away. His gaze never left Dan McReynolds as he moved.

"Jay," Dan began, "Jackie, I need to know what's going on."

"It's better if you don't know. By getting involved, you continue to risk the *Fair Damsel.* I can understand why you don't want to do it. You didn't agree to become a hero: I did."

"But you need—"

"I don't *need* anything else from you. Remember what you told me when we came aboard: how you'd given up two crewmembers to make room for us, how you didn't want to go out of your way for us—"

"That was before a member of my crew tried to flush *another* of my crew into jump. That was before someone tried to destroy my ship. Whatever you're trying to do, whoever is trying to stop you—it wasn't my problem. Now it is."

"Nothing has changed."

"*Everything* has changed. Now, tell me what's going on and tell me what I can do to help."

T HE DOOR slid open. Jackie and Ch'k'te stepped into the room. Around the table sat several people: Dan, Raymond Li, Pyotr Ngo, the *Fair Damsel*'s chief engineer Erin Peterson and Karla Bazadeh. Dan gestured them to chairs, and without preamble began to speak. "Activate security program six." The comp acknowledged.

"I've gathered you all here for a specific reason that includes, but isn't restricted to, the cargo-bay hull breach. This isn't a court of inquiry. There are no charges against anyone. If anything, this is a consensus meeting of the *Damsel*'s major shareholders. The Sultan's on the bridge; he'll get briefed later."

He looked over at Karla, who looked somewhat uncomfortable. "You're here because I trust you," he said, smiling, "and Jackie has to trust you, too.

"There's been some speculation about what happened and about our two new crewmembers." He gestured to Jackie and Ch'k'te. "I won't address the scuttlebutt. Instead I'm going to take you into my confidence because you could all find out anyway. As part owners of this tub, you've got a right to know.

"The 'accident' that opened the cargo doors was no accident. Someone deliberately tried to kill Jackie, or at the very least drive her mad. This person, identity unknown, seems to have lured Ray and Karla off the deck, and then overrode security interlocks to open the doors.

"Whoever he or she is"—he looked at Jackie and then Ch'k'te pointedly, and continued—"he or she is an enemy of the zor High Nest, and it's the opinion of the High Nest that humanity is also in danger. Jackie and Ch'k'te are currently working for the High Nest, on detached service from His Majesty's Navy." Before any of the others could interject, he continued. "I'd like to introduce to you Jacqueline Laperriere, Commodore IN, and Commander Ch'k'te HeYen, also of the Imperial Navy."

Jackie looked from face to face. They all appeared angry or resentful. Among the Navy's duties was the regulation of piracy; that sometimes led to overzealous prosecution of legitimate commerce. Merchants and regular Navy were not the best of friends inside the Empire.

Of course, they weren't inside the Empire now.

"Captain?" Karla Bazadeh asked. "Can I make a comment?"

"Don't see why not."

She caught the glances of the officers. "We're all sitting here staring down these two people like they just slithered out of a nightmare. The Navy's supposed to be the good guys, no matter what we think of 'em. Shouldn't we hear them out?"

"No doubt," Pyotr Ngo said at last, "the *captain* had some reason for getting us entangled in the Navy's business. Perhaps he'd like to explain it to us."

"The High Nest paid us a healthy commission." He named a figure that drew appreciative noises from the others in the room. "They—and, interestingly, not the Navy—perceive a threat of some kind outside the Empire. For reasons I only barely understand, Jackie and Ch'k'te have been chosen to undertake a mission out there, and it was intended that they sneak out of the Empire without anyone knowing they were gone.

"Needless to say, someone knew—or found out. Now we have a choice: We can either drop them at Crossover, as originally agreed, or we can keep them on and help earn that commission. Unless you have objections, I'd like to hear them out."

"If it doesn't commit us to anything," Pyotr Ngo said.

"It doesn't so far. Ray?"

"I'm curious what all of this is about, though I have the same concern that Pyotr does."

"Noted." He toyed with a stylus, noting something on the comp before him. "Erin?"

"Two things. First, anyone who threatens the ship because she is aboard might well threaten it after she's gone. If we don't know what we're dealing with, we don't have much chance of fighting it. So much for pragmatism.

"My second point is that a member of *our crew* was attacked. Now, maybe the two of them"—she gestured toward Jackie and Ch'k'te—"maybe they came aboard under false pretenses, but they're crew now. We don't pick and choose who's protected by the radiation shielding or who gets to breathe the air. Crew is crew. Anybody who attacked one of us is the enemy of all of us."

"That's not a majority position."

"Tough. That's how I feel."

"All right; it's noted. Karla?"

"I get a vote?"

"You get a say."

"Okay. I don't—" She knotted her hands around one knee and drew her foot up into her lap and rested her chin on it. "Erin's right; we'd better know what's going on before another day passes, especially if the ship's at risk. But I think Pyotr's naive if he thinks we can sit and listen as if we're not already involved. By inviting them aboard, the captain's already committed us."

"How do you figure that?" Pyotr rounded on her. "We drop them at Crossover and sail off into the sunset. I don't see how we're *already* involved."

He glowered at Jackie, and she felt the unspoken message: *If I were captain, that's what I'd do with the likes of you.*

"If the enemy is as ruthless as I think it is," Jackie responded, "you'd never make it to jump."

"*I* don't see any enemy. You're asking us to risk the ship—" He glanced angrily about, landing his glance on Dan, then Karla, then back on Jackie herself. "You're suggesting that we've already been risking the ship—to an enemy I don't even know *exists*?"

"*anGa'e'ren* exists," Jackie answered, folding her hands in front of her. "There's an enemy out there; there's an enemy in *here*. The enemy controls Cicero, where I used to command."

"*Cicero*? The big naval base?"

"That's right. Cicero was taken by the enemy a few weeks ago and was abandoned on my orders."

Pyotr looked around the room again, then he leaned back and resettled himself in his chair, placing his hands on the table in front of him. "All right, Commodore. I'm listening."

Jackie swallowed and nodded. She'd reviewed the events of the last several weeks and knew that they'd begun to make a perverse sort of sense. Now she would have to clarify them for others. Dealing with subordinates at Cicero, or with a court-martial, had been easier than dealing with this crew; she knew that they might end up sympathetic, but they also might decide they had no stake and put Jackie and Ch'k'te ashore at the next opportunity.

"Things began to happen several months ago. Two exploratory vessels, based at Cicero Starbase, had gone missing while on charting expeditions. The two ships weren't unmanned probes or small advance scouts: they were fully armed and crewed starships, commanded by veteran pilots. These vessels regularly report their position and submit logs describing their activities; in each case, the ship had last been recorded at the Sargasso system—what you call Crossover.

"The Navy sent Admiral Horace Tolliver, a desk officer, out to see what was going on. He was accompanied by an important representative of the High Nest: Sergei Torrijos, the *Gyaryu'har*, the holder of the Talon of State."

"Sonja's great-uncle," Ray Li said.

"Right. He was—is—the inheritor of whatever authority the High Nest vested in Admiral Marais after he completed his conquest of the zor eighty-five years ago. This authority apparently extends back millennia, all the way to the very first *Gyaryu'har*, a legendary zor hero named Qu'u. We'll get back to him in a moment.

"Admiral Tolliver decided to take direct command of some of my squadron and go to Sargasso—Crossover—to see what was really going on. The *Gyaryu'har* warned against it. I went on the record as opposed, but he did it anyway. Mr. Torrijos told me that the High Lord had begun to perceive that there was a malevolent force out beyond the border of the Empire. This was why he had been included in this inspection tour. The admiral brushed it all aside.

"Some days after this, one ship returned to Cicero, mostly wrecked, with every Sensitive aboard dead. They were killed by their fellow crewmembers." The people at the table were listening intently. "The survivors claimed the Sensitives had turned into 'monsters' ... their words. According to them—including Admiral Tolliver—something attacked them out there, and those that escaped got out barely alive.

"As it turned out, my command had already been undermined by the enemy, an alien race with Sensitive capabilities far beyond anything we or the zor understand. Their powers include the ability to alter their perceived appearance. Only a very few Sensitives can pierce the illusion of one of these aliens; they can take the role of anyone. Several of my officers had been replaced—my own replacement was planned as well. I found out about this almost by accident, but with Ch'k'te's help I was able to regain control of Cicero long enough to get most of my people and my squadron to Adrianople. We were able to rescue the *Gyaryu'har* as well, but he was in a deep coma, apparently because the aliens had taken the *gyaryu* away.

"Let me clarify that point. The *gyaryu* is a sword like a zor warrior's *chya*. It gave Mr. Torrijos the ability to perceive the threat posed by the aliens and imparted certain other capabilities to him as well. I ... don't know the full extent of its powers, but I know that it's very important to the High Nest. Having it in the hands of the aliens is a matter of concern at the highest levels.

"So. Aliens had seized control of Cicero, and I'd gotten away, taking as much as I could and almost all of my people. The Admiralty convened a court-martial out at Adrianople and sent some heavy hitters out to fit me for leg-irons. But here's where it became strange.

"A zor VIP, the High Chamberlain T'te'e HeYen, had come out to Adrianople as well. He claimed to be there to examine Ch'k'te about the alien contact. Ch'k'te asked me to stand with him in this examination and I accepted, but as soon as the trial had started, it became apparent to me that the purpose of this trial was to test *me* rather than Ch'k'te. The High Lord himself had directed that I be tested as a candidate to go out and fetch back the sword from the aliens."

"Why you?" Dan asked quietly. "I mean, it's not that you were a particularly *bad* choice, but you aren't a zor. Or a Sensitive, as I recall."

"The zor don't believe in coincidence. To put it another way, they move according to the patterns of the High Lord's dreaming. There is some evidence that the High Lord knew that I would make contact with the aliens, though he saw them as demons in zor mythology—the *esGa'uYal,* or servants of *esGa'u* the Deceiver. It also means that the disappearance of the ships was no accident."

"You mean that—" Dan rubbed his chin and frowned. "You're suggesting that the High Lord knew that it was all going to happen."

"That's what the High Chamberlain implied." She rubbed her hands together, then seemed to realize it and feel self-conscious. Instead she folded her hands again in front of her on the table. "What the High Chamberlain did in the trial was to introduce an *esGa'uYe* into the mental link. I found myself in mental combat with it.

"This servant was named Shrnu'u HeGa'u." The lights in the room dimmed again, just long enough for the people sitting around the table to notice. "He addressed me as Qu'u, the legendary zor hero, a turn of events that seemed to surprise no one but me. I defeated him somehow—and the High Chamberlain told me that the High Lord had foreseen even *that.* In fact, he explained that even the *Gyaryu'har* had known what was going to happen, and had agreed to go to Cicero to set it all in motion."

"Meaning—" Dan began.

"Meaning the High Nest had set up the whole play. Sergei Torrijos was sent out to Cicero to cause the *esGa'uYal* to show their hand, delivering the *gyaryu* into the hands of the enemy so that the situation would come about that Qu'u ... that I ... would surface to go and get it."

"They threw away this important artifact so that someone would turn up to go after it." Dan looked at her like he didn't believe it; Jackie held his gaze steadily.

"They did it so that *Qu'u* would turn up," she said at last.

"Why Qu'u?"

"It comes down to the legend. According to the story, Qu'u journeys to the Plain of Despite, a sort of cold hell where an eternal war is fought. Qu'u confronts the Deceiver and gets the sword from him; then he returns it to the High Lord A'alu. She unites the zor with it. The zor believe that right now this is a crucial point in history and that Qu'u is needed again.

"I'm following the quest now. Every major step of my journey corresponds to some part of the legend. Even the opening of the cargo-deck doors has an analog: there's a point in the story where Shrnu'u HeGa'u confronts Qu'u with *anGa'e'ren*—the Creeping Darkness. Before the doors were opened, I heard the voice of Shrnu'u HeGa'u in my mind.

"And that's where I'm at. I'm not an Imperial Navy secret agent; I'm not sure just what it is I *am.* I resent it and I'm angry that I've been manipulated along this line, but I believe there's no choice but to continue. I'm walking the Qu'u path now and I can't turn back. Behind me is a court-martial, and who the hell knows what else. Ahead of me is …"

She paused and looked around the room, ending at last on Ch'k'te. His wings were in a neutral position, as if he were hesitant to convey his feelings, even to her.

"How does the legend end?" Dan asked, and the tone of his voice didn't give assurance that he really wanted an answer.

"That's the last problem. Like everything else, I don't know whether *everything* is supposed to correspond. If I were a zor, rather than just playing one on 3-V … Well. At the end of the Qu'u story, he comes face-to-face with the Deceiver, and gets hold of the *gyaryu*—and the Deceiver kills him."

"He *dies*? What the hell good is that?"

"When the Deceiver blasts him to bits, the Lord *esLi* raises him from the Plain of Despite, sword and all, up to His Circle of Light. This thwarts the Deceiver. In the end, Qu'u is brave enough and honorable enough and—what? —suicidal enough to let himself be destroyed to prove a point. I don't know if I'm able to fulfill that particular aspect, but otherwise I think that I have to follow this to the end."

The conference room was quiet for several moments, as if everyone were groping for some pithy comment to make. Apparently there was none appropriate to the situation.

"I've got a question," Karla Bazadeh said at last, breaking the silence. "What happens next?"

"Next?"

"In the story. In the legend of Qu'u. What happens to him right after this demon confronts him with the darkness?"

"Qu'u and Hyos reach *Ur'ta leHssa*, the Valley of Lost Souls," Ch'k'te said, the first words he had spoken since entering the room. "This is the place where souls captured by the Deceiver are kept. The hero discovers that most of them do not even know that they're trapped."

"Damned souls," Dan offered.

"Your analogy implies free will," Ch'k'te continued. "Many of the *Hssa* are not in the Valley by choice; in fact, some of them simply were unlucky enough to be in the wrong place at the wrong time. The Deceiver is not bounded by the strictures of propriety or fairness, nor does he require willing cooperation of his victims."

"So it's the Valley of Lost Souls, and some of them are prisoners of conscience. I assume you've concluded that the valley corresponds to …"

"Crossover," Jackie said, as Dan let the sentence trail off. "Though what it means for us is anyone's guess."

"What does Qu'u do there?"

"In the Valley? He is shown the base of the Perilous Stair, the way to the Fortress of Despite. When he begins climbing the stair, he knows there is no turning back ... there is no means of descent."

"And in the real world?"

"There's a clue at Crossover that will direct us toward where the *gyaryu* is being held—and toward the person, or being, who represents *esGa'u* the Deceiver."

"Who kills Qu'u," Dan said.

"I draw the line there. I refuse to go to the slaughter; as I said, I'm going because it's the only direction open."

"Like this 'Perilous Stair,'" Karla said quietly. "You've pretty much reached that stage already."

"I suppose you're right."

The room was quiet except for the hum of the ship's machinery. Jackie looked around at the familiar faces of strangers, now taken into her confidence, her upended life laid out for them.

"Do I need to summarize our options?" Dan asked, and when he got no answer, looked down at the notes he'd made during Jackie's exposition. "All right. Jackie's going to Crossover to find some clue that leads to finding the sword. We have two choices: to back her up or just to drop her off. It all comes down to one of those two directions. We're either in or out.

"Pyotr, you've heard her out. Are you still for tossing them ashore?"

"I'm not cut in the hero mold, Skip." Pyotr shifted in his seat, frowning. "I don't mean to be cruel, but if there's a gunfight going on, the last thing you do is stand up and wave a flag and shout, 'Come on, I'm over here, shoot me.' The enemy—*her* enemy—will go after her. I don't see as there's much we can do about it." He set his face in a grim expression. "Put 'em ashore."

"Erin?"

"I'm for following this through. I was before I heard the details; I am now."

"Ray?"

"We're not innocent bystanders anymore, regardless of what Pyotr thinks. I'm with Erin; let's go through with it. There's an enemy aboard this ship, maybe even in this room. I can't let it lie."

"And I can't either. Out past Crossover there's plenty of business opportunity; we can take the *Fair Damsel* wherever the legend or the clues suggest. Pyotr, we're going to go ahead with this. Are you on or off?"

The question was a serious one. What Dan McReynolds was asking was whether Pyotr's objections were such that he would rather leave the ship and sell off his share in it than accede to the decision of the other stockholders. It told

Jackie something significant about Dan, too: while as captain he was absolute master of the *Fair Damsel*, he wasn't a dictator. He wouldn't preside over a wardroom in which there was dissent. Given what it might cost him to buy out his chief pilot, it was a clear sign of his adherence to principles.

"I don't think it has to come to that, Dan. We've been business partners for six years. If I didn't yield to your opinion at least occasionally, I wouldn't trust you to be captain. I've registered my objections; now I'm ready to move along."

Dan looked relieved. "That's it, then. Everyone's got their duties to do; let's get on with it."

chapter 21

Dan McReynolds leisurely raised his hand and caught the attention of the bartender and signaled for another round. Then, as if he were commenting on the weather or the traffic patterns, looked across at Jackie and said, "Well, Jay, this is about as far from the Plain of Despite as I could imagine."

They were sitting in a bar named, interestingly enough, the Steps. It was located on the outermost ring of Crossover Starport; it was a prefab metal shell built near the top of a flight of metal steps that went nowhere. Dan had promised the best beer on-station, leading them through the labyrinth of Crossover, which appeared to be in a constant state of renewal—internal walls were being torn down or installed everywhere. The Steps had been there for only six months or so, according to the *Damsel*'s captain; before that, the bar had been located near the main cargo bay under a different name, but someone had decided that it was in the way and had had it dismantled.

Music blared from the sound system; some off-duty merchanters were playing some sort of space-combat game in a holo tank. There was a commentary program on the 3-V screens scattered around the room, the contents of which were inaudible to Jackie, but which was receiving rude commentary and jeers from the patrons who were disposed to give it any attention at all. The smells and sounds of people relaxing swirled around the room, occasionally washing over their table, intruding on their privacy but guaranteeing it as well. Dan was totally relaxed; Jackie was on edge, waiting for something to happen.

"What do you mean by that comment?"

"I mean … look. We've been here at Crossover almost two days. We've watched and waited; we've been looking out for clues in every direction. We've conducted a search of the ship and we still haven't found any indication of who tried to vent you into jump—there's not even a log entry of the doors being opened. With all that, you're still not sure where to go or what to do next."

"No one's tried to kill me for the last two days, either."

"Point taken." A tray hovered into view with two transparent mugs on it. When it reached the table, Dan inserted his comp into the base; after a moment he lifted the mugs from the tray to the table. He removed his comp and the tray whisked away. "Maybe that's not such a good sign. Are you sure we're in the right place?"

"This is the right *star*. It's the *wrong* planetary system—it matches the old IGS data, not the system where Tolliver and my people were … where they found the vuhls.

"So no, I'm not sure of anything. I've been pushed to this point. Now that I'm *trying* to follow the legend, you'd think I'd feel like I'm in greater control—but I don't. I don't know what's supposed to happen next or what I'm looking for." She lifted her mug and took a long drink.

"I'd like to know, too." He leaned forward, rubbing his chin. "Has it occurred to you, Jay, that this might *not* be the Valley of the Damned after all?"

"Lost Souls. Valley of Lost Souls."

"Whatever."

"I don't have the answer to that, either. There are too damn many parallels, too many indications that this should be the place. Ch'k'te told me that anyone *esGa'u* grabs lands in the Valley of Lost Souls whether they belong there or not. There were two ships grabbed out here—or what was here at some point."

"I find it hard to imagine that planets got moved or changed around. It's either here or it's not. Right?"

"We know the enemy is capable of fooling sensing equipment."

"Is the enemy capable of fooling navigation equipment, or communications equipment? There must be dozens of systems in a hundred-parsec radius that have never been visited, only surveyed by robot probes. What's more, this is outside the Empire—even the worlds that have been surveyed haven't been completely mapped. Think about it: How easy would it be for one of those ships to misjump?"

"Two Imperial starships?"

"Yeah, *two Imperial starships.* Navigation isn't a perfect science, as you know. Maybe they got lost somewhere else."

"I don't believe it."

"Look, Jay, it's not my job to strain your sense of credulity, but I'm not going to try and explain what's going on out here, either. Occam's Razor applies, doesn't it?"

"It's fit well so far."

"All right, let's approach this scientifically, no mystical stuff. I'll accept that you're out here as some sort of avatar and you're supposed to find this sword and hustle it back to Zor'a. Everything you know about this situation is based on S'reth's, or Ch'k'te's, or your own, interpretation of the legend.

"Suppose you're off base? Are you going to continue with the theory you have if it doesn't give you the information you need, or are you going to come up with a new theory to fit the new evidence—the evidence that this doesn't seem to be the First Circle of Hell here?" He leaned back in his chair and waved around him. "Does this look like the Valley of the Shadow of—"

"The Valley of Lost Souls. Your point is taken."

"Okay. So you agree with me."

"No, I *don't* agree with you. I concede you have a point. I haven't seen any of the evidence I'm looking for; Crossover is a navigationally simple system with eight almost perfectly coplanar planets with no asteroid belt. It corresponds exactly with the Imperial Grand Survey data. The system that the *Negri Sembilan* and the *Gustav Adolf II* reported is nowhere to be found. As for what the *Singapore* and the other squadron ships encountered—well ...

"But if you're willing to accept *me* and the mission I've been given, then you have to accept the premise that there's an enemy out here. Maybe it's here on Crossover, maybe not. The enemy is more powerful, more dangerous, more—more *evil* than anything we've ever seen. They're extremely potent Sensitives, and there may be no defense against them."

"If there's no defense, how did you get away back on Cicero?"

"I—"

There is a way, and you already know it.

Jackie whirled in her seat, looking around the bar in alarm. Dan pushed back his chair and went around to her side, grasping her hand. The expression on her face was almost unreadable. She tried to mask it right away.

"What is it, Jay?"

She carefully disengaged her hand from his and carefully stood. "I heard the voice."

"What voice?"

"I ... I don't know. I started hearing it back on Cicero. It's been pushing me all along, even before this Qu'u thing began."

"Great." He walked back around to his side of the table, sat down, and took a drink from his mug. "You're hearing voices. You didn't mention *this* in your briefing."

"Why should I have? You wouldn't have believed it then. You don't believe it now." She leaned over the table, placing her hands out in front of her. "All right, you want some proof? Let's go back aboard the *Fair Damsel.* I'll give you proof, from an authority even more responsible than me."

"What—"

"Not here. Back aboard."

Dan shrugged his shoulders. "Okay, it's your game."

I N PLACE of her regular coveralls, she had put on the crimson robe from the *Dsen'yen'ch'a* and had made a comfortable place to sit on her cabin floor. She didn't know if it was necessary, but it seemed to fit the mood. Ch'k'te was standing behind her, his right hand resting lightly on his *chya*. Karla was perched on her bunk and Dan McReynolds was lounging in an armchair.

"All right, Jay. I'm ready to hear about this voice."

She closed her eyes. *Th'an'ya?*

I am here, se *Jackie.*

I need your help. Would you make yourself visible?

Jackie opened her eyes and saw Dan standing up suddenly. Near the closed cabin door, an image of Th'an'ya had appeared. She sensed Ch'k'te tensing behind her as usual and heard a sharp intake of breath from Karla. "What the—Who—"

"Permit me to introduce *si* Th'an'ya *ehn* E'er'l'u *na* HeYen. In addition to other distinctions, she was once the mate of my companion and friend Ch'k'te."

"Honored," Th'an'ya said, bowing slightly toward Dan.

"Where did you come from?"

"As I understand the import of your question, I 'come from' the mind of your former mate. I ... reside there."

It wasn't clear what had rendered Dan speechless: the term "former mate" or the idea of a zor personality living in Jackie's mind. He looked several times from Jackie sitting on the floor to the image of Th'an'ya and back, each time trying to start a sentence but failing utterly.

"You'll want an explanation."

"I—well, yes."

"While Ch'k'te and I were on Cicero we performed a mental link, and during it Th'an'ya appeared. She was a powerful prescient Sensitive who had seen this quest coming many years ago; she mated with Ch'k'te and put her image in his mind, along with the key to bringing forth."

"So she was inside Ch'k'te and now she's inside you."

"Basically."

"She's some kind of memory, then?"

"Not exactly," Th'an'ya replied for herself. "I am the *hsi* of my former self. A mental representation of my ... 'soul,' as you might say. *se* Jackie is not only my host, but also my student and my friend. There is even a place for me in the Legend of Qu'u—that of the spirit guide."

"... Okay," Dan said after a moment, and flopped back into his chair. "So what about this 'voice'?"

"You are referring to the voice that *se* Jackie has been hearing intermittently since Cicero. She originally incorrectly attributed it to me. I have not reached any conclusions as to the source of the voice, though since it speaks in allusions and metaphors it is clearly well steeped in our racial culture. It could be the Lord *esLi* Himself, to whose will I humbly bow."

"*God* is talking to Jay?"

"Is there some reason why a divine being might not speak to your former mate?"

"Listen here, spook," Dan said, pointing his finger at her. "Get off the 'former mate' bit. We weren't mates; we were friends and lovers, and that was a long time ago."

"You still address her by another name—"

"I call her what I used to call her! Why are we discussing this?"

"You objected to my use of a term," Th'an'ya replied quietly. "I referred to *se* Jackie as your 'former mate,' and you said, 'Get off the—'"

"I know what I said! What is this, a self-analysis seminar?" He rubbed his chin. "A ghost. I'm arguing with a ghost. Can we get on with this?"

Jackie couldn't help but grin at Dan's annoyance. However, unlike on other occasions, Th'an'ya's image did not waver or blur. She waited patiently for Jackie's concentration to return.

"What has the voice said to you, *se* Jackie?" Th'an'ya asked at last.

"We were discussing the enemy." She tugged at the hem of the robe. "I said they were powerful enough to radically alter reality as we observed it. Dan then asked me how I could have escaped them myself.

"At that point the voice told me that I already knew the answer."

"And do you know the answer?"

"No, not at all. I—I was almost taken over, replaced, by one of them."

"'Almost'?" Dan looked at Th'an'ya, suspicion clouding his face, and then back at Jackie. "If these things are so all-fired powerful, how did you stop it?"

"She—it—was distracted."

Poor John Maisel, she thought to herself, feeling slightly sick in the pit of her stomach. "Then Ch'k'te shot it."

"Was that the only one you actually met, face-to-face?"

"No, there was one other." Jackie felt Ch'k'te shift nervously behind her, his wings rearranging themselves in a pattern she could not see but could guess at. "He took control of me to learn about dispositions." She clenched her teeth, remembering the pain.

This time Th'an'ya did waver and almost disappear. Dan looked around, alarmed. "I couldn't see, couldn't move," Jackie continued. "It was like someone was driving a stake into my head. I couldn't fight him off, really, all I could do was struggle ..."

"I would not have expected Sensitive talent of you, Jackie ... But you will not live long enough to use this secret."

He raised his hands and a wedge of pain was driven into her forehead. She screamed as it drove farther and farther into her skull, growing white-hot ...

"What happened then?"

"I fought him—them—off. I tried to get to a window, to jump out."

"You resisted the probing. How did you do it?"

"I don't know."

"You have to remember," Dan replied, insistent. "This is important, Jay. The voice told you that you already knew how to fight it. How?"

"I don't know, damn it!"

"What were you thinking? What went through your mind?"

She was afraid. Still, the point of paralysis had been reached and passed and left far behind. She had known worse, though her mind was now open to all of the horrors and fears she had kept concealed behind a wall of reason.

She had known death on the battlefield. She had watched a starship disintegrate and explode under concentrated fire.

She had watched John Maisel collapse and die at a single thought.

Hatred fueled anger, an awful, growling thing forming first in her chest, making her hands clench and her arms and legs tense.

Jackie's arms and legs grew tense at the memory. "I was past pain, past fear. All I could think of was how John Maisel had died." Dan shot a questioning look at Ch'k'te, but the zor did not seem to notice. "All I could feel was anger and hatred. The creature that was ripping my mind apart was the most evil thing I could imagine."

"*anGa'riSsa,*" Th'an'ya said. "The Shield of Hatred."

Jackie emerged from her memories, willing herself to relax. "I don't remember that from the Qu'u legend."

"It is a later tradition," Th'an'ya said. "It comes from the epic *seLi'e'Yan,* or 'Standing Within the Circle.' In the story, the *esGa'uYal* seek to assault the Lord *esLi*'s Circle of Light; the Army of Sunset, commanded by He of the Dancing Blade, Shrnu'u HeGa'u, comes to the gates of the warriors' city of Sharia'a … the city of my birth … and uses their powerful weapons of Despair to sap the will of the people there. The lord of the city goes all about and finds that everyone from the highest to the lowest is overcome by lassitude and unable to act. A young warrior, trapped by the advance of the host of Despite, goes to the lord of the city and exhorts him with tales of all of the Deceiver's misdeeds, reminding him how much evil has been done in the past. With this Shield—*anGa'riSsa*—the lord of the city is able to protect his people against the Deceiver's minions, which saves the city."

"Hatred." Jackie sat forward. "The ability to resist is based on hatred."

"Just so," Th'an'ya answered. "But many will not be capable of such a strong emotion. You have been touched by the *esGa'uYal.*"

"And lived to tell about it. *And* to have a mysterious voice remind me about it. I believe that if we were in the wrong place, the voice would tell me."

"So …" Dan said, "that leads me back to the question: How are you going to find the way to the sword?"

"Well, actually," Jackie said, turning to look up at Ch'k'te, "there is an alternative. Ch'k'te and I can create a mental link and search around."

"Search around the station?"

"Something like that." Jackie looked at Th'an'ya, who nodded at her.

"Is that wise?"

"I think it's worth a try. We have Th'an'ya to help protect us while in the link and you folks standing by to protect us on the physical level. We might be able to find out if this is where we're supposed to be, and we might be able to locate the base of the steps leading to the Fortress of Despite."

"Whatever the hell that means. All right." He exchanged some kind of knowing look with Karla. "What do you want me to do?"

W HEN SHE opened her eyes this time, she expected to see some sort of construct Ch'k'te had built for her. She was prepared for the pastel nothingness of the void. Instead it was as if she had been awakened by a large, loud noise echoing nearby. She found herself leaning against an outcropping of large, misshapen boulders. The sky above was hazy and smoke-filled; the air was filled with explosions. She was still wearing the crimson robe; where her skin was exposed, it was grimy and the dirt wouldn't rub off.

She wore no sword, but her belt had an empty scabbard hanging from it. It was the scabbard she'd seen on *se* Sergei's belt; she knew what was supposed to go in it. Ch'k'te and Th'an'ya, similarly attired and standing nearby, seemed to be waiting for her to take action.

"This is a hell of a mental construct," she said to them. "Couldn't we have tried something a bit easier to deal with?"

"We are on the Plain of Despite, *se* Jackie," Th'an'ya answered. "The pattern of this mental link is not under our control."

"Does that mean that we can't break it? Or can it only be broken the way it was broken last time?"

"Perhaps, perhaps not. There is no ready answer," Th'an'ya answered.

"I wanted to find some real-world analog, not to act out the Legend of Qu'u in my mind. This doesn't seem to be any help."

"*esLiHeYar,*" Th'an'ya answered cryptically, arranging her wings in the Posture of Polite Deference. "The Eight Winds blow where they will."

"But I don't know what to do."

Th'an'ya did not answer. Both zor drew their *chya'i* and crept closer, prepared to follow.

She shrugged and began to make her way forward.

The standing boulders seemed to be poised at the edge of a steep slide. As she moved forward, she could begin to make out a wide valley below, with tendrils and streamers of fog traveling through like living creatures that had no particular destination. She could see zor traveling about on foot, also aimless, their gazes directed downward as if they were incapable of lifting their heads.

Beyond the valley was the huge, imposing backdrop of a blackish-blue façade … the Icewall. It stretched left and right as far as she could see; its base was lost in the fog below. Somewhere near the middle she could make out an impossibly steep stair. It was actually less a stairway and more a series of platforms, clawholds for flying creatures ascending from the Plain of Despite to …

She looked up. It was an act that seemed to drain almost all of her energy; far above on the wall she saw an imposing fortress, overgrown with towers and outbuildings. Lightnings from nowhere, cascading toward nowhere, played around its parapets and turrets: the Fortress of Despite.

"Is this the Valley of Lost Souls?"

"Yes," Th'an'ya said. "If you can find the base of the Stairs, you can begin your ascent. The legend says that the inhabitants of the Valley fail to notice the passing of the hero. Only the guardian of the base of the steps recognizes him because he had known Qu'u from the World That Is.

"The guardian was only there to warn him that *esGa'u* could be defeated but never destroyed," she continued. "Still, you must not assume that the *esGa'uYal* will play by the same rules. We may well be attacked."

"I seem to be unarmed."

"No," Th'an'ya answered. "You merely do not possess a *chya*."

HUNDREDS OF parsecs from where Dan McReynolds and Karla Bazadeh stood guard, and infinitely far from the internal landscape that their three companions inhabited, an alien queen turned to listen to the words of her advisor.

=The prey approaches the trap,= the advisor said. Its words were a combination of speech and thought, but the queen understood the remark and all of its undertones. The advisor appeared as a box containing a multihued cloud of gas with a silver sphere floating on the top.

The Ór had been the guide and counselor, the near-omniscient tentacles and listening membranes for many of her predecessors, since it had catalyzed the unification of her race and instilled in them the will and desire to conquer.

It was the Ór, after all, that had directed her attention to the capture of the device that the winged meat creatures so highly prized. It was the Ór that had directed the thought patterns to follow in order to try and get it back. The idea of it was laughable, of course: neither the winged meat creatures nor the far more populous wingless ones that they served could even hope to attempt such a thing … their minds were so weak, their science so primitive, their resources so limited.

Conquering both of them, despite what the other advisor had said twelves of years ago, would be only marginally more difficult than conquering either of them alone. The queen, as well as the Ór itself, had been surprised at the way in which the two species had been able to reconcile after being at each other's thoraxes for so long … but, no matter.

She had the Sensitive device; it would only be necessary to spring the trap on the foolish primitive sent to fetch it. Then the conquest could begin. Even to a creature as alien as the Ór, it must seem to be a sign.

S HE HAD nightmares like this, in which she had walked through the streets of a city while its inhabitants did not or could not notice her. In her dreams, the city and its residents had been human: here they were zor. But it made it no less unnerving to move in the midst of so many souls that seemed to be oblivious to her presence.

Under a canopy of iridescent fog, the indigenous population of the Valley of Lost Souls moved as in a dream. The Valley was like a large, spread-out *L 'le*, except that it rarely climbed higher than a second story. The inhabitants seemed to crouch, afraid to lift their wings into the pervasive cloud cover. It had a terrible wrongness to it that she felt; she could read it openly in Ch'k'te and Th'an'ya's troubled eyes as they followed her.

At first, she had used the shadows and moved stealthily from building to building, but as she moved further into the *L 'le*, it hardly seemed to matter. Near the outskirts of the settlement, the inhabitants seemed to be mimicking zor daily life, but deeper in the Valley they were less and less active—as if proximity to the center rendered them as lifeless as statues.

Jackie and her two companions passed through a wide, octagonal town square under the gaze of—but unobserved by—hundreds of zor, their only movements resulting from a tenuous breeze ruffling their wings, half-arranging them in new yet more despairing positions.

Ch'k'te and Th'an'ya also seemed to be caught up in this dreamlike lethargy, requiring her to stop several times while they gathered the energy to continue. Lassitude mixed with genuine fear gazed up at her each time she caught their eyes. The meaning was all too clear to her.

When they finally seemed unable to rise and follow she said, "I'm going alone to the center. If you follow, you'll only be trapped here."

Reluctantly, as if it required a great effort for them to reply, they both nodded and took up a position of guard, back to back.

She moved on alone. To her surprise, the terrible lethargy seemed not to be affecting her as she moved through the silent streets, now peopled only by zor statues whose wings drooped in positions that indicated their despair. Shortly she could see a huge wall with wide stairs set into it. At its base was a zor with its back to her, unmoving like the rest—but at her approach, it turned to face her.

She was stunned. She stopped in her tracks as it did so, for it had a human face: one she recognized.

"Damien?"

"*ha* Qu'u," the human-faced zor said. "Mighty hero, I am stationed here to warn you." The figure that bore the image of Damien Abbas, captain of the *Negri Sembilan*, did not seem to recognize her except as the zor hero.

It figures, she thought.

"Warn me?"

"You have come," the Abbas-zor said, "to ascend the Perilous Stair to the Fortress of Despite. You believe you have come far, but all of your journeying thus far is but a fraction of the task compared to what lies ahead."

She reviewed the Qu'u legend in her mind, casting about for the correct response. "Still, I am bound by oath to continue."

"Even those condemned to life may die the true death," the Abbas-zor replied.

"The Lord *esLi* protects me and commands that I follow this quest to its end," she answered.

"Have you questioned why such a powerful Lord would choose one so young and inexperienced? You are unarmed," the Abbas-zor said, gesturing toward the empty scabbard at her belt. "Surely you do not expect to fill that scabbard with the blade the Lord of the Fortress possesses?"

"That's what I had in mind."

"The Deceiver, and all of his minions, will seek to destroy you at the moment you touch it."

"That's what they've been doing all along."

"You do not understand, mighty Qu'u. That is the honor and the burden of the sword. Once taken up it *cannot* be laid down. This responsibility that you will undertake is not one of conveyance but rather one of commitment."

"I still don't understand." She didn't remember this exchange. She was listening intently now, wishing Th'an'ya was here to interpret.

"This is the Perilous Stair." The Abbas-zor gestured to the worn steps behind him. She looked up and saw the Stair ascending, impossibly high above her; a few dozen meters above she could make out another zor clinging to the stair; it also had a human face, but the mist obscured the other's features. "By it you may ascend to your eventual destiny. It is a stair which only has one direction." He pointed upward, where the steps disappeared into the weirdly luminous fog. "If you step onto it you have committed an irreversible act, one that ends with you standing within the Circle. All of those that preceded you will be there to help, but the burden is ultimately yours alone.

"This is a *shNa'es'ri,* a crossroads, mighty hero. A step away—or a step forward. It is up to you to choose."

"I'm not going up there alone."

"You deceive yourself if you believe differently. In the final analysis, mighty Qu'u, you *must* be alone. It is your destiny."

"Why do you have a human face?"

"It is a sign to you, *ha* Qu'u, a guidepost so that you might find this place again. As you know, *this* place is fixed, but the time is not yet decided. You may retreat now as you wish: the *esGa'uYal* have not yet determined your guise. But if you place one step upon the Perilous Stair, it will only lead to one place."

"The Fortress of Despite?"

"Standing Within the Circle, mighty Qu'u. While all about you is torn to ruin."

She felt an impulse to place a foot on the stair behind the Abbas-zor but hesitated: she had left her companions behind her and she didn't completely understand the situation.

One step, she thought. *Like everything else before, my destiny is set by an agenda I don't even understand.*

"The time is not yet decided," the Abbas-zor repeated.

With a great effort of will Jackie stepped back from the foot of the stair, retreating slowly. The Abbas-zor arranged his wings in a posture of deference to *esLi,* the first time she'd seen something like that on the Plain of Despite.

It was only a short distance back to where Ch'k'te and Th'an'ya waited, back to back, their *chya'i* drawn and ready against the army of statues that gazed, unseeing, upon them.

"I think I got the message I wanted," she said. "Let's go home."

chapter 22

The actual number of people that could fit on a gig was nearly thirty. Only a few crew members had come down from the *Negri Sembilan*; Marcel Liang, the *Negri*'s chief surgeon, had come planetside to replenish the *Negri*'s medical stores, under the watchful eye of one of the aliens.

"There are only a few aliens aboard," Liang said as they slowly moved through the upper atmosphere with Owen in the pilot's seat. "The captain is one."

"No kiddin'," Abbas said from a rear seat. "Glad you noticed."

"The day the *Negri* destroyed the *Gustav* we noticed." Liang looked at Abbas. "The day the captain spaced a dozen members of the crew we noticed. We thought you were one of them, Cap."

"They dumped us on Center," Abbas said. "Are there aliens to replace everyone they've offloaded?"

"Truthfully," Liang said, "I don't think so. The Sensitives are under their control"—Abbas shot Owen a *told you so* look—"but I think there are no more than five or six on board. And they don't get along very well: they're in competition. Each one has an agenda, or belongs to some faction. They've had direct confrontations on the bridge and at least one of them was killed by the others."

"How do you know?"

"A month or so ago I got orders to clear out part of sick bay." Liang exchanged a glance with one of the med crew. "A wounded officer was brought in—I only got a quick look: She—it—could hardly hold a human shape. I went to help but two Marines were ordered in my way by the captain. It didn't come back out."

"Is one of them stronger than the others?" Owen asked.

"The captain." Liang looked from Owen to Abbas and back.

Outside the shuttle the sky had gone dark; they were in the upper atmosphere. On the pilot's board in front of Owen, there were several ship icons visible, including the *Negri*'s. He corrected course toward it.

"Tell me about him," Owen said.

"He's very sure of himself," the doctor said. "The bridge crew is pretty scared of him; one of the junior helm officers landed in my sick bay in a state of nervous collapse—he hadn't made a course change quickly enough, and the captain had made him believe he'd been spaced. He's never been right since."

Owen thought about this for a moment. "What do you think, Captain? Could you scare 'em enough to make them believe you were an alien?"

"I don't know how long I could keep it up."

"They only have to be fooled for a few minutes. We'll do the rest."

J ACKIE MOVED through the corridors of Crossover Port with grim determination. Ch'k'te walked alongside with his eyes shielded from the glare by his sunglasses, but she didn't have time for amusement. She knew what she was looking for now: When she'd asked the Abbas-zor why he had a human face, he had replied, *"A guidepost so that you might find this place again."* It was a calculated hunch, but it made sense. According to the Qu'u tradition, the base of the Perilous Stair was guarded by someone Qu'u knew in life.

Maybe Damien Abbas was here at Crossover. The mental link had given her no other clues other than Abbas' face, but it was more than she'd had beforehand.

The last thing Dan McReynolds had said before she and Ch'k'te went ashore was: "You want some help on this?"

She'd said no. Another hunch ... Or was it that she didn't want him to get into the line of fire? She'd even tried to dissuade Ch'k'te from coming along, pointing at the piece of the legend they'd most recently experienced—that only Qu'u reaches the Perilous Stair. It wasn't to be. Ch'k'te merely belted on his *chya*, as if to ask, *What do we do next?*

She couldn't even say what it would mean to find Abbas here. If she found him, what would she say to him? *What happened out there? Where's the* Negri? *Can I buy you a drink?*

Truth to tell, she didn't really know *what* she'd do. It was tactically foolish to go into a situation without having a plan, but even that didn't seem to matter anymore.

I T MADE sense to start at the Steps. The coincidence was too much for her to stand, so she began her search at the bar where she'd last heard the voice. Some heads turned when a human and a zor entered together, but no lingering gazes followed them. There were a few zor on the station; they moved about almost oblivious to each other, and of course didn't fly. A zor, even in human company, was a curiosity—but not for very long.

The Steps served *egeneh*. It wasn't very good; perhaps it had been jostled about in transit, or was left to age a bit too long. There weren't many who drank it at Crossover.

There were no *esGa'uYal* in the Steps, and Damien Abbas wasn't there either.

They moved on, trying bars, eateries and other off-duty spots first. She was accustomed to the Imperial Navy's data access and realized that she was at a loss to look for someone, even someone she knew reasonably well, without even a vid image. How could she distinguish him from any other member of the human race? He was tall, but not especially so; dark-skinned with high cheekbones, full lips and a rather small nose. He was clean-shaven with a slightly receding hairline; his speech was clear and clipped. He cracked his knuckles.

Narrows it from one in a million to one in ten thousand, she thought. There were dozens of people they saw that would match the description but who were not Damien Abbas.

"WE WOULD have noticed it already," Ch'k'te said as they walked slowly along the pedestrian way, past cargo dock after cargo dock. They had circumnavigated the hub of the station, nearly reaching the Steps again.

"It's worth checking again. Unless you have a better idea."

"I do not. But I do not expect a ship the size of the *Negri Sembilan* to have escaped our notice."

They walked along in silence for the next few minutes, examining each berth in turn. A few were empty, showing the scheduled arrival of some ship that had made it insystem and was navigating into the gravity-well. Most were full, warrens of activity, loading and unloading cargo. It was unnerving how much business was being done here, away from the inspections of Imperial customs. The normalcy of it all was bringing her slowly around to Dan's position: This *couldn't* be Sargasso, the place that had made two Imperial ships disappear, had destroyed the squadron, and where Admiral Tolliver had gone mad.

At last the *Fair Damsel* came into view and she stopped walking and turned to Ch'k'te. "All right," she said. "We've walked all the way around. The *Negri* isn't here, but maybe it *has* been here. Dan thought it had gone pirate, remember? There must be some record of it berthing here."

"Agreed."

"We'll need a public comp—there." She pointed toward the main deck where there was a public booth. They rode a lift down and stepped into it. Ch'k'te had his hand near his *chya* and kept his attention toward the deck as Jackie gestured toward the screen, her own comp in her hand.

"Query commercial records," she said to the blank screen. "Arrivals and departures of vessel *Negri Sembilan*, Imperial Navy."

Somewhere far off in the station she imagined the request being processed. There was no sound to indicate it, but the screen showed the request in process. Then it went dark and the screen began to display text.

You have come to ascend the Perilous Stair to the Fortress of Despite. You believe that you have come far, but all of your journeying thus far is but a fraction of the task compared to what lies ahead.

Go to the Center, Mighty Hero. The Icewall awaits.

"What the—"

Ch'k'te shot a glance over his shoulder and quickly scanned the text. He looked from it to Jackie and then returned his attention to watching behind them.

The text disappeared. The comp seemed to be offline. As she turned around, she could see someone coming toward it with a satchel in his hand.

"Broken," he said. "Out of order. I've come to fix it."

"Broken? But I just—"

"It's *offline*," he insisted, coming up to the booth. "Broken. Out of service." He wore a set of coveralls with the Crossover emblem at the left lapel. He gave Ch'k'te a long look, sizing him up and down, and then said, "I got a call from the Center less than half a Standard hour ago. You got any complaints, sister, take 'em to the Center."

Go to the Center, Mighty Hero.

"The Center," she said. "How ... How do I get there?"

"Past that bulkhead," he answered, gesturing. "Next side corridor on your left. Take the moving walkway and get off when it ends. They'll know what to do with ya." He began to make a comment about what he'd like to do with her but stopped a few words along, looked at Ch'k'te again, shrugged his shoulders and began to take out his tools.

IT WAS a blur of scenes that Owen Garrett only remembered imperfectly afterward. At the hangar deck Abbas played his part: he refused to answer questions from Marines on the deck as he emerged with Liang and the others; none of the crew were aliens, and as soon as Rafe and the others came off the shuttle it was clear that something was up.

With some of the hangar-deck crew in tow they made their way to Engineering Section. Owen hadn't wanted to split them up, and from Engineering they could power down the whole ship if necessary. It was there they met—and killed—their first alien. That was surreal as well: An alien had replaced Cam Enslin, the *Negri*'s chief engineer, and there were thirty crew members who knew it. The Enslin alien was dead before he hit the deck, without the need for Owen to focus his attention.

Then they reached the bridge, and things took the strangest turn of all.

IT WAS no surprise that Damien Abbas—or something that looked like him—was sitting in the pilot's seat. He turned it to face the lift doors as they opened; two other aliens disguised as humans—Owen could tell that right away—took up positions behind him. Everyone else on the bridge was still and rigid, locked in whatever position they'd been in last.

"Garrett," the Abbas-alien said. "At last we meet. And I see you've brought along my twin." Abbas looked at the alien sitting in his seat and surged forward; Owen held him back.

"I'm glad I have a reputation to uphold," Owen answered.

"Oh, you do, you do. And when the *Negri* reaches home you'll be quite a specimen to study."

"I wasn't planning on that."

"I'm sure you were not. I must say you've impressed me, though: I wouldn't have expected you to reach the bridge of the *Negri Sembilan* even with whatever *k'th's's* power you've developed. The Great Queen will enjoy studying you ... and then consuming you."

There were a dozen *Negri* crew on the bridge now, arranged behind Owen and the real Captain Abbas. Others were making their way up the access ladders, but only so many had been able to get into the lift. Without turning his head, Owen could tell that none of them were moving now—no one but him.

"I'm not scared of you," he said. Anger coursed through him; he had the urge to wipe the smirk off the Abbas-alien's face, but he knew he couldn't take out the other two as well.

"You should be, Garrett. This charade is almost at the end. You and your *k'th's's* power will be taken to First Hive and digested."

Pressure began to form in his mind, and his anger rose to meet it. Around him the others were crumpling to the deck, one after another; the Abbas-alien—and perhaps his companions—were focusing on Owen alone, as if none of the others mattered at all.

Then, suddenly, the deck lights on the bridge went out.

Owen heard snatches of conversation or thought—he couldn't tell which: *meat-creatures*—k'th's's—*Or will tell.*

Then there was a flash of rainbow-colored light streaking through the bridge compartment. The sudden darkness, followed by the sudden brilliant light, blinded everyone; in the commotion Owen felt himself being thrown to the deck. Where his hand touched, he felt an incredible smoothness as if the deck had been sanded flat.

The event had broken whatever control the aliens were exerting. Shots rang out in the darkness; people were diving for cover. The pressure on Owen's head had stopped abruptly—the eerie quiet that had prevailed just moments before, had erupted into shouts, cries of pain and noises no human voice could make.

The lights came back on. All three aliens were sprawled where their human images had been; comps showed evidence of energy-weapon hits; two or three crewmembers were lying on the deck injured. Dr. Liang moved first, checking the wounded.

Owen looked around, slowly getting to his feet. Everyone was accounted for but one person. The real Damien Abbas was gone.

IT WAS all too perfect. They had walked all around the outside of the station but had neglected the administrative section at the hub. It was connected to the torus of Crossover Port by six corridors so long they had moving walkways to keep the pedestrian from having to make a half-hour journey. As they stepped onto the walkway it began to move: Shortly they were traveling at close to thirty klicks through a long, dimly lit tunnel. Ch'k'te had his claws extended and was making no secret of his discomfort with the situation; Jackie was on edge, feeling as if she was finally moving toward resolution. She remembered the Valley of Lost Souls as she'd seen it in the mind-link and wondered what she'd find at the Center.

The walkway took them there quicker than she'd have thought. It slowed to a stop near a reception area. To her surprise it seemed abandoned: no one was there to greet them or ask them their business. The ambient light was even dimmer than in the tube and was tinged slightly red—more comfortable for a zor, more difficult for a human. Comps were online but there was no one there to look at them.

"Where are the *Hssa*?" Ch'k'te asked no one in particular. In one sinuous motion he unsheathed his *chya*.

She didn't answer, but instead let her senses try to absorb the scene.

Hearing: It was quiet except for life-support systems and the occasional acknowledgment from a comp. Whatever noises were normally associated with a smooth-running admin office were conspicuous by their absence.

Sight: The dim light showed a shut-down office. Actually, it was more like a crude caricature of an office, like a 3-V stage from which the actors and the stagehands had walked away; they had turned down the lights and left the furniture in place. Everything seemed like a prop—not real, but standing in for the real thing. It chilled her even more to think of it this way; it made her feel like a chess-piece, moved to its final position on the board, awaiting capture.

Smell: Instead of the antiseptic, sanitized air of a space-station, there was a stench of decay that sent a shiver down her spine. In a sudden flash, she remembered where she'd smelled it before—in the garden of the residence building on Cicero, where ...

"Come now, Mighty Qu'u," a mocking voice said: Damien Abbas' voice. "I'm growing quite impatient."

Jackie and Ch'k'te exchanged glances. The voice had seemed to come from all around them. They now noticed an office door slightly ajar; the light from within was somewhat brighter, but still red-tinged.

Ch'k'te stepped past her and toward the door. She thought to hold him back but his wing-posture did not brook disagreement. She wished she had a pistol in her hand, but she realized that it wouldn't do any good against an opponent capable of taking control of her mind.

A step at a time they approached the room. Its contents came into view: a crowded office with furniture, documents and equipment distributed in equal proportions. Damien Abbas sat behind the desk, leaning back in his chair. He beckoned them to seats.

"I'll stand, thanks," Jackie said, and Ch'k'te, his *chya* held out in front of him, took up a spot to her right, slightly farther into the room, and a bit closer to Abbas.

"As you wish, *se* Qu'u," Abbas added, turning his attention to Ch'k'te.

Ch'k'te didn't answer but looked instead at Jackie. It was clear to her that Abbas had been addressing Ch'k'te when he said the name *"Qu'u"*—and not her! Ch'k'te apparently hadn't realized this yet and was waiting for her to say or do something.

"It has been a long chase," Abbas continued. "Our effort to direct you here has almost exceeded our resources. The futility of this quest is something we could have foretold from the beginning, but it still surprises me that the High Nest chose one so weak to fulfill a role so important."

Ch'k'te's claws extended around the hilt of his *chya,* which snarled angrily at Abbas. Not knowing exactly why, Jackie caught Abbas' attention and looked into his eyes. They were full of anger and burned with an alien light.

She remembered the garden and the smell of death.

"Noyes," she whispered.

Abbas' image melted and flowed, re-forming after a moment as Bryan Noyes. "If you prefer. It's all the same to me, these misshapen meat-creature images. If this one pleases you better, so be it. I am sure it matters very little to the *hero.*" The last word was propelled by contempt, aimed directly at Ch'k'te.

"I did not kill you before," the zor replied softly. "I will not fail to do so now."

"Such melodrama becomes you well, Mighty Qu'u. But I assure you, cloaking yourself in the trappings of a great hero does not cause you to *become* one. You are not here to kill me or even to redeem your worthless honor: You are here because you have been led here, trapped in the spirals of your own primitive legend.

"We have the sword. We threw away the old man; the coming of the hero has been foretold. We did not know your name or Nest, but we knew that you would come. You even bear the soul of the spirit-guide—not that it truly matters anymore.

"Good old Ch'k'te. Not human enough to fit into human society, too far from his zor companions to retain his own identity: only suitable to be a pet for his commander."

Noyes stood up and walked slowly toward Jackie. Ch'k'te, obviously angry and disturbed at the alien's words, started to interpose himself, but he froze in midstride. Noyes didn't even miss a step.

"And Commodore Laperriere. 'The Iron Maiden,' isn't that what they call you behind your back? You've gotten yourself involved in something you don't understand. This is far beyond inspections and parades, and hasn't a *thing* to do with regulations. And this second-rate hero"—he gestured toward Ch'k'te, still frozen, stepping forward—"thought you could play Hyos to his Qu'u. So like a zor."

From Jackie's perspective, Noyes seemed to be walking toward her in slow motion. His mouth didn't move in sync with his words.

"When you were Dominated before, Commodore—all we wanted was information on the disposition of the fleet." The room was narrowing as he spoke, though she couldn't break away from his gaze.

"I complimented you—do you remember? I told you that had you been of our species, you might be considered a worthy mate. It cannot be, of course, but for a Sensitive of sufficient skill, any effective illusion is functionally equivalent to reality. For the subject, at least."

His hands/tentacles reached toward her from out of the gloom. She could not move; she could not turn away. The depths of his eyes grew to drown and encompass her, as they had before …

"You?" A curious expression crossed his face. "*You* are—"

The alien writhed in sudden pain as Ch'k'te's *chya* drove into him. Energy flashed up and down the blade as it seemed to cry out in delight and triumph. Ch'k'te, somehow freed for a moment from the alien's casual Domination, thrust it farther and farther into the alien's midsection until it began to emerge from the front. Blood welled up and gushed out as he grabbed hold of it, his face transformed in surprise and horror.

Jackie found that she could act. She snapped a kick directly below where the blade protruded. Noyes staggered back, dragging Ch'k'te with him. Noyes' features began to melt and his body began to assume its true shape.

He looked at Jackie for a moment and then turned his wavering attention to Ch'k'te, who held on to the sword with both clawed hands. It was clear the alien had suffered grievous damage—perhaps enough to kill him, perhaps not.

What he hoped to gain with his next action, Jackie would never understand.

"Die," he said to Ch'k'te.

John Maisel had been completely helpless against such an attack, but Ch'k'te by comparison was a trained Sensitive. He had expended almost all of his will in the attack he had just made; still, he had enough strength to reach out and grasp Noyes' neck. He dug his claws into the transforming body and pulled, drawing out a huge chunk of something that was not even close to human skin.

As Jackie watched, the light left Ch'k'te's eyes and he collapsed to the deck. Before she could even move to check on him, the alien, now mostly transformed to its insectoid form, fell beside him still clutching its midsection. There was a sharp report as the *chya* snapped beneath his weight. Then all was silent.

Now. Quickly. Th'an'ya's voice, cool and dispassionate in her mind.

"Ch'k'te—" she cried out, but she heard Th'an'ya repeat herself. *There is no time, se Jackie. My mate has transcended the Outer Peace. The* esGa'uYe *has killed him.*

"No! He can't have—" But she knew that he had.

He can. He has. His honor is returned to him, se Jackie. You must understand that and let him be. There is danger if you do not act at once.

The voice sounded strained and far away. The alien has transcended the Outer Peace as well, but he has left behind knowledge of the location of the gyaryu *and the means by which you can reach it. I obtained this information from the alien's mind as he returned to the Plain of Despite.*

"Information," Jackie said numbly. The hair on the back of her neck began to stand up, as if something was happening nearby. The smell rose to meet her: the terrible odor of decay, of death …

The gyaryu *is here.* A star map marked with alien script appeared in her mind's eye. The green-white star with many notations was Crossover; nearby was another star, also well annotated. The sense of the map indicated that the alien had intended to take her and Ch'k'te there for some purpose.

The alien hadn't meant to kill them—not even Ch'k'te. Poor Ch'k'te, lying broken on the station deck, the snapped haft of his *chya* still clutched in his hand …

The alien had a scout vessel at his disposal. It is berthed at a private dock on the deck below this one. These are the access codes; it is of Imperial issue. Th'an'ya communicated a set of standard-sounding codes. *You must go now.*

Jackie wanted to run from the place and back to the *Fair Damsel*—but she knew the Perilous Stair was ahead of her, not behind. She bent down and retrieved the broken hilt of the *chya,* sliding it from between Ch'k'te's claws. "Forgive me, old friend," she heard herself say from some distance.

She tucked it into her belt and stepped away from the body. "*esLiHeYar,*" she added almost as an afterthought.

THE ALIEN queen was not happy with the report. The death of a drone, especially one so skilled and experienced, was a poor sign; but the information indicated that the winged meat-creature was dead as well. That, at least, would satisfy the Ór that the threat of this unknown hero was ended. Perhaps the meat-creatures would try again to obtain their prize, perhaps not; but they would certainly be disheartened at the bad end of their foolish quest.

But the Ór told her: =The hero Qu'u has been shown the base of the Perilous Stair and climbs it even now.=

=I am told that the winged one was killed—against my orders, but he has decidedly been killed. How can the hero approach?=

=Your servant has aided the quest, not thwarted it. Something is not what it seems to be.=

And on that subject, that was all that the Ór would say.

WITH SLOW and painful strokes of his nearly transparent wings, S'reth made his way toward the highest perches of the Chamber of Contemplation where the High Chamberlain, T'te'e HeYen, waited patiently for him. It was a tremendous effort for him—more flying than he'd really done in years. Still, to concede that he was unable to reach the perch he now approached was to admit that he was no more than an *artha*, a wingless one, and no longer a warrior of the People. He had not actually worn his *chya* for years; it had sat in an ornamental stand next to his favorite perch. Still, it was an obligatory part of the costume even though its weight dragged against him as he slowly ascended.

He wondered what thoughts were going through the High Chamberlain's mind as he flew upward. Pity perhaps, or concern, as this pavane was played out: The ancient sage struggling with the restraints of his worn-out frame, while the dignified envoy of the High Nest feigned indifference. He and T'te'e had been friends for a long time, but S'reth remembered other High Chamberlains from generations past, now gathered within the shining Circle of *esLi*.

S'reth turned his attention away from the effort of flight and considered what he felt at that recollection. T'te'e—*ha* T'te'e, he reminded himself—had been High Chamberlain for many turns, long enough to remember the last few sorrowful years of High Lord *hi* Ke'erl's father's administration. As a young Councillor, *ha* T'te'e had had to observe the Flight of the People without the guiding talon of *esLi*. It was a difficult prospect even for a Sensitive of exceptional talents. Then, as now, he had had to settle his wings in a posture of contemplation and wait for events to come to him without conveying the void he no doubt felt.

Of course T'te'e did not remember the time before *esHu'ur*, when at least the direction was clear if misguided.

He was now just a few meters below T'te'e's perch. He saw the concern in the younger one's eyes as he raised himself level and slowly executed the Posture of Deference to the Servant of *esLi*—no easy feat in midair at his age!—and settled himself onto a wide perch a few feet away from the High Chamberlain. His ritual duty done, he reached for an ornate flagon and with trembling hands poured himself a cup of *egeneh*. He dipped a talon into the liquid and drew a figure of obeisance in the air.

"*esLiHeYar*," he half whispered and sipped at the liquor, looking over the cup at the High Chamberlain.

"I am gratified you could come, Elder Brother," T'te'e said formally, arranging his wings in the Stance of Courteous Deference.

"I am always at the disposal of the High Nest," S'reth replied. His wings settled into a configuration that had no name, but was meant to convey delicate irony. "Though it would gratify me, Younger Brother, if you would give me enough warning next time that I might be able to enter a physical training program before I pay my respects."

T'te'e snorted amusement. "Eight thousand pardons, old friend. I have my reasons for inviting you formally, rather than simply visiting your eyrie on Cle'eru."

"One hears tales." S'reth set the *egeneh*-cup aside. "So. How is the High Lord?"

"Officially? Or in truth?"

"I did not abandon my familiar apartments and travel eights of parsecs, and then fly all the way to the top of this *esLi*-forsaken Chamber to receive *official* news, my friend. I assume this room is guarded and warded. What is really happening in the High Nest?"

"*hi* Ke'erl is … his Inner Peace is gone. He can feel the *esGa'uYal* everywhere, even in the Home Stars; he sees conspiracies behind every wing. He has abandoned the daily ceremonies of course, though Nest business continues as it can."

"Who knows this?"

"The Inner Council; the Imperial envoy; *hi* Ke'erl's mate and heirs. And now you."

"Not the Council of Eleven?"

"In *esLi*'s blessed Name, *se* S'reth! There is not a single one of the twelve Councillors I could trust with the knowledge. They must not be told, until—"

"Until when? You cannot keep them in the Darkness forever, old friend. No matter what your motivations, they will be consumed with anger if they are kept too long from the knowledge. Even if you wish to discount the eleven Lords of Nest, the Speaker for the Young Ones will be hanging around your neck—!"

"When you were Speaker for the Young Ones, *se* S'reth, the Council of Eleven was strong and powerful. Now it is old and toothless. I do not feel it necessary to treat with fools."

"'Fools.'" S'reth picked up the cup and drank a mouthful of *egeneh*. It burned its way into the back of his throat. "Is that how you feel now, *ha* T'te'e? That in the Nest there are only two groups: conspirators and fools?

"What category would you place me in? Do not cast me as a conspirator, Younger Brother: that is a role I will not play. That only leaves one choice."

T'te'e growled but did not answer. Instead he rose from his perch and flew about the Chamber for several moments; S'reth could see the tension and anger in his frame. Finally the High Chamberlain returned to his perch and crossed his arms in front of him.

"So tell me," S'reth said quietly. "Tell me what you want of me."

"I had hoped you might be able to offer me some advice. Now I see that all you wish to do is tell me that I conduct my office improperly."

"Is that the only conclusion you draw? Tell me, *ha* T'te'e, old friend. What possible motive would I have to criticize your position? I am too old for struggles, too old for ambition. All I can be is a teacher."

"So you would be my teacher again."

S'reth settled himself on his perch. "I was your teacher once, half a lifetime ago. Yes, I would be your teacher again, Younger Brother T'te'e. Perhaps I can help your situation."

T'te'e caught the old one's gaze and held it for a long time. Like any Sensitive, the High Chamberlain was well trained in reading body-language and the slightest change in wing-positions; like any Sensitive, S'reth was well skilled in concealing his feelings and intentions.

"All right, old friend," T'te'e said at last. "Be my teacher."

At S'reth's urging, T'te'e reviewed the entire flight from the first contact with the *esGa'uYal* to the departure of Jackie Laperriere aboard the *Fair Damsel* a few weeks before. T'te'e was impatient but concealed it from both his voice and wings. He knew that S'reth sought a *sSurch'a* from this exposition, but he could not see where it would lead.

At last the discussion turned to *si* Th'an'ya, who had chosen to be the spirit-guide for Qu'u in this incarnation.

"She could not know how it would come about, but she placed her faith in the grace of *esLi* and gave a great portion of her *hsi* to the young warrior when they mated a few months later. Within a year she had disappeared, and the evidence of her awakening within *se* Ch'k'te some weeks ago demonstrates most clearly that she has transcended the Outer Peace, and all that remains now is the memory he carries of her."

"That statement is untrue in two important particulars," S'reth interrupted. T'te'e's wing-position sought an answer, but S'reth did not seem inclined to offer an explanation.

"We could not have known what would happen to *si* Th'an'ya," T'te'e continued after a moment. "Though it is clear now that the High Lord did. He specifically prohibited a search-and-rescue effort when she disappeared; indeed, I did not understand his motivations until recently. Similarly, until I learned of *si* Th'an'ya's awakening, I did not realize that our visit to Sanctuary many years ago actually contributed to the building of the Qu'u legend.

"After *si* Th'an'ya disappeared, the High Lord informed us that it would be necessary to await a sign. By the time the two Imperial ships disappeared several months ago, we had almost exhausted our patience.

"It was then *hi* Ke'erl indicated that the time had arrived, *se* Sergei was dispatched to accompany the human admiral to Cicero; the *esGa'uYal* seized the *gyaryu*; *se* Jackie surfaced, passed the Ordeal of Experience against the One of the Dancing Blade, and ..."

"And?"

"And here the story ends, Elder Brother. I know she is capable of withstanding attacks by the *esGa'uYal* and that *se* Ch'k'te can play the role of Hyos as well as she can play the role of Qu'u. But that is all I know."

"And *that* statement is incorrect in one very important particular."

"What would that be?"

"Younger Brother Ch'k'te has transcended the Outer Peace. He was killed by an *esGa'uYe* at Crossover Station several suns ago. The *esGa'uYe* is dead as well, apparently by *si* Ch'k'te's *chya*."

"Then *si* Th'an'ya is lost."

"As I understand it, *si* Th'an'ya transferred her *hsi* from Ch'k'te to *se* Jackie Laperriere some weeks ago."

"That is impossible!"

"I can only point out to you that it is not. As you indicated earlier in this flight, *si* Th'an'ya saw much more clearly than you did and must have known it was the human, and not the zor, that would attempt to climb the Perilous Stair, *si* Th'an'ya's *hsi* is bound to the avatar of Qu'u, who now travels alone to the Fortress of Despite."

"Alone."

"Yes, though we knew that was how it would be all along. Is that not true, Younger Brother?"

T'te'e HeYen, High Chamberlain of the High Nest, returned the sad gaze of S'reth the Sage, and settled his wings in the Posture of Polite Resignation.

In jump from Center to Port Saud, another world outside the Empire, the crewmembers from the *Negri Sembilan* took stock of their situation. Lacking a captain, chief engineer and chief navigator, as well as several other key officers, the crew largely deferred to Owen Garrett as chief pilot. Owen designated Rafe Rodriguez as chief engineer.

The ship's comp had a chart of the stars beyond the edge of the Solar Empire, with various annotations they couldn't understand—though the same symbols were used to mark both Center and Cicero. Other worlds within the Empire, such as Corcyra and Adrianople, had other markings. The possibility that they might fly the *Negri* into another alien-occupied system kept them from setting course for a world inside the Empire itself.

Whatever it had been before, it was war now: The aliens had begun to attack the Empire in earnest. Owen's ability remained a mystery, but it gave him celebrity status aboard the *Negri*. Still, as he sat watch-and-watch in the pilot's seat of the recaptured starship as it traveled through the darkness, he realized he had no idea where he was going or what to do when he got there.

As for the mysterious force that had plucked him from the alien ship and deposited him on Center, and which might have given him the ability to see through the aliens' deception (and had then, just as mysteriously, taken Damien Abbas off the bridge of his own ship), Owen couldn't manage any sort of opinion. He was being moved like a piece in some game he couldn't understand.

He believed the aliens had to have counted the ribbons of colored light as an enemy. But he wasn't ready yet to count them as friends. In the end, he had no choice but to watch and wait.

JACKIE SETTLED back in the cushions of the pilot's seat, trying to hold off anger and despair until she could get the ship safely into jump. Th'an'ya had given her directions to get to the scout ship; it had been unguarded, and she'd gotten off the station without warning or interference. Still, a worry gnawed at her: *This was too damn easy. It happened too fast, and the outcome was too convenient.*

Then she thought of Ch'k'te, left behind on Crossover, dead in the process of redeeming his honor. It hadn't been convenient for *him*, except how he had righted himself with regard to *esLi*. She pulled the broken *chya* from her belt, all she had left of him—all she'd ever have again, other than memories.

If you step onto it you have committed an irreversible act, one that ends with you standing within the Circle. All of those that preceded you will be there to help, but the burden is ultimately yours alone.

This is ashNa'es'ri, *a crossroads, Mighty Hero. A step away—or a step forward. It is up to you to choose.*

One step onto the Perilous Stair and there was no turning back. She had already chosen: As the Abbas-zor had told her on the Plain of Despite, she would have to ascend the Stair alone. Somewhere out there *esGa'u* the Deceiver held the *gyaryu,* and it would be up to her to recover it if she could.

If she could.

On the Plain of Despite, the voice said inside her, *warriors travel with their gaze directed toward the ground. Only heroes can cast their eyes upward and thus see the signs and portents of their guest.*

She cast her eyes upward, toward the distant stars beyond the viewport of her tiny ship. She saw no signs or portents, only questions and uncertainty. Perhaps, she told herself, it was because her eyes were full of tears.

Walter H. Hunt is a science fiction and historical fiction writer from Massachusetts. His first published novel, *The Dark Wing*, originally appeared in 2001, and was favorably compared to *Babylon 5* and *Ender's Game*.

He has written four novels in the Dark Wing Universe, as well as a historical novel about Rosslyn Chapel and the Order of the Temple, *A Song in Stone*, also available from Fantastic Books. He has several projects in preparation, including historical projects set in the seventeenth and eighteenth centuries.

An active Freemason and baseball fan, he lives in eastern Massachusetts with his wife and daughter.

CPSIA information can be obtained at www.ICGtesting.com
Printed in the USA
LVOW13s2224061013

355675LV00001B/172/P